THREADBARE
Volume 3:
The Right to Arm Bears

by Andrew Seiple

Cover by Amelia Parris

Edited by Beth Lyons

Warning: Contains profanity and violence

ISBN: 0692086641
ISBN-13: 978-0692086643

DEDICATION

With thanks to Piers Anthony, for teaching me that puns and fantasy *can* mix!

CONTENTS

AUTHOR NAME

ACKNOWLEDGMENTS

To my roleplaying groups. Look what you made me do!

PROLOGUE

Once upon a time, there was a teddy bear.

He became a golem, a thing animated by magic, and had many adventures. And at last, he was reunited with the little girl who loved him.

And there, in his moment of triumph, she died.

But he would not let it end that way.

For in his travels he had learned to defy death itself and grant his friends a new existence, as golems. And he saw no reason his little girl could not be so reborn.

He practiced hard, drove himself to new levels of skill to give her the body she deserved, the best he could make her.

And when all else was ready, he checked himself and spoke the word **"Status."**

And this is what he saw.

Name: Threadbare
Age: 5

Jobs:
Greater Toy Golem Level 15
Cave Bear Level 12
Ruler Level 11
Scout Level 7
Tailor Level 11
Model Level 8
Necromancer Level 11
Duelist Level 6

Animator Level 12
Enchanter Level 10
Golemist Level 12
Smith Level 10
Sculptor Level 12

Attributes	**Pools**	**Defenses**

Strength: 124 Constitution: 138 Hit Points: 330(410) Armor: 52(59)
Intelligence: 216 Wisdom: 201(208) Sanity: 417(545) Mental Fortitude: 42
Dexterity: 147(154) Agility: 112(126) Stamina: 269(373) Endurance: 62
Charisma: 110(145) Willpower: 199 Moxie: 309(424) Cool: 20(47)
Perception: 112 Luck: 89(96) Fortune: 208(295) Fate: 15(22)

Generic Skills
Brawling - Level 35 (+8)
Climb - Level 13
Clubs and Maces - Level 9
Dagger - Level 9
Dodge - Level 8
Fishing - Level 1
Ride - Level 8
Stealth - Level 13
Swim - Level 5

Greater Toy Golem Skills
Adorable - Level 30
Gift of Sapience - Level NA
Golem Body - Level 26
Innocent Embrace - Level 14
Magic Resistance - Level 7

Bear Skills
Animalistic Interface - NA
Claw Swipes - 24
Forage - 13
Growl - 2
Hibernate - 37
Scents and Sensibility - 20
Stubborn - 8
Toughness - 19

Ruler Skills
Appoint Official - NA

Emboldening Speech - Level 16
Identify Subject - Level 10
It's Good to be King - NA
Noblesse Oblige - Level 26
Organize Minions - NA
Royal Audience - Level 17
Simple Decree - Level 8
Swear Fealty - NA

Scout Skills
Alertness - Level 2
Best Route - Level 2
Camouflage - Level 2
Firestarter - Level 4
Keen Eye - Level 5
Sturdy Back - Level 6
Wind's Whisper - Level 5

Tailor Skills
Adjust Outfit - Level 4
Clean and Press - Level 13
Recycle Cloth - Level 1
Tailoring - Level 51(65)

Model Skills
Call Outfit - Level 1
Dietary Restriction - Level 40 (+80 to all pools)
Fascination - Level 4
Flex - Level 16
Makeup - Level 3
Self-Esteem - Level 16
Strong Pose – Level 5
Work it Baby - Level 40

Necromancer Skills
Assess Corpse - Level 12
Command the Dead - Level 28
Deathsight - Level 8
Drain Life - Level 1
Invite Undead - Level 12
Mana Focus – NA (+11% to sanity)
Soulstone - Level 45

Speak With Dead - Level 20
Zombies - Level 3

Duelist Skills
Challenge - Level 4
Dazzling Entrance - Level 8
Fancy Flourish - Level 7 (14)
Guard Stance - Level 8
Parry - Level 6
Swashbuckler's Spirit - NA (+13 to cool)
Swinger - Level 2
Weapon Specialist - Level 17 (Brawling +8)

Animator Skills
Animus - Level 35
Animus Blade - Level 10
Animus Shield - Level 4
Arm Creation - Level 7
Command Animus - Level 19
Creator's Guardians - Level 26
Dollseye - Level 18
Eye for Detail - Level 20
Magic Mouth - Level 10
Mend - Level 40

Enchanter Skills
Appraise - Level 30
Boost+5 - Level 9
Boost +10 - Level 2
Disenchant - Level 1
Elemental Protection - Level 8
Glowgleam - Level 26
Harden - Level 28
Soften - Level 30
Spellstore I - Level 9
Spellstore V - Level 1
Spellstore X - Level 1
Wards - Level 2

Golemist Skills
Clay Golem - Level 1
Command Golem - Level 10

Golem Animus - Level 46
Golem Guardians - NA
Invite Golem - Level 11
Mend Golem - Level 15
Program Golem - Level 40
Toy Golem - Level 56
Wood Golem - Level 9

Smith Skills
Adjust Arms and Armor - Level 7
Refine Ore - Level 10
Smelt Down - Level 1
Smithing - Level 46

Sculptor Skills
Detect Clay - Level 8
Mend Ceramic - Level 5
Refine Clay - Level 16
Sculpting - Level 58

Equipment
Journeyman Tailor's Apron of fire resistance (+6 Armor, +10 Tailoring, Resist Fire 9)(+2 Armor, +4 Tailoring, +3 Resist Fire from WIB)
Okay Quality Bling
Ringtail Master's Coat (+5 CHA, +5 LUCK, +5 Armor, +5 Fate)(+2 CHA, LUCK, Armor, Fate from WIB)
Rod of Baronly Might (+5 CHA, +5 WIS, +10 Cool)(+2 CHA, WIS, +4 Cool from WIB)
Yellow Belt of Bravado (+5 AGL, +5 DEX, +5 to the Fancy Flourish skill)(+2 AGL, DEX, Fancy Flourish from WIB)
Toy Top Hat (CHA +10)(+4 CHA from WIB)

Inventory
A Finely-Made Dagger (Dagger Level 5)
Tailor's Tools
A small jewelry box with a few reagents and crystals, most minor.
1 bead of Mend Golem (Level 15)
Minorphone (Enhances voice and social skills focused through it twice per day)

Quests

Unlocked Jobs
Berserker, Cleric, Cook, Cultist, Grifter, **Spirit Medium,** Tamer, Wizard

Cecelia's new body would only be the first step, he knew. To save her, to save himself, to save everyone, they would have to start a new journey.

And this time, the teddy bear swore that everyone he loved would get through it alive...

CHAPTER 1: SPARKS IN THE NIGHT

"Golem Animus."

The teddy bear spoke, and everything changed.

Threadbare watched, worried, as the invisible pressure built, stronger than he'd ever felt it before when he animated a golem. But he had done this many times, and his skill was high, high enough that he could focus his will. Focus his will, and ensure that his best and oldest friend had the body they'd gone to so much effort to prepare.

And with joy in his heart, he watched as the ceramic dolly under his paw opened her eyes and tried to move her mouth.

Your Golem Animus skill is now level 47!

"Afgart." She vocalized. "Umf. Ango. Ahng on. Hang on."

"Newborn's Mercy," hissed Zuula, laying her head on Cecelia's red, frizzy hair.

"Yorgum's blessing of luck on Cecelia!" Fluffbear squeaked, slapping her hand on the ball-jointed doll's ankle.

"Status," Cecelia said.

Threadbare smiled and offered her a paw up.

And the porcelain doll took it, testing her new legs, and finding them graceful enough.

"It's fine, I hope?" Threadbare asked. He'd put a lot of work into learning and skilling up the sculptor job, which was evidently what you needed to make clay things and pottery things as well. A LOT of work, knowing that they only had one shot at this. There was a makeshift kiln out back, filled with his failures, and after a full week of grinding, his successes.

"It is."

"So what didja get?" The three-foot-long wooden dragon who'd been watching through the doorway pushed herself into the bedroom. "Tell me the racial skills are totes bitchin'."

"Well, the stats are way better than starting toy golems," Cecelia told Madeline, smoothing her green cloth dress with fingers that Threadbare had crafted individually then worked into tiny ball joints, with Fluffbear's help. "Better than wood, too. I've got a few triple digit attributes, mainly from my adventuring job levels, I think."

"Nice!" Madeline said, nuzzling her with one oaken cheek. "I shoulda held out fah clay. Be a pahttery dragon or something."

"Well, one of the skills would do you no good. I'm immune to fire, which is of no use to you." Cecelia said, easing herself down from the wrecked bedframe. Like most of the rest of the farmhouse, it was ruined, long gone to seed, with mold and vines growing over and through it. "And I have Gorgeous, which is like your Adorable skill, evidently. I skilled it up a bunch when I woke up."

"Yeah, I'm thinking you're beautiful," the two-foot-tall wooden minotaur said, hooking thumbs through his belt. "Not that, uh, well. I mean... ah, let's not make it weird," Garon finished.

"No worry. I know what you mean." Cecelia studied her pale hands and shrugged. "I guess. It's... this is going to take some getting used to." She frowned, as something on her status screen caught her attention. "My hit points aren't much better than a wood golem's, but my armor is over a hundred. Some of that's probably from my Human job but not much." Cecelia said, rubbing her chin with one ceramic hand. "I wonder if I'd stayed unfired, if it would be reversed? High hit points, low armor?"

"Yeah yeah," Zuula said. The plush half-orc doll eased herself from the foot of the bed, dropped down next to the armored black teddy bear. "Skip to important part. How many of you jobs and levels you get back?"

"Five animator, five enchanter, five knight... and five Steam Knight." She smiled.

And Threadbare felt joy well up inside him. It had been a lot of work and time to figure out how to make her face flexible enough to do that, with the tiny joints and the interplay of her wood skeleton and stuffing 'muscles'. But it had been worth every bit of grinding to see his little girl smile again.

"Then we have what we need." Garon relaxed, adjusted the harness slung over his wood-and-fur chest. The hatchet he'd found kept tugging it down.

"I'm thinking of askin' for an upgrade," Madeline said, turning glass eyes on Threadbare. They were marbles, catseye marbles they'd found in the attic while casing the ruin. Probably the closest thing they'd get to a dragon's slit pupils, Madeline had said. "Bettah stats are okay wit' me."

"Not right now. We only had the one pinch of green reagent. And that was risky enough to get." Threadbare shook his head. "But speaking of that, we need to go thank Graves. I think he'll appreciate the results of his sacrifice. And his hard work."

The doll haunters and their golem friends filed out of the room, making their way around the big gap in the floorboards, stepping carefully as the floor creaked and groaned.

They followed the faint sound of music. Eerie and in no tongue that anything on this plane spoke, it wound its way through the old house from outside. The late, unlamented Pastor Hatecraft would have called it eldritch, but then he always was an excitable one.

No, there was nothing eldritch here. The assorted constructs knew it was only their friend Glub, barding it up.

They found him outside the barn, which was moderately better preserved than the house and intact enough to hold Annie Mata's wagon. A fire crackled not far from the barn doorway, and the rest of their friends sat around the campsite, watching them approach with relieved eyes. They were five in number, a big black bobcat and a cougar about half his size, both cats sound asleep by the warmest part of the fire. Next to them was a black-haired man wearing a padded cloth tunic and trousers, so thin that his bones were flush to his skin in places. Sitting on a nearby log was a little wooden doll that could only be described as a fishman, down to its leather catfish whiskers and big googly eyes.

And then there was the catgirl.

"Oh wow!" A wooden marionette, of a black-haired woman with two kitty ears sticking out of her head and a tail poking out through a hole in her pants jumped up, stringless. She grinned at Cecelia, showing tiny fangs. "Captain, you're gorgeous! Desu, desu."

"You're still saying that word, Kayin?" Garon snorted. "Seriously?"

"Shut up. I swear it gets me racial job experience," the assassin who'd once been human but was now an undead spirit haunting a wooden catgirl golem walked up to Cecelia and knelt. "Captain! Reporting for duty!"

"Oh get up. Come on, come on," Cecelia took her shoulders and straightened her to her feet. Her ball-jointed body was one of the larger golems here, standing two feet high, towering over her companions. "Pretty sure that oath was only until death."

"Kayin swore a new one," offered the sole living human in the group from the comfort of the fire. Graves leaned his withered body over his cane, studying Cecelia. "I'll swear to a new code myself, as soon as I get another knight level. My armor's gone, so I'll need all the defense boosts

I can get."

"I still feel guilty about that," Cecelia looked away. "That was enchanted armor."

"Don't be. I'm just glad we guessed right, and one of its components was green reagent. And after the bear gave up his pants for the task, I couldn't do any less."

"It does feel a little strange without them," Threadbare said, looking down to his paw, and the golden, bear-headed rod he now had to wield without the benefit of his hammerspace pocket. "My scepter's out in the open now, for everyone to see."

There was a pause, then everyone but Threadbare and Fluffbear and the cats were laughing.

"Um," the teddy bear said, puzzled.

"It's probably a fart joke. Or about poop. Or a sex joke," Fluffbear explained to him.

"It de last one. Sex joke." Zuula said, winding down and proceeding to explain the meaning of the joke in detail.

Threadbare still didn't see why it was funny, but whatever. If his friends got a good laugh out of it, he didn't mind.

"Besides," Graves said, "the armor would have made me stand out more. I'm sure that the inquisitor has reported me as a traitor by now. And it would've... hm... have you heard of the swordsman's curse?"

"Oh. That." Cecelia snorted. Kayin nodded.

"I don't think we have." Threadbare glanced back to Garon, Madeline, and Zuula, who were three of his big touchstones for worldly knowledge. They all shook their heads.

"It's a dumb, macho thing. So it's mainly bored noblemen and soldiers, is who you see it in," Cecelia explained. "If someone is openly carrying a sword you kind of expect them to know how to use it. And if you think they might not and YOU can use your sword, you call them out to see who's better. Then you fight, and if you win you look good, and if you lose you can kiss up to the winner, and maybe they'll be your friend. And then you'll have a friend who's better than you at fighting."

"It seems like a big waste of time," Threadbare said. "Why not just be friends at the start of it all?"

"Because the swords get in the way, for certain types of people," Cecelia said.

"Some people had to go through a lot to earn those swords," Kayin said. "Not that I'm defending it, but... they see someone else with a sword, they maybe want to test to see if they're at the same point. Been through the same stuff."

"My point is," Graves said, settling back onto his broken chair, "if I go around wearing really heavy armor, then when we get into a fight people are going to assume I'm a very hard target and try to hit me really hard. Whereas if I'm wearing cloth, they'll go oh, a mage. And probably send someone sneaky to shank me while the tanks batter at each other. Which is where Always in Uniform comes in. An invisible, weightless chain mail-equivalent, you know how that goes, Cecelia."

"Thanks for reminding me," the doll smiled. **"Always in Uniform."** Her eyebrows rose, and Threadbare sighed in relief to see it. Those had been tricky to rig. "Oh! It stacks with my golem armor!" Cecelia said.

"Good. We need you alive and as hard a target as possible if this is going to work," Garon said, leaning on one of Madeline's wings as she played with the fire. "Which means that if and when we get a higher golem option possible, we have to consider transplanting you. So don't get too comfy."

"Thanks again for letting me try that out," Graves said to Kayin. "Good to know we can swap people around without destroying the golem bodies first."

Bored by all the talk about swords and challenges and stuff that was self-evident to every orc, Zuula wandered over to Glub, who was merrily humming along more quietly, now that his pals were back and chatting. "He eating?" She said, jerking a cloth thumb towards Graves.

"Oh yeah dude," Glub broke off singing, and pointed to a pot, set next to the fire. "Some kinda furry critter stew. Kayin killed the fuck out of it."

Graves had been afflicted by the kiss of a succubus. It had essentially withered his strength, and he needed help with a lot of things. Teaching him animator levels let him move around without too much pain, by dint of turning his clothing into something like temporary golems, but hunting and foraging his own food was a lot to ask of the guy. Especially since he'd been born a street rat and thought the woods were something you moved through as quickly as possible when you traveled to different settlements.

"I'm going to need to work on soulstones more," Threadbare said finally, "before we do any more spirit transplants. Otherwise you're going to lose levels you'll need later."

"And I'll keep working on that refine soulstone skill," Graves promised. "Fortunately we've got a lot of volunteers to experiment with, and extra soulstones to transfer them to when I get failures." He jerked a thumb spasmodically back at the wagon and the crate of soulstones within it. "It worked, didn't it?" He said, worried, looking to Cecelia.

"Level five across the board, in four adventuring jobs. Also got all my crafting jobs." She smiled, and Graves sagged in relief. "But I'm not a scout, so four's the maximum, I'm guessing."

"It might be that a higher soulstone skill affects that," Threadbare said. "At any rate, no one die again until we know more about it, okay?"

Everyone promised to do their best.

"Are they doing all right?" Threadbare glanced over at the crate.

"Some grumbling, but yes," Graves said. "An advantage of them all being cultists, I suppose. They'd expected some form of weird afterlife down the road, this is actually probably a bit better than their prior expectations. They do want to get into new bodies as fast as possible, though."

"Once we get more reagents, yes," Threadbare said. They'd burned through all the rest of the yellow dust animating wooden shells for Kayin and Garon and Madeline.

"And there's only one likely source for that and all the other things that we'll need, so we need to figure out our approach," Cecelia said. "Garon, could you?"

The minotaur nodded. **"Secure the Perimeter,"** he said and glanced around. "Yeah, we're good. Or they're good enough at hiding that it doesn't matter, and we can't stop them anyway."

"Good." Cecelia scooted in closer to the fire. "We need to ally with the dwarves. There's only two real points of resistance left in Cylvania, and they're the bigger side."

"Easier ta find, too. Not like the othah guys. The ranjahs are all over the place," Madeline said.

"And there's no guarantee they'll talk to us, since they don't need help as badly." Cecelia nodded, her frizzy red hair swaying against her porcelain scalp. She reached up and touched it. "What is this stuff, by the way?"

"Blisterweed pod silk," said Zuula. "Relax. We boil it to make it frizzy, get de poison out. Zuula got better uses for dat stuff.' She indicated a barrel in back of the cart. "Added it to de poison stores."

"I'm going to have to have a long talk with you later about those poisons," said Kayin, ears twitching. "Sorry to interrupt, desu. So, dwarves?"

"Dwarves." Cecelia spread her arms. "I've spent the last half a year reading the intelligence reports and preparing to battle them. They're sturdy, they're stubborn, but they've been hard pressed by the last five years. If we approach them the right way, they won't turn us down. Especially when we tell them we can convert reagents into troops. Three hundred and some golems can turn the tide in just about any battle on that front, with four exceptions."

"The Hand," Graves said, and Madeline and Garon whistled, low and worried.

Cecelia nodded. "Right. We're not set up for open battle against any of the Hand. Not yet."

"What hand?" Threadbare asked.

"Ah, right, you ignorant," Zuula said, patting his paw. "Four of de King's most elite servants. Powerful adventurers. Maybe."

"Or they might be demons in disguise. There's always been talk," Garon said. "That Melos killed his old adventuring group, murdered his friends, and traded them in for high-level demons."

"My father insists that he didn't kill them," Cecelia said. "But I wouldn't put it past him to recycle their corpses if someone else did. If he did it to my mother, he wouldn't hesitate to do it to anyone else. He's pragmatic that way. But yeah, the Hand are the reason that the dwarves can't win without help, and they're a problem we'll have to face sooner or later. There's four of them. And that's one advantage we can give the dwarves straight away." The ceramic doll grinned.

"Oh?" Graves asked.

"Remember I told you I read up on intelligence reports? The best ones were from The Lurker, the spy and infiltrator of the Hand. He's infiltrated the dwarves, and he spies on them nonstop. We were well on our way to losing before that, even with the Hand's help. Since then, things have been turning around. But I know enough about him that if the dwarves believe us, we can probably help them ferret him out."

"But first we have to reach the dwarves," Kayin said. "How are we gonna do that?"

"We're not far from the main roads," Garon said. "This is the outskirts of Grubholm, so a couple days north should get us there. The front's only another day or two east, unless it's moved on us."

Cecelia rubbed her hair. "It's not enough. We could get to the front, but we can't approach the moats without the Crown's army noticing. They've got observation posts every mile along there, with people looking west watching for rangers, and people listening east, for sappers. If we want to break the lines we need to get up to one, disable the watchers, then scoot before they notice. Otherwise they'll call in fire support, and that'll mean anything from Wark Riders to Dragon Knights to Steam Knights to one of the Hand themselves. We're not really set up to survive most of that."

"So we need to sneak in among them?" Threadbare asked.

"Yeah. But we need to do it against folks who have a good chance of spotting rangers in the wilderness." Kayin sighed. "Even at my old levels, I don't know if it'd be doable. At level five? No. And not with you guys along, no offense. Most of you are no good at it." She shot

Madeline an envious look. "Except you, you're scary quiet for what should be a big clattery wooden toy. What's up with that?"

Madeline's carved reptilian jaw fell open in a smile, and she lifted a paw to show Kayin the cloth pads sewn on under it.

"Fucking sweet!"

"Inorite!"

"Eeeeee I'm totally doing that!"

Threadbare cleared his throat. The catgirl and dragon fell silent, and the rest of the group looked to him. "Who goes to these observation posts, normally?"

"Supply shipments," Graves said.

"Personnel rotations, groups of infantry and specialists cycling in and out," Cecelia added.

"Regular patrols," Kayin said, eyes still on the sweet little sneaky dragon feet, her tail and ears twitching.

Garon shook his wooden-horned head. "I'm going to go out on a limb here and guess that the guys at the observation posts know the schedules for all three of those types of visitors."

"Oh yeah," Cecelia said. "The rangers are sneaky, so the staff on duty know to keep security tight. As soon as a convoy is ready, coded messages get flashed up along the line with semaphore flags with the rest of the day's messages, telling them what's coming, who's with it, and when it'll arrive. And the code changes weekly."

"No shit?" Madeline peered at her. "That's some pretty smaht stuff. We talkin' about the same Crown that overreacts and slaughtahs villages over minor shit?"

Cecelia rubbed her hair, Graves sighed, and Kayin shook her head. "The thing to realize," Cecelia said, "is that the Crown forces, for the most part, are people who have put a lot of faith in my Father because to do otherwise would be to admit that they've been wrong for years, and they're very afraid of what would happen if he fails. He's the devil they know. And..." She looked out into the darkness, gathering strength. "... and some of them have been fooled pretty thoroughly. I was. And it only took a few years of him and... her... working on me. So a lot of the soldiers and a good part of the officers are smart, motivated people trying to make the most of a bad situation and win the war quickly so that everyone can go home."

"But it won't work that way," said Threadbare. "There will always be an enemy, won't there?" He'd spent a great deal of time thinking this over, trying to figure out how a very bad King and some obviously evil demons could keep making good people do what they wanted them to. "As long as there is some other enemy to fight, then most people won't fight the King. So he has to keep making enemies or keeping some around or else his own subjects will be very upset with him."

"They already ah," Madeline said. "But yeah. People get restless in peacetahm and forget about how horrible wah is. They go lookin' for fights, and the King's a big fat tahget unless he shifts blame like a propah cowahd."

"Yes," Cecelia said, picking up a stick and poking the fire. "I see it now. I fought for peace, but any peace we could win was a lie. It wouldn't last. We need a good one, one without demons and murders and skipping trials, and we won't get that with my Father in power. Heck, it might be a moot point even with him in power. We're running low on food, have been for..." She stopped. "Supplies."

"Yes?" Threadbare knew this tone. This was her 'idea' tone. And he smiled to see the beautifully-sculpted face he'd given her twist in joy. She'd figured something out!

Evidently Glub recognized it too, because he switched from soft humming to dramatic drumming on a nearby log, knocking out an uplifting, hopeful beat.

"All supplies go through Fort Bronze," Cecelia said, slowly, eyes gleaming. "Which is a heck of a lot easier to get into than the observation posts and has people and things coming and going all the time. Garon, Madeline, how far is Pads Village from here, do you think?"

"Pads? That craphole? A couple of days in the wrong direction, through some bandit-filled wilderness," Garon said, consulting his knowledge of the local geography.

"Less bandit-filled now," Graves grinned. "I see where you're going with this."

"I know how we're going to get in," said Cecelia. "And once we're in, we can get ourselves assigned to an observation post shipment. All we have to do is get a look at the logistics records and find a good one."

"That'll be the hard part, desu," Kayin threw in. "Probably have to break into General Mastoya's office, for that."

"Wait," Zuula said, whipping her head around, and putting down the makeshift drumsticks she'd been using to backup Glub. "What you say?" Her voice was hoarse and tense, and her button eyes practically burned as she stared at the little catgirl.

Kayin shrank back from the small shaman's sudden intensity. "That we'll have to break into the General's office, and—"

"General Mastoya," said Garon.

The circle of friends went silent, staring as Garon and Zuula shared a long glance.

"You know her?" Cecelia said, confused. "She is a half-orc too, I guess. But I didn't want to assume."

"Yeah," Garon and Zuula said, simultaneously. "We know her…"

A quick accounting followed. Cecelia listened, covering her mouth with her hands as Zuula told of the fatal duel she'd lost to her own daughter and how said daughter had murdered Garon inadvertantly.

Garon filled in the blanks on the last part. "…and then Madeline found me and vamped me. Then *that* got resolved…"

"Messily," Madeline added, "but it worked out okay in the end so whatevah."

"…And now I'm here. And I know what I have to do."

The friends looked at Garon, who spread his hands. "My reason for keeping on here, is to talk with Mastoya again. To let her know I forgive her. To let her tell me she's sorry, if that's what it takes, because I know it's eating her up inside."

"This might not be the best opportunity," Graves said. "We're trying to run a covert mission, here. At least, I'm assuming that's where you were going with this, Cecelia?"

"Yes. The Alderman of Paws owes me a favor. It'd be easy to get a wagonload of food from them, take it to the front and pack us in with the food. You'd be driving, of course. Posing as an older teamster, since, well…" Cecelia indicated his wasted frame. "Sorry."

"No apologies needed. I'll need to shave," Graves said, rubbing his goatee. "Pity. But this doesn't change my point. Talking to General Mastoya at this time, *General* Mastoya, the High Knight of the Empire herself, is a really, really bad way to stay covert."

"But what if I can turn her?" Garon asked.

"No," Zuula said.

"Mom, look. I know what you think of her—"

"No you don't," Zuula said, and the toys and their token human looked at her in surprise. Even through the voicebox that she used to speak, her words held raw pain. "Zuula failed her. She grew up wrong, but she grew up strong. She will not change."

"She seemed strong to me, when I met her," Cecelia mused. "But tired. And a little sad. Right in the middle of a briefing, she hauled out a bottle of booze and started drinking."

"Wait, you're serious?" Garon said, leaning forward, and studying her with bovine carved eyes. "Yeah, something's wrong. The Mastoya I used to know would never drink."

"Yes. Which is why you idea is bad idea now," Zuula said. "She is not Mastoya you used to know. She is Mastoya of now, General Mastoya, and Zuula got no idea how you talkin' with her would go."

"Isn't that why you're along, Mom? To get me this shot?"

"Yeah, but if it's at the risk of Cecelia's lives and our own, she's got a point, desu," Kayin piped up.

"Would you can it with that word?" Garon snapped. "Gah. Sorry." He rubbed his snout, rattling wood on wood. "Look. What if it isn't at the risk of your lives?"

"Why don't you tell us what you're planning?" Threadbar offered. "And if we don't think it will work out, you wait until another time to talk to her?"

"That's a bad idea," Garon said. "Because right now we're *not* her enemies. Look, I know how she thinks. Once you're her enemy, it doesn't matter what you say or do, she'll beat you or die trying. But once we ally with the dwarves, we *will* be her enemies, and everything gets orc simple then. Uh, sorry, Mom."

"Is fine," Zuula said. "The words, anyway. This idea, not so much."

"My point is once we ally with the dwarves, we either beat the Crown forces or we fail, and either way I lose my shot at talking with her in any sort of situation where she might hear me out. This is it. This is my chance... our chance to get her to listen. To save my sister's soul."

The fire popped and cracked, as they considered it.

"Tahning the High Knight would be a right kick in the pants for the Crown," Madeline said. "And losing the general would give the dwahves a chance for a win."

"You like this idea?" Kayin shot the dragon a glance.

"It's risky, yeah, but if Garon can do it..."

"And what if it's just risky for me?" Garon asked. "Look, we'll have to break into her office anyway. Leave me behind after we do, and I'll talk with her. If it comes to a fight, I'll fight to the death, then go run back to a soulstone."

"Make sure you get the right one, if that happens," Graves added. "There are sometimes other necromancers rotating through the fort. It'd be *unlucky* if that happens." He glared hard at Garon, who looked away.

"Yeah. I need more luck. I also need the best charisma I can get. Hell..." Garon looked at Threadbare. "We've got a bit of prep time, right? Can you montage me Ruler?"

"I could. Are you sure?"

"Positive. I only ever had two adventuring jobs when I was alive, and thanks to Graves refining the soulstones, I've got two more job slots open. Ruler is charisma, luck, and wisdom, right?"

"Yes." Threadbare nodded. "I could loan you my scepter too, if you want."

"No. That's fine. Just the job and some grinding should do fine. If we've got time for it."

"We should," Cecelia said.

"To a point," Graves added, glancing back at the crates. "I told you I used to be in the Royal Necromancers, right?"

"Yeah," Garon glanced at him. "Is there something going on with them?"

"The royal necromancers? No. But a few times I got access to their vaults, to borrow magic items or read old texts. We've got a few boxes of soulstones down there, traitors mainly. Some of them have been in there a while."

"And?"

"Once, out of curiosity, I cast speak with dead on them. And for the next three days I was deafened. They were screaming, Garon. Screaming endlessly, without lungs."

"Shit," Madeline said.

"Yes. No body, no senses, and unless someone casts speak with dead, no way to talk to anyone else. Just eternity in your own little crystal prison, with no one but yourself for company." Graves shot another look back at the wagon. "It hasn't sunk in to most of them, yet, but I've been making sure to cast the speak with dead spell three times daily, and let them chat with themselves and myself. But sooner or later it won't be enough. We need to get them bodies, and the longer we take on that, the more pain and suffering it's going to cause for them."

And then, everyone, Threadbare included, looked to Cecelia.

She closed her ceramic eyelids. "Even after death I don't get to escape these kinds of decisions, huh?"

"You can if you want," Threadbare offered. "Nobody's really in charge here. We could talk it over and put it to the vote."

"Calling frogshit on that one, boss," Glub piped up for the first time, and everyone else looked over to him, surprised. "What you say usually goes. You're kind of the most important dude here. I think it's the hat. It's totally because of the hat, isn't it?"

Threadbare took of his top hat and looked at it. "It's nice, and I like it. But if anyone else needed it, they could have it."

"No," Cecelia said, patting his head. "Keep it. It looks nice on you. And I gave it to you, a long time ago, so no takebacks. So how long do you think we should take to grind, how long do you think we should ask our soulstoned people to wait?"

"Why don't we ask them?" Threadbare said.

Graves blinked. "Er. Well, it might get them thinking about it if they haven't already."

"But hey, they're cultists, like you said earlier," Kayin threw in. "Probably used to hard questions anyway, right?"

"Probably a bit more inured to the notion of existential dread. Yes, let me go ask them." Graves headed back to the wagon, muttering **"Speak with Dead,"** along the way. "Hello!" he said and got a chorus of happy voices back, gabbing and babbling at him as he settled in to listen, throwing in small talk as needed.

The minutes crawled on. The toys watched, then drifted off to their various business, until it was just Cecelia, Threadbare, and Kayin waiting by the fire.

Threadbare took off his top hat and rubbed his head again, then decided to risk it. "Celia?"

"Yes?"

"If it's not too much of a bother, could I ask you to hold me please? Like you used to do?"

He watched her face shuffle, resolve into a sad smile. "Oh, Threadbare." She scooped him up, settled down on one of the fallen logs, and Threadbare sighed in happiness as he settled into her embrace as best he could.

He'd waited five years for this, and it was good. Finally, he was in his little girl's arms again, and it didn't matter that they were ceramic, or that she smelled different, or that she was smaller than she used to be. She was still Celia, and he was still her teddy bear, and all was right with the world.

That lasted for a few minutes, then Cecelia shifted, surprised. "What?"

"You look comfy. Do you mind?" Kayin asked.

"Um. I guess not."

Threadbare turned his head, as wooden legs poked against him. Kayin had settled in Cecelia's lap, curled up in a catlike ball.

"This isn't like you, that's all," Cecelia said.

"I know. But it feels right," Kayin said. "I... tell the truth, I didn't expect shifting over to a catkin to influence me this much. It's like thinking through jelly, my impulse control is all screwy, and my attention span is shot all to hell."

"If you want, when Graves isn't busy he could try that Evict Spirit skill on you, transfer you to another body."

"This is the last wood golem we've got though, right? And Threadbare, you're out of the reagents to make another?"

"Yes," Threadbare replied, shortly. He was a little cross with her for interrupting cuddle time.

"Besides, I think it'll get easier once I get my mental stats up," Kayin sighed. "Didn't expect catkin to be so low. Or to be so... it's like everything's way more fun, and the less seriously I take it, the better I feel. Catkin are a weird race, I guess. I'm thinking the one I ran into when I was a contract killer was a really experienced one. And I shouldn't gripe anyway, because I got the skill I wanted out of it."

"Oh?"

"It's called Nine Lives. I THOUGHT something was screwy about that catgirl. I should've killed her three times over, but each time she got back up."

"Did you get her, in the end?"

"No, she managed to escape. I heard she ran off and started a dungeon somewhere, then got punked by the royal guards eventually. Or maybe not, maybe she still had some lives left. Seriously the skill's THAT good."

"Oh." Cecelia settled back. "Sorry, just trying to get comfy."

"If you want me to move, that's fine. I... know we didn't have this sort of relationship. Or any, really, beyond mutual respect and being knights together. I'm not looking for anything, just..."

"Friends?" Threadbare offered.

"Friends," Kayin decided. "Friends is good. Yeah, let's do that."

"I'm game," Cecelia said. Her hand strayed down to rub between Kayin's ears, and the catgirl emitted her first surprised purr. "I never had too many of those. I'm glad you're one of them."

Friends, Threadbare thought. *Yes, that would do.* His little girl was back, but he had to share her, now. But that was fine, because she'd still cuddle him, and that was all he wanted, really was for her to be happy and give him lots of hugs.

And as they waited, a heavy, black weight settled in to one side of them, as Pulsivar moved over to join the nap pile. "Um..." Cecelia said, flailing for purchase with her free arm and bracing herself against a wooden bole.

Then Mopsy moved in on the other side, and it got easier.

For a while, the toy golem and the two doll haunters just lay there with the cats in the cuddle puddle, with the fire burning down, and the stars overhead. And it was right.

Eventually, Graves finished his discussion, moved back to the fire, and saw what had become of his friends.

Your Adorable skill is now level 31!

Smiling, Graves turned his back, and started shuffling off, taking it slow, his animated pants moving his wasted muscles along while he balanced with the cane. "See you in the morning, then."

"No, it's fine," Cecelia said. "We don't sleep like this, do we? I mean, golems don't sleep, right?"

"Not normally," Threadbare said. He sighed, and wiggled down, out of the cuddle pile. "What did they say?"

"I'll get the others, first," Graves yawned. "You may not sleep, but I do, and it's been a long day so I only want to explain it once."

Soon, the toys were reconvened, much to the disgruntlement of the cats who had enjoyed sleeping next to a fire-warmed porcelain doll.

"Most of them are fine with waiting," said Graves. "They put their trust in you, and you didn't disappoint them. Their friends and neighbors and relatives who aren't in the cult are safely away, and you spent a ton of resources making toy golems to protect the ones who are braving the wilds. But the problem lies with the children. Oh not the really young ones, those all got evacuated, but some of the teenagers were old enough to be cultists, and they're taking the angst a bit harder."

"Figures," Kayin said.

"Yes. I'm pretty sure a lot of them had body issues to start with, and this isn't helping. It's not so bad, not yet, but given time, it could cause major rifts. Which is rough, because when they're having a bad time of it, it's harder for the adults."

"How long do they think they have?" Threadbare asked, concerned. Of COURSE the children were the first priority!

"I talked with the parents privately. Maybe a few weeks. Maybe a month if we're really lucky, and I start animating spare toys and letting them take them out for a spin, work out some of their issues with temporary animi. Even so we're still probably going to lose a few to madness."

Cecelia rubbed her hair. "A couple of days to Pads. About a week or more up the main roads to Fort Bronze. Then a day or two out to an observation post. It leaves us two weeks, at the most."

"Then let's take one," Threadbare said. "One to sort out what we need and grind as best we can." He looked to Garon. "Do you think you can do it?"

"Yeah. Give me command of the training group, and it should skill up the ruler skills nicely." The little minotaur nodded to Zuula. "She scoped out ruins of Grubholm while Graves was busy. Goblin sign all over."

"Goblins?" Kayin said, straightening up. "Didn't think there were many left in the kingdom."

"Not in de settled places," Zuula said. "But in de empty spaces, still lots of dem. Dey stay out of sight, live in ruins. Everyt'ing eat dem. Dey find a place to nest, den breed, den expand out until people or stronger monsters come an' kill dem." Zuula grinned. "Stronger monsters like us."

"Are you sure we should be doing this?" Fluffbear squeaked. "Just going in and killing them for the experience?"

"We'd be doing the kingdom a favor," Graves said. "Goblins have about sixty-three different recipes for cooking human babies."

"What?" Fluffbear shouted, then jumped up. "Where'd I put my whip!"

"Patience," Zuula consoled. "Goblins be darkspawn. We go in day when we go. Kind of surprised they haven't come to see our fire tonight. But we behind a ridge, and dey lazy, so maybe dat it."

"So you need to be a Ruler." Threadbare pointed a paw at Garon. "Does anyone else need a montage? I can do two per day." That was roughly correct. Each one took about ten to twelve hours.

"Yeah, we're about to do a covert mission, right?" Kayin spoke up. "I've been thinking that over. We need more scouts in the group. I'll take one of them."

"I can teach ya while Threadbeah's montaging Gar." Madeline offered.

Threadbare twisted to look at her, in surprise. "You learned scout?"

"Hey, I had a long and exciting unlife befoah I met you guys, just didn't have no jahb slahts to use all the stuff I unlocked. So I had two more open when I got my soulstone upgraded, then re-embodied. I figahed, why wait? Yer looking at not only a faiah elementalist, but a scout and a merchant!"

"You didn't tell us you were taking that stuff," Garon said.

"I don't have to. That's mostly my business." Madeline looked at him, glass eyes glittering in the firelight. "I like you guys, but ya not the boss of me."

"Right, right, I didn't mean anything by it... wait, merchant?"

"Yeah! Check this out!" Madeline headed off into the ruins of the house and returned with a backpack, dragging it along with her mouth.

"I wondered why you asked me to sew that," Threadbare said. "Does it have some significance to merchants?"

"Watch!" Madeline grinned, stuck her head in the pack, and pulled out a sack of coins, the ones that the villagers had given them to hang on to. Then a set of golden candlesticks from Hatecraft's ritual room. Then several stuffed toys. Then one of the wooden cats they'd originally used to pull the wagon.

"There's no way all that fit in there," Cecelia said. "May I?"

"Shuah!"

Cecelia went over to the pack, stared into it. Then stuck her head in, and abruptly she was gone.

"Celia!" Threadbare charged up to the pack, and Madeline hastily put a wing in his way. "It's fine, watch." She reached her head in again, and the wooden dragon drew Cecelia out, Madeline's maw holding one ceramic hand and drawing her forth.

"That was weird," Cecelia said. "It's like a room with black walls and floor, but there's light coming from somewhere. And there's random junk on the floor. It's not that big, maybe closet-sized?"

"Yeah. Skill says it gets biggah as I level it. Should be safe to be in theah so long as the spell doesn't expaiah."

"What happens then?" Kayin said, tail twitching. "Because I'm seeing some possibilities for infiltrating the fort like this."

"If it expaiahs whatever's inside explodes outward and the pack's ruined. Lasts like an howah per merchant level thoah. Not too bad to cast, either, just some sanity."

"Why Merchant? Why Scout for that matter?" Garon asked. "I'm not seeing a combo for fire elementalist or dragon in there."

"Nice broad range of attribute boosts. Int and Wis between 'em foah boosting sanity." Madeline shrugged. "And it turned out we didn't need jewelah and with no thumbs I'm crap at crafting anyway, but I figga handling gold and hoarding it will help me level dragon. Besides, with Scout, I can fly recon and message back to you and be invisible when I need to. Invisible dragon? Pssh, that's a no brainah."

"With three scouts in the party that'll let us split up if we have to," Cecelia said. "Does anyone else have any job slots to fill out?"

"If you want to try the Evict Spirit soulstone upgrade combo we discussed, I could maybe give you more jobs," Graves said to Glub.

"Dude, I dunnno. Bard's pretty sweet by itself." The little fishmen thought it over. "Besides I've only got like a few unlocks."

"Well, what are they?"

"Cultist, Explorer, and Water Elementalist."

"I'm going to say please don't be a cultist," Threadbare decided.

"Yeah, that's really not my thing. My old one's cool and all, but I'm not about to worship the dude. Wouldn't feel right."

"Explorer's kind of weak," Garon said. "That's what I always heard about it, anyway."

"I don't know about that," Cecelia said. "Explorers from outside made the greater waymarks when they passed through and left us the waystones so we could use them. That's what's let the Crown maintain the front, by teleporting the Hand and other important people and supplies from Waystone to Waystone one person and packload at a time. If we had more of them, or the cooldown wasn't so bad... if my father had more of them, then the war would be over by now."

"How high level is that?" Garon asked. "That's got to be like a twenty, twenty-five. I don't know if he can grind it high enough to be useful in time."

"Yeah, but theah's gonna be a time AFTAH, raht?" Said Madeline.

"If he wants it, then let him take it. And watah elementalist would be totally bitchin' ta have around. Be like synergy with my faiah and all."

"It'd also give you water resistance so your parts don't degrade underwater," said Kayin. "Otherwise your leather bits will need a lot of mending or replacing eventually."

"Oh? Oh yeah, that'd be a hassle," Glub nodded. "Sure dude man, let's try that spirit shuffle trick while they montage."

"Absolutely," Grave said. "It'll be worth it to skill that up, if nothing else."

"Then yeah, I'll do that. After all, I'll have a job slot left, right? So I might as well go all in here. Uh, except for Cultist."

"Thank you," Threadbare said.

"How about you, Mom? It'd probably take a spirit eviction, and you'd lose a few levels, but it'd open up more jobs."

"No," Zuula said. "Best you can do is five, right Graveman?"

"Graves. And yes, that's the best I can do right now with the skill I've got."

"Then no. Zuula just got level ten. Not worth it to go back to being weak. Not wit'out bitchin new body." She glanced over to Threadbare. "Still got the picture she drew you?"

Threadbare took it out, and showed it to the group. Silence fell around the fire, as Graves struggled not to laugh, Kayin hid her face, and Cecelia looked away, coughing desperately.

"Are those battleaxes for hands?" Garon asked.

"And is that faia yoah breathing?" Madeline said, grinning wide.

"No. Dose be lighting bolts. De fire be coming from Zuula's ass." The little plush half-orc pointed with her spear.

Graves lost it then, waving his hands as he headed into the barn "All right, all right, it's late. Good, heh, goodnight. Talk to me in the morning if you need something."

"It's the heaps of skulls that you're crushing that have me confused," Missus Fluffbear said, leaning in closer. "Are those things we have to make for you?"

"What? No. Zuula provide her own skulls." She considered. "Maybe you make a few clay ones just to start. Starter skulls. So her enemies know what is in store."

"Oh, I'm pretty sure they'd know just from one look at you." Garon said, shaking his head. "All right. Let's get montaging. If we start now, we should be finished before noon tomorrow."

CHAPTER 2: HECK COMES TO FROGTOWN

Noon rolled over the village of Grubholm. Once a trapping and farrier outpost at the edge of the marsh, it had fallen a decade ago to monsters. Evacuees had spoken of eyes in the night, twisted little men striking from the dark places of the marsh in the dead of the night. Enough had died that the surviving families threw up their hands, packed up their supplies, and headed out for greener pastures.

Abandoned by civilization, filled with monsters, it was now only really useful to adventurers looking for experience and loot. Like the seven toys, and their mounts, who moved slowly along the old road, eyes wide for trouble. Threadbare, Graves, and Pulsivar had remained at the old farm. The first two did so because they'd siphon too much experience, and they could spend their time animating toys and letting soulstoned villagers romp around and Pulsivar because he didn't seem to care to come along. Dude had some serious napping to catch up on.

Zuula led the way, glancing around, following goblin sign, looking for signs of the twisted little baby eaters.

Kayin and Madeline took the flank, with Keen Eyes up, ready to Wind's Whisper back if they ran into something that required silent warning.

Garon and Glub backed Zuula up, walking in step with her.

And Fluffbear rode Mopsy, guarding the rear, glaring around for goblins to smite or babies to save. She wasn't picky. And her Inspiring Aura buffed the Moxie of her nearby friends, so it was a good spot for her.

Cecelia rode one of the wooden wagon-pulling cats, animated, and about the only thing they had that was suited to her greater size. The parties had been sorted out... Garon had Zuula, Glub, and Madeline, and she had Kayin and Fluffbear. That seemed like the best split and ensured that Mopsy got experience too and that each leader had a scout to listen for.

It didn't mean they couldn't work together, just that they wouldn't eat into each other's experience too much. Cecelia and Garon had spent most of the walk up towards goblin turf planning out scenarios and strategies.

But for all their troubles and preparations they weren't ambushed on the way.

Not when they moved past shoddy barricades, broken and covered with moss, old skulls on pikes now rusty and shattered.

Not when they crossed over into the edge of town, past fire-blackened and crumbled hovels made from bits of other buildings but now abandoned.

And not even when they came to the town square, at the edge of a shallow pond that stretched off to more marsh in the distance. The silence rolled on, quiet and unbroken save for the clattering of Garon and Glub's steps. Zuula halted there, turning around, squinting at the buildings and checking the burned sigils on their side, rubbing them with her cloth fingers.

Finally, Garon tapped Zuula's shoulder. "Well? Where are they?"

Though he tried to keep it quiet, his voice echoed across the marsh. In the distance, a bird took off, hooting.

"Dis sign be old. Way older den de stuff inland." Zuula said, shaking her head. "And de ruins... dey wrong."

"Yeah," Kayin said, fading in from the left. "I looked through a few. Goblins WERE here, but... well, you'd better come see this." She motioned, and the group followed her around from the square to what had once been a town hall. Now the roof was gone, fallen in or fallen apart, leaving only a foundation, a few wooden walls, and a few floorboards.

The cellar below was filled with slimy water, weeds and goop and round spheres as big as beach balls. Gelatinous, with some sort of greenish embryo curled up within each, they were clustered together six or eight in a bunch. They twitched and pulsed in the noonday sun, and as soon as Zuula saw them, she nodded once, and said a single word.

"Run."

"What?" Garon said.

"RUN!"

And from the pond, from the marsh, and from other dark, wet places, came the sound of dozens of large throats croaking, as giant green THINGS hauled themselves out of their hiding places...

Grubholm *had* been raided into ruins by goblins; it was true, and for a time the twisted little creatures had celebrated their victory and bred happily in that lush place, with plenty of food and empty 'bigger' houses to infest. Access to the main roads of the kingdom also let them send out raiding parties when their population got too high for the area to support, which was about every four months or so. The raiders either came back with shinies and bigger meat, or they didn't come back and that was less mouths to feed, so it was all good.

And for a few years, it had worked.

But the weakness of goblins is that they have no real loyalty to each other. It's all they can do to be a tribe or even a family. Goblins live in a society where everyone is always out for themselves, for everything they can get, and no one else truly matters.

Which is why the Gribbits had broken them like a rotten twig.

Gribbits aren't much taller than goblins but are quite a bit wider and longer. They can swallow goblins whole, which is bad enough, but worse than that, they're *organized*. When a Gribbit attacks, he or she does so knowing that his entire tribe is right next to him, hitting the enemy all at once with everything they've got.

Even though they're physically weaker than humans, the fact is that Gribbits don't do things by halves, and they don't run unless the whole battle line runs. Unlike goblins, who will gleefully abandon each other at the first sign of trouble.

And worst of all?

Like goblins, and raccants, and other smart tribal monsters, Gribbits could sometimes have *jobs*.

Zuula had recognized what they were dealing with.

And the other golems trusted Zuula enough to follow her lead, which is why they bolted, which probably saved them casualties right there and then.

"Get to cover!" Garon shouted, as wolf-sized frogs waving spears and clubs burst out of the water. "We'll find a safe place to **Fight the Battles!**"

"I'll pick up rearguard!" Cecelia called. **"Shield Saint!"** She hauled out the old pot lid she'd found in the farmhouse's kitchen, and readied the small sword Threadbare had made her, bounding over on the wooden cat animi. The faster Gribbits closed, aiming for Glub and Garon, the slower members of the parties. But Cecelia got in their way, slashing at them, making them hop back to their front lines, their rapidly-closing front lines.

Garon glanced back, saw they wouldn't make it. If they were caught out in the open, they were dead. Fortunately, he knew what his people could do. "Mom? Shaman slowdown two-fer?"

"**Call Vines!**" Between Cecelia and the Gribbits, vines tore loose from the crumbled ruins and burst up from the marshy ground, flailing and wrapping the oncoming Gribbits. Zuula smiled, slowed a bit, ignoring Kayin as the catgirl assassin tugged on her arm, and waited. Waited until Gribbits were hopping over, working to get their tangled brethren free. Waited until she had the most within her affected radius. And then... "**Call Thorns,**" Zuula whispered and grinned with half-orky glee as the Gribbits' croaks turned to screams. And scream they should! Every vine or piece of vegetation within that area had just grown two-inch thorns.

"Hahahhaha! Take dat!" She laughed. "Go up against a shaman, you get—"

WHACK!

Kayin hadn't been trying to get her to run faster. Kayin had been trying to tell her that the Gribbits on the flank had moved in while she was busy dealing with the ones behind.

The club knocked the little plush shaman across the street, where another Gribbit waited, stretching his maw open wide...

...to be denied, as Missus Fluffbear leaped Mopsy in the air and caught Zuula, whirling the cat around as soon as she hit the ground, and speeding toward the others.

Meanwhile, Kayin snarled at the one who'd clubbed Zuula. "**Hindering Strikes!**" Three quick tendon-slicing slashes with her little dagger later, the Gribbit was in no shape to jump after her as she ran.

But it didn't have to run. Kayin made it ten feet when she heard a whiplike snap behind her and felt something wrap around her waist as she was jerked backward. "No!" She yelled, as the Gribbit snapped her into its fleshy, slimy mouth...

...and paused.

Toy golems are adorable and give healing hugs.

Baked clay golems are immune to fire and can be gorgeous if made in a certain way.

Wood golems? They're splintery. Every time they're struck or grappled, some of their outer layer spikes into their attacker's flesh.

And this Gribbit had just stuck her into his mouth, which was way, way softer than his skin.

The little assassin found herself spat out, covered in frog blood. With catgirl agility she hit the ground, rolled, and came up running. "**Faster Than Death!**" she yelled, outpacing the Gribbits who were moving in on both flanks.

"Get up here, man!" Glub called back to the stragglers. "**Heartening song! Move those muscles, run those feet! Keep on fleeing, or we're**

dead meat!"

Didn't really have a beat, but they were strengthened nonetheless. The ones in his party, anyway.

Cecelia's group didn't have to worry about that now that Kayin was out of danger and booking it. Fluffbear was mounted on Mopsy, and Mopsy could *move*. The wooden animi was a bit slower, but Cecelia's Horsemanship skill made up for that.

That only left one more member of Garon's party unaccounted for, up until she came down out of the sky like a red streak, divebombing the closest pursuers. **"Bahninate!"**

Fire exploded from the little dragon's maw, carving a streak through the first third of the Gribbit horde, and they screamed and fell back, some falling, dying—

—up until a Gribbit wearing a mitre hopped up from where he'd been observing the fight and started croaking. And as he croaked, Gribbits healed, falling back to the lake and getting out of the fight.

"They've got a cleric? No fair!" Kayin screeched.

"Get up to tha inn!" Madeline screamed back from above, her voice fading as she looped around the sky. "You can... hold on...."

Garon stiffened as she wind's whispered him. "There's an inn down that road!" he said. "It's mostly intact; we'll make our stand there! Follow me! **Forced March!"** Garon, Glub, and Mopsy sped up. The shaman poked Fluffbear, hopped down from the mini-cougar, and paused to take a look back at the chaos.

Some Gribbits had fallen, perhaps a dozen or so between the worst of the vines and the dragonfire, but the wounded ones were being hauled back for healing, including the one who'd tried to swallow Kayin, who was pointing at his tongue and pointing at the little toys.

"Damn..." Zuula said, turning and running.

Gribbits were a threat, and that was true. They worked together, and that was worse. But the main reason they were a problem for her little coterie? Gribbits *learned*.

The inn was on a rise. It wasn't much to look at, and, like the rest of the buildings, its roof had rotted and fallen in years ago. Goblin graffiti sprinkled throughout suggested vulgar things in their crude language, which was why Glub was laughing and taking notes, but nobody else really cared. Garon stomped around, testing the creaking floor, and checking the walls. **"Secure the Perimeter."** he nodded, in satisfaction as his skill told him what was what. "There's a family of raccoons in the basement, but that's it."

"Raccoons means Gribbits don't come up here much," Zuula hissed, waving Kayin and Fluffbear and Mopsy in through the doorway, before she grabbed one end of a mossy table and strained to try to shove it in front of the entrance.

"I got yah," Madeline said, wings clacking as she clattered to the ground, and got the other end of the table with her jaws. Between the two of them, they got it into place just as Cecelia leaped her animi through the window.

"They're slowing down, I think," Cecelia said.

"Yeah. Zuula, on a scale of one to ten, how bad is this?" Garon said.

"Eight," Zuula decided. "Gribbits pretty smart. Dey also nuts about protecting territory. Gonna be hard to get out of here wit'out casualties."

"We could just pile everyone into one party except for Madeline and the wooden cat, put up forced march, and book it," Garon said. "We outran them on raw speed that last time."

"Outrun them ta where?" Madeline said. "They'll chase us to the wagon and Graves. Then they'll have someone to attack who is actually capable of dyin'. And if he goes, then we got problems."

"We'll have problems if any of us die here too," Cecelia said. "We're out of reagents for making new golems, even toy golems. If anyone dies they'll be in a soulstone until we can find the dwarves. So no heroic sacrifices, okay?"

"You have plan?" Zuula asked, moving from window to window, hopping up and hoisting herself to peer out of each. "Cause dey do. Dey setting up circle—"

"Perimeter, Mom," Garon interrupted.

"—circle around inn. Back a ways, but dey makin' it clear dey watching."

"I could go burn 'em out," Madeline said. "I don't think they gaht a countah to me."

"Don't bet on that," Cecelia said. "I learned about these things in my suppression classes."

"Your what now?" Glub asked.

"The Crown has a problem with nonhuman races. We get taught the most efficient ways to kill them. It's... yeah, it's not very nice. But on Gribbits, the doctrine made it clear that they adapt to the tactics that people throw at them. So if you use a strong one early on, then odds are good they'll come up with a counter. And there's no way they'll ignore a flying dragon that can roast them wholesale."

Garon nodded. "Okay. Madeline, go back to the camp and tell Threadbare we need him and Pulsivar. Then come back with them, stick low if you have to."

"You sure, Gar?"

"Go. We'll be fine." Garon held up a handful of soulstones. "I grabbed one for each of us." He put them in the dirty hearth, then swept ashes over them. "Anyone dies, they'll be here."

"Smaht."

"Wait," Zuula said. "Before you go, get Zuula's barrel out of de pack, yeah?"

Madeline shrugged and squirmed her pack free from her back. Kayin helped her get it down, and they drew out the small keg emblazoned with poison symbols.

"Dat be our endgame," Zuula said. "We get dat in de pond, every one of dem die. But... only want to use it if really, really necessary."

"Yeah," Fluffbear said. "They're just defending their homes! It would be bad to kill all of them and their little babies too! I'm proud of you, Zuula!"

"Actually Zuula was gonna say it would mess up de plants and poison de land here for a few years. But sure, whatever."

"Oh." Fluffbear sagged down a bit. "Still proud of you."

"Tanks."

"How territorial are they?" Garon asked. "Do we know that? Do we have to wipe out every last one to get away clean?"

Zuula rubbed her chin. "Haven't fought Gribbits since Zuula was child. Ah... half. Get dem down to half, dey usually call it quits. I t'ink. But pond dis size, spawning pool dat big... need to take down four, five dozen to do dat."

"Hey, am I free ta leave? Go get help?" The dragon asked Garon.

"Yeah, go Mads, it's cool."

Madeline got to the clearest part of the room. **"Scaly Wings!"** she flew up and out—

—and swerved, as two volleys of javelins, some of them on fire, hissed up towards her. Madeline yelled as a few raked along her side. But she got away, heading south, back towards the camp and aid.

"Countered," Cecelia nodded grimly. "Those fire javelins, those are an archer trick, right? Shouldn't they be using bows?"

"Nah. Works with any ranged weapon. Bows and crossbows are just more efficient," Kayin said, staring out from the cracks in the table that made their makeshift barricade. "Had a girlfriend once, back in our guild. She was an archer/assassin who sniped, killed from a distance. Had a blowgun for emergencies, and her tricks worked fine with it."

"Girlfriend?" Cecelia looked at her in surprise.

"Yeah. Um, is that a problem?"

"No, no. Just... huh. Didn't know that."

"What's to know? I used to like women. Back when I had parts to do something with, anyway. But we've got killer frog guys right now, desu."

"Right." Cecelia cleared her throat. "We're up against a horde. Kayin, please see if you can find me some knives or stabby things. Fluffbear, I'm leaving the party; you're the leader now."

"Why?"

"Because if I'm alone I can have six animi, and this should help make up for them outnumbering us."

"Smart," Garon said. He popped open his chest, and drew out stacks of coins, slotting them into the holes carved into his sides. "Zuula, is there anything you can do with that poison barrel that isn't genocide?"

The little shaman pursed her cloth lips and considered. "Maybe. Gonna depend on whether or not we got a kettle all up in here. Still got to be careful. We don't breathe. She does." Zuula pointed at Mopsy.

"If she gets poisoned I can cure her," Fluffbear said. "So long as it's not too nasty."

"Glub, do you have anything that might help?" Garon said. "I don't know Bard stuff too well."

"I'm new to this myself, mister boss dude. Got some water elementalist stuff, but it's all level one. Still that'll get us an elemental so booyah. As far as bard stuff goes... Uh... I can sing a song that distracts everyone who hears it."

"That'll hit us too, so pass."

"Heartening Song makes you all stronger and sturdier. Rejuvenating Song makes you heal slowly and regain stamina faster. Just that Cool makes me cooler. All the time. My borrowed skills are Knack for Languages and Mend. Fortune's Fool makes me be more fortunate, don't know why I'm a fool for it... oh, hey, Salty Song! This might work!"

"Yeah? What's it do?" Garon asked.

Glub told them, and Garon nodded, as the starts of a plan started to form inside his bovine noggin.

"Found a kettle!" Zuula announced, just as Kayin came up from the cellar, dragging along a cluster of butcher knives.

Garon nodded in satisfaction. "How they looking out there, Celia?"

Cecelia paced around the common room, peering out the windows. "I see the one with the mitre. I can't exactly tell, but I think he's buffing a few of them that are wearing furry hats and metal helms. Like helms that cover half of their bodies."

"Berserkers and Knights, probably," Zuula said. "Dis be bad."

"There's also a couple on the rooftops wearing pointed cloth caps with feathers. Archers." Cecelia said.

Then she ducked, as a javelin sped through the window, narrowly missing her face. "Yep, archers. Wow, pity my dodge skill is maxed."

"You didn't get a few levels from that chase?" Garon asked. "I upped Ruler twice."

"Different skillset. And that's upping your level one, I'm trying to rebuild level fives. Anyway we're running low on time. What's the plan?"

Garon grinned and beckoned the toys in close. "Here's how we're going to turn this thing around..."

*****

A few minutes after they started their desperate plan, Threadbare sent a Simple Decree, used in a manner that most rulers wouldn't.

The decree was simple.

Your Ruler has declared a Royal Decree!
"Nobody die. Again."

"Now!" Garon called. "Everyone, get to your places!"

Zuula poured a flask into the bubbling kettle, then slammed the lid over it as smoke started to roil up. She beat feet into the kitchen with Kayin following.

Garon nodded to Glub, as they climbed into the chimney, leaving the blob that was Glub's least water elemental bouncing happily in the main room.

Cecelia smiled and settled back into the cupboard they'd found for her, leaving the wooden cat outside. She held her hands over her ears and said **"Dollseye!"**

From the chimney, Glub fired up his bardsong, using the one he hadn't had occasion to try yet.

It was called Salty Song, and it was ANNOYING.

And thanks to the acoustics of the chimney, every Gribbit within a three block radius was subjected to it.

It ground at their Moxie, tore at it, not much at first because Glub's skill in it was very low, but the skill only improved as he sang.

Inside her cupboard Cecelia grunted and tried to ignore it. It wasn't easy, and some of her own Moxie drained. But knights and steam knights both had charisma as a boosting attribute, and she had the Moxie to wait it out, she thought.

The Gribbits didn't.

The Gribbits attacked, just as Garon had hoped.

They would have anyway; those were definitely pre-battle buffs their cleric was handing out, but this made them jump the gun a bit. That was the first part of Garon's plan, draw them in before they were good and comfy.

And so after a few volleys of javelins arcing over the roof, which didn't do much beyond splatter Glub's elemental, the Gribbit Knights rushed the barricade, using their armored helms as battering rams, clattering in through the wide doorway. The table took a few hits then shuddered back, as the three armored Gribbits looked around, saw the wooden cat, and frogpiled it.

That's when the Frogzerkers gave mighty bounds and leaped over the walls, running on pop-eyed rage and croaking battle cries, holding salvaged wood-chopping axes in their hands and looking around for unengaged targets.

They found none.

Behind them, hordes of regular, unjobbed Gribbits poured in, spears ready, and lidless eyes open, staring around. The wooden cat rocked and fell, battered to pieces, but the song still echoed.

They looked to the chimney, and the steaming kettle in it, with the fire merrily going. The song was loudest there...

And just as Garon had hoped, one of the Frogzerkers knocked the kettle aside with a contemptuous blow.

Green smoke exploded throughout the inn, and the Gribbits croaked in dismay and coughed, trying to back out. They jammed the entrance and the windows, screeching in dismay as red numbers rolled up from their fat bodies—

"Now!" Garon shouted. **"Fight the Battles!"**

—Cecelia burst from the cabinet, butcher's knives whirling, pot lid and sword in hand. **"Shield Saint! Dolorous Strike! Dolorous Strike!"** She wasn't as strong as she'd been as a human, but wherever her sword stabbed, a Gribbit died. The butcher's knives focused on a single target at a time, hacked it down, then moved on with gory efficiency.

"Backstab!" from the direction of the kitchen, and then Kayin was among them, using the smoke for cover and shanking with a poisoned steak-knife in each hand. **"Poison Blade!"** She'd call, whenever the green sludge that Zuula had helped her prepare started to fade. Whenever the skill kicked in, one of the vials tied to her back would vanish, and her blades would re-coat with venom.

Garon fought the Frogzerkers, weakened from their poison but no less deadly. But his wooden form was sturdy, and he was about as strong as they were, without needing rage to boost himself. And every time they dealt him a good hit, he'd go defensive, and call out **"Blood is Gold!"** One of the coins set into his side would clink and vanish, and he'd heal.

For his part, Glub stopped the song, dropped from the chimney, and started hauling Gribbits corpses toward the most cracked part of the floor.

And whenever he dropped one off, Fluffbear's little black paw would come up out of the crack, touch it, and say **"Zombies!"**

The dead Gribbits rose and, without directions, went after the nearest living things with delicious brains.

Which happened to be living Gribbits.

It was glorious chaos, and though to the Gribbits it probably felt like a hellish eternity before the survivors got clear, it was probably only a minute, at the most.

Garon dispatched the last of the Frogzerkers with Cecelia's help and glanced up, as water splashed down from above.

"Dude, they've got a Water Elementalist!" said Glub, as large balls of water catapulted in to douse the smoke, arcing from the direction of the lake. "A really good one!"

"Start up the song again! Everyone, phase two!" Garon bellowed. "Archers next!"

"Okay dokay!" Fluffbear squeaked and left the party. **"Invite Zombie!"** she said, following it up with four more castings, then commanding the ones that remained to go and eat archers.

The rest of the toys barreled out the door, with Glub switching back to his salty song, and Cecelia pausing to grab one of the Frogzerker's axes and animating it. They ran straight into the Gribbit Knights, who desperately tried to break their charge.

"As if! **Rammit!**" Garon bellowed, lowered his horns, and bulldozed one through the adjacent ruin's wall. Then Cecelia was on the other ones, with Kayin flipping over them to stab at the froggy bits the helms didn't cover.

Javelins came at the golems, clipping and wounding them, hindered by the archers having to aim around their friends.

And then the remnants of the mob that had rushed in croaked hearty cheers as a dozen of their surviving friends stumbled out of the remnants of the fog.

Cheers that died in horrified throats, as they saw the bloody wounds of the 'survivors.'

Cheers that turned into screams as the zombies, with Fluffbear and a mildly-poisoned Mopsy in the middle, made a beeline straight for the Archers' perches. Hastily the javelin tossers hopped for cover as some of the regular Gribbits turned and fled, having quite enough of THIS, thank you very much.

Some of them didn't flee far.

"Call Vines! Call Thorns!" Zuula said, grinning, as from the mossy and overgrown roofs, plants grew spikes and lashed out at the Archers.

And as they fought, the Gribbits retreated. They'd been put on the back foot, ran into too many surprises at once, and needed a few minutes to figure out how to adapt and overcome.

But that was a few minutes that Garon wasn't about to give them. "To the pond! Bring the barrel!"

Cecelia nodded, then ran to grab it. It was still a bad solution, but if things went poorly, they'd need it.

They fought their way after the Gribbits, who were low on Moxie now, low thanks to the salty song, and disheartened by the surprise the friends had sprung on them. The friends hacked and stabbed at the ones they could catch, downing them then moving on as fast as they could, keeping rolling, trying to turn it into a rout...

...which lasted until they reached the town square again, and saw what awaited them.

"Dey gots a queen!" Zuula yelled.

Eight feet tall it towered, as fat and long as two draft horses together, glaring down at the golem friends with beachball-sized eyes. She wore a crown on her head, and the rolls of fat underneath her maw shook as she pointed a massive webbed paw at them and croaked deafening words.

"Uh," Glub said, pausing his song. "She says we are not amused."

Then the queen turned to her fleeing subjects and belched out a rapid fire series of words that spoke of duty to tribe, queen, and damply, and the routed Gribbits slowed... stopped... and started to regroup. Behind them the Gribbit cleric followed, healing the wounded, and glaring at the friends.

SPLOOSH!

And then a robed Gribbit was there, perching on the queen's back, resplendent in a wizard's hat, and waving a bent staff with a goldfish bowl on the end of it towards them. The water of the pond roiled, and lifted up, forming itself into a ball.

"Oh, there's the elementalist," Garon said. "Shit! Watch out!"

The ball arced toward them, and they scattered— not fast enough, as Cecelia took it head on, and it knocked her back down the street. A red '84' floated up from where she fell, and she got up, glaring.

"No! **Slow Regeneration!**" Garon yelled to her, and then he had no time for words as the rallied Gribbits charged him, and Zuula and Kayin fell in next to him, covering his flanks. Glub switched to his heartening song and tried to stay clear, punching with tiny wooden hands whenever a Gribbit came after him. Fluffbear and Mopsy brought up the rear.

The upside was that at least the Gribbits weren't trying to swallow the friends. They'd learned their lesson from the last time they tried it, and while they didn't know if all of them were as splintery as Kayin, they weren't about to take the risk.

"This is bad," Garon whispered, as spear after spear rattled off his chest, gouging and forcing him back. They were in the open again, and the Gribbits were all around them, but even then they'd have a chance. The tribe was wounded, depleted, and most of their combat job elites were down.

But the queen was here, and to his horror he saw her wading forward, massive bulk shifting as she stepped almost daintily towards the battle. And up top the elementalist grinned in froggy glee and manipulated up another ball of water, readying it for a throw...

"**Bahninate!**" Madeline howled, and the watery ball exploded into steam. The water elementalist shrieked, stared up, then hopped down into the pond again. The queen screamed, bulk shaking as the dragonfire just tagged her, searing her wide back. She opened her mouth to tongue the tiny dragon out of the sky but hesitated. These things were splintery, right? Then Madeline was past and up, and away.

And Garon smiled, as a black form sprang out of a nearby ruin, and two of the Gribbits in the back of the mob died. He fought harder, laying about him with his axe, dropping a Blood is Gold as necessary.

From the lake, water lashed up at Madeline, and she answered by dropping gouts of fire, as the two Elementalists lashed out at each other. The Gribbit had levels and skill, but Madeline had much greater mobility and the whole sky to dodge around in. Eventually the Gribbit would fend her off and return to the fight, but that was fine. She was buying them time, and that's all they needed.

"**Call Vines! Call Thorns!**" Zuula hissed at the queen. This was draining, but she'd leveled up back there a couple of times and refilled her sanity, so that was fine. The queen snapped through the vines without stopping, taking the scratches on her hide, glaring at the little dolls that had so wounded her tribe, hurt her people. Zuula sighed. "Fine. **Fast Regeneration. Beastly Skill Borrow: Owl.**" she rose into the air, spirit wings shimmering from her back, as she called upon her totem. Darting toward the queen with her well-practiced triple digit flight skill, she harried her, slowing her down, and causing the giant ruler to thrash about with her paws. For once the frog couldn't eat the annoying little fly, and oh, did it gall her!

"Excuse me," Threadbare called, through his Minorphone.

The battlefield paused, as the fighting stilled, and everyone looked back.

"Is there some way we could work this out? I'm very certain this is definitely a misunderstanding."

"You want me to translate that?" Glub said, taking the opportunity to pick up one of his severed arms.

"Yes, please." Threadbare said, strolling down the street, with every buff active, adjusting his jacket as the Gribbits stared at the sharp-dressed bear.

He was very glad he'd used Dazzling Entrance before coming into sight.

You are now a level 9 Model!
AGI+3
CHA+3
PER+3
Your Work It Baby skill is now level 41!
Your Work It Baby skill is now level 42!
Your Work It Baby skill is now level 43!
Your Work It Baby skill is now level 44!
Your Work It Baby skill is now level 45!
Checking Dietary Restrictions time counter...
Your Dietary Restriction skill is now level 45!
Buff adjusted accordingly.

Oh, well, that was nice.

Glub croaked out words to the Gribbit queen, using his knack for languages. The queen croaked back.

"She says your people threatened her eggs and killed many of her tribe. She wants to know why she should not keep fighting here."

"Back off a bit, Mads," Garon called up, and the little dragon wheeled away. A watery globe arced after her, but the queen turned and slapped her consort lightly, and the ball dispersed into droplets.

"Did you threaten the eggs?" Threadbare asked Cecelia.

"No, we found them and were looking at them when they attacked us."

"Ah. I see. Please tell her that we mean her eggs no harm and would have left them alone, regardless."

"Well, actually—" Zuula began.

"Would have left them alone, *regardless,*" Threadbare said, with long experience in dealing with Zuula.

The little shaman shrugged and returned to shore.

The queen considered that, running her eyes over the remnants of her tribe, and croaked.

"She says this may be so, but her people are dead, and she does not see why she should spare you."

"Spare us?" Threadbare said, moving up to where ten Gribbits lay dead in a heap. "Mercy, no. We're sparing *them.*" He beckoned, and

Pulsivar oozed out of the shadows, purring, and rubbing a bloody cheek against the bear's paw. "Please let her know that if she wishes to continue the fight we will, but we came here to fight goblins not her people."

That seemed to make her happy. "She's bitchin' a lot about goblins and telling me the awesome tale of how they won their home," Glub said.

"Ah, okay. Listen to her. Please tell me when she's expecting me to be appreciative." For his part, Threadbare smiled and nodded whenever Glub gave the signal. It really wasn't too different from his early days, listening to Cecelia's stories and woes back during the tea parties, before he understood what she was saying.

And it worked.

CHA +1

"All right," Glub said, much later, after some negotiations. "Boss, you're gonna repair and forge their armor and weapons, since they don't have a proper smith and montage the smith job to one of their own. In return they'll forgive us our trespass, and the deaths, and let us leave in peace."

"And we get nothing but departing safely, but that's all right," Garon said. "We came in here to grind levels, and sweet Ritaxis, did we ever."

"There's still a few more we could get," Kayin said, glancing back to the barrel Cecelia was sitting on, now. "I mean, it'd be kind of a jerk move, but... we are up against the Crown, and if we don't pull off that very sneaky mission, we're gonna die in Fort Bronze. A little more experience could give us an edge."

"Mm." Threadbare said. "You're thinking of using Zuula's poison stocks?"

"If we dump it in the lake, then they all die. And their kids. And the pond and the land around it are poison for years," Cecelia said.

"And what do you think of that?" Threadbare asked.

"I think my father would do it without hesitation, to make us all stronger. So fump that noise." Cecelia's mouth set into a line of determination. "If you can't get strong without being evil, you don't deserve to be strong."

"Works for me," Garon said. "I was going to try to threaten them with it if we got in a bad spot, but I really didn't want to use it. It really was a last-ditch maneuver."

"Let's agree to not do that or things like that, then." Cecelia said. "No matter how bad it gets, genocide isn't an option, okay? I made that mistake last life, I want to start fresh with this one."

"I think we're all good with that," Threadbare said. And the rest of them nodded, one by one. Kayin and Madeline were a heartbeat behind the others, but no one called them out on it.

"All right," the dapper teddy bear decided. "Tell her I agree to her terms. Everyone else, feel free to hang about if you want or go get the camp in order. After I'm done, we'll pack up and leave peacefully."

"I almost feel guilty," Garon said. "We got these levels, and you're going to have to lose a day montaging."

"I got a level of golemist while you were fighting," Threadbare said. "And model because evidently they like my hat." He hadn't missed the fact that the tribe had spent most of the negotiations staring at his headware. Given that the sole concession that Gribbits made in the way of clothing was hats, it wasn't too hard to figure out the object of their gazes. "And besides, the stronger you all get, the better off I am. It's good to be king, after all."

"I agree," croaked the queen, in heavily-accented common tongue, and the golems stared at her, mouths wide open.

"You understood every word we said, didn't you? All this whole time?" Garon slapped his wide wooden palm to his muzzle.

"Yes. It seemed best to hide that until I was certain of you. Now I am. I am glad you decided to avoid treachery. You are good people after all, and I am sorry that we misunderstood your intentions. Now what is this about fighting the Crown and sneaking into Fort Bronze?"

CHAPTER 3: LOUDEST INFILTRATION EVER

A one-day trade with the Gribbits turned into three days, then a whole week. Threadbare and his friends montaged jobs, traded favors, and established a lifelong peace between themselves and the Smallgronk tribe, which was this group of Gribbits' formal name.

And all of the negotiations were presided over by a grinning Madeline, who used Haggle to great effect and had the time of her life grinding merchant levels.

The Gribbits also shared knowledge of their favorite hunting grounds and the local monsters, which the rest of the group eagerly adventured through while Threadbare montaged and spent his off time teaching the Gribbit queen the finer etiquette of tea parties.

He was also busy making them a boatload of hats. They were very taken by his chapeau, and he was happy to show them how to make similar hats. Then of course he had to show off each one, and that was good for a Model level and all new skills. Negotiating with a fellow head of state and signing treaties was also good for both of their ruler levels, and he thought very hard before he turned her down when she offered an heir's betrothal to one of his.

The rest of the group spent the week grinding as hard as possible, and he was happy to gain a golemist level from their actions. Then they came back with scavenged reagents and crystals, (mostly red and orange reagents, and level 1 crystals respectively), and he turned THOSE into items useful for the infiltration of Fort Bronze.

Threadbare also replaced his pants, while he was at it. He really did feel strange without pants on anymore.

But there were limits, and every time he checked with Graves, the man's reassuring smile got smaller and smaller. He'd allocated a week to training up, but the longer it went on, the more he realized that had been a hopeful estimate. They needed yellow reagents, and they needed them now, and Zuula, who had been harvesting the most reagents, confirmed his fears when he consulted her.

"You not gonna find yellow around here. Zuula been gettin' dem from places nature be strong, untouched herbs and places sacred to life and every'ting. But it take months to grow de red flowers for red reagents, and months more for dem to ripen to orange. Yellow takes a year or two, as do de crystals when dey bud from de main stalks. Don' even be askin' bout green."

"Oh. Bother."

"Dere odder places to get reagents and crystals. Can get dem from ground. Fluffbear been diggin' for a few. She good at de mining. But dis marshy land, ain't many places to mine. No, we want any better den basic, we gots to get to dwarves or find a dungeon to clean out. Or kill a bunch of soldiers an' you crumble dere armor and stuff..."

So with a heavy heart, he gathered the group that night and took the barrels full of smoked fish that the Gribbits had supplied them. Then Fluffbear got to work on the wagon, taking down Annie Mata's cover and assembling a proper yoke for the lone oxen that the Gribbits had... obtained... from somewhere.

Privately, Cecelia checked the tattoos on its ears and kept silent. Gribbits WERE monsters, but they were monsters that the band of golems needed right now.

But after this was all over and done with, she made a promise to track down the oxen's owners and reimburse them for their loss.

Fluffbear gleefully adopted and named him Oxey McOxenface and would have tamed him properly had it not been pointed out that it might shrink him down a bit. Though Mopsy had grown some in the last week as Fluffbear leveled tamer, she still wasn't back up to her former mountain lion size.

Finally it was done, and Oxey was roped to the wagon. A shorn and shaven Graves, now clad in a peasant tunic and breeches and boots that Threadbare had made himself and artfully smeared with mud, clambered into the wagon seat and settled in for the trip.

In the case of the toys, this meant packing Madeline in a false bottom of one of the barrels and putting everyone else in, well, her pack. It had gotten a bit roomier in there as she leveled the skill, now up to the size of a bathroom rather than a closet. They'd taken the precaution of putting tools, supplies, and more barrels of fish in there, in case one of the Crown wizards detected it as a merchant's pack. Any questing hands that came in would latch onto the merchant stuff first, was the hope. They'd also put the crate of cultist soulstones in there, and Threadbare had promised to speak with them a few times every day.

They had to have a tiny hole in the bottom of Madeline's barrel for her to reach out and poke the pack every few hours, but that was no big deal. And anyone could reach into the pack and pull them out, they just couldn't get out on their own. Worst case, the pack would blow up and send all of them free at once.

"That's how I think it'll wahk, anyway," Madeline said, taking once more glance at the barrel she'd be coiled inside for the trip. "Yeesh. Really glad I don't have a sense of smell anymoah."

"Wait!" Cecelia said, turning back to look at Graves. "What if they scout you? There's no way you're not on a wanted list by now."

"I thought of that." Graves smiled. "Fortunately, level five Spirit Medium has the solution for that. You know how cultists have a skill that falsifies their status screens?"

"Yes, but you're not a Cultist."

"No, but I can talk to dead ones. And as a spirit medium, I can borrow their skill for a little while. Or others, for that matter. Level ones, only, right now, but that's okay, because it's a level one skill." He held up a soulstone and smiled. "Marva here's going to talk me through it once we get to the fort. Doesn't last long, but it should get me past the door if they're looking. I'll be a merchant with farmer and carpenter levels, that seems safe."

"All right. Just..." Cecelia hopped up to the backboard of the wagon and gave him a hug. "Play it safe, all right? This golem thing has its downsides. Stay alive."

"Believe me, I've no desire to shed this mortal coil anytime soon." Graves hugged her back. "Sit tight. We should be there in three days. I'll pull you out if things go to plan and it'll be Madeline if things don't."

"Okay," Cecelia muttered. "Okay, okay..." She headed into the pack, joining the others.

"Oh, there you are. I was beginning to worry," Threadbare said. He waved from the big grindluck circle that the others had settled in for. "Shall we deal you in a hand or three?"

"We could do that," Cecelia said, then shook her head. "But I'd rather practice. We can't kill monsters in here, but we can use some of our skills. And Zuula can dream quest us."

"Dat might be a little weird in here," Zuula said. "No nature. Dreams gonna be screwy."

"They're screwy anyway, desu," said Kayin, neatly stacking the deck and setting it back. "All green and stuff with weird things moving in a light that's actually darkness."

"That's what you see?" Garon said, grabbing the deck from the cheating assassin and shuffling it again, before slapping it down in the middle of the circle. "I see trees, usually. Just trees on a hillside, bending in a windstorm."

"I see fish mostly," Glub said. "Some real hotties."

Cecelia didn't want to say what she saw. It was pretty disturbing, to her at least. "But we'll still get the rest, right? Full pools?"

"Yes," Zuula conceded.

Glub put down two blues and won the hand. "I also got something new at tenth level. Song of Clarity, dudes. Should help refill Moxie and sanity for people, so we don't have to wait on dream quests so much."

"Nice," Garon said. "Has Explorer gotten you anything nifty yet?"

"Yeah. I can make waymarks and waystones."

The circle fell silent, and everyone put their cards down and stared at Glub. "What?" Cecelia said. "That's huge! Why didn't you say something earlier?"

"Dudes, it's lesser ones." Glub put up his webbed hands. "They're not permanent or anything. They just last like an hour."

"Can you set them anywhere?" Garon asked.

"Not in here. It gives me beef about illegal geography. But outside, I think so, yeah."

"What are these exactly?" Threadbare asked.

"He set de waymark, and anyone he hand de waystones to can use dem to teleport to it."

"That would have been very handy to know before we got in here," Threadbare said, glancing at the darkened space that was the 'door' to the room, impassable from this side of things unless they were drawn forth.

"It only lasts like an hour, man," Glub said, waving his hands. "I didn't think it'd be useful!"

"Peace, Glub," Kayin said. "We can use it in the fort. Carry a few to get out of tight situations."

"It's best if we keep them for emergency use only," Cecelia said. "If they're anything like the greaters, there's a cooldown on those, right?"

"Nah, no cooldown. But you can only carry one at a time and using it breaks it." Glub shrugged. "And when the waymark expires all existing waystones break."

"Hm. Well it's a good idea for you to make a waymark once we're out and in a safe spot in the fort and to give us waystones while we're sneaking," Threadbare decided. "In the meantime, yes, let's practice. We can grindluck when we're tired, and Glub can sing to us to make us regain faster, or Zuula can tuck us in, or both."

And so they whiled the time away in the small space, practicing on each other and themselves, in the case of buffs. Threadbare was happy to try out the new model skills he'd gained. The others weren't so happy, especially the first time he tried out his 'Sexy Pose' without warning them about it. Adjust Weight went over a bit better, even if he did look bizarre when he went too far toward one end of the spectrum or the other.

Still, he could see the uses. He was tired of being kicked or knocked away by strong foes. Being able to add on a few pounds so he could stand his ground now and again, that was good stuff. Even if it did debuff his agility if he added too much.

But in the end, he fell back on his golemist, ruler, and scout skills, along with a broad range of utility buffs. The scout skills were sorely underdeveloped, and they'd be very helpful for sneaking around. Golemist was fast becoming his focus. The others were counting on him to upgrade them as soon as possible, and if this could knock out some easy experience, then so be it.

Ruler now, ruler had been very useful when negotiating with royalty. The dwarves had royalty too, Cecelia confirmed. They'd need to talk with them as well, sway them to his side. So he got to work giving those skills a workout, throwing around decrees, organizing minions, and identifying his subjects. Also dropping silly quests for small experience rewards and emboldening the others with speeches.

Most of his stamina went into buffs or duelist moves, sparring with the others. There was only so much that peaceful practice could do, so they stepped it up a bit, tearing into each other with brutal force and using mend, repair golem, and slow regeneration to fix each other up. So long as he or Cecelia were on the sidelines with Eye for Detail up so they could monitor the fighters, the risk was negligible... but there WAS risk, and whatever mysterious force governed the universe judged that to be worth extra experience.

But it wasn't all fun and games. Especially for Pulsivar and Mopsy, who *hated* being stuck in such a small space. The litter box that the toys had prepared for them was way too small, and the big cats spent most of their time annoyed and irritable, even with Fluffbear.

After about two days of this, the toys called the practice session quits and got dream quests from Zuula, getting ready for what was hopefully their decanting from the pack. Then there was nothing save for a few nervous hands of grindluck, and quiet conversation. Threadbare spent most of it sitting on Cecelia's lap, enjoying her arms around him as she reached past him and sorted her cards.

That was worth a few adorable levels, but it really wasn't the point.

The point was that they were going into their most dangerous situation yet, and he wanted all the hugs he could get from his little girl.

A thought occurred to him, as they wrapped up about the thousand and third hand of grindluck.

"You're not upset we didn't use your suggestion to go to Pads village, are you?"

"What? No, no," Cecelia said. "It would have been poetic to get their help, but the more I think about it, that would come with problems of its own. If the Crown investigates, the trail would lead back there, and it might risk people getting tortured. Besides, Graves will lie and tell people he's from Pads, and he knows enough about the place to fake it. But the wagon's not really from there and everyone there is ignorant of our ruse."

"Yeah, and I trust the Gribbits more than I do those peasants, desu," Kayin threw in. "Less chance of the froggies selling us out for a handful of turnips."

"I'm sure the peasants of Pads wouldn't do that," Cecelia said.

"Look at it this way, we're taking the Gribbits' food, and not theirs, so we're not tempting them to do so either way." Garon added. "And whoa, that better be Graves."

They turned to see a withered hand groping out of the darkness, questing around, and poking the various items they'd dragged in as cover. "It is," said Threadbare. He walked over, tapped its pinky finger, and stood still while it drew him out.

Threadbare found himself drawn into a dingy barracks room, with beds lining the chamber, open footlockers sitting empty, and narrow slits in the walls letting in sunlight. The wooden floor was grubby, and many of the blankets were stained. But the walls were solid stone, and it was empty enough for their purposes. Graves put Threadbare down and reached into the pack for another toy.

Threadbare took a long look around, then turned back to Graves. "Did everything go—"

BOOM!

The room shook from the explosion. The noise was loud, close, and it was all Threadbare could do to not leap under the bed and take cover.

"What," he said, when the stuffing between his ears stopped throbbing, "was that?"

"Siege cannons," Graves said, drawing Cecelia out, then following up with the rest of the toys.

"Siege cannons? Oh, good!" Cecelia smiled. "Well, maybe. Shipments are going to be delayed, but there won't be as many eyes watching for us."

"What is a siege cannon?" Threadbare asked, rubbing his temples so hard that he smushed his head in a bit.

"We're in the western block?" Cecelia asked Graves.

"Yes. Above the infirmary."

"Come look." She hopped off the bed and beckoned Threadbare to one of the arrow slits, then lifted him up so he could see clearly.

Threadbare looked down into a vast, curving courtyard, partitioned by smaller walls, each of them with patrolled ramparts and guards, most now clustered on the outer walls. Wagons and groups of busy men, hauling around crates and barrels and other supplies, filled the courtyard directly below, moving into a main building about twelve times the size of Caradon's old house. From that main building, stone wings spilled off, winding their way around inside the walls of the vast Fortress. They were in one such wing, he realized, about three stories up from the ground floor.

And in among the wings, breaking up part of his view, were great stone towers, five of them, each with a massive gleaming dome of bronze topping them. From each dome a black metal cylinder protruded, smoke rising from them in gouts and billows. As he watched, gears ground on the side of one bronze dome, and the cylinder started to retract.

"Do you see them?"

"I think so. You mean the big things up on the towers?"

"Yes. They can drop shells full of gas or geek's fire or anything else the alchemists whip up, anywhere in Brokeshale valley. So long as we-the Crown, I mean, can keep the battlefield confined there, keep the dwarves from breaking out, we can shoot at them whenever they surface."

"Dwarves prefer fighting underground," Graves added, drawing out Kayin and putting her next to Zuula, who was already clambering down the bedpost. "But occasionally they launch a raid, cracking open a tunnel and assaulting the lines. When that happens, the guns—"

BOOM!

The room shook, and Threadbare fell off Cecelia's shoulders. "Sorry, could you?" he asked.

"What?"

But she didn't protest as he climbed back up on her shoulders again and peered out. One of the other cannon had erupted in smoke and flames, and as he watched, black clouds poured upward from its dome.

"I heard about those!" Garon said, coming over and hoisting himself up. "Took years to build, even with the best tinkers the Crown has working on it."

"Yes, I studied them." Cecelia threw in. "But since they're firing, most personnel will be watching outward, and below, for surprise attacks to make sure the dwarves aren't going to get sneaky. Which means we'll have a little more room to sneak around."

"Oh dear," said Threadbare.

"Oh dear?" Glub looked at him, fishy eyes goggling. "What's wrong with more sneaky room?"

"No, not that. There's that Steam Knight again."

"Oh, is one of the Steam Knights back from the front?" Cecelia added. "Which one? Fedifencer? Goliathan? Inkidoo?"

"I don't know, but it's the one you were driving around back at Outsmouth. You tell me what it was called."

"What? Reason? Impossible! Garon, take him, would you?"

Garon shifted Threadbare over to his shoulders, as Cecelia clambered up, porcelain feet scrambling for purchase on the rough stone blocks of the wall.

And there below her, battered and a bit burned-looking, but still very much intact, was Reason. Its massive helm passed not ten feet below the arrow slit, giving her a very clear view of the cloth covering that no other steam knight in Cylvania had.

"Impossible! Impossible!" she said, putting her hands on her hips. Then she hastily scrambled down, as one of the guards on a distant parapet glanced her way. "That... no. Can't be done."

"What can't be done?" Kayin asked.

"Steam Knight armor can only be piloted by the Steam Knight who made it. You CAN'T use another Steam Knight's suit. The magic doesn't work. Worst case, you botch it, and the suit tries to kill you."

"It looks like it's not as impossible as you think it is," Threadbare said. "Because there it goes right now. Could they have animated it?"

"No. It... animating things willy-nilly on them is dangerous. You need the right spells and sequence, and only Steam Knights get those. I... suppose someone could have completely taken the suit apart and reassembled it, but that would take a month, even for a top-tier tinker. It hasn't even been half that. And I don't know any top-tier tinkers who could be spared for that." Cecelia frowned. "Something's going on here."

"It went through a big portcullis in the eastern wall," Threadbare said, then hopped down from Garon's shoulders. "Thank you."

"That'll be the machine bay." Cecelia sighed and rubbed her chin, ceramic rasping on ceramic. She glanced around at the assorted doll haunters, golems, and one very worried necromancer. "Graves, how secure are we here?"

"The fish were an out-of-cycle shipment, they told me. I get to spend the night here, then it's off with the wagon tomorrow at dawn. I've been here an hour, and no one else has come by, so it's probably pretty safe here."

"No problems getting in the gate?"

"No, though they did wonder why so many fish were coming from Paws. There's no big bodies of water down there. I told them that a bunch of fishermen had passed through and traded for stuff, but the village found the fish not to their taste. That got some picky peasant jokes tossed my way." He shrugged. "They checked the barrels and decided not to turn down free food. The only problem is that I don't know where they've taken Madeline's barrel. They wouldn't tell me."

"That's a problem. But it's a problem we anticipated," Threadbare said. "Garon? Time for a King's Quest."

He sent the details across. It was very simple, when all was said and done, as was the monetary reward. Just enough to synergize with Garon's mercenary skills.

"Find Madeline, huh? Works for me." The minotaur grinned. "Sure, I'll **Do the Job.** And **Follow the Dotted Line.**" He glanced around, and over at the door. "Goes right out the door. One minute."

He hoisted himself up to the window again.

BOOM!

The toys waited for the explosion to fade, and Garon dropped down, spoke a few times until he was sure they could hear. "...Testing, testing... yeah, okay. The line doesn't cross the courtyard, so I can probably get to her without going outside. Piece of... No wait, hold on. I have something I need to do. I need to talk to Mastoya."

"Can you do dat, bring her here, and den go talk to Mastoya?"

"Mmm... bad idea." He held up a pouch, and jingled it. "I only have so many of the enchanted camouflage beads. I don't know how many it'll take to get to Madeline."

"How about this?" Cecelia asked, coming out of a long rumination. "We split into two groups. One group goes and gets Madeline loose and raids the General's office. Garon, you go with that group so you can hang behind there and talk with Mastoya. Glub, you go with that group so you can give Madeline a waystone. You Waymark this room, and everyone Waystones back here when they're done. Including you, Garon, if the talk doesn't go so well. Promise?"

"Promise."

"I'll lead the other group. We'll go see if I can get Reason back."

The toys would have blinked if they could. Graves did blink. "With all due respect, Captain—"

"I'm not your Captain anymore. But I am a Steam Knight, and if I can get Reason back, I can beat feet all the way to the front, with everyone safely inside the cockpit."

Garon shook his head. "And the guns firing on the rogue Steam Knight every few—"

BOOM!

"—thank you dramatic irony, for making my point."

"No, they can't target anything as small as Steam Knight armor," Cecelia shook her head. "Besides, the shells are hollow, used for gas and alchemical dispersion. Reason could take a near hit, no problem."

"And what if they call in the Hand to deal with you?" Kayin pointed out.

"It'd be overkill. I don't see why. Besides, they're probably busy with whatever assault the dwarves just launched."

"Zuula tink dis be bad idea."

"Look. I'm..." Cecelia raised her hands, and smoothed down her green dress, fingers shaking with agitation. "I'm not stupid. I know it's a long shot. But I at least want to go and see if it's possible. If it's not, then we'll wait for you guys to check the ledgers, and pick a shipment to put us in. Then we'll see about getting over with that convoy's goods."

"And assigning me as a driver," Graves said. "I'm guessing I'll wait in here until you all send word?"

Threadbare nodded. "I think this is close enough to the original plan. It should be dark soon. Who wants to go with which group?"

"You'll need someone who knows where the commander's office is, Garon," Kayin slid over to join the tiny minotaur.

"Zuula don't want to get nowhere near Mastoya. Not go well for anyone if she see me," said the plush shaman, trudging over to plop down next to Cecelia

"I got to go with you to give Madeline a waystone, right?" Glub said, holding up a hand to Garon. "High five, Team Sneaky!"

"Um..." Said Fluffbear, looking back and forth between Cecelia, then Garon. "You said she was a cleric?"

"Yeah, of the goddess of war."

"I'm a cleric too. Maybe I can help you talk with her."

"I don't know if that's such a good idea."

"I'll pray once we get there and ask Yorgum about it. If he says it's a bad idea I'll leave with the others."

BOOM!

The doll haunters and golems were starting to get used to the thunderous shots, by now. They simply waited half a minute, then Garon resumed. "All right, just make sure you're ready to use that waystone the second things go south. Because they might."

"That leaves me with you,' Threadbare said, patting Cecelia's shoulder. "You'll need a scout to whisper to the others, just in case."

"And I've got the easy job," Graves said, reaching into the pack and pulling things out, one by one. He nearly dropped the barrel of fish, before the others went to help.

"Why empty it?" Threadbare wondered. "Oh. It's going to burst at some point when Madeline's spell wears off, isn't it?"

"Yes. And also... ha!" Graves said, as they hauled out the crate of soulstones. "I'll need to keep them company. And it gives me access to a hell of a lot of skills if I need to borrow anything. Like oh, that wind's whisper thing so I can call you for help if something goes wrong here. Because it might. There are so, so many ways everything could go wrong, here."

"Yes," said Threadbare. "Sorry."

"Don't be, man," said Glub. "Savin' the world, right?"

"The Kingdom, anyway," Cecelia said. "And he's got a point. If we don't take the risks, other people have to. And we've got a backup plan if we die. Again."

"Might I remind you that I never took my last decree down?" Threadbare pointed out, and they chuckled.

For yeah, they had all pledged to the little bear, to be his subjects and reap the bounty of his Noblesse Oblige. And there on their status screens, the simple message remained—

"Nobody die. Again."

"Almost dark," Garon said, glancing toward the window. "No better time. Glub?"

"Create Waymark. Create Waystone, Create Waystone, Create Waystone..." The fishmen solemnly handed out the weirdly-marked rocks that appeared with each chant.

"All right." Garon sighed. "We've got one shot at this. Let's make it —"

BOOM!

*****

Fort Bronze never slept.

The pinnacle of the Crown's might, the coordinating headquarters of its most grueling war, hummed with activity at all hours. The Siege Cannon never stopped firing, shaking the walls with each discharge, and the stone chips littering the halls that Threadbare passed through seemed to suggest that this was a regular thing.

Not that he had much time to study them. One of his eyes was currently synced up to a small cloth mouse that he'd animated and kept behind them, watching out for trouble or oncoming traffic. Cecelia had her own mouse animi up ahead of the group, since she was more skilled with the trick.

Zuula, for the most part, slunk along and tried to be patient with the slow pace. Five levels ago it would have been impossible, but shamans got wisdom, and it made all the difference.

And luck, too, which helped out immensely when people passed by, and the three golems had to scramble for cover. But whenever there was no cover they could reach in time, the toys had to dip into their stock of camouflage beads... all save for Threadbare, who could use the skill with a single soft word.

And use it he did. They passed through two guard posts, and at the second one, Threadbare had to pick up Cecelia and run for it. Although they'd made her cloth slippers to muffle her ceramic footsteps, she just didn't have much stealth skill at all, and agility was a secondary concern to her, now that she didn't have access to her scout levels.

Finally, they reached the machine bay. Blocked off by a metal grille, the space between the crosshatched bars was easy enough to squirm through. Threadbare winced as his head smushed through, deforming a bit. The smarter he got, the more uncomfy that was. He didn't exactly have brains, he didn't think, but form seemed to follow function and he wasn't sure if he could survive decapitation. It seemed best to leave that as an unanswered question.

With his good eye, he saw Cecelia bend down and scoop up her mouse animi, tucking it into the pocket of her dress. "I'll need both eyes for this," she whispered, staring around at the piles of junk, and racks full of tools scattered haphazardly around.

No one else was visible in the vast, open bay. Chains hung silently, with bits of war machines, geared contraptions, and spare Steam Knight parts arranged in separate lots, separated by chalk lines on the floor and portable barricades.

"What dose for?" Zuula said, wandering over to a barricade and nudging it. Basically several slabs of metal on wheels, it was solid enough that she could barely move it, even with her fairly-good strength. Compared to a human, it'd be about chest height. For the doll haunters and Threadbare, they were huge barriers that thankfully weren't in the way right now.

Cecelia kept her voice to a whisper. "Those are for dangerous projects and devices. The Tinkers and Alchemists move them around as needed to partition the shop and get cover if something explodes. Please keep your voice down; we don't want to draw guards." The courtyard was right out THERE, just through a huge portcullis. It was lit by glowstones and still bustling, though down to about half the passers-by that they'd seen during the daylight hours. The lighting didn't extend to the machine bay, though, and half of it was in shadow. And there were at least four doors and a winding staircase heading up into the cannon tower above, and any of those exits could have people within earshot.

"Can you see all right?" Threadbare asked Cecelia. She didn't have Darkspawn, like he and Zuula did.

"Yes." She looked back to the corner, where a hulking form squatted down, arms just visible in the light from the courtyard outside. "Mostly. Hang on." She rummaged around in a nearby workbench, pulled out a metal tube, and capped one end. Then she grabbed a screw, whispered **"Glowgleam,"** and dropped it into the tube before it could flash into light.

Threadbare and Zuula looked up at the spot of light on the ceiling, then down to Cecelia, who grinned. "A little trick I learned from Dad." The grin faded. "One of the nicer ones, anyway. So long as I don't point it to the courtyard and keep the spot out of view nobody should see it. Give me five minutes to go examine Reason."

The half-orc plushie nodded. "Okay. Zuula go check doors, listen for trouble. Shouldn't be—"

BOOM!

The echoes were pretty bad in here. If he'd been organic, Threadbare thought he'd have a headache by now.

"I just got a golem body level from that one," said Cecelia, rubbing her skull as a red '18' drifted up. **"Mend."**

"I'll keep watch on the portcullis. And the grille." Threadbare said, glancing around through the mouse's dollseye. He glanced over to Zuula, but she was already gone, lost in the shadows. Of the three of them she was the most skilled at sneaking, and he supposed she could borrow rat skills or something to help out if she needed it. At any rate she was off being Zuula in a good way, so he trusted her to keep doing that. "Be very careful, okay?"

"Absolutely." Cecelia took one last look up at the light on the ceiling, then covered the end of the tube with her free hand, and slunk across the floor towards Reason.

She disappeared between the rows of barricades, and Threadbare hunkered down, glancing back and forth.

And a few minutes later, he heard something very close by.

CLANK.

Threadbare glanced around, and froze.

Something big was moving, back in the far corner of the shop. Moving slowly, but that was definitely a 'clack' as it put a foot down and a scrape of metal on the stone floor. It looked for all the world like someone very tall in very heavy armor, tiptoeing.

Maybe he hadn't seen them? Threadbare slunk back into the shadows, ready to camouflage himself at the first opportunity.

And then he gasped, as the armored figure moved into the first edges of the light coming through the portcullis. He knew that helm. He knew that armor.

It moved up near him, glancing up at the ceiling, and Threadbare realized that it was trying to figure out where the spot of light had come from. It had been in the bay when they'd entered, and he'd mistaken it for just another war machine back with the rest of the strange contraptions.

Opportunity warred with common sense, caution with nostalgia, and Threadbare realized that he could probably take a risk here, if he took a precaution first.

"Command Golem – please whisper when talking and be generally quiet," he told the figure—

—and instantly it was as if his mind had slammed into a brick wall. The pressure was immense, as SOMETHING fought the spell, but Threadbare, initially surprised, rallied and PUSHED, using the willpower that he'd trained and boosted with level after level of caster jobs, and managed to get the command through.

WILL +1

Immediately, the figure whirled— but slowly, and with grace out of proportion to its size, taking care to remain quiet.

Behind its helm, two gems flared to glowing life, shining red. Threadbare knew those gems well. He'd seen them every morning, when he came downstairs with Celia, back in Caradon's house.

"Hello Emmet," he said, stepping out of the shadows. "Do you remember me?"

"Yes," the armor golem ground, in a rasping voice that was probably as quiet as it got but still about as loud as regular conversation. "You are Threadbare. You are family."

"Good," sighed Threadbare, glancing back to the courtyard. Loud enough and far enough away that another discussion might not draw attention. Maybe. "So what have you been up to these last few years?"

*****

Madeline puffed in air, as her barrel shifted. *Moment of truth now*, she thought, with a word ready on her lips to unleash dragonfire on whoever was decanting her.

But it died unspoken, as the top half of the barrel finished unscrewing and a horned wooden head loomed over her. "You got our message?"

"Yeah." Her neck rattled a bit as she uncoiled it, poked her head up past the rim of the barrel's secret compartment, and nodded toward the catgirl in the back of the group. "Thanks for the whispah."

"Shh," Kayin said, leaning out the door, holding out a wooden palm. "Twenty seconds. Then you can come out."

It was hard. Madeline had spent days coiled in that barrel, and though she didn't have flesh anymore, she FELT cramped. But she waited until the catgirl switched from an open palm to a beckoning wave.

Garon helped her out, and Fluffbear cushioned her fall.

"Feels weahd to see you without Mopsy," Madeline said.

"We left her back with Graves," the little bear squeaked. "I'm hoping he can convince her and Pulsivar to come out of the pack before it explodes."

The whole trip had been harrowing for the mini-cougar and Pulsivar. They'd had to share a litter box and hadn't THAT been fun.

"Create Waystone," said Glub, handing her a little green rock.

"What's this?" Madeline squinted at it.

Garon answered. "It'll teleport you back to Graves. Please go. We'll need the pack re-enchanted if it hasn't blown up by now. And you're sneaky, but you're big, and we need to run up and get into the general's office and that's past three checkpoints—"

BOOM!

"What is that, anyway?" Madeline asked. "Been hearing it for a while now."

"Look, just go, please. And Glub, go with her, okay? No offense but you're about as sneaky as a bowl of bananas."

"None taken, dude. What's bananas?"

"This whole mission. Gods, nevermind. Just go, okay?" Garon glanced back at Kayin at her sudden chopping movement, as she eased the door shut. The little toys waited, until footsteps passed the door and receded. Kayin eased the door open again, peering out. "This is a heavily guarded area," Garon continued. "All the storerooms are."

Madeline craned her neck around, took in the floor-to-ceiling stacks of crates and barrels. "I'll say. Hm, anything good here?"

"We don't have time."

She looked at him then nodded. And came to a decision that she'd made weeks ago, just hadn't acted on yet. Swift as an arrow, she darted forward and bumped her muzzle against his. "Good luck."

"What?"

"Come back alive, okay Gar? Be a shitty undead existence without ya."

"Oh. Uh." Garon's hand clattered to his muzzle as he realized that had been a kiss.

"So how do you use this thing?" She turned to Glub, and after a few whispered questions and answers, they dissipated as the waystones activated.

Madeline smiled as the two of them faded in on a cold, empty barracks... empty save for a very tired-looking Graves and two upset cats. Mopsy crouched under a far bunk, her tail sticking out and very puffed up, showing extreme displeasure. Pulsivar peered out next to her, yellow eyes gleaming with rebuke.

"Oh!" Graves said and fumbled for his cane. "Thank goodness. Can you?" He hauled up Madeline's pack.

"Of cawse. Pack of Holding."

"Good. I need to rest, then I can see about getting the rest of this stuff back in." He gestured at the dummy payload and junk strewn about. "I could have borrowed a merchant level from our dead friends, but I don't think any of them have the skill at a higher level than you. Most of them were pretty settled, didn't go on many trips."

"Why do ya need to put it back in?" Madeline shrugged her wings. "We're in. They ain't likely ta search us on the way out. We'll just push it under the beds and you can just say it was heah before, if anyone asks."

"All right, I guess that works. Mostly." He glanced over at the very full and very stinky litter box.

"On it, dudes!" Glub started moving junk around. "Man, why are the cats—"

BOOM!

"—right, stupid question," the fishman doll said as soon as they could hear again.

"I've been trying to get them back in the pack, but they won't go," Graves said, miserably. "Can they spare Fluffbear? You could whisper her, since you're here now."

"Herbie, man, you never did know much about animals, didya?" Madeline grinned. "Streetrat like you nevah had the chance, huh?"

"Hey, I like animals just fine." Graves shrugged. "Rendered into sausage and smeared with mustard after they're thoroughly cooked. Not my fault living ones are stubborn."

"Theah's a trick with cats. Heah. Help me get the pack open an' square it as much as possible."

"What? Why?"

"Just do it."

She coached him into making the pack as boxlike as possible, and sat it on the ground.

Mopsy crept out first, sniffing, then settling into it and fading from view with a surprised "Mrp!"

Pulsivar, though, was made of sterner stuff. He didn't budge. Glub tried to convince him and got some gentle mauling for his trouble. The bobcat was NOT happy about this place and wanted his new hoomin to know it.

Graves watched Glub and Madline try for a bit, but after about the fourth BOOM, his head snapped up. "Trouble."

"What?"

"Get the pack over here, we need to stow the soulstones. Ah shit... **Borrow Skill, Conceal Status**." He blinked a few times, as Glub helped him manhandle the soulstone crate into the pack. "Pulsivar. We need Pulsivar in here. There's no time!"

Someone pounded on the door.

Madeline grabbed the pack, raced under the bed, and as the cat howled in protest, shoved Pulsivar into the pack. "Get to covah!" she stage whispered at Glub, who dove into an empty footlocker and pulled it shut.

Just in time, too, as the door flew open. Graves tottered to his feet, tapping the floor with his cane. "Eh?" he warbled, in a querulous voice. "Who's there?" As emaciated as he was, he didn't have to fake shaking as one hand cupped his ear.

A black-robed man swept into the room, glancing around. "Deathsight. Speak with Dead." he murmured, and Madeline pulled back under the bunk, avoiding his view as the world turned monochrome.

BOOM!

"Camouflage," she hissed, as the cannon fired, thanking heaven that she'd gone the scout route and practiced it back in the swamps.

The man stopped and knelt, peering under the bed straight at her, but didn't seem to see her. "Hello? Is anything here?"

Behind him, she saw Graves staring down at the man, eyes wide. Wide and full of recognition.

"Is everything alright, young man?" Graves rasped, voice creaky and doing its best to sound forty years older.

"Perhaps," the man said. He was thickset, with mutton chops and a black moustache, greased to neat points. He had small eyes, in a broad face, and an insincere smile as he turned it upon Graves. "High Magister Arxan Arcane. I'm with the necromancer corps. I was experimenting downstairs and caught some residual chatter from above. Tell me, old man, have you noticed any apparitions about? Free-floating? Class Threes, if you know the term?"

"No, no, I can't say I do," Graves said, coughing, and holding his hand in front of his face. "Just a humble farmer, sir."

Madeline watched, as Arxan stepped toward him. "Now that's odd. You sound a bit familiar. Why is that…"

*****

Garon sighed with relief, as the window broke silently. He waited for Kayin to slip in through the busted pane, waited longer while she forced the window open. Then it was over and down, with Fluffbear clinging to his back, and through the open window, letting go and falling in a clattering heap to the floor.

"Easy," Kayin whispered, dropping her Silent Killer skill. Useful for her, since it made herself and most things she did completely noiseless but not so good for Garon.

Garon didn't answer. He froze, listening, and holding his breath. He'd made noise, and this office was guarded.

"Relax. Two triple thick doors between here and the guards," Kayin said, easing the window back down, half an inch at a time. "We need to avoid shouting, but a little noise will get lost in the—"

BOOM!

Garon rose, looking around the room that his sister had spent years in. Cold, spartan, with weapons on the walls and a fireplace that looked barely used. She always did like it cold. The few tables in the place were cluttered with plans and diagrams, and little wooden figures of royal troops lay scattered in among pewter dwarves, with a few three-inch-tall steam knight miniatures looming among the fray.

"Mom should have just let you have those dolls," Garon said, finally. "Would have saved everyone a lot of trouble."

"Where's the ledgers?" Fluffbear squeaked.

"They'll be in her desk, probably. That's sensitive information," Kayin said. "I think. Still got a head that's kind of like jelly, desu. At least scout helped with that a little."

"It's alright," Garon said shooting a glance at the main door, then at the smaller door on an adjacent wall. "Where's that one go?"

"Beats me, but it's quiet in there," said Kayin. "Private bathroom, maybe?"

"Maybe," Garon said, uncertainly. "But she's never been much on luxuries. Not when I knew her, anyway."

"People change, maybe," Kayin said, poking around the desk, before hauling out a set of tiny lockpicks. "Wow, this is a lot easier with tiny hands. Give me five minutes, and-"

"And you'll do what?" said Mastoya, opening the side door.

The toys froze.

Mastoya lowered the sword in her hand and squinted down at the two wooden dolls and the tiny, armored bear. She blinked twice, glanced back to the small bed that filled most of the cramped bedroom. "Am I dreaming?"

BOOM!

"No," she said, eyes unwavering as she snapped her gaze back to the intruders. "No I'm not dreaming. **Always In Uniform. Shield of Divinity. Holy Smi—**"

"Heya Nasty Masty," Garon said, swaggering up, hands on his hips. "You forgiven me for putting mud in your hair yet?"

The buff died on Mastoya's lips, as her eyes went wide, white against her green skin. "Garon?"

"Yeah. Can we talk?"

"What the hell is this? What the shitting hell is this?" she whispered, the sword dropping to point at the ground. With her free hand she tucked her nightgown closer around her. It was pink, with ruffles, Garon noticed, and he smiled to see it. *Yeah, it's still her. I've got a shot.*

"It's... a little weird." He jumped, pulled himself up onto her desk. "I hear you're drinking now."

BOOM!

As the echoes faded Mastoya moved in, grabbing a ring of keys off a nail on the door as she did so, and settled in at her desk, giving Fluffbear and Kayin hard stares until they backed off. Unlocking a drawer, she reached in and pulled out a bottle, then two cups. She poured a shot for herself, slugged it back, then poured another. Then she tilted the bottle over his cup and hesitated, glancing at him.

"We all got stomach cavities put in so we can drink. Doesn't do anything, but hey." Garon thought it best not to tell her it was Cecelia's idea, so they didn't offend the dwarves if the issue came up.

She poured him a shot and he picked it up carefully, sipped it carefully. "Whoo, that's some varnish gone," he lisped, and twisted his tongue to wring the alcohol from the cloth. "Your throat must have more holes in it than cheese."

"My original question stands. What. The shitting. Hell. Is this?" Mastoya said again.

"Basically I got a second chance at life, sort of. I'm a ghost haunting a golem."

She digested it for a bit, then swallowed. "So I did kill you."

"That's where it gets weird. No, you didn't kill me. A vampire came across me while I was bleeding out and turned me. Then an old friend showed up, and I died as a vampire, and he helped stuff me in a golem shell when I asked him nicely."

"And you honestly expect me to believe that?"

"I don't care if you do or not, sis. It's me either way. I'm just here to tell you it's fine."

"What... this?" She waved a hand at him and took another shot. "Because from where I'm sitting that looks like some sort of tortured existence as some other guy's pet monster."

"No, no, it's not like that. He's pretty cool. Seriously, great guy. But also that's not what's fine. What's fine, is that I'm fine with you attacking me when you were killing Mom."

She slammed the shot glass down on the table, so hard that it cracked. Kayin winced, and shot a glance toward the door.

"Fuck. I'm muddling this, aren't I?" Garon asked. "Shit. I'm sorry. I just..." he sat there, staring into the cup she'd given him. "I needed to tell you that. I forgive you, okay? It was the rage, not you, and—"

And then her arms were around him, the sword clattering to the ground, as High Knight Mastoya, Western General Mastoya, the badass mother to her men and hammer of the Crown, was hugging Garon to her chest and bawling heavy, racking sobs.

"Ma'am?" A voice said, muffled through the outer door. A gauntleted hand knocked, and Kayin and Fluffbear looked at each other, spread out to either side—

"Go away! It's fine!" Mastoya yelled.

BOOM!

And Garon relaxed into her arms and hugged her back. *Maybe this will work. Just maybe.*

Finally, she put him down, and mopped the snot from her crooked nose with one sweep of a fluffy pink sleeve. "This guy who brought you back, is he around?" She looked over at Kayin and Fluffbear. "Gonna assume you're dead people, too."

"I'm not!" Fluffbear squeaked, and Mastoya giggle-snorted in surprise at the sound of her voice. Fluffbear's adorable level rose accordingly.

"I am, desu," Kayin said, shrugging. "And he's not around right now. We're here because of Garon. He needed to talk with you."

Garon considered the word. "Yeah. My... savior? Huh. Weird, but I guess he is. He's busy." *And hopefully things are going as well on his end,* Garon thought.

CHAPTER 4: REASON FAILS

"These past few years," Cecelia heard Emmet rumble and nearly lost her footing on the crates she'd stacked together. She knew that voice well!

Sure enough, a backward glance showed a somewhat-familiar armored form, half visible in the light coming in from the portcullis. Right about where Threadbare was.

"Yes," she could just make out the tiny bear's voice in the darkness. "The last time I saw you, everything was on fire, and you were falling over a bannister. Well, through it, I suppose. It was rather flimsy to you I think."

"It was. Then there were soldiers, and I fought them. But then King Melos was there, and I could not fight him, for he was stronger than I. And he took me back to Castle Cylvania."

"I see. I was stuck under a lot of rubble for a few years. Then I got out and found my old friends and made some new ones, and now I am here."

Oh, Threadbare. Cecelia palmed her face with her free hand. Then she shook her head, and looked up at the boxes. She had a job to do, and he was... buying her time? Having an innocent conversation? Hard to say.

Emmet. Emmet was a surprise. She'd never thought to ask after him, assumed he was sitting deactivated in a storeroom somewhere. But here he was, talking, and his words sounded an awful lot like he was smart now, too. *Another Greater Golem...* She thought, as she scrambled up the boxes.

And then she was hopping off the last box and scrambling up Reason.

"I was not done," said Emmet. "King Melos told me of my destiny and personally took me through many dungeons. I fought many foes at his side, and learned to become strong. Even though I must pretend to be stupid, and follow Anise Layd'i around and obey her commands, I am smart, too."

"Anise Layd'i. Is she about? That could be trouble," Threadbare said.

"She is in the Fortress somewhere. Speaking with the Hand. And Princess Cecelia."

Cecelia froze.

What?

BOOM!

Once the echoes faded, the little bear continued. "Princess Cecelia? Are you sure?" Threadbare asked.

"I am sure. I was awaiting here as ordered when she came in her Steam Knight suit which is strong but not as strong as me. She came out, and Anise bowed to her and smiled in a way that should have been pleasant, but I thought seemed unpleasant."

"And you are certain it was her?"

"I have seen her face, her armor, heard her voice many times before. King Melos told me I must guard her with my life and do as she instructs, even if Anise Layd'i does not want me to. And I am certain that was Princess Cecelia."

Cecelia felt a sick premonition welling up in her gut. She remembered rumors, barracks whispers, and old tales.

Old tales about daemons, and what they could do with people.

But I'm here! My soul is here in my new body, right? Sick to her stomach, she scrambled back to the hatch and wrapped her fingers around the handle.

"Oh. That's strange. I saw Anise Layd'i kill her." Threadbare said.

Metal shrieked, as Emmet stirred, restless. "Impossible. That would be treason."

"And yet she did."

Cecelia's hands shook, and she pushed hesitation aside, twisted at the handle, and got it half open...

And then her eyes opened wide, as something inside twisted back. The handle ground shut again.

"You are fooled or lying. I am a representative of the Crown. It is treason to lie to me," Emmet ground out, and there was a hint of frustration in his voice.

"I think Anise Layd'I has been fooling a lot of people," said Threadbare.

"And she has told me that is what traitors would say. Are you a traitor to the crown?"

"No," Threadbare said after some consideration. "But the King killed

Caradon, you know."

"Caradon?"

"The old man who made us."

BOOM!

Cecelia closed her eyes, let the old sorrow wash over her, to be replaced with new resolve.

Reason was hers, dammit! And since Reason was dormant, she had a trump card.

"Animus!" She whispered, touching the hatch. **"Invite door!"** And then she gave it a sharp tug, putting her will into the animi as she did so, and it sprang open—

—as flesh tore, and a spray of blood hit her face.

Something inside screamed, louder than any steam. She staggered back, got the glowgleam rod up, and shined it in…

Into a mass of writhing tentacles, and wires, and nonsensical gears, and glowing sigils that she'd never seen before. Eyeless faces sobbed at her, as the thing that filled Reason like a hermit crab filled its shell, whined and shrieked over the tendrils that she'd torn free with the hatch and lashed out after her.

She fell off Reason, hitting the ground, feeling her body crack a bit, as a red '34' floated up.

"What?" Emmet said, voice gaining volume as he rose. "No! I must guard Reason!"

The hatch slammed shut, and gears groaned, as Reason stirred, rising in jerky motion, turning toward Cecelia as she crawled backward, watching the parasite-filled mecha up its massive blade.

Reason needed no guards, as it turned out.

Not that it was Reason, any more. No, they were far, far past reason here, Cecelia realized…

*****

"So you're Graves' old man," Arxus smiled, as he paced around the barracks, looking over the junk scattered hither and yon. "I hear he turned traitor."

"I wouldn't know. He don't exactly call home no more." Graves said. "Ran away to the big city cause he was too good for pickin' beets the rest of his life."

The necromancer chuckled as he nudged the overfull catbox with his toe. "Looks like someone's been keeping pets against the rules. Sorry for the mess. It was here when you got here I suppose?"

"Yes. Eh, it don't smell worse than the barn on a hot day. I reckon."

Gods, he was laying it on thick. Madeline kept her camouflage going, feeling the sanity drain.

"Well, it's no worry," said Arxus. "The Crown makes war on traitors, not their relatives. So you were bringing supplies in?"

"Yessir. Bunch of fishermen came through Pads and traded for stuff. We're simple farm folk and fish disagrees with us so we decided to tithe it to tha troops."

"How patriotic. You know, I'm from Riversend, myself. My folks weren't peasants, but they weren't far from it, and I don't ever recall knowing any peasants who would give up food."

Graves shrugged, uncomfy. "Well, I didn't make the choice. New Alderman's a shit, probably wanted to kiss up to the Crown."

"New Alderman?"

"Baron down there went bad. Royal Knights rooted him out. Put in an Alderman in his place."

"Oh? See, that's interesting. Because I heard that my old colleague Graves was one of those royal knights who did that, back before he went traitor."

BOOM.

Madeline studied Graves' face. He was sweating, and using the time to think, she could tell. But if she could tell, she rather thought Arxus could, too.

"Yeah. I did talk to my son after he did that," Graves said, bowing his head. "Didn't want to mention it to ya because he went traitor a few weeks after."

"Mm. I know why you're here." Arxus said.

"You do?"

Madeline shifted slowly, slowly under the bed, angling for a good pounce.

"You're here looking for news of your son."

She relaxed a bit.

"I am," Graves admitted. "Do you know anything?"

"Honestly, I don't know if I'd tell you if I did. He thought he was better than us. Felt bad about the soulstone archives. Kept asking questions about where the bodies came from." Arxus chuckled, an oily sound. "First rule of the necromancer corps, you never ask about that. He thought he was above that rule. Better than us. But we got him back."

"Did you?" Graves asked, and there was something in his voice, something that Madeline had never heard from the thoughtful, nervous Necromancer she'd come to like.

"Oh yes. His fiancée came back from the front, dead. One of MY friends had a contact in the morgue. Guess which body we had shipped over for training, when Wight day came?"

"You— *you* did that," Graves said, forgetting to put the quaver of old age in his tone. There was a quaver there all right, but it wasn't from age.

"And guess which trainee ended up with her body, staring up at him, when he pulled the sheet off?" Arxus said, sneering.

"You son of a bitch," Graves said, standing.

"Hello, Bertie," sneered Arxus, whipping a wand from a holster, and pointing it straight at him. "How's tricks?"

BOOM

"Chomp!" Madeline lunged. Arxus screamed as Madeline's fangs went into his calf. The wand fired and black energy went wild, and Graves shouted words that were lost in the thunder of the cannon, as red life burst from Arxus and flowed into him. Over and over again he stomped forward, pounding his cane on the ground, shouting until the echoes of the cannon faded, and Arxus was a shriveled husk on the floor. **"-Life! Drain Life! Drain Life!"**

"Stop!" Madeline howled, crashing into him, and sending him off balance.

"You jackass!" howled a spectral voice, and both of them whipped their heads around to see Arxus' spirit, standing over his corpse. "You are so fucked!" And then he dove through the floor.

"He'll get help," Graves said, and from outside, down the corridor, shouts were already starting to rise. "I'm sorry. I'm..."

"Glub!" yelled Madeline, grabbing up her pack. "Get ready to move!"

Wind's Whisper Threadbare, she thought. "We're made! Need an escape route!"

And then it was Garon's turn...

*****

"She hated me," Mastoya said, slurring her words. The second bottle, empty, crashed to the floor as she fumbled for it. "Nuts. That's alcohol abuse, it is."

"She didn't hate you," Garon said. "She loved you; she was just awful at showing it."

"No. It was... it would have been fine, I guess, if it was just us, y'know? But she let Dad take me into th' town to play. An' I had friends. An'..." Mastoya slumped back in her chair. "An' they got to play with dolls, and wear pretty dresses, an'... but not me. Not Nasty Masty. Had to wear furs and loincloths, an' get my ears pierced early even though it hurt, and fight off the rats she called to eat me. The rats. Garon. She tried to eat me. With rats."

"Yeah. We, uh, we got her to stop doing that after they nearly got Jarrik that one time."

"I... shit. And Dad... what's he do? He like acted all supportive and stuff, but whenever it was him 'gainst her, he'd crumble. Weak. Just... good man. She didn't deserve, him, him. Hm?" She reached for the bottle, found nothing there. "Shit."

"Yeah. Listen, do you believe me? Believe what I said about what Anise is doing?"

"Oh yeah. She's a shit. Thing is..." Mastoya chortled. "The King is strong. He's just... just giving her rope. He needs 'er now. Needs 'er till the dwarves'r dead. Then she's nexx, nexp on the chokking blopp."

"But what if she's not? What if she's playing him? From what you told me about Taylor's Delve, it sounds like SHE was giving the order to scrub it."

"You. You have no idea how much that hurt, Gar." Mastoya said, staring at her hands. "My ol' friends? Gone. Dead. But... it was... final test. It was what I had to do, to finish HER. To move on from 'th past. In the end... Anise, the King... in the end it was gonna happen. An' if I didn't, then someone else would. So why shoodn't I benefit from it?"

He opened his mouth...

...and Fluffbear squeaked up. "Because it's wrong. It doesn't matter who ordered it, it's wrong either way. Killing innocents is never okay."

"Yeah, well, Ritaxis don't care. War happens," Mastoya said, glaring at her.

"That's bull hockey! Those were the people you were fighting to protect! What good is a war if you kill your own people? That's worse than losing!"

"Wash your mouth, li'l bear!"

"You'll never be a paladin that way!"

"Psh, what'd you know ovvit. Ain't no paladins no—"

"Clarifying Aura!" said the little bear, and the office filled with light as she glowed, holy radiance easing in and around the toys and the drunken half-orc.

BOOM!

"There are," Fluffbear said, as the echoes faded. Her aura did its thing, buffing mental fortitude and restoring sanity, bit by bit. "And I am one. And I tell you now, there's good ways to wage war, but the ends never, ever, ever justify the means."

Mastoya looked at her, mouth opening and closing.

And Garon stiffened, as Madeline's message screamed in his ear. "Oh hell. Look, Mastoya… this isn't right. You know it. At the heart of it, you haven't changed!" He said, the words tumbling, coming faster. "You're still my sister, you still don't deserve the crap you go through, and you still want to be an awesome paladin! You can! Come with us! We're fixing things! We're putting it right! Come with us and help!"

Mastoya looked at him. Then she stood, wobbling. "Gar…" She sighed, and put her hand to her head, rubbing the crewcut black hair, and the scars under it. **"Curative."** She said and instantly straightened up, cold sober. "Innocents. Good men. Yeah. Thing is… I'm commanding a lot of'em. Not all innocents, but…" She moved around to where she'd put her sword and picked it up. "They're relying on ME."

"Masty… don't do this…"

"They swore to the Crown, but they're my family now, Gar. The one I chose. And if I turned? I could never look them in the eye again. Yeah, I killed my mother, and it didn't help like I thought it would. I just felt bad. I killed you too, and I'm sorry, and I can never make that up to you. But them? They're my redemption. They're the one good thing I did, the one thing I tried that hasn't turned to shit. They TRUST me. They know I'll have their back. Just as I know they'll have mine." She sighed. **"Holy Smite. Divine Conduit!"** She said, and light burst from her, eyes erupting with holy glow, as a halo formed around her head, and she raised the shining golden sword high.

"Now surrender, Garon," She said, in a voice that reverberated like thunder. "I don't want to have to kill you a second time."

And then Reason screamed, and all hell broke loose.

Long and high, like some sort of undersea crustacean thrown in a fire, Reason screamed, and the wail tore out of the machine bay, breaking the silence between cannon shots. And like everyone else in the fort, Mastoya's head whipped around toward the window.

"A distraction!" She assumed, turning back toward Garon and the toys…

…to find an empty office and dissipating green flickers, as the golems' waystones did their work.

Garon materialized at the foot of the bed…

…which was no longer there. Graves was rummaging inside the pack, pulling out different soulstones, looking for the right one. Glub and Madeline were shoving the bed, along with a few others, in front of the only door out.

From beyond the makeshift barricade, the group could clearly hear approaching metal-shod feet.

BOOM!

For a bit, anyway. Reason might be wailing, but the guns weren't stopping.

"Threadbare's not answering!" Madeline shouted.

Garon thought quickly. "Trouble. He'll need our help and we can't stay here."

"I'm sorry," Graves said. "I fucked up."

"It wasn't your fault," Glub insisted. "Dude had it out for you. Speaking of that, here." The fishman grabbed the withered corpse on the floor, jumped up, and slam-dunked it into the pack. Graves nearly dropped the pack and cursed.

"What the heck?" Fluffbear squeaked.

"Evil dude. Magic items. Search later," Glub summed up, then went back to building the barricade. There was hammering against the door now and angry voices.

Garon growled low in his throat. "Right. Graves, Madeline, get in my party." He threw invites, then he threw a quest.

"Follow you?" Madeline said.

"Yep. That simple. **Do the Job. Organize minions to follow me!**" He pointed at the barricade, and the door slamming against it repeatedly, as the guards battered against the recalcitrant portal. "Burninate that, buy us some time."

"**Bahninate!**" Madeline yelled, and then there was fire. Glub screamed and jumped clear, barely.

"Dude! Warn a bro first!"

The angry shouts outside turned to panicked shouts, and Garon nodded, pointed to the window. "Out we go. We get to Threadbare as fast as possible."

"We're four stories up, give or take!" Graves said, gesturing at his withered arms. "I can't climb!"

"Fff... can you fit in the pack?"

"No," Graves said, sparing it a glance. "It's just a bit too small. Pulsivar barely got in there."

"I could adjust it with tailoring." Fluffbear offered.

Graves coughed, as the smoke from the burning beds started filling the room.

"No," Madeline snapped. "Can't alter the pack when it's enchanted or it'll lose the magic. No way weah getting the cats back in now if they get out!"

"Okay. Waystone shenanigans with Graves, would they work? Get clear, make a waymark somewhere else, and get him a waystone?" Garon looked to Glub.

"Dude, those things cost fortune. I'm low. And we'd still have to get him the waystone, how are we gonna do that?"

"Shit." Garon hopped up, looked out the window. The courtyard below was distracted, with civilians getting clear and armored men advancing on the portcullis of the machine bay. A flash of metal, then the portcullis groaned and bent outward, as something heavy slammed against it.

"I have a different idea," said Graves, coughing. "Fluffbear, can you quickly sew me a pair of gloves? Garon, please kick me out of the party."

A minute later, Graves was coughing helplessly, unable to move a muscle as he cleared his lungs of smoke.

But he didn't have to, because he was an animator, and his gloves, shoes, pants, and tunic were all animated, and they climbed him down the wall with slow and careful grace.

Garon watched as a few fleeing civilians paused, then came over to help, offering hands up to the rogue necromancer and helping him down once he got to the courtyard. He pointed up to the window, which now had smoke oozing out of it, and Garon ducked. "We're good! He can blend in with the crowd. Madeline, you ready?"

"Get ahn!" She said, just as the door sizzled and burned to nothing in the space of a second. A bare female hand pushed through the ashes where a door had been, and a beautiful woman wearing a diaphanous red halter top and harem pants pushed through the barricade contemptuously, black eyes narrowed behind her red domino mask...

...just in time to see a small wooden dragon with its back full of toys go careening out the window.

The creature who the knights knew as the fifth member of the Hand, called only "The Cataclysm", sighed and turned her attention to extinguishing the flames. Really, calling her in here had been like asking a sledgehammer to crush a cockroach.

As to the culprits who had fled, well, she'd leave them to her friends. That should be more than enough to take care of the matter.

*****

Reason screamed, the sound filling the machine bay with the shrieks of the damned, and Cecelia ran for cover.

"Celia!" Threadbare shouted, staring as the great Steam Knight suit rose, and started stabbing its sword into the piles of junk around it. "No!"

"Cecelia?" Emmet rumbled, loudly this time, voice rising as he managed to shake off the command keeping him quiet. "She is here?"

"Yes!" Threadbare said, running toward Reason...

...which turned.

Yellow light glimmered inside its helm, and tendrils poked out, slimy tendrils, with glowing orbs like eyes that trained down upon the little bear as he smacked his scepter on the moving barricades. "Hi! Over here!" he called. "I challenge you! Er, **Guard Stance!**"

Your Challenge skill is now level 10!

Your Guard Stance skill is now level 20!

But as he did, there were heavy footsteps behind him.

"No!" Emmet said. "I must guard Reason!"

"That's not Reason!" Cecelia wailed, as the massive machine turned from her and glared its eyestalks down at Threadbare. "There's a monster in it!"

Emmet stared at her, gems glittering under its helm. "You... are Cecelia!"

"Yes!"

WHAM! Threadbare twisted desperately to the side as Reason shuffled toward him and tried to kick the little bear. It missed, barely—

Your Dodge skill is now level 9!

I don't have nearly the skill to keep doing that, Threadbare knew. So he ran past a row of barricades, slapping them with his paw. **"Animus Animus Animus Animus, invite barricades one through four,** get that thing," he said, calming a bit now that Cecelia was out of danger.

Your Animus skill is now level 36!

Your Creator's Guardians skill is now level 27!

The heavy barricades rolled on their sturdy wheels, slamming into Reason's legs as it stepped back, surprised.

"What has happened to you?" Emmet said, gazing upon the little porcelain doll. "You are smaller and not armored!"

BOOM!

"It's a long story and we don't have-"

WHAM! Reason brought its wrecker blade down on an animated barricade, splitting it asunder and sending a red '303' up into the air. Then it turned to the rest of the barricades and drew back the ten-foot-long sword for a wide sweep. Hastily Threadbare directed them to scatter, but Reason just turned toward Threadbare, lunging forward and sending more barricades into the air, chopping through chains and resting siege engines alike as it tried to skewer the little bear.

"I command you to kill the monster inside Reason!" Cecelia shouted, desperation making her voice squeak as its strings stressed to their limit.

"Alright," Emmet decided. "I can do that."

On anyone else it would be a boast. But there was nothing boastful in his tone, nothing save for quiet confirmation of a thing self-evident.

And so as Threadbare ran from Reason as it wrecked its way across the machine bay. The little bear used barricades to slow it down and animated new ones just as fast as they were destroyed.

Emmet thumped his chest with a hollow CLANG and started toward the infested machine that stood twice his size, speaking with his booming voice as he went.

"Always in Uniform. Shield Saint." Emmet said, for his forearms WERE shields, with gauntlets on the end of them. **"Unyielding. Fight the Battles. Take the Hits. Get that Guy! Build up—"** he finished with the first run of buffs, drawing a hand back as he broke into a sprint. **"The Bigger They Are... Fast as Death."** He intoned, running through all the applicable tier one melee buffs.

And then he switched over to his melee tier two skills. **"Ablative Armor,"** he commanded, and barricades flew up to coat him, along with broken chains and other surrounding metal items. He continued as they slammed into him, forming a shell of his own. **"Unbreakable. Unmoveable. Unstoppable. Always Angry..."** Then a dip back into tier one, for the last skill. **"Rage!"**

Emmet roared, and Reason twisted to face him and nailed him point-blank with an arbalest bolt.

It hadn't shot at Threadbare because the target in question was tiny. But Emmet? Emmet was big.

The bolt, which could punch through plate armor like a longbow through cardboard, hit Emmet... and sent a spray of barricades from the armor golem's back.

A big, fat '0' drifted up.

Realizing too late its danger, Reason twisted, tried to get out of the line of Emmet's lumbering charge—

—to no avail. **"Clench!"** Emmet roared and latched his hand around one of the pistons in its calves.

The wrecker blade bounced off his head, as Reason tried to cut him down. A red '17' drifted up, and more barricades sprayed away.

"Siegebreaker Strike!" Emmet roared and drew back his free arm. Then with terrible, slow force, he punched towards Reason's knee.

Reason wanted to dodge it.

Should have dodged it.

And it would have, if it could have. But Emmet had it in a deathgrip, and no matter what the heavier machine tried, it couldn't shake the armor golem free. He was unmoveable. Desperate, Reason slammed the Wrecker blade down between its leg and the oncoming fist, trying to parry it.

But Emmet was not only unmoveable, he was unstoppable.

In slow motion his fist hit the Wrecker blade. And went right on through six inches of forged steel as the blade crumbled and splintered, went right through Reason's knee beyond, snapping through clockwork and armor, and tearing through the fleshy thing inside it.

Threadbare and Cecelia watched Emmet pull his fist back, sighed in relief as Reason toppled, bloody tendrils whipping from the stump of its thigh.

"End Rage," Emmet said, stomping up toward the cockpit, ignoring the flailing arms. "Please stay clear, Princess Cecelia!" he called. "I shall end its threat."

"Holy shit," Garon gasped, and Cecelia and Threadbare turned to see the rest of the group dismounting from Madeline's back.

"No wondah you didn't ansah yah whispahs," Madeline said, watching in mixed horror and awe as Emmet slowly, relentlessly, beat in Reason's helm with his metal fists. The tainted machine whined as it scrabbled, trying to drag itself away from him, but every time it made headway Emmet just grabbed it and yanked it back to him.

"That's Juggernaut stuff," Garon said. "Got to be. Knight Berserker hybrid stuff, holy shit."

"That's my brother, more or less," Threadbare said, dusting himself off, and dismissing the barricades. "I'm sorry to say we can't take Reason out of here."

"Where's Graves?" Cecelia asked.

Shouts from outside, as a figure ran up to the portcullis, wiggled through some of the warped bars from Reason's kick and ran to them. "I'm here!" Graves shouted. "What the..."

"The Hand is here, too!" Cecelia yelled back. "We need to escape!"

"Too late," someone whispered in her ear, and she jumped in surprise, as a knife stabbed straight through her skull—

—and she gained another golem body level, because you can't kill golems that way.

The toys whirled to see a woman clad in tight-fitting black clothes from head to toe, all save a scarlet sash around its waist. The figure stepped back in surprise as Cecelia tore the knife from her skull and tossed it in the air.

"Mine now!" snarled the porcelain princess. **"Animus Blade!"** Then the red '124' drifted into the air, and she staggered. "Woo." But the dagger arrowed after the figure, who suddenly exploded into smoke and was gone.

"Mend Golem!" Shouted Threadbare.

You have healed Cecelia 120 points!
Your Mend Golem skill is now level 28!

"That's the Ninja! That was the fucking Ninja!" Garon freaked out. "Yeah, it's escape time!"

Fire flared from behind them, in the courtyard, and the portcullis started to melt.

"And theah's tha Cataclysm and why ah we still sitting heah talking?" Madeline said, rushing toward the doors on the far side of the room.

BOOM!

In the afterechoes, the central door out of the machine bay slammed open, and Cecelia gasped as a white-armored form pushed through. She knew that armor well, from the horn cresting its helm to the royal crest on its greaves.

And then she saw who was behind it.

Anise Layd'i stepped into the room, her face roiling with rage, staring around at the mess—

—and fixing on Threadbare's silhouette as he stared back at her.

"Can't go that way!" Madeline shouted, skidding to a halt and coming back around.

"Up here!" Zuula called from the stairs. "Quickly!"

Graves and the golems ran, ran for their lives, all but Threadbare. He paused, on the last step, looked toward Emmet. **"Invite Golem,"** he finally decided.

Emmet looked up, surprised.

Your Invite Golem skill is now level 12!

Threadbare stretched out his free paw, offering it...

...and then a shuriken blossomed in the center of it, as stuffing sprayed.

CON+1
Your Golem Body skill is now level 27!
Your Toughness skill is now level 20!
Max HP +2!

"Stop! Emmet, stop you stupid thing!" Threadbare heard the other Cecelia say and jumped in surprise as the white-armored form lifted her visor and ran forward. "Oh what did you... oh rot, there go the ventral flukes! I'll be days repairing that!"

Reason whimpered and stretched its hand toward its mistress.

And as Emmet stopped pounding, Threadbare sighed. **"Mend Golem,"** he said, on the way up the stairs, as another shuriken whizzed past his head.

WILL+1
Your Mend Golem skill is now level 29!

As soon as he got all the way up the long stairs, Zuula and Garon slammed the hatch down behind him and shot the bolts. **"Animus! Invite Shelves!"** Graves yelled, and a heavy set of shelves, with gears and parts falling off of it at every step, shufffled over to weigh down the hatch.

"That won't stop Emmet for long," Threadbare cautioned. "He's their warmachine now."

"And the fucking Hand's behind him!" Garon said. "Once the Legion shows up we're dead!"

"Where are we, any... way..." Threadbare drifted off, as he looked around and realized that the room was full of dead people.

A great cannon stood in the center of it, and a bronze dome capped it up top, its workings filled with chains and pulleys, with metal spheres the size of Zuula's hut suspended and swaying like evil, looming fruit.

The shelves all around were filled with mixtures and jars, metal jars. But from several of them, evil-looking thorny vines extruded, growing into the shelves and walls, and through about ten men wearing goggles and facemasks and heavy aprons. Some of them were still twitching, but all were plainly dead.

"Zuula been busy. Tanks for distraction downstairs." The little half-orc said, mopping blood free from her tiny spear. "Now what escape plan?"

Threadbare stared toward the view slits at the far end of the room. They could fit through them. Graves couldn't.

Cecelia was investigating the shells and the cannon. "Huh! This isn't complicated. The firing solution's the trickiest part. Looks like these guys were Tinkers. Maybe a few Alchemists. Uh, Graves, stay away from those vines. Don't touch anything."

"Yes, dose vines from poison seeds," Zuula said. "Only vegetation stuff to work with up here."

"It's gone silent downstairs," Kayin said, cat-ear pressed to the floor. "I think."

Threadbare shook his head. "I'm open to ideas. This is a bad spot. We could waystone back to the room."

"It's compromised; I'm sorry," Graves said.

"Oh. Hm."

"Wait," Cecelia said, glancing up at the spheres overhead. "I have a crazy idea... Madeline, how tough is that pack?"

"What?"

"Your merchant's pack!"

"Eh, it's leather."

"I mean if it gets destroyed, what happens?"

"Everything inside comes out at once."

Cecelia gnawed her lip. "Can you put a pack inside a pack?"

"Oh sweet Hoon no, the skill's explicit about that. And I can only have one at a time anyway."

"What are you thinking?" Threadbare asked.

"That you all get inside her pack; we stick the pack into one of the shells, and fire it past the lines over to dwarven territory." Cecelia started cranking levers and wheels, and the counter-weighted cannon swung around.

"Whoa." Garon said. "Don't you need someone outside to pull you out, though?"

"Yeah, or yah stuck waiting until the spell expires."

"Could one of us survive the impact?" Threadbare said, looking up at the giant brass orbs.

"Maybe." Cecelia said. "It'd be one big hit, but I mean a BIG hit. They're not made for force, they're made for delivering gas and other stuff." She took a breath. "But we don't have organs, or bones, so if one of our plush types does it... oh shoot. Graves."

"Yeah," he said. "It's all right. I'll stay behind to fire the cannon. I fucked it up; I'll pay the price."

"No, you didn't!" Garon and Cecelia chorused. They shared a glance.

"It went wrong on my end," Garon said. "Maybe. I have an idea of how to reach Mastoya now."

"It went way wrong on my end, too" Cecelia said. "Besides, you're not a Tinker. You need to be one to fire this thing."

"Feet on the stairs!" Kayin called back. A siren started up, wailing throughout the fort. "And there's the general alarm," Cecelia said. "We're out of time. Graves, get in the pack."

"I can't. It's not big enough."

"No," Threadbare decided. "Nobody stays behind. Nobody dies. Unless..."

"Unless?" Cecelia said.

"Glub, do you have enough fortune left for another waymark and waystone?"

"Yeah. Why?"

"Graves, do you have any merchants you can borrow skills from in your soulstone collection?"

"Yes." He rummaged around in the pack, drew out a soulstone. "Why?"

"There's no time, so I'll try to be concise." Threadbare said. "Here, hold my pants."

And with that, the little bear started stripping, as he told them his plan...

Two minutes later, the cannon belched, and filled the room with BOOM.

Threadbare grimaced, then relaxed as Kayin's whisper filled his ears. "Survived the launch," the catgirl whispered. "Also, OW."

"Get in!" He motioned to his side, and Cecelia dove into the very large pack below him, vanishing to join Graves inside. The sturdy pack was some of Missus Fluffbear's best work. Though not the only bit of work she'd done in the last minute, since the rest of their cloth supplies had gone into the padding necessary to keep Kayin alive. Fluffbear had made her a very, very thick pillow, since Kayin was a wooden type.

This part had actually been the biggest gamble of the whole affair.

CLANG! "Ow!" a woman called. He turned in time to see the shelves fall through the burned-out hatch, and listened as they crashed down the stairs.

Sighing, Threadbare sat on the large pack that he'd had Fluffbear make, and waited. Maybe not the biggest gamble, he thought, as he waited. Waited and counted.

Tendrils of fire burst from the hatch, clearing away the vines and wreckage, rupturing pots and spraying poison smoke into the domed chamber.

But Threadbare had no lungs.

Your Golem Body skill is now level 28!

Emmet was up and through next, a massive arm raised to shield himself, peering over the edge with his gemstone eyes. Threadbare waved to him.

"The bear is alone here," Emmet ground out.

"Oh, yes. My name is Threadbare, actually. I don't remember if I mentioned that or not." He held up a teapot. "Would you like to have a tea party?"

Emmet's free hand snapped forward, and the teapot shattered. Threadbare looked at the handle in his paw, over to the hollow finger that Emmet had used to fling the bolt, then back to the bronze dome, and the footlong iron spike buried into it. "I would have taken no for an answer," he said.

"The real Princess Cecelia tells me you are a traitor who tricked me."

"No," Threadbare said, shoving the two teacups he'd set out back into his pack before Emmet could get trigger happy again. "You can only betray something if you were on its side in the first place. I am on Cecelia's side, and not the King's side. The King killed our maker. I don't like the King very much."

"That is still treason," Emmet said, taking a step forward, training his finger on the bear.

"Command Golem. Please stand down," Threadbare said.

And he felt the spell fizzle. He remembered how Caradon had griped about the magic resistance skill, many a time. "He was right. It is annoying."

Emmet advanced upon him, and Threadbare simply sat, staring up at him with button eyes.

"Do you surrender?"

"I will not fight you," Threadbare said, hoping that Emmet didn't question him further.

"It is safe," Emmet called back.

"Wait for the smoke to disperse first," Anise said. "Unless..."

"I'm on it," a man said. He was nobody Threadbare had ever heard speak before.

Doors slammed open in midair, above the hatch, doors to someplace full of blackness broken by red light. THINGS crawled out of the holes, things like wasps made of metal that darted upward, slamming into the roof, and tearing at it with mandibles. Bronze shrieked and gave way, and the smoke eddied up, as the draft drew it out.

And all through it, Threadbare counted. He hit the goal he was trying for, hesitated, then decided to give it a bit more.

"Kill the fire, dear," Anise said.

"Aw. Wasting so much of my time stopping fires," a woman griped, in an exotic accent.

Fifteen seconds crawled by as the fires shrunk and vanished, and the draft pulled the smoke out and away.

Then wind whipped past Threadbare, and he turned to see the black-clad woman who'd thrown a metal star through his hand, crouched behind him, twenty feet away and ready to cut him down.

"Hello," he said to her. She squinted at him, over the mask that covered everything but her eyes.

"Well well well," Anise said, heels clicking as she strolled up the stairs. "The little bear. Naked and alone."

"Not alone. You're here." Threadbare said, placidly. "But I am naked, yes."

"I suppose you wanted to leave your magic items to your friends." She smiled, then glanced down at the pack. "What's in there?"

"Two of my friends. We had to stay behind for this to work."

"Stay behind?" She arched an eyebrow.

"Oh yes. Everyone else went into the cannon shell."

"Desperate," the ninja whispered.

"And you would be one of the Hand?" Threadbare asked. "Or is it the finger? I'm not sure how this goes."

"Three fingers, I suppose, is a good way of putting it," said the red-robed man as he walked through the hatch. An iron, grilled mask covered his face, and scar tissue showed around the points it didn't cover. "She's the Ninja. I'm the Legion. The Cataclysm is waiting to cook you if you escape."

"And the Princess is waiting below," said Anise, smiling. "Trying to salvage some Reason from the situation. And here I am, Amelia Gearhart, ready to unmask myself to the kingdom... with Emmet's help, to sell it, of course."

"Of course," Threadbare said. "It seems very clever. But isn't there one more?"

"He's busy," said the Legion, gesturing the wasps down to patrol around the dome, blocking the vision slits out. "You're a clever one, aren't you? You see how we're going to play this?"

"Garon told me about the Hand. How the entire country thinks they're the surviving heroes of the Seven, yes. I suppose you're all going to unmask and show them that yes, that's true?"

"A new Seven. Now that Cecelia is grown enough to take her place with us," Anise smiled. "I'm the secret thumb, you could say. And she's two extra digits, her and Reason combined."

"Except she's not Cecelia, is she? Just as you're not Amelia?"

Emmet shifted, restless.

"Don't be ridiculous, who else would we be?" Anise smiled, but her eyes were hard now. "And you're a little bear who knows too much."

"All I know is that you're not a nice lady, not at all."

"No dear. That's part of the irony." Anise smiled. "Ready to die now?" She asked, eyes flicking past him, looking for the trick, looking for the trap.

"I suppose so." Threadbare hopped down. "Do you mind if I put my clothes on? I'd rather not die naked."

"Be my guest. Ranshax, kill him if he gets stupid."

The ninja nodded.

"Call Outfit," Threadbare said and was clad in his clothes once more. He lifted the pack up and settled it on his shoulders.

"Your hat," said Emmet. "It was different before."

"Yes," said Threadbare, putting his paw to the waystone that had been sewn into it. "I suppose it was. Goodbye."

He saw Anise's eyes widen, and then everything was green, and his view distorted as shurikens whipped through it...

...and he was fading in, right in the middle of a crater.

Kayin, battered and scorched, grinned happily at him and waved. "One life down, boss! Glad to see it was worth it!"

Next to her, a burned, holed, but intact pack was open, and Glub was pulling a very cranky Pulsivar out. Next to him, Fluffbear put away her sewing supplies. Then Madeline was hugging him.

"Ah! Thank you!" He pushed her away after a second. "I need to get Cecelia and Graves out. Excuse me. Oh, hold on. **Clean and Press**."

He did himself and the pack, raising levels twice. Both it and he had been dosed with toxic smoke, after all. No sense to going to all this trouble just to kill the man as he emerged.

Threadbare rummaged around in HIS pack, and pulled them out one after the other. First Cecelia, then Graves.

"Everything went to plan?" Graves asked, sweat stained from the evening's efforts.

Threadbare looked at Kayin.

She grinned. "Perfectly. I shoved the pack into the padding, and when the shell hit I used Nine Lives to survive the impact. Then I pulled Glub and Fluffbear and your clothes out. He made the waymark and the waystone, and she sewed it into the brim of your hat."

"I finished like ten seconds before it disappeared," Fluffbear squeaked. "You cut it really close. What happened?"

"My teapot got broken." Threadbare sighed. "Too scattered to mend it, I fear. Oh, and the Hand are going to reveal themselves as the surviving members of the Seven and reunite the kingdom."

Everyone went silent.

Then Pulsivar hissed and backed into the center of the group, as a man cleared his voice from up above the crater.

"Aye, perhaps ye'd better tell us more about that?" A stranger said, and Threadbare looked up, to see about a dozen dwarves in heavy armor, leveling guns down at the golems and their living friends. "Later. After ye're properly in a cell."

"Oh, good!" Threadbare said. "NOW we can surrender."

INTERLUDE 1: THE GENERAL

For a second, Mastoya stared at the empty air. *Waystones. Holy shit,* she thought, and dispelled her divine conduit before it ate up too much of her fortune. Not that she'd needed it in the first place to kick their little toy asses. But shock and awe might have gotten them to surrender, and she really, really wanted a chance to talk to Garon on her own terms.

But none of that mattered right now. Gauntlets pounded at the door. "Ma'am?"

"General alarm!" She called back. "We've got intruders, saboteurs! Find them! Capture them; I want them alive."

With that she headed back into her room to change, hands moving with long practice, donning her arming underlayer, then her plate, and sliding her sword into its sheath. She debated on the shield and took it. All told, the process took two minutes.

And as she did, something felt wrong.

What was it?

"Ma'am! There's a fire in auxiliary barracks twenty-five! The Cataclysm is putting it out! There's signs of violence, and the necromancers say an angry ghost found traitors up there!"

"The fuck? Get a perimeter around that barracks," Mastoya commanded. Something was off. What was off?

Leaving her pauldrons loose and half-tied, she shouldered the door open and found her honor guard awaiting her. "You're with me. Let's move."

They fell into step behind her, blades out, glaring around at the rough-cut halls of the fort as she stomped through them. The West Wing was a ways, the barracks in question was pretty remote.

BOOM!

And Mastoya stopped, so quickly that Hicks almost ran into her from behind.

That was what was wrong!

The cannons had skipped a beat! She knew the rhythm by heart now, heard it in her sleep; it had worked its way into her dreams. It was always Two, One, Three, Five, Four. And since the explosion had come from Five's direction... Three. Three had skipped a beat.

"To the machine bay!" She yelled, pushed past Hicks and Wedge, and flat out ran.

A messenger imp caught up to her as she went. "Trouble in the machine bay!" The yattering thing screeched. "Captain Dontalus is keeping a perimeter! The Steam Knight's gone berserk!"

Cannon Three was right over the machine bay, and chock-full of steam ballistae and tunnel thumpers, and other engines of destruction that Melos had ordered to the front over the last week. It was going to be a big push, Mastoya knew, and she had been waiting for the word.

And now, one of the Crown's most effective warmachines was ripping it all to hell and back. Mastoya's lips twisted against her tusks. Her brother couldn't have found a more effective target to sabotage.

"The barracks. The barracks were their staging point; they're long gone. Call off the cordon and tell the captain to secure the machine bay. If Reason can't be stopped, evacuate the courtyard until I get there. Go back to Captain Dontalus and tell him that!" She shook her head. Garon had distracted her with a heart-felt plea, while simultaneously sabotaging the war effort. Damn, he was clever. Also alive.

She believed it was him, now. This was something sneaky, just the sort of thing that Dad would have taught him. She wondered if Jarrik and Bak'shaz had parts in this... they'd been missing for years, but she'd heard rumors of a mighty tamer working with the Rangers.

After a frantic, scrambling minute she burst into the courtyard, to find Captain Dontalus forming a perimeter around the warped portcullis. Beyond it, in the darkness of the bay, something inhuman whimpered and screeched.

"Why is that bay not secured, Captain?" Mastoya snapped.

"The Princess ordered us back, ma'am!"

"Fuck that noise! She's not in your chain of command!"

"Ma'am... the Hand and the Inquisitor were in there, and and the High Inquisitor said to do as the Princess said..."

Mastoya glared at him for a full second, but she understood. The Inquisitor was a special case. Mastoya hated special cases.

She also hated uppity young officers who she'd thought had more common sense than this.

"Hold position. Back us up if trouble starts," Mastoya said, flipping her visor down and waving her honor guard forward. Her buffs were still up, so there was no need to reset them. But around her, her honor guard muttered their own.

"Yes Ma'am. Uh, she told everyone to keep clear, Ma'am," said Dontalus.

"That's nice." Mastoya said, pushing through the perimeter, and clambering through the warped bars, looking around the room...

...and freezing, as she saw the pulped remnants of Reason, and the Princess kneeling over it. Tendrils, fleshy THINGS swayed out of the Steam Knight's broken shell, and groped for Princess Cecelia, questing, trying to find a way through her armor... Surprised, the princess looked back at Mastoya, showing pale skin, and fearful eyes, somehow unaware of the danger trying to eat her!

Hell no!

"Get that thing!" Mastoya called to her honor guard and charged it. She didn't know what the fuck it was, but it had tentacles, which meant old one or something eldritch like that. And she had a trick against supernatural evil, now didn't she? **"Back, You Fiend!"** She bellowed, slamming her sword against her shield.

Ritaxian clerics had an edge here. Most other clerics had to present their holy symbol to do this. But Ritaxis had adopted the sword as her holy symbol, because putting down your weapon or your shield in the face of extraplanar evil was pretty idiotic.

The tendrils whipped back, and *something* writhed in the ruins of Reason. Unable to escape the oncoming holy rebuke, it shrieked as its unnatural flesh burned.

And the princess, startled, screamed and ran the other way.

Mastoya grimaced. "Wedge! Hicks! Get her to safety!"

Then there was no time, as the creature, unable to escape, fought. But it had already been wounded, she saw, by whatever had broken Reason. She went down its length, hacking until the ridged, slimy meat of it stopped wriggling, stopped trying to gut her. And all the while it burned, as the holy fire she'd called to herself cooked it.

"General Mastoya!" A voice snapped from the stairs, and Mastoya took a few more hacks, then stood next to the cockpit as red steam billowed out, and the thing in there screamed its last.

Mastoya waited until she was certain the monster couldn't rally, and lifted her gaze to meet Inquisitor Layd'i. Next to her, the rest of the Hand filed down the stairs, followed by Emmet, who stopped above the Inquisitor, too big to push past her.

"Inquisitor," Mastoya said. "I'm glad to see this abomination didn't hurt you. Or anyone else?" She glanced over at the Princess, safely surrounded by her honor guard—

—and caught a look of pure loathing from Cecelia's red and burned face.

Mastoya blinked under her visor.

"We're fine." Layd'i snapped. "Everything's FINE. Except it's not. The cannon's personnel are dead, and the saboteurs have escaped. I want to know how the hells they got into the Kingdom's most secure facility on *your* watch."

"That's a good question," Mastoya said, staring at the Inquisitor. "I'd like to know how the hell an eldritch abomination got into this Steam Knight armor and wrecked my machine bay on *your* watch."

"Me? Me! You're accusing me!" Layd'i put her hands on her hips. Below her, the three members of the Hand present looked at each other and started to spread out.

"Maybe." Mastoya said. "King's daughter goes out on a mission to stomp old ones, and comes back with an old one spawn hiding in her armor. You were present throughout that. Seems an odd thing to miss," she said, staring hard at Cecelia and watching the girl's eyes slide away, and her face go blank. *The girl I spoke with a few weeks ago had excellent emotional discipline. Now it's gone. What happened out there?*

"This is a classified matter," the Inquisitor snapped. "I order you not to speak of it, in the name of the Crown."

Mastoya gritted her teeth. "Yes, Inquisitor."

"As to these other witnesses..." Layd'i smiled with pure malice. "We can't risk—"

"No, Ma'am," Mastoya said, moving up to join her men. At her approach the princess cut and ran, surprising the hell out of Wedge and Hicks. They moved to grab her, and the Hand tensed. "Stand down!" Mastoya bellowed, and everyone stopped. "We're all loyal here, ma'am. Hicks, Wedge, Dyson, Myers, I order you to silence on every event that's transpired and will transpire here tonight. Go rejoin Captain Dontalus and tell him to pull his men back and await my orders to secure and cleanup the area."

"Ma'am!" They saluted simultaneously then hurried back to the portcullis. Mastoya held her breath as the Hand looked to them, then looked back to Anise, who was visibly swallowing her fury.

But she didn't speak, and Mastoya's honor guard reached the portcullis alive. Mastoya let out a breath. The Inquisitor wouldn't dare have them killed in full view of the courtyard. Even that sick little daemon wouldn't dare.

But she could make trouble in other ways. It was time to toss her a bone, though."Your orders, ma'am? Regarding the creature?"

Layd'i descended the stairs, then strode up to her, raising a finger—

—and gasping, as it sizzled. A red '5' floated up and she fell back, looking at her red, burned flesh. "Turn that fucking thing off!" Anise Layd'i shrieked.

"Of course, ma'am. Slipped my mind." Mastoya lied, and shut down Back, you Fiend. "May I heal you?"

"No! No. That will *not* be necessary." Anise ground out. She glared around at the ruins of the workshop. "I ask again, how the hell did saboteurs get into YOUR fort on YOUR watch."

"Because we weren't keeping an eye out for puppets," Mastoya said.

"Puppets?"

"More specifically, ghosts inhabiting golem bodies. If my brother was to be believed."

On the stairs, Emmet clattered as he whipped around to face her. Mastoya blinked, then returned her gaze to the Inquisitor.

"Your brother?"

"Dead in the cleansing of Taylor's Delve, ma'am. I saw to it personally. He turned up in my office tonight with several others, and tried to convince me to join him in treason. I tried to arrest them, and they waystoned out. That's about the time that thing was wrecking my machine bay."

"Ghosts in golem bodies. Ghosts in... golem..." The Inquisitor's eyes slammed open, and her already-pale skin blanched even further. "Oh. Oh you... you little... you BEAR!"

"Yes, they did have a bear with them. Funny thing, she said she was a paladin."

The Inquisitor's jaw worked, and she hissed, turning her head to the side. "I'll want a full debriefing on my desk tomorrow." She finally said, turning and walking away, shaking with every step. "Clean up this mess. The assault will be delayed now, due to your incompetence."

"My apologies, Ma'am," Mastoya said.

"Insufficient," Anise barked, reaching the princess' side and putting her hand on the girl's shoulder.

The princess looked from the Inquisitor's hand, back to Mastoya.

Her face was as red and burned as the Inquisitor's hand, Mastoya realized. And a cold feeling ran down her spine. "I'll go and get that ready for you." Mastoya husked, and saluted.

A few steps toward the door, and she expected Anise to order her dead.

Just at the door, and she expected the command to be given, and the Hand to spring into action.

Then she was through the door, and out, and sweat rolled down her face as she realized how close she'd come.

It was only a suspicion, no proof at all, but those burns had been way too similar. And the implications that arose...

I have my duty. I have no proof. I have to move carefully here, she knew. *And before all of that, I have an assault plan to salvage.* She sighed, as more mundane concerns trickled down. *And also a letter to write to the King, to try and save my career.*

She rather thought the odds were good. She was the best general he had, and he needed her for the assault that would end this fucking war for good. But the Inquisitor was a thing of malice, and whatever had happened here tonight, she'd never forget the insults that Mastoya had given her. Blood would come of it.

Blood.

She looked down at her blade, which still dripped with ichor. Taking a cloth, she swiped it along the sword and sheathed her holy symbol. Then it was a quick turn, back to the Courtyard, picking up her honor guard along the way.

"Ma'am? Everything alright?" Myers said, saluting, slamming her fist into her breastplate.

"Walk with me," she said. Once they were back in the keep, in a lonesome hallway between checkpoints, she gave the gory rag to Wedge. "Go to the enchanters. Get them to analyze this. It's darkspawn blood, but I need to know what kind."

"Ma'am?"

"No one else is to know of this. Especially the Inquisitor."

"That's... yes Ma'am."

If it was from the old ones, well, that was problematic, but it was the Inquisitor's problem.

If it was from something daemonic, though...

If it was daemonic she had a great, big problem, and no clear way to solve it.

"Garon, you little shit," she muttered to herself. Things weren't *perfect* before he'd shown up, but they'd been simple, and that had been enough. With the booze, and her duty to lose herself in, that had been enough.

Now she stood on the edge of a deep, dark precipice, with not just herself, but everything she'd built, everyone she'd trained and supported, everyone who looked up to her, all at risk. And worse, was the possibility that she'd erred, badly. No general likes to face that possibility. But the bad ones hide from it, cover it up.

Good ones owned what they'd done and adapted the strategy so they didn't make the same mistake twice.

Mastoya desperately hoped that when this was all said and done, that she had been a good one.

*****

Crouched over her desk, midway through the Inquisitor's report, at the darkest hour of the night, she looked up as heavy metal footsteps clanged on the hallway outside. Heavier than any of her guards. She reached for her sword.

Then metal rapped on wood. Knocking.

"Enter," she called, keeping her hand around the sword's hilt.

Emmet stood there, literally filling the doorway. Mastoya let go of the sword. If the Inquisitor had sent him to kill her, it wouldn't help. She shot a glance at her window and scooted her chair to the side for easy defenestration if it came down to it.

"Does the Inquisitor need me?" Mastoya asked.

Behind him, the two of her honor guard on duty did their best to peer around him, faces looking to her, awaiting her order.

"No." Emmet ground. "The message I am to deliver is private."

She glanced back at the honor guard and nodded. "Hicks, Myers, turn in for the night. You, big guy, come in, shut the door, and lower your voice."

Emmet did, moving oddly daintily for something so massive, something that she was pretty sure could punch down her entire Fort one wall at a time.

"Your message?"

"It is not actually a message," The golem confessed. "I have doubts. I must speak of them. And you are the only other person in this fort that I am permitted to talk with freely if the need arises."

"I am? Who told you that?"

"King Melos. In his secret instructions. I am permitted to reveal my sapience to Princess Cecelia, Anise Layd'i, and you. You are the only three confirmed one hundred percent loyal to the Crown here."

"Before tonight I'd agree with that," Mastoya said, opening up her drawer. "Do you have an extra stomach compartment for drinking?"

"No. Why? Such a thing seems foolish to install upon a golem."

"I'd figured there was more to you. You don't move like the old war golems we have down in the Machine bay... had." Mastoya sighed. "Shattered to bits without even being able to react, since their handlers told them to stand still until ordered otherwise. You're a pretty shitty actor, Emmet."

"Charisma has not been a priority in my training. Aside from my Knight levels."

"What all do you have, exactly?" she said to buy herself time to think.

"Archer. Alchemist. And Grenadier for ranged attacks." Emmet rumbled, his voice as low as it could go, and still filling the room. "Berserker. Juggernaut. Knight. And Mercenary for close-combat engagements."

Sweet fucking Ritaxis' assplate. *Yeah I wouldn't make it out the window.*

"And just to be clear, you follow the orders of the Inquisitor? So she could order you to tell her about anything we talk about here, and you'd have to obey?"

"Yes. Although..." he leaned forward. "I have been ordered to put the orders of Princess Cecelia above hers, and not tell Anise Layd'i about this fact. You are third in order priority."

"Okay. I'll watch what I say." Mastoya kicked back a shot, feeling her spent Moxie restore a bit. "So why are you here?"

For a while, he was silent, the gems behind his helm flickering.

"Your brother came to you tonight. And he is now a golem."

"Yes." It had been Garon, she was sure of that. Not a trick, not a test. That had been Garon, she'd stake her command on it.

Shit, maybe I'll have to.

"My brother came to me tonight as well." Emmet said. "I did not know I had one. He is also a golem. And I very much wish to know more about him, and I thought that since your brother came to YOU tonight as a golem, that perhaps you could tell me more about this, and help me decide how to resolve the conflict."

"The conflict?" Mastoya asked.

"Per Inquisitor Layd'i's orders, confirmed by Princess Cecelia, the next time I see my brother I am to quote unquote rip his fucking head off and burn all his remains and make him suffer if at all possible through every step of the process and kill or destroy everything that he ever loved within his sight before he dies if at all possible you massive metal meathead."

Mastoya laughed, sardonically. "Yeah, sounds like one of my brother's friends, all right."

"But my earliest command, was to protect my family. And he is on the list."

Mastoya sighed, got up, and looked out the window. No imps, the courtyard was bare, save for the watchers she had stationed to make sure nobody spied on her.

Then she nodded and turned back to Emmet. "Okay. First thing I should tell you? I am absolutely the last person you should be asking on how to NOT kill your relatives..."

CHAPTER 5: A NOT-SO-LONELY MOUNTAIN

Brokeshale Mountain rose above the Eastern Reaches of Cylvania like the stump of a massive tree. Large, jagged-topped, and untouched by trees, legend in fact said that it had once been one of the World Trees, destroyed by greedy giants in their war against a pantheon of gods long-since fallen. Or reborn. Or mostly gone, with one or two remaining. Or there was an apocalypse or something, BUT the world recovered so it wasn't the end of the world after all. Or something like that.

What WAS known for sure, was that over a century ago, back when Cylvania carved its way to freedom and withdrew from the Cane Confederation (before all that slavery nonsense,) a clan of enterprising dwarves made their way south from Mighty Hallas and liked the look of the place. They knew why it didn't have trees, and it wasn't because of a curse or giants or gods or anything like that. It was because of what was there, hiding below the soil, keeping vegetation from growing on the place...

They knew it held riches. They hadn't realized just how MUCH. Dwarves being dwarves, when they found out how much metal was under Brokeshale and the surrounding valley, they sent messages back to their relatives. Who got in touch with their relatives. Who called in *their* relatives. And in a relatively short time, (in dwarven terms anyway,) no less than four clans migrated down to set up new lives and turn Brokeshale into a major mining hub of western Disland.

Eventually the humans in the more central part of Cylvania noticed "Hey, there's dwarves over there now," and the usual messages and envoys were sent. Tables were thumped; voices were raised... and then envoys were received; handshakes were offered, coins changed hands, and the dwarves, under King-Grundi-Under-This-Mountain-Here-No-

Not-That-One-The-Big-One-You-Idjit, (The transcriber was later fired,) walked away with the rights to the land UNDER the remote branch of the Skygrope mountain range, so long as the dwarves didn't expand their holdings horizontally, and represented Cylvania to the rest of the dwarven communities in Disland and beyond.

It seemed uncommonly generous, to many of the disgruntled human miners who'd called Cylvania home. But in actuality, it was more than fair. By making the dwarves *their* dwarves, they staved off future incursions. The truth of the matter was that being at the confluence of two mountain ranges, Cylvania was rich in mineral wealth, and more dwarven clans were already prepared to move in on the new nation to see what they could wring from below their soil. But with a formal agreement in place, the oldbeards of the remaining clans knew they'd be moving in on Grundi's turf... a thing which dwarves do NOT do lightly.

So when dwarves wanted to own land or mine or do things in Cylvania, they went to King Grundi. King Grundi would talk with whoever the human in charge aboveground was at the time, negotiations would happen, and everybody got their cut. It worked pretty well.

Up until everything changed, the humans got stupid, and it didn't. "...and that's why we can't have nice things," Garon finished.

"It was more than just the humans getting stupid," Cecelia said, just a touch defensively. "I mean, if you're correct, then Anise tricked my father into slaughtering Taylor's Delve. So yes, Grundi's claim against the Crown was correct on THAT. But they pretty much did the same thing to the Hornwoods and refused the Crown's requests for evidence."

"What kinda evidence they supposed ta show?" Madeline asked, resting her head irritatedly on stone. She'd been out of sorts since the dwarves had confiscated her pack, along with the rest of their items, even down to the cloth mice Cecelia could have used to scout out their prison. "Empty mineshafts? A place where gold ore ain't?"

To be fair, they'd given the toys who had been clothed replacement clothes for their confiscated magic items, but the gray prison shirts were much too large for them, and they'd refused to allow the bears tailoring tools to fix that situation. At least Cecelia's clothes *sort* of fit.

Kind of.

If she held the neckline pinched shut, anyway.

"I'm just saying, that mistakes were made on both sides," Cecelia said. "Though admittedly, more on my father's side."

"Yeah. I don't know the details, not exactly, but Beryl told me the dwarves were NOT happy about the Oblivion. It didn't work at all like they were promised it would." Garon sighed. "It was supposed to be a thing where we could raise or lower it. Was never supposed to be always up."

"You know a lot about this, Gar," Madeline said. "Why?"

"Eh, some of it's from Beryl, a lot of it is history I studied. If you're going to be a Mercenary you have to know what opportunities are out there for profitable conflicts. I figured that it'd end up the Crown against the dwarves at some point and wanted to know the history of my potential employers."

"Nice!" Madeline said, admiringly.

"The Crown doesn't use mercenaries," Cecelia rubbed her chin.

"No, I would've fought for the dwarves. Precisely for that reason." Garon smiled. "Well, that and Mom and Dad would have disowned me if I helped the Crown."

"Beh. You t'ink too little of you parents," Zuula said, as she continued roaming the cell, poking at the walls. "We forgave Mastoya, didn't we?"

"Yeah, AFTER you died. At her hands. See, I didn't want it to come to that with me, at least."

"Technicality!" Zuula snorted.

"I hope Graves is okay," Kayin said, her ears flat against her skull. Her clothing, like Zuula's, had been sewn on, so she was spared a prison shirt at least.

"I just hope I can feed Mopsy on time!" Fluffbear waved her paws. "My code's gonna break if I don't!"

"Surely the gods won't mind?" Threadbare asked. "These seem like, oh what's the words... extenuating circumstances? Yes, those fit."

"It doesn't matter," Fluffbear said. "I swore it so I have to do it. That's the paladin's way."

"Wow. That sounds rough, man." Glub said, offering her a pat on her back. "I couldn't do that. I mean, I'd try, but stuff gets away from me, you know? More of a guidelines type than a rules guy."

"I'm sure Graves is okay," Cecelia reassured Kayin, giving her a one-armed hug. The catgirl leaned into it, even purred a bit as the porcelain princess scratched between her ears. "As are the cats, wherever they took them all. They're probably getting fed right now." She nodded to Threadbare. "So she's getting fed on time."

"Yes, but I'm not the one doing it."

"Look at it this way," Threadbare said. "If someone else is caring for them, then the cats are on THEIR time. Not yours. It's only while they're with you that they're on your time. Otherwise how could they hunt?"

"Hm..." Fluffbear scrunched her little black furry face up, so hard that her eyes flattened upward a bit. "I guess... Maybe?" She sighed. "I'm really new to this job. At least I've got Oops Sorry."

"Desu?" Kayin stirred and looked over to her.

"What?"

"What did you do?"

"What do you mean?"

"You said oops sorry."

"That's the name of the skill."

"Seriously?" Garon said.

"Oh yes! It lets me talk to my god or the nearest applicable deity for the crisis of faith at hand and seek forgiveness! But I get a black mark on my status for a while, and if I get too many, I lose the job."

"BAHAHAHHAHA!!!"

"It's not that funny," Fluffbear frowned at him.

"I uh, I didn't laugh," Garon said, glancing around.

"GAHAHAHHAHAH!" The laughter echoed through the room. "HAHAHAH! Heee, okay. Bring it down, Graf," said a deep and burly voice.

The walls of the cell faded.

The group found themselves standing, sitting, laying about, or in one case, abruptly falling over. (Zuula had been shoving against a wall.) They were in a great hall, wide and vast, broken by support pillars every hundred yards that stretched up to a vaulted ceiling. Glowstone chandeliers hung down, countless numbers of them, bathing the entire place in dim, silvery light. Light that glinted and reflected off the armor and weapons of the forty or so dwarves surrounding the golems.

And in what might have been the back, front, or center of the room, were three circular slabs of stone, atop which sat a fat throne. Made of some silvery metal, with plates and rivets and gadgets festooned all over it, carved with runes, the seat of it was buried in pillows and quilts. Graves sat at the foot of the throne, with two glowering guards next to him, halberds crossed above his head.

On the throne sat an old, old dwarf, buried beneath cloth, with only his face and beard poking out. He had a gold crown on his bald pate, eyebrows that would have put Garon's father to shame for their bushiness, and a beard that stretched down six feet, well off the throne, and coiled neatly on the floor in a pile of braids.

It was hard to tell, but it looked like he was smiling.

"Have we been teleported?" Threadbare asked.

"No. The floah's the same," Madeline said, looking down. "Carrara marble with a two-chisel cut, holystoned regularly. I recognize some a' the nicks that I saw in the cell. What we thought was the cell."

"Do you now?" The old dwarf leaned forward. "You're a Mason, then?"

"Nah. I'm a stonecuttah. Taught myself the old fashioned way. Used to be I couldn't have craftin' jobs."

That caused a stir. Many of the dwarves around them stirred and muttered, and the King laughed again. "Wahahahhaha! Oh, this is good. Alright young man, you may stand."The guards uncrossed their halberds. Graves stood, and Cecelia gasped, for he was no longer emaciated. "You're better!"

"They were kind enough to ask one of their high priests to see to me," Graves said, wiggling his feet a bit to wake them up. "Thankfully it went off, just like a curse being removed." He shivered and pulled his prison tunic down, trying to keep his nether parts covered. "I assume that you're satisfied, your majesty?"

"Mostly." Said the King. "Sorry for tha trick, children. Your man Graves here said some pretty outlandish things. We had ta be sure."

"You put us in a cell that wasn't real and listened to us talk," Threadbare realized.

"Aye." The King nodded. "With a barrier to let your sound out and keep ours from comin' in. Wasn't the first time we've used this trick. Won't be the last."

Cecelia stepped forward. "Then... Graves, did you tell them everything?"

"More or less. He stopped me midway through."

"Ghosts in golem bodies I could buy." The King shrugged. "Seen weirder, though na for a while. No friends to the Crown, that needed a listen. Paladin? Well, few of those nowadays. I knew one once, before tha Oblivion. Oops Sorry ain't something most know! And most important of all, he talked about yer father, the King." Two large, thin hands emerged from the quilts and steepled under his chin, combing through his braids. "And ye confirmed that."

"So you believe that we're who we say we are?" Cecelia said.

"I believe ye think that. I believe that's what yer statuses say, since my scouts have confirmed it. Ye're either them, or the greatest cultists what ever existed in Cylvania. And that last bit don't seem likely."

Cecelia let out a sigh. Then she straightened up. "Your Majesty. I stand before you now as a Princess of the Realm. My Father has been—"

"No."

Silence fell throughout the throne room.

"Your majesty, please, we have risked so much to journey here—"

"Aye. But yer no longer princess of the realm. My dear, yer dead."

"Oh. Oh." Cecelia said, putting her hands to her mouth. "I completely forgot. Oh no."

"Aye. Our laws are clear on undead. Even if ye've got a nicer husk than most."

"Cecelia?" Madeline said, stirring restlessly. The dwarves nearest to her raised shields, and leveled weaponry at the little dragon.

"No, no, relax. It's not that bad," Cecelia said. "It's just that... we don't count as who we were before."

"Can't inherit, can't hold titles, can't hold property or wealth, all existing debts owed and receivable null and void. Up to you if you want ta stick around, but ya don't get a single copper from yer past life. Give it to yer heirs or to yer thane, and enjoy yer fresh start." The King nodded. "Which is a point in yer favor, because honestly, if you WERE still King Melos' daughter, you wouldn't be leavin' here until we ransomed you back to yer Father for peace. Assumin' we found a way we could trust that fucker."

"He's only half of the problem," Cecelia said. "The Inquisitor—"

"I wasn't finished!" The King thundered, and Cecelia fell silent, along with the rest of the hall. Threadbare moved up to her and took her hand in his paw. Someone in the crowd went "Awww..." and turned it into a cough.

Your Adorable skill is now level 32!

The King sighed. "The point is, you ain't his daughter no more. The point is, you're enemies of the Crown now. And that makes you welcome here, to stay for a bit, purchase what you need, and be our guests for now. So long as y' stay out of the way and don't cause trouble, we'll bring none to you."

Cecelia's face twisted, the ceramic plates of it shifting along with the 'muscles' under her 'skin'. "But... we want to help. We want to end this war."

The dwarves around them muttered, shared looks varying from scorn to sadness. The King nodded. "I know. But... it ain't as easy as all that. Come on. Walk wi' me. I'll tell you why. We owe you that much, I think, and no man, or dwarf, golem or ghost can say that Grundi Embergleam doesn't pay his debts." He glanced up at the rest of the 'court'. "Right. Bazdra, Gudrun, Montag, Hidon, yer wi' me. Rest a' ya, get back to it then!"

The golems looked to each other. Graves coughed. The dwarves dispersed, save for two women and two men who stepped forward, moving to flank the throne.

As soon as they were next to him, the King started fiddling with something under the pillows. Pipes on the back of the throne puffed to life, belched out clouds of steam, and to everyone but Cecelia's amazement the throne slowly revolved and started moving away. Stairs and all.

"Nice!" she said, leading the rest of her friends in a quick jog to catch up to it, then falling into a walk alongside as the King tooled through the vast halls, the wheels on the underside of the throne driven by internal mechanisms. "Is that... no, it can't be a Fizznocker engine, not even a mark four. That's at least half a ton of marble, not counting the throne itself."

"Not really a throne. I call it my Kneelchair." He rasped a laugh, then continued. "Nah, each wheel has its own engine. And you're looking at Burlstrads there, not that weak Fizznocker bullshit. So you're in the trade?"

"Yes. As much as I can be, with only the Royal Archives' books on it, and the few tutors the Crown has left. I'd hoped to learn from your people here someday, to round out the parts I was ignorant of, but... well..."

"Still possible," said the King. "If we win."

"Or if we can achieve a peace."

"Mm." He sighed. "My son thought as you did, once. My son Dhurlem. He knew this war would do us no good. He went to fight, aye but always held out hope... No. No, not anymore, lass. It's the Crown or us, now. We can't trust Melos, and that's all there is to it."

"The Inquisitor is fooling him. She's the one that killed me. She's a daemon with the face of my mother. And... I think she's made my corpse into a daemon." She closed her eyes. "I thought it took souls, but I'm here and I'm pretty sure I'm me, and—"

"Celia," Threadbare said, and the four dwarves pacing the throne looked at him, two with expressions of revulsion, two with fascination. "You are you. Eye for Detail's confirmed it. Whatever's in that armor isn't."

The King nodded. "We knew she was a daemon. As are the Hand. Melos did something forbidden, and damn our eyes, we didn't call him out on it, didn't join the fight when Balmoran rose up." The old dwarf sighed. "If we had, we wouldn't be in the spot we are now, tell you that. But no, we decided to wait and stay out of human affairs, let them settle their own squabbles." The King spat. "Blind, damned, fools. The wrong man won in the North. And it was because of those godsdamned daemons. And now you're telling me there's one more out there, wearin' yer face?"

"Yes."

"Grand."

"And they've corrupted my Steam Knight armor somehow."

"A Steam Knight? Well now!" said the King. "So we'll face a daemon war machine on the battlefield. Even more grand."

"Probably my brother, too. Though he's not a daemon," Threadbare said. "Yet. Hopefully whatever they did doesn't work on him."

"Mmm." The king sighed. "Well, you can talk that over with my ministers." He turned the throne, heading toward a wide archway in the wall, identical to the six they'd passed in his wake. They followed, and he gestured down the hall, to a series of numbered doors. "Your possessions are in room Nineteen. As are your captive souls."

"Not exactly captives," said Graves. "Think of them as refugees, who even lost their bodies. Temporarily, we hope. That's one of the things that you could help—"

"Ministers. Talk to them," said the King, holding up a hand. "And after you're dressed, come and join me in the Hall of Heroes. And I'll show you why negotiating peace won't work."

Without another word, he turned and motored away, the heavy stone plinth revolving with the Throne and rumbling across the floor on its myriad unseen wheels.

Threadbare and Cecelia and the rest of the companions watched it go, then turned back to the four dwarves looking them over with curiosity, and in two cases, a little bit of hostility.

"I'm Gudrun Scarstone. Priestess of Yorgum," said one of the friendlier ones, a lady in an apron with tools sticking out of every pocket, her hair gray and back in a long braid. "It's amazing to see real golems in the... flesh? Plush? Ah, ye know what I mean."

"Bazdra Coaler." The younger dwarven woman introduced herself. She wore gray armor inscribed with an hourglass across its breastplate. "Temple guard of the shrine to Aeterna." She was one of the ones who'd scowled at Threadbare earlier.

"Hidon Fingers," the older dwarven man said, a scowl still on his face. "Minister of Lightless Matters."

"Which probably doesn't mean what you think it does," said the young, blonde-bearded man next to him, a smile on his broad face. "Montag Steelknife. I run the Ministry of Dangerous and New Devices."

"He won't take that last part out of the name of it, no matter how much we tell him they mean the same thing," Hidon said. "Ha ha ha," he said without laughing.

"Ha ha ha." Montag echoed. "Still as funny a joke as it was seven years ago." His voice held a distinct lack of enthusiasm.

"Nineteen," said Madeline, pointing at the door. "Loot, sweet loot, come back to Momma!"

Garon opened the door, and the group spent the next few minutes sorting out their items, digging them out of the chests they'd been put into, and in Pulsivar and Mopsy's cases, releasing the irate cats from two cages. The dwarves backed off warily as Pulsivar growled and snarled in their general direction, but Missus Fluffbear placated them with Monster Treats.

For his part, Threadbare shrugged and said "Call Outfit," adjusting his clothes as they snapped into existence around his body. "If you see my scepter, please bring it here," he told the others, and turned to the ministers. "What does your King want us to discuss?"

"Different matters," said Montag. "I'm to see if you can contribute anything useful to the war effort and offer you a useful price for it."

"If you've got any information useful to us on the covert side of things, that's my department," Hidon said. "We'll pay you if you tell us anything interesting."

"And I'll arrange anything you need during your stay! And be your liaison for day-to-day matters," Gurdun said. "You'll be staying in Yorgum's house while you're here."

"Oh. Fluffbear will like that. I didn't know he lived so close. Is he as nice in person as he is when she prays?"

The two clerics looked at each other and clamped hands over their mouths. "She means a temple to him. He doesn't actually live there. Most of the time," Montag said, while they fought to keep straight faces. "Maybe visits every few centuries or so, so to speak."

"Right," said Threadbare. And he turned to Bazdra, who'd remained silent through most of this. "And what are you here for?"

"I'm here to make sure you don't die or get yourselves killed."

The rest of the group slowed, half-dressed, and looked back in confusion. "Excuse me?" Cecelia asked.

"The Lurker's among us again," Hidon said. "We've had two officials die of mysterious causes in the last month. He's in deep this time."

"You know he's here? That was one of the things I was going to tell you, once I was sure it was safe!" Cecelia burst out.

"What do you mean, again?" Threadbare said.

"We've killed him twice, and he keeps coming back." Hidon said, simply.

"How?" Garon said.

"Daemon shenanigans, we're assuming," Bazdra said. "We've killed other Hand members before, and they've come back, too. This war would be over by now if they'd only stay dead."

"I see." Threadbare rubbed his head. "I'm glad I didn't risk killing Anise when we might have had the chance."

"Who?"

"The Inquisitor. She's Amelia Gearhart's daemonic form."

"Oh. Her. I've heard of her, never met her," Hidon said. "She hasn't been in action yet."

"She will. She's got Emmet with her now, and Cecelia... Evil Cecelia, I mean. They're going to reveal that the Hand are the survivors of the Seven and rally the kingdom around them. Oh!" Threadbare said, toddling over and reaching into a nearby cubby. "There's my rod. Good, I was beginning to worry."

Silence from the dwarves for a bit. The other three looked at Hidon, who nodded. "Okay, that's worth a bit." He pulled out an abacus, tallied a number, and wrote it down on a scrap of parchment before handing it to Gudrun. "Anything else we can use, information-wise?"

"We'd better talk as we walk," Montag said. "The first reports should be coming back now."

"Reports?" Threadbare asked.

"We launched an assault last night," Bazdra said. "Come on then."

Reclothed and re-armed, the toys and their living companions followed the ministers back across the main hall, through another archway, and down several long flights of stairs. Madeline looked on as they went, snout swiveling as she examined the architecture. "Nice. Most of it. Some of it's too smooth, though. Magic?"

"Earth Elementalists, to smooth the rougher parts out," Montag said. "This is young as dwarven holds go, and we had to shift to war footing in a hurry. Don't worry, we've made drawings of how it was before, and we'll put it back that way after we're on a peacetime footing again."

"Why would you do that?" Fluffbear squeaked.

The four dwarves stopped and stared at her, as if she'd asked how tasty dwarven babies were.

"What?"

"You're pretty ignorant, aren't you?" Bazdra said.

"Sometimes, yes."

"Dwarves must build, but we can't take permanent shortcuts and have to do it right, because nothing lasts so we owe it to creation to do the best we can while we're here."

"Say what now?"

"Keep moving. I'll explain it," Gudrun offered. "If I can. Okay. So... hm. You know Aeterna is the goddess of time, yes?"

"I think Yorgum told me that."

Gudrun smiled. "Hee hee! He told me about you, dear!"

"Did he now..." Bazdra shot her a suspicious glare.

"Oh hush. He told me when I prayed at Grundi's request, the same as you did. Canceled each other out, we did."

"Say what now?" Glub flared his fins. "I'm lost."

"So the two most venerated gods in our hold are Aeterna and

Yorgum," Gudrun said. "They're also rivals. Aeterna insists that nothing survives given enough time, and Yorgum says hold my beer."

"All the fucking time," Bazdra rolled her eyes.

"They're rivals. But we honor both, most of the time. Though rarely there are occasions we can't, like with you all." Gudrun said.

"With you so far. Kinda," Fluffbear said.

"Today we found we might not. See, the King asked us to pray to our gods for advice about necromantic golems. Now the thing about gods is the more secrets they give away to mortals in prayers, the more their rival gets to act. In this case they got asked about you simultaneously, so we know all about why Aeterna doesn't like the notion of you one bit, and why you're very dear to Yorgum."

Cecelia frowned. "What? But we adventured with a cleric of Aeterna, years back. She was entirely fine with Threadbare."

"It's not that," Bazdra said. "And it's not who you are, personally. It's what some of you are. See, you're undead, and she dislikes those to begin with, but they're not anathema because all undead fade with age. It just takes longer. But those of you who are haunting golems? You're in forms that will never decay, provided you give them a little maintenance, and you don't require sustenance, ever. Golems are acceptable because they grind down over time. Takes ages, takes forever, but eventually they stop working. You? You can ensure near-immortality with a little effort or the right class feature. Just hop golem bodies endlessly." She sighed. "And that's not good at all."

They walked in silence for a bit.

"I never even thought of that," Garon said. "Immortality, I mean."

"Zuula did," the half-orc spoke up for the first time in a while. "Is one reason why she going to die after she see dis business done. Too tempting odderwise."

"Good on you," Bazdra smiled. "Which is why Aeterna has nothing against YOU per se. It's..."

"She's worried that some of our own people would be tempted," Gudrun said. "And she's right to worry. Dwarves have had problems with undead for millenia, it's why our laws are what they are."

"And our own dead, who need bodies?" Graves interrupted. "They've been in there long enough, they're going to start going mad, unless we can get yellow reagent and lots of it."

"We don't care what you do there, so long as they don't cause trouble," Gudrun said. "But... it would cause serious problems with the King, the Clan Heads, and the temples if we just gave you yellow reagents. That's not our way."

"Right. Dwarves take gifts very seriously. But if we buy them?"

Garon spoke up.

"That's just trade." Gudrun grinned, sharklike, with bad teeth. "Though a lot of our reagents are going to the war effort right now. So it'd cost you."

"Mind you you've earned about four or five vials from what you told me about that Hand," Hidon said.

"What if they eahned it back?" Madeline said. "Like a couple of hundred gahlems to help you fight? They get the bahdies fahst, then eahn it back in battle?"

Montag sighed. "Wouldn't work. Undead are a touchy subject to begin with. That would be seen as the King compromising the laws out of desperation. I'm sorry, but we can't do that. But... we can help you earn the reagents you need. You ah, you mentioned you were a Steam Knight?" He looked down at Cecelia, his eyes aglow.

"Yes. And Threadbare's a golemist, and we'll be happy to montage them to anyone you want—"

"For a reasonable fee, of course!" Garon interrupted.

"Just one apiece to start," Montag nodded, pulling out his own abacus, and writing down another number before handing it to Hidon.

"I'm not their merchant contact. Sweet Nebs, you're offering THAT much?" Hidon scowled and handed the two slips on to Gudrun. She read them and whistled. "Okay, so you're up to twelve vials, assuming the market hasn't shifted since this morning."

"Nah, I think I'd like to **Haggle** that if I may," Madeline grinned. **"After all, these are two unique tier-two jahbs we're talking about heah..."**

Five minutes, three halls, and two staircases later they settled on enough coin for fifteen vials of yellow reagents. Graves nodded, happy. "That should take care of the ones who are worst off." He shifted the crate full of soulstones in his arms. "Really, that'll buy us even more time. They'll see we're following through on our promises."

"Alright," Threadbare smiled. "Let's have a sit down with them later and see what bodies they want, so we can build them something that will make them happy."

"I'm assuming you're Caradon's work?" Montag blurted out. "Because seriously, you're amazing. If we can get a few dozen like you made..." he glared up at Bazdra, who glared back, "...BY a dwarven Golemist or two, WITHOUT undead inside..."

"I'm sorry. I can only make unintelligent golems so far," Threadbare said. "It's probably a higher level skill. And also most of us are... born... with horrible luck. It's very dangerous. For us and all around us."

"Speaking of that," Hidon said. "We're almost there. If you value your lives, stay silent and be respectful."

"What?" Zuula said. "You t'reaten us?"

"No." The black-haired dwarf sighed and pulled his hood tighter around his head. "If you piss them off, we won't be able to save you."

And with his warning ringing in their ears, they entered the Hall of Heroes.

A long gallery, low, with golden plaques glimmering on the walls. Each one had a name. Each one had a clan sign. And each one had a simple slot engraved in it, just a small lip, sticking out of the metal.

Looking down the hall, which stretched a good way back into the mountain, Threadbare could see that perhaps half the plaques had their slots filled, each by a single silvery coin.

The center of the hall was packed by dwarves, older dwarves, some standing with canes or with the help of others who were obviously family. They faced the front of it. Faced the King, who had parked the Kneelchair next to a series of tubes that ran down the wall and opened up next to him.

TONG

An unseen bell chimed, and the tube rattled. The King sighed and reached a large, emaciated hand out, taking a cylinder from the opening in the tube. He opened it, and coins cascaded out, followed by rolls of paper, falling onto the sheets that covered his vehicle.

And the crowd murmured in dismay. An old woman in back started sobbing.

King Grundi unrolled the scroll and bowed his head. "Agni Durable," he said, and the crowd sat silent. The Kneelchair ground and clanked as he rolled down the gallery, next to a plaque. There he took one of the coins and placed it in the slot with trembling hands. Then he read the next name on the list. "Jasper Motherlode," and moved across the hall, fumbling another coin out. Three more names he read, and then—

TONG

Another cylinder clanked in the tube, and the crowd groaned.

"They're the dead," Cecelia whispered, and Threadbare grabbed her, hugged her as she held him back, as the ancient king read the names of the dead and gave them their final due. All this while their relatives, the ones who couldn't fight, who had stayed behind, stood and waited and hoped against hope.

Some sobbed. Some cursed and wailed or stomped away flushed with anger, pulling beards or biting back tears.

But almost worse than that were the ones who were silent. Who reacted when they heard a name, but simply stood there, watching, as the hope drained from them. It left them hollow, like dwarf-shaped outlines in the world.

Four cylinders came down the tube in total. Each had perhaps fifteen to twenty names, all told. And when it was done, and the crowds had gone to grieve or enjoy the relief that their kin were still alive and hadn't been named, only then did the King clatter up to them.

"My son thought peace possible," King Grundi told Cecelia. "He fought with that hope. And he fell with it." The King's hand stretched, out to point at one section of the wall, with two plaques.

GRUNDI EMBERGLOW

DHURLEM EMBERGLOW

And in Dhurlem's plaque, sat a coin.

"So no," said King Grundi, "There will be no peace. We will win, or we will die here. Do you understand me, she who was Princess Ragandor?"

"I do," she said. "And I'm sorry. But more death won't help you or your son or your people."

"No, but about seven will. King Melos. His Hand. And that thing wearing your mother's face. Will you help me with that, Cecelia?"

"Kill my father..." She looked away. "I..."

"Mm. No, it is too much to ask." The old dwarf's face twisted with compassion. "Tell you what. Help me handle the others, and you leave him to us. A trial and justice if we can take him alive and death in battle if not."

Cecelia let out a long breath. "He killed Caradon. His own father in law." Behind her, Hidon's eyes widened, and he pulled out the abacus again. "Yes," Cecelia decided. "I won't kill him, but he has to answer for his crimes."

"Good. What do they have so far?" The King asked.

Hidon handed Gudrun another slip of paper, and Grundi looked them over. "Hm. Decent start. You, Cecelia. Steam Knight? You'll need new armor, then."

"Yes, but our bodiless refugees are the first concern. We need to get them settled before we help ourselves."

Grundi smiled. "You would've been a good queen for your people. Tell you what..." He rolled the Kneelchair up to the Emberglow plaques...

...and as his ministers gasped, he took out his son's coin.

Cecelia caught it by sheer reflex, as he flipped it to her. "This should cover the components she needs for a new Steam Knight suit. And if it doesn't, talk to the tallyman and take mine."

"Sir... no..." whispered Bazdra.

"My heir's dead; I'm the last of my clan here. I've got no blood who might need it after I die," Grundi snapped. "What are two pieces of Adamant in the face of all that, hm?"

"Adamant!" Garon shrieked and stared around the room. At the hundreds of coins, filling hundreds of plaques. Just sitting there, next to the candles... "This is... the cost must..." He snapped his mouth shut. "This is the safest room in the hold, isn't it?" He said, conversationally.

"Oh yeah," Hidon confirmed, recovering from his shock. "Little doll girl, I hope you know the honor the King just paid you."

"Why?" Cecelia said, staring down at the coin and up to the King.

He smiled then, eyes misty. "Because he, too, believed in peace." He glanced over to Gudrun. "Get them settled. Bazdra, keep them alive. The rest of you, come with me."

*****

Two hours later, in a simple chamber decorated with hand-woven rugs and tapestries, ranging from children's first attempts to masterpieces that must have taken years to finish, Graves and the golems and their cats stretched out behind a closed door and huddled together to discuss matters.

"So we've pretty much got free run of the place, so long as Bazdra or the other ministers are with us, right?" Kayin asked.

"Yes," Threadbare said. "Though we need to be careful. The Lurker is probably going to try to kill anyone of us he can catch."

"He can try," Zuula said.

"He can do more than that," Garon said. "If the Hand are actually the remnants of the Seven, then The Lurker's probably what remains of Graham."

"Oh shit," Madeline said. "That's wahse than just assassination."

"What's worse?" Fluffbear squeaked.

"Graham was a con man, a grifter for the greater good," Cecelia said. "The first one to unlock the gambler job... well, in Cylvania, anyway. He favored range attacks, bluffs, and cons that usually put the Seven's foes in a bad tactical position. If the daemon has any of his skills, he's going to come at us using people, and in a way that we won't be expecting. He was also a master of disguise."

"Can he disguise himself as a doll?" Graves asked. "If there's size limitations we might be good."

"Except for you," Zuula pointed out.

"Right." Graves sighed. "Groups. Nobody does anything alone until this is over."

"That's going to be a bit rough," Garon said, glancing toward Zuula, then quickly away before she could see him. "I mean, some of you have valuable jobs to montage and armor to build, but some of us won't have much to do. I... I'd really like to help here, but I don't know how."

"I've thought of that, actually. I think there might be a way you could help, you all could if you're willing," Cecelia said. "I'm going to be stuck putting together my new armor and montaging."

"I'll be montaging as well." Threadbare said, then frowned. "Maybe not. I taught you golemist."

"You did, though I've barely used it. But I see where you're going with this." Graves nodded. "I could montage it to other people easily enough."

"I'm down for being useful," Glub said. "Beats staring at the walls."

"Good." Cecelia leaned forward. "Gudrun tells me the two coins will cover the new Steam Knight armor and the reagents to golemize most of our dead, but there's about forty or so left-uncovered. So we need a lot of money... or we need more sources of reagents. And since we're free to roam the city, we've got every legal reason to enter the dungeon that they've got down here."

"Wait, whoa, dungeon?" Garon said, leaning forward. "I've never heard of one here."

"Oh yeah. It's a well-kept secret outside these halls. I only knew about it because of The Lurker's intelligence reports. It's legal to go in, unlike a lot of the Crown-controlled dungeons were. The downside is that it's way more dangerous than Catamountain was. You know how that one was all about cats? This one's themed around giants."

"Worth a shot," Zuula decided. "Ogre went down pretty easy, all t'ings considered. How hard giants be?"

"Mind you, that's also going to be a lure. We'll raid in and out of the dungeon, and try to tempt The Lurker into ambushing us when he thinks we're weakest- emerging from a dungeon." Cecelia explained. "But I've got an ace to play, there."

"Yeah?" Kayin said, scooting in closer.

"I couldn't say anything before, because there were too many people listening, but we've got an old friend, one who'll probably be happy to help us. If she's alive, and if she's here. But I can't imagine she WOULDN'T be here."

"Oh?" Garon asked. Then, *"Oh."*

"Yeah. Once things are quiet, let's break out the dollseyed mice, Threadbare, and do some exploring. And if we're very, very lucky we might be able to track down Beryl Wirebeard..."

CHAPTER 6: GIVE THE DWARVES THEIR DUE

"You've been awfully quiet," Cecelia remarked to Threadbare, as they sat waiting in the darkness of Madeline's pack.

"Have I?" Threadbare asked.

"Yes," Zuula said. "Dis whole time we down here talking wit de dwarves."

"Oh. Well..." He turned in Cecelia's arms, snuggled in a bit as he stared up at her from an inch away. "This was pretty much your idea. I figured you had matters well in hand, and you did. The King was very impressed by you. And I used the time I didn't have to talk to look at people."

"Okay. That's good." Cecelia snuggled him closer.

"Looking at people. Yeah." Garon said, tossing his hatchet up and down and catching it one-handed. The overall effect, given the proportion of his size to his weapon was of a minotaur juggling a greataxe. Threadbare supposed it was good for his dexterity, if nothing else. "The Lurker's out there somewhere, probably wearing a friendly face."

"Or an unfriendly one," Threadbare said. "Those ministers are pretty highly placed officials, with lots of things to keep them busy, aren't they?"

"Yeah. I caught that too," Cecelia said. "And here we get FOUR of them. I initially thought it was him showing us good faith, showing that he was taking us seriously, even with the problems in my plan, and the downsides I hadn't foreseen. But it's not that at all, is it? He doesn't trust his ministers. Not completely."

"Oh. Oh shit, I think I see it. Wow, that's clever," Garon said, catching his hatchet and sliding it back into its harness. "He's doing three things at once. He *is* showing us good faith. At the same time he's putting four of the most likely ones to be false in a place where they've got three others *and* us watching them at the same time. And to top it off, he's tempting The Lurker to take a whack at us, rather than one of his people."

Zuula whistled. "Okay, dat's almost orky. Zuula approve."

Cecelia sighed. "I'm liking the idea all save for the last part. The notion that it's a minister makes a lot of sense. The reports I saw were from about this level of official. Any of them could be compromised, or worse, replaced. A legendary grifter and master of disguise could easily be a dwarf for a few months or more."

"It could also be a test of *us*," Threadbare mused. "To see how we handle the situation."

"Well, how would dwarves handle the situation?" Cecelia asked.

"They'd shut up, get on with their business, and try to survive the Luker's sudden-but-inevitable betrayal," Garon said. "Dwarves are Sturdy, and if you want to impress them, you have to take hits and not complain."

"Hand," Zuula said.

"Yes, we know The Lurker's with the Hand," Cecelia said.

"No. H*and*." Zuula said, pointing.

And indeed, a gloved hand had entered the pack. None of the toys recognized it. It dropped a single piece of parchment and withdrew.

Threadbare hopped out of Cecelia's embrace and went and read it. "It's Beryl. She says not to resist or try anything funny, or we'll get our... heads blown off. There's more words than that but most of them are not very nice."

"Yep, that's Beryl," Garon grinned. "I'll go first."

The hand returned. Garon plopped himself into it and vanished.

A minute crawled by. Then two. Then three more.

Zuula was practically vibrating with impatience and frustration by the time the hand reappeared and beckoned. They went along peacefully, one at a time—

—and reappeared in a room full of junk.

A purple-haired dwarven girl who had to be Beryl was there, talking with Madeline off to the side...

...and there, with Garon riding on his shoulder, was a tall, green-skinned man with solid yellow eyes. He was clad in leather from head to toe, most of it a greatcoat broken up by bandoliers, with metal contraptions hanging off of it. He had a short, floppy hat that looked a lot like Mordecai's old hat to Threadbare's eyes, and he was looking down at the three of them with amazement at friends and family he'd thought long gone.

"Hullo Mom," Jarrik said, swallowing hard. "Long time no see."

"Jarrik!" Zuula leaped into the air, grabbed his shirt and buried her face in it.

"Give us a few, okay?" Garon stage-whispered to Threadbare and Cecelia.

"Of course." Cecelia smiled, and headed over to Madeline's side.

"Motherfucking shitcrackers," Beryl shook her head as Cecelia strolled up. "I guess this is an occupational hazard for animators, huh?"

She hadn't changed much. Her hair was in four purple-and-black braids, not two, and she wore a simple black haltertop and pants with wide pockets. The boots were about the same, thick enough to walk across beds of nails without her noticing or caring, but the goggles were new. Propped up on her forehead, they were smeared with ash and grime, as was most of her face below it, save for the white patches around her eyes where her goggles had covered.

"Hazard?" Cecelia asked.

"Being turned into a toy. Though daaaaamn, you're a quality one. Someone put a lot of work into your face."

"That would be him." Cecelia jerked a thumb back at Threadbare, who doffed his hat and bowed.

"Holy shit! The little fucker himself! Man, it's all reunion up in here." She slid her hand out from behind her back and put an ugly twist of metal and wood up on a nearby shelf.

"Is that a pistol?" asked Cecelia, craning her neck to look at it. "I've never seen one before."

"Yeah. Don't have to be a gunslinger to use one."

"But if ya are then they're pretty badass," Jarrik threw in, then turned back to whispering with Zuula and Garon.

"Shaddap, braggy," Beryl scooped up a wrench out of a nearby junkpile, hucked it at his head. Without looking at her he caught it, put it down, then kept on talking with his family.

"That's some serious dextahrity," Madeline remarked.

"And it ain't limited to his hands," Beryl leered, as she waggled her tongue between two spread fingers.

"Is that supposed to mean something?" Threadbare asked.

"Holy shit you talk now?"

Your Adorable skill is now level 32!

"I made my own voice after I got frustrated with being silent."

"After that one time in Catamountain I can't say I'm surprised." Beryl's face lightened. "Man, that was a good run. Even if things did turn to shit just after."

"So... what happened, exactly?" Cecelia said, hopping up on a nearby overturned crate. "After we dropped you off in Taylor's Delve, I mean?"

"I wanna hear this too," Garon announced. Jarrik strolled over, balancing his mother and his brother in his arms, kicked a pile of gears out of a chair, and sat down.

"Not much to tell," Beryl shrugged. Then she grimaced. "Not much good anyway. I got back told Da, and he gathered the family. We stopped long enough to let our neighbors know what was going down, then it was down the escape tunnel we'd dug years ago, with the ones who believed us."

"People didn't believe you?" Threadbare asked.

"Taylor's Delve was full o' folks who went there to get away from civilized places, an' resistance fighters," Jarrik said. "The first kind of folks didn't believe 'er, and forted up. The second wanted ta fight." Once a little high-pitched and reedy, his voice had deepened as he'd matured. There were muscles under that coat too, his former gawky slimness growing into the full weight of his mixed heritage. "Can't blame Beryl for th' ones what stayed. The ones what died."

"Like me," Zuula said, and Jarrik winced.

"I'm sorry, Ma. By the time me an' Bakky got there, it was all done, and you were... Well."

"Is okay. Work out for best."

"He and Bakky got to us just as we were about to collapse the tunnel," Beryl said. "We let 'em come with."

"Bak'shaz!" Zuula and Garon said, simultaneously. "He alive too?" Zuula grabbed Jarrik's collar and shook it, while Garon tried to pry her fingers loose from his brother's clothes.

"Yeah. He was. Probably still is," Beryl said. "He left a few years back, got tired of living in cramped tunnels. Went looking for the Rangers."

"A few years? We— the Crown had the observation posts set up early in the conflict. How did he get past those?" Cecelia frowned.

Jarrik shrugged. "I'd montaged him through Scout by then, done my best to train 'im like Da would, and shadowed 'im through. By that time Porkins was dead so it was just 'im ta worry about, and 'e got through easy."

"I think losing Porkins was what got him to move on, honestly," Beryl sighed. "The little guy was never the same after that."

"Wait," Cecelia said. "How did you get to Taylor's Delve in the first place? The last time I saw you the woods were on fire, there were enemy soldiers and scouts all around, and you were going to save your father."

Jarrik fell silent. Beryl sighed, moved over, and reached up to rub his shoulders. He slipped a hand back over hers, covering it completely, and squeezing in thanks. "Long story short, we failed. Saw 'im get taken down by one a' his best students. Feller named Jericho."

Madeline inhaled, sharply. "Wait..."

"Yeah. *That* Jericho. At tha time he was still loyal. He tracked us to Oblivion Point, told us he was sorry, and that he'd try to make sure that da survived. Told us to escape, keep our heads down, and tell no one of what happened that night. He also said that the wilds were crawling with scouts and soldiers clearing the place, and we'd never make it through if we went reg'lar ways."

"Yeah, that's about right," Madeline said. "Why do you think I was on the outskirts of the Delve ta begin with, Gar? Buncha gahds stahted hunting around my graveyahd."

"Then how did you escape?" Threadbare asked.

"We walked tha Oblivion."

The toys stared, stunned.

"You can *do* that?" Cecelia asked. "I thought nothing could cross it."

"Oh y'can't cross it," Jarrik said, tugging at one of his gloves. "But if ya go a little ways in, and walk ALONG wiff it, and don't go too far towards or away from it, ya can run 'long it like a bearing in a track. An' if ya walk in tha right place, it cuts right through solid fings... mountains, trees, whatnot, an' crosses right over gorges an' drops and suchlike."

"I had no idea," Cecelia whispered. "That's... incredible."

"It's fucking unsafe, is what it is," Beryl snorted. "Show 'em, Jarry."

"I am, I am, hold yer knickers..." He tugged the glove up, and held off his hand. His pinky finger was a stump, gone to the first knuckle. "It's dangerous 'cause you got ter stay in exactly tha right middle part. Get too far out, an' you don't come back. But walk too close to tha inside edge, an' ya walk over air an' fall, or worse, walk out inta something solid." He flexed his finger. "Like I almost did. Most of me pinky's part of a mountain or summat now."

"You no do somet'ing dat stupid again," Zuula said. "Howling darkness out dere. Green numbers eat you alive."

"We might 'ave to," Jarrik said, sighing. "If the war goes bad, it's a last-ditch plan for th' hold. Our backs are lit'rally up against it. Me an' tha other scouts been training, as careful as we can. Still lost a few. And if yer add tha rest o' the hold's folks inta it? No way we won't be countin' our dead if we do it, which is why it's a bad idear."

"Which is why winning the war seems to be the best outcome," Threadbare said, staring up at a friend he'd never expected to see here. "We want to help you do that."

"Yeah, why *are* you here? What's all this about ghost golems? We filled you in, let's hear your story." Beryl said, scooting around to a chair, flipping it around, and straddling it while she leaned her head on her hands.

Threadbare told her about the mess at the house, and how he'd come to start his epic quest to save Cecelia, with Zuula and Garon joining in on their part of things. Cecelia took it after that, explaining how she'd been fighting for the wrong side, and how she'd died.

"Ouch. Shit. Ah..." Beryl ran a hand through her hair, tugging on her braids. "No offense, but you uh, solved a problem for us when you did that. Remember how we'd named you friend to our clan?"

"Yes. But that debt's gone now, with my old life." Cecelia sighed.

"Hey. Look. It means we can start over, yeah? And this time you're not secretly the daughter of our worst enemy." Beryl smiled and reached down a grubby hand. "Pleased to fucking meet you."

Cecelia took it and her shoulders dropped as she relaxed. "Thanks! To be honest I was a little worried."

"Why?"

"Well, you're a cleric of Aeterna. Bazdra said—"

"Bazdra? Bazdra Coaler?" Beryl snorted. "She's not the boss o' me. She guards the shrine and advises the King, but she's not my clan. Which is good, because she's been a right asshole the last few months."

"The last few months? Really?" Cecelia asked, glancing towards Threadbare.

"Yeah. Ah... let me show you." She kicked through the scrap on the floor, forging a path to the nearest door, and opened it up.

Instantly, glowstones lit up, revealing a long, high-ceilinged hall, with a pair of iron double-doors on the end large enough to admit three ogres abreast.

Inside the hall were five wire-and-cloth-and-wood contraptions, with wooden blades sticking out in front, and metal boxes on the rear. Each had two seats, set into the curving wooden bodies.

"Those look a little like that tinker diagram we gave you," Threadbare said.

"They are. That flyer was a dangerous, shitty contraption that almost got me killed the first few times I flew it." Beryl grinned. "These though... these are about done. About ready. They'll change the war once we get them out there, get us some wins..." Then she sighed. "And fucking bitchqueen supreme Bazdra Coaler is squawking about how they need more testing, first."

"I thought Montag Steelknife was the minister in charge of new weaponry," Threadbare said.

"He is, but the training for it goes through Bazdra. The... oh, we need a word for people who fly this thing. The flyers, the controllers, they need to be approved by Bazdra's ministry. They choose who gets allocated to what jobs, and she's arguing that this is a job. Even though it isn't, you just need the flight skill."

"The flight skill, you say?" Garon remarked. "Hm..."

"Yeah. They're two seaters, and you need someone flying it. One person to fly, the other to drop bombs over the side." Beryl puffed her lips and made a farting noise. "Easy as mud. Still pisses me off... Montag swore he'd back me up on this, ram it up Bazdra's arse if he had to, and he hasn't. Normally the dude's braver, I don't know what's gotten into him the last few weeks."

"Could be he's jus' backed off 'cause Bazdra had a deaf in tha' family," Jarrik said, trying to console her.

"Did she?" Cecelia squinted.

"Yeah. 'er husband died accidental-like two weeks back. Didn't get 'is coin, since it weren't in battle. Word is she's tore up somefing fierce about it."

"Which doesn't matter because she should fucking do her job so fewer of us die!" Beryl thumped the wall in anger. "Bitch needs to calm her tits right the fuck down."

Threadbare listened, the light almost seeming to gleam in his button eyes. "You know, we've talked with both of them recently. And a fellow named Hidon Fingers, and a nice lady who's putting us up in Yorgum's house, called Gudrun Scarstone."

"Hidon? Yer sure?" Jarrik asked, eyebrows rising. "That guy's been out a sight th' last few months. He was in charge a' the Oblivion run training until he disappeared for a while. Word is he was in some deep mission for th' King."

"Black beard, wears a hood, smells of garlic?" Threadbare asked.

"Yeah, tha's him."

"Well regardless, if you got Gudrun looking after you, you're good," Beryl nodded. "Everyone knows Granny Guddy. She's big on the home crafting part of Yorgum's religion. And the most senior cleric in the faith who isn't on the front."

The four toys shared a look. "Probably not de Lurker, den." Said Zuula. "Is good. We probably not come back to house full of dead friends."

"Nobahdy knows we left anyway," said Madeline. "I made sure of that. Stealth, camo, the wahks."

"Yes, but it's The Lurker," said Cecelia. "We have to play it safe."

"Yeah. About that. What the fuck." Said Beryl. "The Hand?"

"Yeah. This is the part it gets complicated," said Cecelia. "We're pretty sure the Lurker's infiltrated this hold. We think he's one of the four ministers. We think the King knows that and is playing some kind of complicated bluff to try and get him to reveal himself by taking a whack at us, or... well, me, because I'd be problematic to the Hand's plans in the future."

"We're here because we need some help stopping that," said Threadbare. "If he just tries to kill her, we can soulstone her again, but there are some sneaky things he could do that would end up with her permanently dead. And that's... unacceptable," said the little bear.

Beryl nodded. "Yeah, all right. How can I help?"

"Some of us are going to run the dungeon soon."

"Whoa. Much as I'd like to go, that's... no. That isn't the Catamountain."

"We know," Garon said. "Which is why we don't want you going in. We want you watching to see who's waiting to ambush us when we come out."

"Tryin' a lure..." Jarrik nodded. "Da would've approved."

"It's a lure what could go wrong," Jarrik said. "This is one a tha *Hand*. You give him a shot at Celia, what's ta stop him grabbing her an' escaping?"

Threadbare smiled. "I have an idea, there. Do you happen to have any green reagent?"

"I can get some. Why?" Beryl squinted at him.

He told them, and Zuula laughed. "Oh! Is perfect!"

Jarrik went in the back and rummaged around. "I'll go an' be yer watcher. I'll foller yer back, then shadow yer when ya ready for tha dungeon run. Jus' wear somethin' red on yer hat, Threadbare."

"Trust me, he's way better at it than I am," Beryl said. Then her eyes narrowed, and she moved up to loom over Cecelia and Threadbare, shaking her finger in their faces. "Just so we're clear. If you get him killed I will fuck you and not in the fun way. I will find a way to screw you so hard your ancestors will be sore in the morning. You'll go in our book of grudges, and if I don't settle it, my children will. We clear?"

"Ber..." Jarrik started.

"Yes dear?" She looked at him and grinned, a manic smile wide on her face as her braids rustled from the sudden movement.

He sighed. "Ne'er mind." He turned back to the toys. "You do yer fing, I'll back yer up when 'e strikes."

"Thanks bro," Garon said, reaching up one wooden fist. "Just watch yourself, okay?"

Jarrik grinned and reached down to bump his fist to Garon's. "Oh, don't worry 'bout me none. Picked up a few tricks since I got here." His free hand found its way up to his bandolier and ticked down the curved wooden handles sticking out from it.

"Pistols?" Cecelia asked.

"Oh yeah. Let's just say I don't use a bow no more."

"Mordecai would not approve," Zuula said.

"Oh!" Cecelia said. "Speaking of him, there's something you should know. He's alive, too. And he's free. I freed him."

Garon, Zuula, and Jarrik all turned to stare at her.

"What?" Garon gasped.

"It all started when Anise fooled me into thinking there was a test..." She related how the daemon had tried to trick her into killing Mordecai, and she'd freed him from his prison instead. "Father sent the Ninja after him, but he escaped. Father was furious after that, but he kept his word, and I went to the front."

"This is the first time you've mentioned that," Threadbare said.

"I know. I'm sorry. We've been so busy, and..." she sighed. "He was mad. They tortured him."

Zuula's spear quivered in her hands, as she shook, rage filling her tiny plush body.

"But he's free now. I'm... I'm hoping he joined up with the rangers. He probably did. If Jericho was one of his old students, I don't see—"

"Celia," Zuula said, her voice low.

"Yes?" The porcelain princess whispered.

"We done with the talky and the planny and the dwarven shit and the plotty bits?"

"I, er..."

"Cause Zuula really want to go kill some stuff, and de sooner de better."

Jarrik laughed, and her son, her son who was a man now, knelt to embrace the tiny doll with both arms. Zuula bit irritatedly at him for a bit, then subsided, sighing. "Welcome back, Mom," Jarrik said. "Missed yer."

"Miss you too Jarrik. You treat Beryl good, yah? Zuula want grandchildren."

"Uh, yeah, about that, it probably ain't gonna happen-" Beryl started, but Madeline bumped her leg with her snout.

"Sh. Trust me on this. Just shush."

"Yeah, okay, whatevs."

"Yes, I think we're done," said Cecelia.

"Let me go find that reagent for you." Beryl said, rummaging around.

Ten minutes later, the toys were back in Madeline's pack, while the little dragon returned to the temple of Yorgum, emerging in through the same upper-story window she'd left from. Zuula spent most of the trip silent and brooding. Cecelia tried to apologize a few times, but Garon stopped her, quietly pulled her off to the side.

Threadbare, for his part, spent most of the trip thinking. They had a lot to do, before they went to the dungeon. Hopefully he could get a head start on it early tomorrow, when the supplies arrived.

As it turned out, though, he didn't get a start at all.

*****

"Ah, there you are!" Gudrun's voice echoed through the work room. "I was wondering why someone had fired up the kiln."

"Oh. I'm just skilling up my sculpting," Threadbare said, showing her the row of pots he'd just finished firing. It hadn't been the main reason he'd started working here, but he'd finished THAT part of things an hour ago, right before dawn. "I'm impressed by your facilities."

Yorgum's temple had every sort of crafting tool and workstation known to men, dwarves, or stranger races. Including a few things that were for purposes and crafts that were hard to decipher just by looking at them.

"Now that you're here, I can make golems. Would you like to observe?"

"Ah. About that..." Gudrun sighed, and flipped her long silver ponytail back from where it rested on her shoulder. "The markets are out of yellow reagent."

"Really?"

"There was a run on it late last night, evidently," she frowned. "If you can wait a few days, the miners should have a new crop when they come in from the Western digs, that's where most of it comes from."

"Hm." Threadbare said. "I don't know if our people can."

"I'm sorry," Gudrun said. "I told them it was King's business and asked them to put the next batches aside for you."

"Hey Mistah Beah, you gaht a bit?" Madeline poked her head around the doorway.

"Yes, of course." Threadbare pointed at the pots. "Here you go Gudrun, I'm donating them to the temple or whoever needs them. Please use them well." He cleaned the tools, sat them down, and headed into the main room, with Gudrun's thanks following.

Once he got back to their communal room, Madeline shut the door behind him, with a snap and a twist of her wooden maw against the doorknob.

"It's The Lurker," Cecelia said, examining a tangle of copper wire. "This is his opening move."

"Buying up all the reagents?"

"Not just that. I gave Gudrun a list of components I'd need to assemble a new Steam Knight suit. The most important ones suddenly sold out just before this morning."

"She says," Graves said. "What a coincidence, that she's the one doing the buying, and we are suddenly unable to get what we need to help with the war effort." He sighed and held up a sturdy steel shield. "At least the commonly available things came through, so I have arms and armor again. But the rest... it makes me wonder about the veracity of our hostess."

Kayin's ears flattened. "You think she's The Lurker? I don't see it. She had plenty of chances to try something last night. She literally knows where we sleep. Well, where you sleep, desu."

"Maybe because she doesn't want to get found out. Moving against us here would be too blatant, if she's The Lurker." Cecelia said. "But if someone else is, then they WILL move against us here, to frame her... Oooh, this is all twisty. I hate intrigue. It's all complicated."

"Then let us make it simple," Zuula said. "We go. We hunt giants as tribe. And when Lurker show, we stomp him to bits."

"Captured alive, if possible," Garon pointed out. "We know he can come back from the dead."

"Right. Threadbeah, you got the thing?"

"Oh yes," The little bear handed Madeline her pack, pausing to pull the object in question from it. "I think it came out pretty well, all things considered..."

*****

After some quick logistics, the group suited up, equipped themselves, and headed out into the Hold. The dwarves they passed in the dim tunnels stared at them, gave them wide berths as the toys, their cats, and their lone human companion marched by.

Four minutes into the trip, Gudrun came puffing up, racing until she fell in next to Cecelia at the head of the group. "What... what are you doing? Where are you going?"

"We've heard good things about Jotunher. We thought we'd try our luck," Threadbare explained. Cecelia ignored her, marched on without a word, face barely visible behind her doll-sized helm.

"I..." Gudrun shook her head. "We need to know when you're going to do things like this. The other ministers need to know!"

"We're old hands at dungeon raiding," Garon reassured her. "We know our limits. We'll be back in a few hours at most, it'll be fine."

"I... Don't go in! I'll let the others know." Gudrun said. "Please just wait until we get there."

"All right," said Madeline. "Run fahst. We have lots to do, so don't keep us waiting, okay?"

Gudrun beat feet down the passage, and Fluffbear sighed to watch her go. "I feel bad for tricking her," the small bear squeaked when she was gone. "She baked us cookies. I mean I couldn't eat them, but they looked good."

"They were delicious," Graves told her.

"You checked them, right?" Garon asked.

"Unpoisoned. Confirmed by my appraise," Graves replied without missing a step.

All told, it took an hour to wind through the hold. The tunnels got smaller and smaller as they went, until Graves was stooping full time and had to put on his helm to minimize the damage from collisions. Some of the tunnels were fairly dusty, and they passed by two guardposts, with suspicious eyes watching through stone slits as they did.

"What ah they gahding foah?" Madeline wondered. "They didn't even challenge us."

"They're not here to keep people out of it; they're here to keep watch out for things that come out," Garon said. "Must be why the tunnels are barely dwarven size. If it's a dungeon full of giants, no way they'd fit through here."

At last, they came to a final corridor. Beyond, the wind howled past a huge archway, built with curves and lines that were much cruder than the ones that filled the dwarven halls. Natural light, the first they'd seen in over a day, gleamed in from outside.

And footsteps rang in the corridor behind them. "Hey!" Bazdra called, barely breathing hard as she ran up to them. "What do you think you're doing?"

Hidon materialized from the shadows behind her, arms crossed, with a disapproving look on his face. "You do know where you are, right?"

"Oh yes," said Threadbare, glancing around from his perch on Pulsivar's back. "We know it's dangerous. We shall be very careful."

Hidon and Bazdra shared a look. "Is there any way we can talk you out of this?" Bazdra asked.

"Nope," Zuula said, folding her arms.

"You have no idea how much of my time you're wasting." Hidon rubbed his eyes. "Fine, let's get this over with quickly. Invite us in."

"What?" Threadbare said. This wasn't the plan.

"Invite us in. The King's orders were to ensure your survival," Bazdra ground out. "We know Jotunher, you don't. We'll even settle for half-shares."

"Hey now," Hidon said. "Don't go crazy there."

Threadbare looked at the groups and rubbed his head. "Ah. Garon, can you take them please?"

The wooden minotaur thought it over. "I... suppose. I'll have to... well, Fluffbear and Mopsy could transfer over to yours. It'll mean that both groups are running without pets. On the upside we'll both have a full seven."

The toys and their friends reshuffled, and Bazdra frowned. "You're sticking me with the group that's all golems? My party heals aren't going to be much good there. I should go with the cats, and the human—"

"No, no, it will be fine," Threadbare said. "He can heal himself, and Fluffbear will look after the cats. Please trust me, we've worked well together before."

"You're sure?" Hidon squinted at Garon. "Because I only count six in Threadbare's group. The two bears, the two cats, Mr. Graves, and Cecilia. She could shift over there easily enough."

"Oh, six, right, six," Garon said. "Slip of my tongue. But no, no, it works better this way," Garon said. "Besides, I'm a shaman and so's mom. There's enough healing to go around. We need you in a more tanky role," he told them, as he led them forward, after inviting them into his party. "So, please tell me about your jobs and specialties, if you would...

*****

A few minutes after they departed, Jarrik heard Madeline's voice whisper in his ear. "We're in. You in position?"

"Yeah," he Wind's Whispered back, keeping his back to the wall, and settling in for the long-haul. His camouflage and stealth skills, long-practiced these last five years, had let him slide past the auxiliary guard posts easily. And his Keen Eye was up, as he glanced up and down the hall, leather coat pushed back far enough that it wouldn't creak and give him away.

Now comes the hard part. Waiting.

As it turned out, he didn't have long at all to wait.

After a few minutes, his ears twitched, as footsteps echoed down the corridor. He looked over to see a hooded figure run past, black beard flapping as he ran for the archway.

That's Hidon. But he just went by... Jarrik started to inhale as realization crashed in, then held his breath. *Can't make a sound.*

Hidon slowed anyway, stopped as he got to the archway, and glanced around. His gaze passed over Jarrik without registering and kept moving. Then a flash of steel as he pulled a dagger free, and he was gone.

Well. That settles that. Jarrik drew one of his pistols, and checked the primer—

—and barely had time to snap the chamber shut and freeze, as another set of footsteps pounded down the hallway.

Silver hair trailing behind her, Gudrun ran like her life depended on it, hands holding her skirt up as her boots trampled the floor, puffing and panting.

She too slowed as she came to the archway. Jarrik held his breath as she glanced around. Then a flash of steel, as she drew a pistol of her own, and she was gone into the dungeon.

Shit, Jarrik thought.

Then he shrugged. Whatever the case, his role hadn't changed. He moved to the corner of the room, dropped his camouflage and drew out his pipe, tamping it full of tobacco. Once it was lit and smoking, he unbuttoned his coat, and faced the archway.

"Hidon and Gudrun just came in after yer, one at a time. Both armed," he whispered to Madeline. "Tell my bro good luck and bring everyone back alive..."

CHAPTER 7: THE LURKER STRIKES

Jotunher was *big*.

A great stone house, hundreds of feet tall, it sat in a shielded mountain valley, on a free-standing pillar of stone that had to be miles wide. Cleft from the rest of the range by force unimaginable in times long gone, and surrounded on all sides by impassable peaks, the house of the giants was reachable only by one large and quite-well-guarded stone bridge.

"Do you think they see us?" Missus Fluffbear squeaked.

"No," Hidon said, curtly, digging out a pair of daggers. "They won't until we get within a few hundred yards, or if we take a shot at them at range."

"Is their eyesight really that bad?" Garon said, looking over the archway the parties had just emerged from, and the large, open steps down to the edge of the circular gorge. "We're pretty hard to miss, out here."

"Some think it's their eyesight or their dimness. Others think that being dungeon monsters does something to their perception." Bazdra said, before she ran through her buffs. "**Shield of Divinity. Shield Saint. And here, Aeterna's Blessing of Constitution on Cecelia.**"

"Hm?" The armored doll glanced around. "Oh, thank you."

"Aren't you going to buff up too?" Bazdra asked her, frowning.

"Right, right. Um... **Shield Saint.**"

"We all should," said Threadbare. "Hm... **Keen Eye. Flex. Makeup. Self-Esteem. Strong Pose. Deathsight. Guard Stance. Harden.**"

Skill ups rippled past his vision, and he dug in his pack, applied makeup to his face.

"A camouflage pattern?" Hidon said, beard twitching as he fought to keep his scowl.

Your Adorable skill is now level 34!

"I'm buffing one of my Scout skills."

"That, uh, that was a lot of Model stuff, wasn't it?" Bazdra asked, curiously. "What kind of mix are you going for here, exactly?"

"Mix?" He said, nudging Pulsivar, as the rest of the party put up their applicable buffs. The cat hopped down a step, and the rest of the party followed suit, clambering down the mildly-icy, four-foot-tall steps with various degrees of trouble. "I'm not sure I understand. Oh, does anyone else want a harden?"

Pretty much all the golems and doll haunters did, and Threadbare smiled as the skill rose, in fits and starts. Long ago that would have drained his sanity entirely. Now it only dented it a bit.

"She's talking about your jobs," Hidon said, hopping from step to step with nimble ease. "We don't see many models among our people. But I guess one of your purposes is to look cute, so it's understandable."

"I didn't plan any of my jobs, not really," Threadbare said. "But they've proven surprisingly useful, so I guess that's all right."

"We're pretty much all alive again, kinda, because of his necromancer and golemist combo," Garon said.

"It's different for us," Bazdra said, dangling her feet over the side and hopping down, repeating the process with each step and grimacing at clatter of her armor with every drop. "Do you know much about dwarves?"

"You like gold and ale and making stuff," said Madeline, fluttering easily from step to step, with Kayin on her back. "That's about it."

"We get five crafting jobs. And five adventuring jobs," said Hidon. "So we have to plan carefully. Unlike humans, who mainly stumble around, and grab whatever looks shiny, we have to weigh our choices carefully, check with our elders, and see what helps the clan the most."

"Five. Geeze. I mean, don't get me wrong, a while back I woulda thought three would be stupid amounts. But yeah, that's pretty rough," Madeline sympathized.

"Well..." Hidon said, sliding down the last step and staring out to the bridge; "The thing to remember is that jobs are still new to most of us. It's only been about forty-three years since they came about, and the whole world changed. To a dwarf? That's not so long. There's a ton of us who still respect the old ways. Hell, some of our kin back north, when last we spoke wi' em, had decided to ignore jobs entirely and do things the old-fashioned way. Which is a bit extreme, in my eyes. We used to have some folks like that down here, but, well..."

"What happened to them?" Cecelia asked.

"They died early in the war," he said simply. "Now it's only the more pragmatic ones left, like me. I've been using my jobs to great effect, and they're the only reason I'm still alive. Because so, so many of them are so good at fighting dirty."

"To tell the truth, I'm surprised you're not trying to get us to ambush the guards over there," Garon said. "That's about what I'd expect from an Assassin/Bandit/Burglar mix."

"This is your run," Hidon shrugged, glancing back to Bazdra. "We don't think you should be here risking your fool necks. So I want to see how you do before I start suggesting complicated tactics and tricks. And if you can't handle the guards, then it's better we know it early so you can go back to Guddy's place and eat cookies and let us get on with more important work."

"That's kinda harsh, desu," said Kayin.

"Yeah man, we got this. Maybe. Dang those ladies are big." Glub stared across the gorge, at the two blue, fur-clad women, standing to either side of the portcullis. Each of them was twelve feet tall, and the parts of their arms and legs that were visible rippled with pure corded muscle.

"I don't like the fact that the gorge is all around us," Threadbare said. "It would be all too easy for one of us to get knocked over the edge."

"See, that's a thing we don't have to worry about," Bazdra said. "Dwarves are Sturdy. We don't get knocked back. Ever."

"Still not too late to turn back," Hidon offered.

Garon shook his horned head. "Nah. Madeline, fly under the bridge, I want you on rescue duty. Mom, those grasses on the edge, are they enough to get vines from?"

"Yes. Is easy."

"Great. Give us some vines and ready them to catch anyone who gets flung. And do the owl thing and backup Madeline."

"But Zuula want to shank a giant bitch!"

"Mom... It's party experience. You'll get a share anyway."

"Not much with greedyguts dwarfs taking big share! Dey be twice our levels, Garon!"

"Greedy?" Bazrda said. "Greedy! We're here to keep you alive, you ungrateful green fool!"

"Bah! We not need you!"

"Guys, save it for the giants. Mom, they'll be plenty of regular fighting when we get inside."

"Better be. Zuula really need to kill some'ting. Been days Garon, whole DAYS."

"Hey," Threadbare said, hopping down from Pulsivar and hugging her. "We wouldn't have gotten here without you. Without everyone. You're all very useful; you're all my friends. And I hope you are, too," Threadbare looked up at Hidon and Bazdra.

The offended cleric sighed and finally nodded. "Friends. Whee." And if her voice held very little enthusiasm, then nobody called her out on it.

Hidon was made of harder stuff. "I'm waiting to see what you can do before I share a drink with you." He glanced across the bridge. "They'll throw snowballs as you come in. Be ready for that."

"Snowballs don't sound too bad," Cecelia said, putting her visor down.

Two minutes later, as chunks of ice and rock and snow the size of footstools whizzed overhead and exploded on the bridge, Cecelia apologized profusely and repeatedly to Graves as he ran alongside her, shielding her from rocky shrapnel.

Threadbare was the first to arrive, leaping off Pulsivar as the black bobcat pounced on one of the giants, wailing. **"Adjust Weight!"** the little bear cried...

...and ballooned into a puffy, oversized version of himself about one and a half times his regular mass.

"Hum," he said, narrowly avoiding a Giant-sized boot.

Your Dodge skill is now level 10!

"No, not much help," he decided and canceled the skill, deflating rapidly and moving in to slash at the very angry giant as she tried to simultaneously get fifty pounds of angry Pulsivar off her head and smash the weird little toy in front of her into teddy bear paste.

The second giant moved up to help her fellow guard...

...and promptly got her own face full of stabby feline as Kayin leaped off of Madeline, daggers slashing. Then Garon's group crashed into her, and Threadbare's party arrived to back him up, and there followed about five minutes of violence. The giants found themselves massively outnumbered, by small targets who had maxed out their buffs and worked together with practiced tactics. Not only that, the tiny terrors were backed up by dwarves who were a lot easier to hit but had much better defenses and were smart enough to back out and heal up when hits go through. Inevitably, the guards really didn't have a chance. They were built like the ogre had been, many hit points but only middling armor, and the toys were much stronger now, especially with Glub's heartening song rocking the beats of that battle.

But it wasn't entirely one-sided.

The giants were a hell of a lot faster than the ogre had been and a lot more accurate. Their hits hurt, and Threadbare found himself splitting his duties, tanking, getting in the occasional slash to keep his giant focused on him, and dropping mend golem spells when his friends fell back. Graves stepped up a few times too, to take the pressure off of him, withstanding shield-rattling hits, hacking with dolorous strikes, and getting off a drain life now and again when the hits got to be too much.

The good news was that his fears about being knocked off the cliff were mostly unfounded. The giants only seemed to be able to do that with a skill called "**Swing for de bleachers!**" When they yelled that, the toys knew to get clear.

All except for Cecelia, who got caught square on and went sailing. Threadbare grimaced and fought harder.

"Got her!" Zuula yelled, and Threadbare let out a puff of relief.

That's about the point he heard the gunshot. They all did, as it rang out behind them.

"What's that?" he called. "Zuula, Madeline, tell me what's going on, please." He said, slapping the giant's club aside. And as they had through most of the fight, his skills rolled on, climbing as he fought against the stronger opponent.

Your Parry skill is now level 14!

Threadbare checked the giant's hit points with Deathsight, nodded and cut her down with a few claw swipes, before turning to look for the source of the shot.

Your Brawling skill is now level 47!
Your Weapon Specialization skill is now level 36!
Your Claw Swipes skill is now level 35!

There was movement, up on the cliff, and something fluttering at the edge of it. He squinted, regretting that he'd never ground Keen Eye that much. Then he caught a glimpse of silver hair. "Is that Gudrun?" he turned, just as Garon brought down the other giant, toppling her to the ground where she lay unmoving.

"It's Gudrun. She's hurt," Madeline whispered back. "I'll escort her in."

"Gudrun?" Threadbare asked. He turned to check on his group, found them intact and healing up. Glub and Fluffbear saw to the golems, which was good because his sanity was down a bit from that fight. Bazdra was busy tending to herself and Hidon.

"**Greater Healing.** Almost lost your princess there," Bazdra shot him a sidelong glance. "Sure you want to keep going?"

"Definitely. I have a question, though. Can either of you think of why Gudrun might be here?"

"What? Why?" Hidon looked down at him. "You're sure?"

The bear pointed back up the stairway descending the cliff, and the two dwarves stared at the red dragon flapping around the elderly dwarf easing her way down the stairs.

"Yeah, we need to search and be gone before the two giants come back," Garon said. "Zuula, Glub, search the corpses. Hidon, are we clear to open the door, or is there another way in?"

"Well, if you want to avoid going flying again—" Hidon shot a glare at a very chastened Cecelia, "—then we'll want to go in the front door. There's a feasting hall just beyond, full of giaunts and giuncles, but they won't engage if you stick to the walls and don't take a poke at them. Getting all their attention at once is suicide unless you can trick them. But we can move into the side passages and deal with things one at a time there."

"Let's wait a bit," Threadbare said. "Graves? Contingency plan four?"

"On it." He moved over to each corpse. "Done searching?"

"Yeah," Zuula said, tossing a pair of large pouches up and down. "Coins. Snacks."

"Good. **Zombies. Zombies.**"

Bazdra flinched as the guards groaned and rose. "Is there a need for this?" she snapped.

"If the guards show up again, then they'll have to fight undead guards. We can escape while they do," Threadbare said, keeping his eye on Gudrun who was stomping across the bridge, brandishing a pistol—

—at Hidon, who raised his hands and looked dumbfounded.

"You!" Gudrun said, shifting her bloodspattered robe around with one hand, as she pointed the smoking gun at Hidon. "What are you playing at!"

"What?" Hidon said. "Nothing. Fighting giants."

"He has been," Garon said.

"Not a minute ago he was trying to kill me!" Gudrun said, her glare not leaving Hidon.

"He's been here with us all this time," Threadbare said.

"Want me to tell her?" Madeline's voice whispered in his ear.

"No..." Threadbare said. "No, I don't think he was trying to kill you." He shook his head at Gudrun and ended up looking at Madeline. "Don't tell her. We don't want to tell anyone about Jarrik," he whispered back, through the wind.

Gudrun hesitated, looking from Hidon to Threadbare to the rest of them.

"Guddy, lower the pistol," Bazdra said, stepping in front of her barrel. "I'm pretty sure I know who took a swing at you, and it wasn't Hidon. Tell us what happened."

"Quickly," Garon said, peering in through the cracked door. Raucous music and giant voices sounded from the aperture. "We need to get moving."

"Montag's missing," Gudrun said, lowering the gun. "There's a lot of blood in his home. And some red doll's hair scattered around."

"What?" Threadbare said, glancing over to Cecelia, who shrugged back.

"Ridiculous, of course," said Hidon. "Almost as ridiculous as me trying to kill you." his eyes were narrowed as he studied Gudrun.

"The King's looking for you," Gudrun said. "He thinks you're in danger."

"Yeah. It's got to be The Lurker after us. But you should NOT be here!" Bazdra said. "You haven't delved a day in your life! This is NOT the place for you, Gudrun Scarstone."

"Hang on a second," Hidon said. "Where did I go after something that looked like me tried to kill you? And how did you survive in the first place?" Hidon asked.

"I ran here," Gudrun said. "Haven't moved that fast in ages. Then as soon as I came through the archway, I saw you on the steps watching the fight. I called out to you, and you waved, came closer, and stabbed me. I fired my gun, and I think I got you. But you disappeared."

Graves tilted his head and adjusted his backpack, while Gudrun recounted the affair. "Did you make that musket yourself?" he asked. "It's ah, some nice work."

"Of course!" she said. "No self-respecting priestess of crafts would use a weapon she hadn't made herself."

Threadbare bowed his head. "Garon, please shut the door," he said. "We're not going any further right now."

"What? Why?"

"Do it, stupid boy!" Zuula bonked her spear against her son's noggin. "It DAT business."

"Oh, oh, right..." he eased the door shut.

"Glad you're seeing reason," Bazdra sighed. "We need to go back and settle this."

"Well... you're half right," Threadbare said, whispering mental messages through the wind. Graves, Fluffbear, and Glub moved behind Gudrun, cutting off her retreat back down the bridge. "We do need to settle this."

"We need to figure out where the Lurker's hiding," Hidon said, glancing around.

"He's right in front of me," Threadbare stared at Gudrun.

Silence, for a long bit, broken only by distant winds howling through the gorge around them.

"Lurker? What are you talking about?" Gudrun said, staring around them, confused.

"You came in disguised as Hidon. But Gudrun was right behind you," Threadbare said. "One of us saw you do that. Then when you noticed her behind you, you killed her. That was probably when the gunshot happened."

She stared at him, eyes wide. "I'm me. I'm not any Lurker."

WILL+1

Your Magic Resistance skill is now level 17!

Threadbare shook his head, as something passed over him. Most of his friends looked confused. Hidon sheathed his daggers.

Bazdra, though, scowled. She inhaled sharply and slid her sword from its sheath.

Threadbare continued. "Your clothes are bloody, but you aren't wounded. And that could be because you healed yourself. But your clothes are still torn. You haven't fixed them."

"Well yes, I'll fix them now; I've got a few seconds and plenty of tailoring supplies to do that—"

"But Yorgum's Godspell is mend," Fluffbear squeaked. "It would have taken a second, and you didn't."

Gudrun's eyes snapped open. "Well what if it slipped my mind! See, **Mend,**" she said, and her clothes drew together.

But there was no flash of golden light, Threadbare saw.

"I suppose that could have been true," Threadbare said, "But when Graves called your pistol a musket you didn't correct him. On top of everything else, it looks very suspicious."

"I.. I was just flustered," Gudrun said, taking a step back, looking at the solemn-faced group behind her. "In fact, I—"

A blur of motion, Threadbare tried to get in its way, but was just too slow. Bazdra shouted a warning—

—and then Cecelia yelled, as she was scooped up, and Gudrun was backing up to the door, teeth bared, holding the little doll high. "No closer," Gudrun said, her voice rippling, and changing, losing the grandmotherly tone, as it was replaced with something oily. "Or she goes over the edge. If she dies down there, you can't revive her, can you?"

Hidon twitched, but Garon slapped his arm. "No!"

"Clever boy. She's coming with me," The Lurker sneered. "I was very glad you came to this dungeon. It's one of my goals with this infiltration. You handed me two of them in one fell swoop, really, how could I resist?" Gudrun's form rippled, swirling and rearranging, growing until it was a handsome, smiling man, nude for a second until fine, flashy clothes swelled out of his skin and wrapped around him.

"Those ain't clothes, are they? They weren't earliah, eithah?" Madeline asked.

"Nope. And that wasn't a mend spell. **I can talk like this at will,**" The Deceiver smirked.

Cecelia twisted, looked to Threadbare for help. "Stay calm," he whispered through the wind. "We'll save you."

With absolute faith she nodded and got shaken for her trouble. "Ah ah ah! Sit still, do nothing, and you might survive this, Your Highness," The Lurker hissed, as he tucked the pistol under his arm and opened the door to the giants' hall with his free hand.

"And Gudrun?" Hidon's hands shook, gloved hands clenching around the daggers.

"I let her go." The Lurker said, gazing back to the steps leading down the cliff... and the misty gorge beyond. "Long drop. Short stop. Down there somewhere."

"You bastard!" Bazdra snarled. "Why shouldn't we kill you now!"

"Because I WILL throw Princess Cecelia, and I'm smart enough to do it where your dragon and witch can't catch her, and where the vines *aren't*. And because if you let me go now, you'll have a shot at me when I leave. One way out, one way in, hm?"

"And exactly what do you mean to do here?" Threadbare asked, but without another word the daemon slipped through the door and slammed it behind him.

BANG!

The muffled shot resounded from inside. Hidon turned to Threadbare, furious. "What! You honestly think you can trust a word that thing said? Your princess is as good as dead if you give that thing time, and you're just letting it go?"

"You're wrong on three counts," Threadbar said. "First, I don't trust it, second, we won't give it time, and third... well, that wasn't my princess."

Graves' pack stirred, and a porcelain arm poked out, followed by the rest of Cecelia. "No, but it's almost as bad. We need to get moving or he might kill Marva."

"What?" Bazdra blinked. "Two of you? Oh. Oh, clever."

Threadbare shrugged. "I baked a new clay golem this morning and asked our dead for volunteers. We just needed someone who had unlocked knight at some point, everything else could be faked. Especially since they could modify their status screens to hide things. Marva was it."

"Your whole dungeon run was to lure him out." Hidon said, as light dawned.

"Don't mean to be a poop, but we need ta hurry," Madeline said, staring at rippling patches of air. "The gahds are coming back."

Cecelia pointed at Hidon and Bazdra. "You two, out. Tell the King what happened. We took care to Lurker-proof our people, so he shouldn't be able to impersonate us, but we've no preparations with you. If you're still around, he'll try shenanigans."

Bazdra started to protest, looked at the now roiling patches of empty space, and nodded. "We'll get word to the King."

"Good. We'll go after The Lurker, try to get him to flee without time to prepare. We've got an edge there; we know what he's doing."

At the edge of the bridge, Hidon stopped and looked back. "What? What's he doing?"

"I have an idea," said Threadbare. "Get in Madeline's pack, everyone except for Graves and Madeline. I'll whisper the plan. Go! Oh, and be careful leaving the dungeon, we've got a friend out there. Go out slowly with your hands up, both at once."

"What's the Lurker doing? Simple. He's going to seal the dungeon," Cecelia said, before hopping out of one pack to another, as the dwarves' stunned faces went pale.

CHAPTER 8: JOTUNHER

Giants, though rare creatures throughout the bulk of Generica, are fairly common in the Northlands. Like the dwarves, this particular batch had migrated down from Mighty Hallas, seeking opportunity and a new start away from their more troublesome associates, enemies and allies alike.

Originally, Jotunher was supposed to be a twin settlement to Jotunhim, a steading ruled by the Jarl's brother.

Then she'd gotten her hands on a dungeon core, and the original plan had gone... a bit out of the window.

Giants have the "Living Large" skill. Which means that they usually alternate between two attitudes: hangry, and lazy.

So when the Jarl, after playing with the dungeon core a bit, figured out how it worked, she'd seen some of the benefits right away. Unlike most giants, who are— to put it charitably— rather slow, she'd managed to grind her intelligence up to a respectable fifty-two.

Which let her realize "Hey, if I stick all these delicious foods and alcohol stuff in the loot pillars and put my friends in the midboss and mob pillars, then we can pretty much eat forever in a never-ending party without doing a lick of work!"

And so when the dwarves finally tunneled back to that end of the mountain, they found Jotunher nestled just inside the Oblivion and full of happy, torpid giants. Dwarves being dwarves and the old enmity being what it was, they sent in raiding parties. Some of them survived; some of them didn't, and the chief shrugged her shoulders and begin setting up a proper dungeon, adding to it as her whimsy took her. After all, the little hairy ones sometimes dropped good loot and that got added to her hall of treasures. And it wasn't like they could REALLY kill her people. Best

Jarl ever!

Okay, so she might not have figured out ALL of how the dungeon worked but whatever. It worked, and that was enough. She'd come to appreciate the benefits of life as a dungeon master.

Her subjects, on the other hand, had not.

Though she had no way of knowing it, being stuck in a dungeon slot for long has a way of wearing on one's perceptions. It ups aggression, tries to mold behavior and urges, and pushes those in the slots into acting in accordance with a script that tries to encourage and provide dramatic conflict with visitors.

All else falls by the wayside.

Some monsters, such as strong-willed undead or daemons can resist it. Dragons don't usually notice, because they're used to the unending weariness caused by the march of time anyway. But for most mortal races, it wears the people in those slots down, especially if they're not mentally strong...

...like, for example, most giants.

The ones in the feast hall, gorging themselves, had barely noticed when the doors slammed shut. They did that sometimes, as people came and went. No big deal.

They hadn't even looked up when the handsome stranger stood there, holding a frightened doll in one hand and a pistol in the other, taking stock of the situation. Nor had they noticed when he shook himself and shrunk down to the shape of a three-foot-tall teddy bear in a red coat and a black top hat.

They sure as fuck had noticed when he shot Hralph in the face, though. Especially Hralph.

The entire long table had gone silent, as the gunshot echoed, and the feasters stared at the murderous stranger.

"My name is Threadbare, and I think all of you are stupid fartsniffers!" He cheerfully announced.

As one, they rose and charged him, bellowing in rage.

And after a few injuries, some broken furniture, and a slight divergence into a food fight after Hregina accidentally beaned Hronda with a hurled ham, they realized that the little bastard had disappeared in the confusion. Angered, the mob of giants spread out throughout the hall and began looking under chairs, lifting the covers of serving dishes, and peering behind tapestries for a small bear who desperately needed to be flattened. And maybe farted on, because who's the fartsniffer NOW, huh?

(That's about the extent of witty retorts among giants, as they go.)

With one shot and a little trickery, the Lurker had created a sticky situation indeed for Threadbare's group.

He didn't realize, however, that they'd been told about the entry hall by Hidon, just prior to his arrival.

And while they didn't know just what he'd done, they'd heard the gunshot through the doors and guessed the gist of his plan.

So when the doors slammed open again, about thirty giants, giuncles, and a couple of ginephews and ginieces whirled around with axes and clubs out, but they didn't see an adventuring group led by a small bear who desperately needed pounding. They saw two badly wounded guards, staggering in, leaning on each other. "Get help..." one of them croaked, before slipping from her compatriot's grasp and hitting the ground.

Well, that wouldn't do!

The giants surged forward to help the fallen one up, firing questions at the still-standing guard, who shrugged.

Unnoticed, a tiny red dragon wrapped around a totally silent knight ran from the door to the nearest side-passage. As they reached it, the knight glanced back, and the remaining guard's eyes rolled up in her head as she collapsed.

They made it down the hall, around a few corners and came to a stop.

"I can't believe that wahked," Madeline said.

"..." Graves replied, lips moving without sound. He frowned and sound returned to him. "I'm just glad the bear had that silent killer bead left over from the infiltration run. I'm not a stealthy person."

Madeline plopped her pack down and started drawing out their friends while Graves listened back the way they came.

"Were there any problems?" Threadbare asked as he came out.

"No. It worked perfectly. The zombies distracted them, and we got past."

"Good. Garon? Can you check?"

"Sure thing. **Follow the Dotted Line.**" He looked down, then shook his head. "The Lurker's resistant or something."

One of Garon's mercenary skills let him find the shortest path to a given quest objective. Before they'd entered the dungeon, before they'd even left their quarters, Threadbare had given them all a King's Quest to take down The Lurker. Then to give himself the quest, he'd sworn fealty to Garon, who had shared the quest that Threadbare had given him BACK to its originator.

They'd done that last part mainly to see if they could. It was possible and raised some interesting notions for ruler-based shenanigans later.

"I suppose that makes sense," Threadbare said, after a bit of thought. "If it were that easy to find him, he wouldn't have caused so much trouble."

Kayin cleared her throat, as she faded into sight, losing her camouflage. "There's one guard at the junction up the hall, and a lot of doors off. It's like a maze back there, from what I can see."

"You think they'll hear us in the main hall if we take him out?" Graves asked.

"It's a her," Kayin said. "I think."

"Nah," Madeline said. "I know how dungeon mobs think. They'll stick to theah paht of things and not go roaming unless we draw 'em."

"There's a question, though. The guard, is she actively searching or hurt?" Cecelia asked.

"No," Kayin confirmed.

"Then it's almost certain The Lurker didn't come this way."

"Or he slipped by with stealth," Garon said. "But we need to go deeper in, regardless."

Cecelia sighed. "Remember, our goal isn't to 'win' this dungeon; it's to catch him before he seals it. We need to catch him before he gets to the final boss."

"Not what I meant. Mads?"

"Dungeons have a way of funneling you to the end regahdless of how you go," the red wooden dragon spoke. "If we don't follow his path exactly that's fine, so long as we can make it in time to catch him when the paths convahge."

"Let's go, then," Threadbare decided, mounting up on Pulsivar's back and waving the rest along with his scepter. "Kayin, any way to sneak past this one?"

"Not without risks. It's a narrow junction and she seems pretty sharp."

"Down she goes then."

There was a time when that would have bothered me, Threadbare reflected as he rode Pulsivar into a charge, ambushing the surprised guard.

AGI +1

Your Ride skill is now level 9!

Most of his early life had been spent fighting for survival. First against the cat who he'd soon befriended, then against a horde of ravenous rats, and eventually graduating to struggles against undead and weirder things.

But giants were people of a sort, and with every claw swipe he landed on them, with every bruise his scepter left on her skin, he was reminded that he was helping kill something that was like his little girl, just on a bigger scale.

Your Clubs and Maces skill is now level 10!

To that end he forgave the occasional axe hit or kick the giantess got in on him, because it was quite understandable, really. But he was happy to switch over to support once the rest of his crew followed him in and took over the slashy duties.

She IS a dungeon monster. That does make a difference. What he'd seen so far seemed to suggest that dungeon monsters weren't truly alive in the first place, that you could kill them and they'd just come back time and again.

Like The Lurker. And a connection teased in his mind there, before he brought it back to the fight.

Garon brought the guard to her knees, screaming, and Threadbare had a very hard time remembering that she was a projection of the dungeon, and nothing more—

But that wasn't quite right, was it? Not all dungeon monsters were that way. Madeline was a dungeon monster who'd developed, escaped, and gone on to be a... well, you couldn't call her a good person, not with a straight face, but a decent one given the fact she knew she was a monster and never felt the slightest guilt about it.

At the end of it, when the guard toppled and fell, swarmed by small foes who overwhelmed her with bodies and attacks, he knew that it didn't matter. This was what Cecelia needed, to save her kingdom, and her people.

He sure would be happy when it was all done, though. Perhaps then they could get back to tea parties and hugs.

Though it WAS good to see his friends rejoice and get more powerful and confident as they went from victory to victory.

Speaking of which...

You are now a level 7 Duelist!
AGI+3
DEX+3
STR+3

You are now a level 15 Golemist!
INT+5
WILL +5
You have unlocked the Bone Golem skill!
Your Bone Golem skill is now level 1!
You have unlocked the Call Golem skill!
Your Call Golem skill is now level 1!

"Anothah one down!" Madeline cheered. **"Goldfindah!"** she chanted, and coins popped out of the giant's pockets. Then Zuula took over searching duties, while Kayin nodded and faded into camouflage again.

"Any route, desu?" The catgirl asked as she stared down three identical corridors.

"Look for the larjah passage," Madeline advised. "Main routes are the way to go." She nuzzled her coins greedily. "There we go! High Dragon level tree! Woo!"

"Cecelia?" Threadbare said, "I think I just got a skill that could save Marva here and now. Do you see any problem with me doing that immediately?"

"Not a bit," Cecelia said. "Please do!"

"Call Golem," Threadbare said, staring at the first Cecelia's name in his party screen.

Your Call Golem skill is now level 2!

Immediately, Cecelia's body double stumbled forward, appearing from thin air. She cringed, then looked around... and immediately glomped Threadbare. "Thank you, lord! I was so scared!"

"It's all right," he said, hugging her back. "Where was he?"

"I... don't know. He's running around looking like you, King Dreadbear!"

"Not unexpected." The teddy bear gently pried the ex-cultist loose, just as Kayin rematerialized. "That way," the catgirl said. "Just past two more guards it opens up onto a hillside for a bit. There's some giant shepherds and herds of giant sheep and goats and stuff. It looks like there's an entrance to a tower of the hall across the way, but if we step careful we might be able to evade most of the herds."

"I, I lost the sword and shield you gave me," Marva said, turning to Cecelia. "I'm sorry."

"No, no, you've got nothing to apologize for!" Cecelia said, taking her shoulder with one hand, and touching her face as Marva tried to look away. "If anything I'M the sorry one. You risked your neck for me, because of me, and it almost went bad. I owe you a big favor. Garon, can we get her spares?"

"Oh yeah. Mads?"

Madeline rummaged in the pack, and pulled out a few spare doll-sized weapons. The temple of Yorgum had been good for grinding their craft skills last night, in more ways than one.

Once Marva was armed and re-equipped, Threadbare slapped a few mend golems on those who needed it, and the group hurried to the next set of guards.

That fight didn't go quite as well.

Even with the same tactics that they'd employed against the gate guards, handling two at a time was rough. Especially without a pair of experienced and sturdy dwarves there to help take the pressure off of them.

And in the more confined space of the hallway, it was harder to encircle and swarm the guards, harder to dance out of the way of their clubs. Threadbare was very glad he'd gained a level and refilled his sanity in the last fight, because he was stuck tanking as best he could and casting mend golem over and over again.

On the upside it was doing wonders for his golem body and toughness skills. And his defensive duelist skills were getting a workout, too.

The downside was that his friends were getting hurt, pretty badly hurt. At one point Pulsivar took a bone-shattering hit, bounced off a wall, and got up and limped away, leaving droplets of blood on the floor behind him, with a whole '1' hit point glaring on Threadbare's party screen. "Fluffbear!" he yelled, as he leaped onto the giant's chest, holding its tunic while he jabbed it in the jaw repeatedly. "Heal him, please!"

"On it!"

The giants went down, finally. And Threadbare went over to hug Pulsivar, who lay there, panting, grooming his bloody fur.

Fluffbear looked up from his side and shook her head. "He lost a life."

"What?"

"He has the Nine Lives skill, just like Kayin. But he's on life number seven now. One more to go, then..." she hugged Pulsivar too, his fur rasping as it ruffled against her armor.

"No. No, I don't want him to die!" Threadbare said. The cat switched from grooming himself to licking them, tongue rasping against their plush hides.

"Maybe..." Cecelia looked over at Madeline. "Maybe we could put him back in the pack? Just for this run?"

"Maybe for more than that," Garon said. "We're up against some pretty tough customers, and bobcat levels aren't going to cut it. I mean..." he sighed. "As a cat, he's totally badass. But he's still a cat. Up against giants, and daemons, and everything else... if we want him to survive, we should maybe stop bringing him into battle."

"That might be good. He doesn't get any of my tamer bonuses, like Mopsy does. And his armor just.. isn't. I used to think we could soulstone him if the worst happened," Fluffbear squeaked, "But I'm not sure he'd be okay with this. Or like living as a golem."

"We should have this discussion outside. Until then let's keep him out of danger," Threadbare decided.

But Pulsivar was having none of it. When they pulled out the pack, he refused to go back in. Even with Fluffbear offering treats.

Finally, Zuula shook her head. **"Speak with Nature,"** she said and snarled for a bit. Pulsivar growled back. Then the shaman shrugged. "He say no."

"No? But... I don't want him to die," Threadbare said.

"Incoming," Kayin said, looking at the rippling air.

"He say it his choice. And he rather die fighting for family, den hide safe while dey all risk. Besides he say you all lost wit'out him, silly hoomin toys."

Without hope of changing the proud cat's mind, they hurried away from the respawning guards and into what the local giants referred to as the 'Sheep Level.'

And there the toys got a rude shock. Kayin's estimate of evading trouble had been far, far too optimistic.

The shepherds weren't a problem as all. The shepherds dropped their crooks and ran as soon as trouble started.

But the things they were herding weren't sheep at all.

They were Wooly Bullies, and the bigger males among them had horns and strong territorial instincts.

"Bah!" they called, as they sighted interlopers.

"Ram!" they shouted, as they used Rammit skills to knock the golems around the grassy fields, sending them tumbling as Threadbare and his friends fought the herds.

"Oh Ewe!" their mates called out, affectionately, as they used healing nuzzles to keep the males fighting fit.

The group had come prepared to fight giants, big slow things that took a lot of punishment and hit really hard. They hadn't come prepared for endless waves of sheep, which were faster things that took a bit less punishment, and nibbled more weakly, but more persistently. And worst of all, the damned things didn't run. No matter how many of the herd had fallen, the wooly bullies didn't stop coming.

But for all that, they were up against golems, with only a few living allies to worry about. Golems had great endurance, and it took a lot to get them tired. Twenty minutes into the fight Graves and the cats were flagging, but with a few shouted orders by Garon and Threadbare, the toys reorganized themselves into a loose square around their living allies.

And for a while there, it looked like it was working. They moved across the field, slowly, sending wool flying and standing resolute against sheep the size of great danes. Glub's song rose above the bleating, a song of clarity this time, so Threadbare and the healers could keep everyone in good shape. The giant fights had been sprints, races to take them down before they killed someone. This was more of a marathon, a grinding ocean of wooly meat that needed to be converted into mutton.

They didn't notice the midboss until it was among them.

Threadbare's head snapped around as Cecelia... no, Marva, screamed.

There, under a white pelt with eyeholes, was something brown, with glaring red eyes, and big, big jaws, all the better to bite Marva with. It was gnawing her, looking very surprised, as its teeth rasped on porcelain and metal. It spat her out and she tumbled, barely avoided a Ram and hurried back to the group.

"Wolf in Sheep's clothing!" Garon yelled, and then the creature was leaping into the center of the formation, howling in fury...

The wooly bullies were acting out of territorial concerns.

The wolf? He wanted MEAT.

Pulsivar and Mopsy smelled like predators, so they weren't his first choice.

No, that honor fell to Graves.

And Graves fell as the enormous, horse-sized wolf leaped on his back and fastened his jaws around the man's head, worrying it. Only his helm saved him from serious damage.

His helm and Fluffbear, as she squeaked a challenge, slammed Mopsy into the wolf, and started raining down Dolorous Strikes that hit all out of proportion to her size. She'd activated holy smite early in the sheep battle, and the glowing, enlarged field of divine energy that trailed after her weapon and left afterimages flashed as it sliced red numbers out of the wolf.

Then Kayin was on the thing from behind, backstabbing for all she was worth.

"Hold the square!" Threadbare called, worried as their formation started to fall apart...

...but he needn't, for to his amazement, the sheep were as worried about the wolf as he was. They backed off, forming a wooly ring, and the ewes in the herd got to work healing up their bah rams.

"Madeline, go toast some healers!" Garon called, as soon as it was clear they wouldn't get rushed.

"On it!" She broke ranks and flapped upward, diving towards the biggest clusters of fluffy ewes. "Hey ewe assholes! **Bahninate!**"

Turns out, wool is pretty combustible. Burning sheep fled the herd, bleating and crying. Though the others didn't follow suit, it did thin out a few of their healers.

The wolf fought savagely, laying into Fluffbear and Mopsy, and Threadbare focused on mending her, while she healed Mopsy.

Then Pulsivar was in there, laying into it with a full pounce and rake, only to get tossed off contemptuously. The black bobcat squalled and came in for another run... but got slammed backward, sent head over tail.

The group closed in, surrounding it, overcoming it by sheer weight of numbers—

—and the wolf grinned, and said **"Where Wolf?"** Then it leaped, as mightily as it had before, leaving the group and vanishing back into the herd.

"Healing? Please?" Graves croaked, blinking blearily at the dumbfounded sheep, who looked around for the wolf...

...and saw it was gone.

But hey, wait! There were intruders in their territory!

The sheep looked at each other, and again the fuzzy tide surged inward.

Garon yelled "Reassemble! Get back in form—"

"RA-A-A-AM!" A wooly bully called, colliding with the little wooden minotaur. Garon went flying. Madeline darted down and caught him and descended to rejoin the formation.

"Zuula got you!" the shaman said. **"Fast Regeneration!"** She told Graves, then hopped up to his shoulder, to get a little more room to cast. **"Call Vines!"** Ropes of plant matter shot out of the ground on their flank, blunting the worst of the charge. But the Bullies were big, and her vines weren't infinite, and it would only hold them for a little while, she knew. No point in calling thorns either, their woolly hides would ignore those.

Graves glanced back to Threadbare, bashing a ram in the head with his shield as he sidestepped it. "Permission to go full death knight?"

"What does that mean?" Threadbare called back, raising his voice over the bleating and screaming.

"The cats need to get clear!"

"Missus Fluffbear, get them out!" Threadbare called.

It took a few seconds, but the little paladin managed to leap Mopsy clear. And where Mopsy went, Pulsivar did as well. He'd learned THAT much, at least.

"All right you jerks," Graves said, raising his sword up high. **"Bony Armor! Graveblade!"**

Bloody bones ripped from the sheeps' corpses, and gathered around him, splattering him with gore. Gray, sickly energy coalesced around his sword, almost like smoke made solid. Leading with his shield, hacking into the herd around him, the Death Knight left the formation and began his gory work.

Glub and Marva started to move to back him up, but Cecelia called them back. "He's got this! Watch!"

The Graveblade didn't seem to kill sheep any faster, but it wasn't meant to.

No, what that buff did, was turn anything that Graves killed into a zombie.

One by one, the sheep he hacked fell down. One by one they rose, baahing "Brai-ai-ai-ains," and doing their best to chew their former herdmates to death.

They didn't turn on Graves, thankfully. His Undead Truce class feature was proof against that.

And as for the golems…

Cecelia stood very still, as a zombie sheep waddled up to her, gave her a sniff, then walked away, bleating for brains.

No flesh, no meat, nothing good to eat.

For a second, all was going well. Graves was killing living sheep; the sheep couldn't hurt him fast enough to bring him down, and the growing tide of zombies was throwing their ranks into confusion and panic. The circle around the toys slipped, started to break—

—and in the sudden gap, Threadbare could see Pulsivar, Mopsy, and Fluffbear, fighting for their lives against the wolf. It stood on two legs now, wooly skin thrown on its back like a cape, lashing down at Fluffbear with sweeping strikes.

Threadbare ran that way with all his might, moving with long-practiced agility, great bounds eating up the grass as he hopped Zuula's vines, but he was far away, so very far, and as he watched the wolf backhanded Fluffbear off Mopsy and turned to focus on the two cats, chasing Pulsivar. A Caterwaul rose up from the bobcat as he dodged for all he was worth—

—but it wasn't enough. The wolf's jaws closed around Pulsivar.

"I **challenge** you!" Threadbare called, tucking his scepter in its loop, hanging it over his shoulder as he stretched his claws.

Your Challenge skill is now level 10!

"Drain Life!" the little bear threw in for good measure, as the wolf turned around in surprise, then yelped and dropped the limp cat as a red '21' tore from him and swirled into Threadbare.

Your Drain Life skill is now level 8!

Mopsy tore at the wolf's flank as Fluffbear ran to Pulsivar's twitching form, but the wolf ignored them both and growled at Threadbare as he loped toward his tiny tormentor.

Threadbare ignored the Moxie damage, and the notice that flashed up.

You have resisted The Wherewolf's Growl!

Your Stubborn skill is now level 10!

No, Threadbare ignored all else, as he rushed straight into the wolf's jaws, as they came crashing down around him, for massive damage.

CON +1

Your Golem Body skill is now level 32!

Your Toughness skill is now level 24!

The wolf tried to shake him. Threadbare felt one of his legs rip free, ignored it, ignored his pants tearing away as they went with the leg, and squirmed, right into the wolf's throat.

The big beast froze, as the little golem's claws jabbed into it, right through the back of its cheeks.

"Adjust Weight," Threadbare said, there in the wolf's gullet.

And the wolf coughed as the little bear swelled up to almost twice his regular size.

Inside the wolf's throat.

The wolf went berserk, shaking its head, clawing at its mouth, unable to get its paws in at a good angle. Not that it mattered. Whenever Threadbare felt a tear, he'd whisper **"Mend Golem."**

He had to ration the air he used to speak carefully. There wasn't much inside the wolf's throat.

Especially since he was blocking any from getting in to the wolf's lungs.

And after a minute, its struggles weakened and slowed. Then it fell over. But Threadbare stayed stuck in.

In the end, the wolf died in an appropriate fashion, choked to death on a mouthful of fluff way bigger than he could handle.

By slaying a creature through suffocation you have unlocked the Air Elementalist Job!

You cannot become an air elementalist at this time!

Only then, did Threadbare dig himself out. It was very messy, but eventually the wolf gave way, and he stared out into the sky... and at the distant figures of his running friends, heading toward him. He glanced around, realized that he was in a different part of the field. The wolf, in its struggles, had panicked and fled, evidently.

"I'm all right!" he called, emerging bloody and torn from the wolf. But it didn't matter, because Pulsivar was one of the ones coming toward him, and he was very, very relieved to see the big cat alive and mobile.

While waiting for his friends he managed a few clean and presses, and a mend for his torn trousers, and then his friends were up to him. He glanced over at the herd of sheep zombies, shuffling slowly towards the group, drawn by the lure of living cats to eat.

"Should we be worried about those?" Threadbare asked.

Graves glanced back. "No. They're temporary, and—" he blinked behind his visor. "Oh my goodness the levels. **Status. Help.**" He blinked again. "Okay, Death Knight only gets nastier."

"I don't think I want you to teach me that job after all," Missus Fluffbear squeaked, watching the zombies who weren't chasing them feeding on their fallen comrades. "That's really not Yorgum's um... style. Ooooh, levels!"

And indeed, now that the rolling waves of sheep were done, the party was reaping the rewards. In more ways than one, as Madeline searched the suffocated midboss for gold, and Zuula hunted for other items.

Threadbare was no exception to the gain.
You are now a level 13 Cave Bear!
CON+10
WIS +10
Armor +5
Endurance +5
Mental Fortitude +5

You are now a level 8 Duelist!
+3 AGI
+3 DEX
+3 STR

You are now a level 9 Duelist!
+3 AGI
+3 DEX
+3 STR

You are now a level 16 Golemist!
INT+5
WILL +5

"You leveled golemist again? So quickly?" Cecelia said, taking a break from checking her own status to look at the party screen. "This has to be because you're double dipping. Taking in experience every time we win a fight."

"More like dipping sevenfold," Garon pointed out. "Besides the cats and Fluffbear and Graves, we're all earning him experience. And that's not counting the Golem Guardians boost that you guys are getting. And the Creator's Guardians boost." Garon sighed. "We need to reshuffle. Marva, would you be upset if you went back in the pack?"

"Not at all," Cecelia's double said. "If you're sure you don't need me anymore, Lord." She smiled at Threadbare.

"It's fine. You've done plenty. Thank you!" He hugged her, and golden light flared.

You have healed Prinses Seselia 140 points!

Your Innocent Embrace skill is now level 15!

Back in she went, and as zombie sheep collapsed in the distance, their animation timers up, the group reshuffled the party.

Fluffbear got tucked in with Pulsivar, Mopsy, and Graves, who immediately animated the Wolf as a slavering, red-eyed ghoul. Zuula talked Pulsivar and Mopsy into letting it be. Graves also rummaged around in the pack and pulled out a black, twisted wand. "It's tight enough in here I might have to drain the charges left in this thing," he decided.

"That's the one from that Arxus guy, who tried to taunt ya in the fort, ain't it?"

"Yep," Graves said. "Just a drain-life wand with a hair trigger. Can suck someone dry in a matter of seconds."

Everyone else went in Threadbare's party, and Garon's old group sighed in relief as Threadbare's twin animator and Golemist buffs amped up their stats. Not by a HUGE amount, but enough to give them another edge.

Your Creator's Guardians skill is now level 28!

Your Creator's Guardians skill is now level 29!

Your Creator's Guardians skill is now level 30!

"Here. De crowning touch." Zuula offered Threadbare a wolfshide cloak.

"Where did that come from?" He glanced over to the slavering, ghouled where wolf, and didn't see any bare patches, beyond a few wounds.

"Don't ask how loot drop. Just put on de cape."

"What does it do?"

"Enhance natural weapons. Like, oh, bear claws."

"What?" Madeline said. "Oooh! I could... I... nah, you eahned that one the hahd way. But if you find a bettah cape, I got dibs on yah old one."

"Adjust Outfit," Threadbare said, and snapped the cloak tight in his hands until it was teddy sized. Then it went around him like a mantle.

Your Adjust Outfit skill is now level 5!

Cecelia got the Sheep's fleece that it had worn, which evidently made the wearer seem less threatening to monsters. Then it was time to get moving, before the wooly bullies and their midboss minder reformed.

The rest of the trip across the field went a lot easier. Refreshed and refilled for the most part by their level-ups, the party dispatched the remaining, fairly-small Wooly Bully herd with little trouble.

About the only thing that gave them pause was a herd of sheep-like humanoids in bikinis pursued by a very excited giant in a kilt waving a barrel of alcohol that Graves announced to be watered-down scotch, after the fight was done. But the wandering scotchman and the beautiful sheeple weren't that hard to put down, and the group was through the distant archway and into the far tower of Jotunher before anything else found them.

CHAPTER 9: LARGE AND IN CHARGE

The party was confronted by a stairwell, with signs pointing up and down. The one pointing up read "Tightens." The one pointing down read "Luusens."

And immediately, Threadbare's nose flared at a familiar odor.

Your Scents and Sensibility skill is now level 21!

"I smell gunpowder," he announced. "The Lurker is close."

"Up or down?" Cecelia asked.

"I don't know." Threadbare said, sniffing at the stairs going in both directions. "All I know is that a gun got fired around here at some point."

"Up," said Madeline. "This dungeon, tallah is bettah, right? So the dungeon wants you to go to the tallest place. That's wheah he's heading."

"If you want, I can scout ahead," Kayin offered. "But…"

"Yeah. It might not be you who returns, just The Lurker wearing your face. Since he's near, we need to stick together. Come on."

"One minute," said Threadbare, patting Pulsivar's back. **"Bodyguard Pulsivar."**

Your Bodyguard skill is now level 9!

The big cat had come way too near to losing another life against that wolf. He might not have many ways to help protect him, but Threadbare would take what hits he could for his fuzzy brother.

Thus readied, he led the way up the stairs, with Missus Fluffbear falling in on the flank.

When they found the first enormous giant corpse, he knew they were on the right track.

"Hurry!" He urged, eyes hunting around, buffed and keen, looking for the sneakiest of the Hand.

BANG!

The gunshot sounded close! Threadbare and the rest upped the pace.

Through an opened set of double doors, past a few wine presses, over a few screws and giant-sized screwdrivers, past a giant-sized set of furniture currently disassembled with some incomprehensible instructions and a plate of meatballs next to it, the group made their way through the now-emptied giant-sized living area that for no reason they could tell had blue arrows on the floor. Occasionally they passed common household items with little namecards next to them, on which were written symbols that were presumably words in the giant tongue. Either that, or someone had really disliked an incorrectly-assembled wardrobe and very much misspelled the name they'd given it when they called it a DOMBAS.

Finally, they burst through a set of double doors, to witness the tail-end of an epic battle.

A three-foot tall teddy bear, with a wicked grin, leaped from floating rock to floating block, dancing around a blue-shirted giant wielding a pick. On the back of the shirt was a simple name tag that read "Steve." Below the ruins of what once was a floor, lay a void of inky blackness... the flagstones that were remaining were floating in midair, suspended by nothing in particular. As they watched, the giant brought the pick down in a flurry of chops, narrowly missing the teddy bear as he backflipped to a new set of blocks. The picked block crumbled and fell into nothingness...

...and a series of knives sunk into the flagstone Steve was standing on, destroying it in a rush of red numbers. Steve fell silently into the abyss, and a door across the hall shuddered open, revealing a treasure chest.

Then, as the toys started to head into the room, hopping gingerly from block to block, the teddy bear glanced over and grinned, quickdrawing his pistol. "Too easy!"

BANG!

Cecelia squawked as her block got shot out from under her, and she fell into the abyss...

"Call Golem!" Threadbare shouted.

Your Call Golem skill is now level 3!

...and instantly appeared in Threadbare's arms. He sat her on Pulsivar's back, as he urged the cat toward The Lurker.

"You cheater!" The bad parody of him yelled, in a horrible imitation of his voice. Then it hopped with incredible agility, making long bounds across widely-separated blocks, before darting through the newly-opened door.

"Don't take risks!" Garon urged, and the toys, along with their living companions, made it slowly around the mostly-intact outer edge of the arena, hurrying through the door just before it started to close.

"What is spleef?" Zuula wondered, as she held up a t-shirt emblazoned with the words SPLEEF CHAMPION

"Where did you get that?" Glub asked.

"Treasure chest tucked in one corner. Shame to let it be."

Garon shook his head, looking around the room. "Mom, that was risky."

"Dis is not risky?" Zuula pointed straight ahead.

Before them lay a long hall, at the very top of Jotunher. The stone room was full of pillars upon pillars, some wooden and some stone. To either side, diamond-shaped windows let in light, lining the hall and casting golden beams down at the end, on the massive throne and its giant occupant. Easily twenty feet tall, with a club half her size at her side, the massive blue woman was draped in a toga and wearing a set of golden laurels. She had one massive foot up on the opposite knee and was busy filing her toenails. Her waistline and stomach betokened many a good meal, but her arms were no less muscled than the guards downstairs had been.

"Where did he get to?" Threadbare said, looking around, at the many, many sight-obstructing pillars, and the countless patches of shadow broken by bright light. It was an ambusher's paradise.

But Threadbare and his party weren't the ones being ambushed, as it turned out.

"Hey! My name is Threadbare!" The Lurker shouted, stepping out from behind a pillar and doffing his hat to the giant.

"No!" Garon shouted, running forward, waving his arms. "He's a—"

The giant lady looked up at The Lurker's disguised form and stared with confusion... that turned to a grin. Such an adorable little thing!

"Fuck you, fartsniffer!" Fake Threadbare shot her in the face, turned around, slapped his bear ass, and ran giggling out of sight behind a different pillar.

"Oh shit," Glub said, as the lady rose to her feet, grabbing up the club, and slamming it against the floor so hard the entire room shook. "It's on!" he went flying, tumbling to the ground... as did most of the rest of the toys and Graves, too.

And Threadbare as well, rolling out into the light and looking up just in time to see the giant matron's gaze fix on his, blood dripping out of the bullet wound in her cheek, and murder writ large in her eyes...

The Giant Jarl strode toward the little bear, club raised high. It was stone, an ancient column of some sort that had grips hammered into it, and it whistled as it came down at Threadbare.

Who, fortunately, was agile enough to not be there when it struck down so hard that the floor shook again.

AGI+1

Your Dodge skill is now level 13!

He looked back to see Pulsivar scrambling away, and sighed, chasing after the cat. Though as giant footsteps echoed behind him, he wasn't sure he was doing Pulsivar any favors at all.

"Over here! Quickly!" He heard his voice call and saw a furry hand beckon from behind a pillar... then looked past him to see Kayin and Graves hesitating.

"That's not me!" he shouted. Then threw in **"Guard Stance!"** because here came that club again—

—and this time he didn't escape.

It caught him in the back, knocking him into the air, to thump against the wall, then bounce to the floor. A red '139' drifted up, and he gasped, rolled to the side, and stood up.

Grinning, the giant pulled her club back and took a few more steps toward him—

—and then his friends swarmed her from all sides.

"I **challenge** you!" He called to her, dusting his shoulder off—

Jarl Greta Sumvonesdottir resisted your Challenge!

—but his efforts didn't get through her Cool. Unlike The Lurker, he hadn't honed his social skills to insanely good levels.

Which was a problem, because he saw, from his slightly removed perspective, that another Graves had entered the fight.

"Look out! A fake Graves!" But his small voice was lost in the din, and the bellowing, and the clamor of the fight. Horrified, he saw one of the Graves move up behind Cecelia and glance down at her unguarded back...

"I **Challenge** you, Lurker!" He yelled through the Minorphone.

Your Challenge skill is now level 11!

Startled, the false Graves and Cecelia whipped around to stare at him, and both caught a giant boot for their trouble—

—as what he'd thought was the real Graves shanked Zuula in the back of the head and ran off giggling, shape blurring as he darted behind a pillar. Zuula, enraged, pulled the dagger from her head and threw it at the giant.

"Um..." Threadbare canceled his challenge against the very real Graves, and started dropping Mend Golem spells instead.

Graves, for his part, stood up painfully and whipped out the wand he'd prepared, triggering a three-charge burst and healing himself up to full.

And also getting the giant's full attention.

The Jarl threw off Kayin, who'd been climbing her with claws out the whole way, swept her club around until the cats and Fluffbear backed off, ignored Garon hacking into her boot, and strode toward Graves and Cecelia. She swung the club high in the air...

...and then the Wherewolf ghoul made its attack.

Graves had kept it in the back, Threadbare realized. Waited until the others were clear. He wondered why that was so, for a second...

...then the ghoul leaped up, grabbed her toga, and spewed rancid filth all over her face, and Threadbare stopped wondering.

The blue giant backhanded the ghoul away, then staggered, and as the party watched, her face turned green. Red numbers started slinking up from her... not huge, but it was having an effect.

"Don't just stand there!" Graves yelled, waving the ghoul in again, this time biting and clawing, "Get her!"

Threadbare closed the distance—

—and a trio of knives sunk into his belly, knocking him across the floor. He rose, glaring past the columns, to see his own face grinning back at him, holding up another set of knives, before juggling them into the air and sending them winging at him one at a time. "Dance, golem!" The Lurker shouted.

He tried, but the guy had good aim. Threadbare managed to make it behind a pillar while he had HP left and skilled up a few times while he mended himself. The fight raged past him while he did so. The little bear winced as the ghoul got turned to pulp under one giant heel and checked out the Jarl's hit points with his deathsight.

She'd lost a fifth, all told. Threadbare shook his head. They needed to coordinate. This wasn't undoable... but unfortunately The Lurker realized that, too.

"New plan—" He heard his voice call through the Minorphone. What? No, the magic cone was still on his belt... This had to be another thing the daemon could do.

"—Everyone scatter, I'll tank her for a bit!" He heard The Lurker finish.

"Ignore that!" He yelled through his own minorphone. "Stay on her together!" He said, running forward... and cringing as his own friends shot him suspicious glares. Glares that faded, as he used the last of the Minorphone's juice to shout at the giant. "I **challenge** you!"

And this time it stuck.

CHA +1

Your Challenge skill is now level 12!

"I've had enough ov hyu leetle bear!" The giant roared, whirling her club in the air and breaking cleanly through a few pillars. **"FIMBULVINTER FROST!"** She bellowed.

And the world turned white.

A snowstorm roared in through the windows, filling the air with flakes and ice, and sending visibility straight to hell.

No! This is the sort of thing The Lurker will…

Will use to get Cecelia, he realized.

"Call Golem," he whispered, and grabbed onto her arm the second she materialized, almost catching her sword in his belly for his troubles.

Your Call Golem skill is now level 4!

She shouted something, but it was lost in the storm.

And then the storm was fading, as fast as it had come, leaving half his party frozen in ice… and a shadow around him, spreading, growing as Cecelia screamed and pointed up—

—then braced herself and shouted, **"Corps a Corps!"**

And it worked.

A foot above Threadbare, her rising blade met the Giant's descending club, and Threadbare gasped as the stone ground on metal above his head, Cecelia's skill allowing her to effectively parry a ten-foot-tall column with an eight-inch-long steel blade.

"Hold her!" Threadbare yelled, heading toward his frozen friends. "I'll free them!"

"I gaht this!" Madeline said. **"Call Faia! Shape Faiah! Minah Elemental!"** Madeline ripped flames into the air, spun them in spirals, de-icing Glub, Zuula, Garon, and Mopsy and Fluffbear, and sending a roiling, bonfire-sized elemental towards the Jarl, who yelped and pulled her club away from Cecelia's desperate clench. The giant backed up, swinging at the fire elemental, trying to simultaneously tag it and stay out of reach of the flames.

"Ectoplasm!" Graves shouted, and a sticky ball of gooey translucent stuff splattered against her boot, binding it to a nearby pillar. The giant stumbled, then shrieked as the flames burned her…

…until knives shot out from behind her, whistling through the fire elemental and dispersing it. Angrily, the giant started to pull her boot away from the sticky ghost goo.

And Threadbare jumped, as wood clattered up behind him, turned as Garon waved. "We need to shut down The Lurker!" he whispered. "We can't fight him and this giant at the same time! Ideas! Give me some!"

Threadbare thought. He racked his brain, put his high intelligence and wisdom to work, ignoring the raging battle behind him, ignoring the yelps of his friends and the bellows of the enraged giant.

And finally, he came up with something he thought might work.

"I'll have to leave the party. For a minute. And I'll need you to do something. Here's what…"

After he heard it, Garon grimaced and looked at the group. "I can give you half a minute. Beyond that we'll have casualties!"

"Half a minute it is!" Threadbare said, rummaging in his clothes and running over to Cecelia. "Tell me when!"

Cecelia was very surprised when he asked for her help, but she nodded when she heard what he wanted. "In my pouch! Just tear the whole thing off my belt!" she said, lunging forward to shield Madeline against a nasty club strike and sucking down a red '52' for her trouble.

Threadbare chased after her, grabbed her pouch, and ran away, rummaging through it.

"Now!" Garon yelled, and Threadbare hoped that it WAS Garon, because if not…

…no time to worry about it. He left the party, and started casting, whispering under his breath, and dropping things in his hat.

"Hold her!" he called back to Garon, as he moved into the light of one of the big windows. "I've almost got the daemon ward enchanted—"

And abruptly the hat was whisked from his hands, as The Lurker darted out of hiding and snapped it onto his own head. "I think not!"

The Lurker's triumphant grin lasted for all of a second.

And then it turned to a horrified rictus, as things squirmed under the hat and bit into his head.

Animated mice. Five little cloth mice. The things he'd used to scout ahead, through dollseye, now animated and with the full force of his will backing their bites.

The hat stuck, as The Lurker found when he tried to remove it, clamping to his head with animated fury. The daemon panicked, twisting and struggling, managing to get part of the brim free as it wrapped around him, struggling to keep him grappled…

"Now!" Threadbare yelled, whipping aside when he heard the hooves clattering behind him—

—And Garon yelled **"Rammit!"** as he collided headfirst into The Lurker…

…knocking him through the window and away.

Garon has invited you to his party!

"Oh good!" Threadbare said, running back to the fight. "Nobody died!"

Though it wasn't for lack of trying, a glance at the party screen told him. He settled in to tanking and healing his friends up.

And without The Lurker interfering, it went much more smoothly.

Fluffbear switched on her Clarifying Aura, using Righteous Taunt to switch attention to her whenever the damage got too much for him. Glub doubled up on that with his Song of Clarity, and between the two of them, the healers had enough juice to keep things going so that the rest of the group could focus on damage.

It still wasn't an easy task. All the knights and the bears had to get a rotation going, swap tanking duties so the rest could recover. And Graves ended up burning every last charge in his drain life wand, recovering from a critical hit. But they made it work, and though there were a few close calls, the Jarl's hit points dropped, and dropped, and dropped.

But while it was going on, Threadbare kept a keen eye on the entrance. The Lurker would be back, he was certain of it. But he'd have to take the long way around. If he could've climbed up via a shortcut he would've, Threadbare knew, but he'd moved through the dungeon like anyone else. So sooner or later, he'd be back.

It did turn out to be later, as Madeline, flagging, and low on Moxie, managed to recharge just enough to get off one last Burninate.

The flames died, and there was a big-sized Threadbare, three-feet tall, looking in at the scene.

He saw a giant on her last legs, a group that was battered and drained but still going, and two resting cats, licking their wounds.

And as The Lurker's eyes fastened on Pulsivar, and his grin widened, Threadbare realized what he was going to do.

Three knives left The Lurker's hands, spinning mercilessly towards Pulsivar, wounded Pulsivar, faithful Pulsivar, who looked up with whiskers quivering.

Time stretched as Threadbare dived, no time to call out, only time to run, run and hope he could get close enough to save his friend—

And Pulsivar leaped, straight up in the air.

The first knife spun lazily around, tore through the bobcat's paw, sending a red '62' upward. Threadbare leaped—

—the second knife missed both of them, whirling just past Pulsivar's head…

…and the third and final knife sunk deep into Threadbare's back, as his bodyguard skill kicked in, blocking the strike that would have taken Pulsivar between the eyes.

They hit the floor together, and knife still sticking out of his back, Threadbare scrambled to Pulsivar and hugged him with all his might.

You have healed Pulsivar for 150 points!

Your Innocent Embrace skill is now level 16!

He reeled as sanity left him, reserves tapped, only the song refilling him now, but slowly, slowly…

And when he turned around, The Lurker was gone.

"Where…" he said—

BOOM!

The stone club fell to the ground.

The Jarl fell to her knees.

"Yes!" Garon whooped.

And then the giant collapsed, slumping to the floor.

"Everyone!" Threadbare said, "I've lost track of The Lurker!"

Then his view was crowded by words, as the levels hit.

You are now a level 16 Toy Golem

+2 to all attributes

You are now a level 13 Ruler!

CHA+3

LUCK+3

WIS+3

You are now a level 8 Scout!

AGI+3

PER+3

WIS+3

You are now a level 10 Duelist!

AGI+3

DEX+3

STR+3

You have unlocked the Disarm skill!

Your Disarm skill is now level 1!

You have unlocked the Riposte skill!

Your Riposte skill is now level 1!

You are now a level 13 Animator!

DEX+3

INT +3

WILL +3

You are now a level 17 Golemist!

INT +5

WILL +5

You are now a level 18 Golemist!
INT +5
WILL +5

"Remember, he's going to try to seal the dungeon!" Cecelia said, looking around. "I'm not sure how you do that, but…"

"There's a chambah, there's a way into a chambah," Madeline said, taking to the air and flapping around the hall. "Look foah green! Green light!"

"Yes!" Zuula cheered.

"You found it?" Garon charged back to her.

"No, she gots dese," Zuula waved the giant-sized set of golden laurels. "Dey let you rest!"

"Not the time Mom!" The wooden minotaur snapped, then returned to searching…

…as reality rippled.

"Oh shit," Graves said, patching himself up.

Then, from behind them, a surprised warble. A surprised FELINE warble.

Threadbare turned, staring…

…at Pulsivar. Pulsivar, whose form was shifting, and flickering, not quite in time with the reality pulse, not to the dungeon's rhythm, but to his own.

For Pulsivar had just hit level twenty-five.

And he'd managed, with one life left to him after The Lurker's botched attack, to rank up.

The rest of the group spread out, shouting, looking for the dungeon core entrance, but Threadbare knew that it was already too late. So instead, he sighed, said **"Call Outfit,"** and put his hat back on his head, then went over and sat down next to his friend and held the cat's paw between his own as Pulsivar worked through the changes.

"Mrrrp?" Pulsivar asked him, stretching out with one black paw, as his hide shimmered…

And though the paw didn't seem to come anywhere near Threadbare, the little bear felt Pulsivar patting his face.

Curious, Threadbare reached out with one of his own paws, and Pulsivar's face rubbed against it… fur wrinkling.

Except the face was a good meter away. And bigger, much bigger. It felt bigger, too, as he petted Pulsivar, going by touch alone. The cat felt like he was twice his bobcat size, or more.

Threadbare reached out with both arms, and the big cat leaned into his embrace, invisibly, while his image flickered and firmed up, showing two disembodied teddy bear arms hugging him. Yep, definitely larger than he had been.

"I wonder..." Threadbare climbed up on the unseen cat's back...

...and his own image appeared, feet away from him, mounted on Pulsivar as Threadbare himself faded from view.

And though the little bear had no way of knowing it, his oldest friend had become that rarest of all feline monsters;

A dreaded Misplacer Beast!

But that was something to ponder later, as blackness winked away, and green numbers flickered...

...and coalesced into a blue crystal, shining with red numbers, in the hands of Threadbare's hatless, three-foot tall evil twin.

And then the world was full of falling giants.

And rains of food.

And kegs and cups full of liquor falling to the ground.

And shrieking sheep.

All these things and more exploded out into the space where the dungeon had once filled, rendered from a scenic, jagged gorge and pillar, with a mighty hall...

...down to a rather small mountain valley, with some half-built huts, a few patches of raggedy grass, and an ordinary-looking hillside.

"Vhat de hell. Vhat de hell hyu done hyu vorthless little bear!" The Jarl bellowed, much shorter and fatter now that she was out of her master's pillar. She struggled to her feet, hefted a club rather more dinged and busted up than it had seemed through her master's projection, and glared around... until her eyes fixed on Threadbare.

Around her, at least two dozen giants, mostly women, lay groaning or comatose. Food and items of loot lay strewn all over them.

"Not me!" Threadbare said, pointing at a running figure, heading upslope. "Him!"

The figure let out a laugh...

...that ended in a surprised squeak, as it crested the ridge.

"Hello there!" King Grundi's voice boomed out. "I brought cannons!"

And then the world was thunder, as The Lurker dodged for his life.

The dwarf lord had come for daemon blood, and he'd brought company.

"I don't know vhat's going on, but I'm still blaming hyu!" The Giant Jarl pointed down at Threadbare...

...who looked up at her, solemnly.

"I'm sorry. Would you like a hug?"

The giant queen paused, confused. "Vhat?"

Threadbare pointed at her side, and the hilts of small daggers protruding from her generous rump. "I'm guessing he called you nasty names like fartsniffer and threw daggers at you until you chased him. He's very good at that."

"Vell hyes, hyes hyu did."

"No, it wasn't him lady; he was with us the whole time," Madeline said, laying a wing across Threadbare... or trying to and missing. "The hell?"

"It's Pulsivar's new thing, I'll explain later." He hopped off and toddled toward the giant, arms open wide.

She raised her club, glaring. "Up hyu lot! Up and get him..." she looked around at the somnolent giants, as they refused to obey. "Vhat's wrong vith hyu?"

And then the little bear was embracing her furry boot and light glowed.

You have healed Jarl Greta Sumvonesdottir for 160 Points!
Your Innocent Embrace skill is now level 17!
Your Fascination skill is now level 9!
Your Adorable skill is now level 35!

"Oh." Jarl Greta said, easing her club down. "Vhell, I guess it vasn't hyu, den."

"It was him. Want to go hit him a bunch?" Threadbare said, pointing at his howling, dodging duplicate, who was having a very bad day of it as canister shot raked the hit points from him one blast at a time.

And as The Lurker managed to stagger down the hill, with the first waves of dwarves in hot pursuit, he slowed as Threadbare's group came charging from behind, the furry little bear clutching the giant woman's frosted braid tightly and pointing at the daemon with one tiny claw.

The Lurker skidded to a stop... glanced around... and headed for the nearest sheer cliff.

He couldn't go back through the mountain, the dwarves blocked that entrance. He couldn't go away from the mountain, he'd hit the Oblivion square on, and he had no clue of Jarrik's trick for navigating it.

But as they watched, he changed, into something that was all spindly arms and legs, and big claws.

"He's going to go over the mountain!" Garon shouted in horror.

"Like fun he is!" Madeline said, pumping her wings harder.

"No, stay back! One on one he'll munch you!" Garon called.

Dwarven musket fire pinged and rattled on the stones around him, as The Lurker, Dungeon core flickering red and blue in one clenched hand, leaped twenty feet up to the sheer cliff of Brokeshale mountain and started to climb.

"Cannons! Get cannons on him!" Grundi called.

"No good! They won't elevate that high fast enough!" A dwarven voice called back.

"Jarrik. Jarrik!" Garon called, and his brother was there, coat thrown over his shoulder, squinting up at the rapidly retreating Lurker. "Swear Fealty to me!"

"What?"

"I'll get you the quest and buff you up just fucking bring that thing down!"

"Sure bro, yer the boss. **I swear.**"

Garon pointed at The Lurker. **"Organize Minions! Fight The Battles!"**

Jarrik measured the distance. Hundreds of yards already, dozens more vanishing by the second. The thing was built to climb and climb fast.

"Musket." He said, reaching out to the nearest dwarf.

"Do it!" Garon screamed, when the dwarf hesitated.

And Jarrik snapped the sturdy dwarven rifle up in front of his eye, sighted down it, and chanted. **"Aim. Far Shot. Crippling Shot."**

Then he sighted a bit more, the musket tracking as he focused, focused—

BANG!

—and fired.

A pause.

Red drifted up from the daemon to the sky. The Lurker stood stock still.

Then the thing stretched and flailed, falling backward, falling downward, shifting as it went—

And Jarrik's coat went flying. **"Two Gun Mojo! Quick Draw!"**

BANG!

BLAM!

KRAK!

KRAK!

BLAM!

BANG!

The coat hit the ground.

Four smoking pistols hit the ground.

And Jarrik stood there, the two pistols left in his hands smoking, his bandoliers empty of guns, squinting as five red numbers rolled out of the falling Lurker so quickly they appeared as one mixed, mangled, mess.

Which, incidentally, best described what happened to The Lurker when he hit the rocky valley floor from his fall.

The dungeon core bounced free, skittered, cracked against a rock, and Threadbare and his friends collectively held their breath...

…but it was made of tougher stuff, and merely ricocheted out to land at the feet of the Jarl.

"It knows its master," she grunted in satisfaction, and reached down for it—

—then froze, as about thirty dwarves brought their muskets up to bear on her, cocking hammers back in unison.

And Threadbare and his party all heard the chime of a quest completed. The Lurker had been taken down. Not alive, as they had hoped, but that was fine.

Garon, though, Garon got a slightly different notification and stood there, jaw open in shock.

"I… oh my gods."

"What?" Zuula asked.

There came the sound of metal wheels grinding through stony dirt, and King Grundi's kneelchair crested the hill, escorted by the rearguard. "Well! That's the bastard dead again," said the king, grimly. "That fucker's taken too many a' mine down, but at least we don't have to worry about him for another month or two."

"Who de hell are hyu! Vhy hyu raiding my stead anyvay?" Jarl Greta said, waggling her club at him and almost getting shot for her troubles.

"Guys," Garon said, vibrating with excitement.

"Your stead? Why did ya put a perfectly good dungeon in my land!"

"Hyour land? Ve vas here first!" Greta scowled and nudged one of her groaning subjects with a foot. "Come on, get up, ve gots some claim jumpers to run off."

"Now hold on here, you great blue tart!" the King snapped, shaking an aged fist. "Pretty sure we were here first, just underground, that's all! It's still our land!"

"May I speak, please?" Threadbare offered from the giant's shoulder.

"Vhat?" She turned to glare at him, a glare that softened as he patted her face reassuringly.

"You're using an outside part of these lands. He's using an inside part. I really don't see the problem."

"De problem is he's on my land, pointing der little boomsticks at me."

"The problem is that it isn't her land in the first place!" the King said, glaring around. "And look at this loot! I know half of this loot! It belongs to my people, who died in your deathrap of a dungeon!"

"Hey, not my fault hyu little guys kept crashing my party!"

"The party that you made illegally in my lands!"

"Ahem," Cecelia cleared her throat. "Sir?"

"What is it, my dear?"

"Guys!" Garon said, jumping up and down.

"Hold on," Cecelia said. "I was going to point out, sir, that you're at war."

"Yes! Which is precisely why we don't need a tribe of troublesome giants—"

"A tribe of troublesome giants who my father definitely would not be expecting to fight."

Silence, then, broken by Garon's wooden quivering.

"Huh. Huh!" Grundi said. Then he looked up at the frowning Jarl, who had her arms crossed, leaning on her club. "That's... a point. Hum."

"Fight who to the vhat now?" The Jarl said, confused.

"Someone we'll pay you a lot of money to fight." Grundi said.

"Bah. Money ve gots."

"Do you have three kegs of Sunfire mead?"

That made her pause.

"Hyu ain't got notting like dat," she said, staring at him like he'd announced that he'd bottled the sun. Which was a pretty apt comparison, as anyone who'd ever been fortunate enough to actually taste the stuff could tell you.

"Oh, I do. It's the last of my private stock, from the northern breweries before we were cut off."

"Hyu svear to me it's real. And mine if ve fight for you. All of dem."

"It's real. By my beard and axe, it's real and yours if you fight honorably."

"Done!" she said, offering her enormous hand for a shake.

That settled, Threadbare and his friends turned to Garon.

"Guys, I just got a job unlock." Garon said. "A tier two."

"Okay. So what's the fuss?" Madeline asked.

"It's for Guild Master."

That brought silence. Silence that spread to where the giant and the dwarf were settling terms.

"I can make guilds. It... I need to read the help screens, there's so much stuff here. This... this changes everything." Garon sat down with a bump.

"How?" Cecelia asked. "Just... how?"

"You have to be a Ruler, enough to assign or share a King's Quest. Then you have to lead a party and use both mercenary and ruler skills to complete it. And it has to be a challenging one, requiring multiple parties to complete, and you have to lead one of them. Well..." Garon gestured around at his friends, and himself. "We did that. We can do this. We can form a Guild. We can crack level twenty five."

"No," King Grundi said, rolling over. "I'm sorry lad, you can't."

Behind him, the Jarl went to try and rouse her people, not realizing just what kind of hangovers they'd gotten from decades of continuous partying.

"What? It says right there," Garon pointed at nothing. "All I have to do is say "Form Guild The Threadbarren, and... what? What the hell?"

"Aye. It did the same thing when I tried," King Grundi sighed.

"But..." Garon looked around, and the valley, and at the Oblivion rolling in the distance. "We're not in a dungeon."

"Garon?" Threadbare asked, as suspicions rose in his mind, "What exactly happened when you tried?"

"It told me that I can't create a guild while I'm in a dungeon."

"Aye. Just as it told me when I discovered the job, four years ago, and tried it myself." Grundi said, looking at Garon with sympathy.

"Maybe this counts because Jotunher was so close?" Madeline said, rubbing her muzzle with one claw. "We could go somewheah else, and —"

"No," Grundi said. "There's no place in Cylvania that isn't in a dungeon. The whole land's a dungeon."

"He's a midboss. That's why he can die and come back," Threadbare realized, pointing at The Lurker's corpse, which was already fading.

"Aye, and King Melos, damn his foolish eyes, is the dungeon's master."

"How?" Cecelia asked, turning her ceramic eyes to the ancient dwarf. "How do you know this?"

King Grundi turned, painfully, staring past them. And as one the group turned, to follow his gaze...

...but there was nothing on the horizon, save for the black sheet of the Oblivion.

"We helped turn it into one," King Grundi said. "They came to us for help, you see. It all started with the Seven, with their wizard, Grissle..."

INTERLUDE 2: KING'S LEGACY

The moon rose high through the ornate stained glass windows, as six heroes and one golem slammed open the heavy wooden doors to the shrine.

Dark, haunting organ music skirled high to the rafters, sending swarms of bats screeching out into the night, flowing through and past the intrepid vampire hunters who had come to put paid to the darkest of vampires; the dread Count Joculah!

"And so you are here..." said the vampire, brown fingers lifting from white keys, as the organ fell silent. The vampire's brown hands wormed his way over his brown suit, and smoothed brown hair, testing and touching as only those who never see themselves in mirrors do, making sure that he looked his best for his would-be slayers.

"Die Monster!" Melos bellowed, leveling a blade that glowed with the leering faces of the trapped daemons within, red and hellish and surging with raw power as he led the charge. "I'm your **Challenge! Come face my Entropic Strike!**"

"You don't belong in this world!" Rezzak yelled from behind the charging demon knight, raising his feathered staff high, and slamming it to the ground. **"Angelic Pact! Summon Greater Cherub! Summon Greater Cherub! Summon Greater Cherub!"**

"Fools! It was mortal men who— gah!" the vampire yelled, dodging as Melos' red blade came way too close to splitting him right down his widow's peak. "Can't a man monologue first?"

"A man? Yes!" The woman in green stepped out from behind Rezzak, pointing at him with a wand in each hand. "A monster? No. Get him, Emmet!"

As glowing, silvery babies with bows and arrows faded in all around the group, a hulking suit of armor shambled through the doorway and came in on Melos' flank. The Demon Knight grinned to see it, grinned behind his helm as he fought the vampire, laying into him with strikes that left dust and scars with every slash. The wounds from Entropic Strike couldn't be healed, not while the spell was active.

Then flames wisped around him, as Sabi went into business. The red-silk-garbed woman slid out from behind a tapestry, twisting her hands, as she directed the flames to sear the elder undead. Brown cheeks quirked in a smile under a red veil as the creature burned... burned until he folded his cloak around him, and his flesh started to ripple.

"You think you have a chance?" Count Joculah chuckled, then exploded into bats. Melos brought his shield up, and the daemon faces in it gobbled and chomped at the flying rodents as they swirled around him. *So long as they stay out of my helmet, it's good. It's fine. Besides, the fool's played right into our hands. Come on Sabi...*

"Fireball!"

Even with his flame resistant gear, he felt the blast wave, grunted as a red '146' whipped out of him. But as bad as it was for Melos, it was leagues worse for the vampire. Bats shrieked and screamed and swirled in all directions.

"This is the point where I miss Grissle the most!" Graham shouted, as he put down a rain of crossbow-flung stakes. **"Rapid Fire! Rapid Fire!"** Vampire bats shrieked and fell, dead or paralyzed from their wood allergies. "Grissle would have been telling us how many hit points the thing had left by now!"

"Oh, I'll just pick up Necromancer then!" Melos called over, jauntily. "Got to give you SOME reason to hate me, after all."

"Don't get me started," Rezzak sighed, as his summoned cherubs went about their business, flapping after the farther-ranging bats and shooting at them with arrows of angelic light. "That's like a drunkard switching over to chewing brainburn weed."

"Leave the arguments for the tavern!" Amelia snapped, keeping her wands going and firing lightning bolts through the few bats that came her way, crisping them with scarcely a glance. In among them, Emmet swung his massive metal gauntlets, trying to catch and crush what bats he could.

And occasionally, from the shadows, a throwing star would spin out and catch a bat on the wing, turning it into a bat pinned to the wall. It was Jane, Just Jane, doing her thing.

Melos simply waited.

And when the Count reformed, the demon knight yelled "Ears!" before dropping his weapon and shield and clapping both gauntlets to his own ears, then ordering the demons writhing within his armor to scream.

And scream they did, as the sound ripped through his skull at point blank range, scrambling his sanity, sending him to his knees...

...but safe, as he saw the count mouth words, words he couldn't hear.

The Count's Command had been the doom of many an adventuring party. Many had fought their way up through the secret entrance in Cylvania City's catacombs, up to the impossible castle that loomed over a nightmare version of the city, up to the very topmost tower through hordes of vampires, bats, werewolves, lesser undead, and weird snake-tentacled heads that always seemed to try to attack you when you were climbing narrow and slippery stairs.

It was easy to die in the Count's domain, to any number of horrible monsters.

But those who managed to survive until they'd found the Count himself?

All too often, they died at the hands of their friends. The count's charisma was undeniable and his patterns well-mapped. After he went to bats, then would come the commands...

Once the count finished speaking, Melos popped a pill from his pouch and swallowed it, scooping up his sword and shield, and his hearing returned...

...just in time to hear a man's voice laughing maniacally.

"Oh for fuck's sake Graham," Melos said, taking a big risk and taking his eyes off Count Joculah. "This is what happens when you don't wear earplugs!"

"Everyone dies! So commands the master!" Graham hissed, dropping his crossbow, and making a yanking motion with one arm.

No! "Slot machine!" Melos yelled, and he and the four remaining sane friends jumped clear, as a metal slot machine as tall and broad around as an elephant slammed through the roof, right onto the ground. The handle jerked, and symbols clicked by...

...8...

....9....

Melos held his breath. If it was a ten, they were all dead. It was that simple.

...8... DING!

"We'll need heals! Get healing!" he called to Rezzak—

—and then the wave hit. He watched '160' rise from everyone's skull, then the pain struck him, and he gasped. Straight through armor, straight through everything. The cherubs poofed back to their home plane, and even Emmet groaned in pain.

"Muahhhahahhahha!" wheezed the count.

"I'll get Graham! The rest of you on the old bastard! Watch it, he'll go full daemon when he starts to lose," Melos shouted over his shoulder.

Graham under the enemy's control wasn't a worst-case scenario. But it was close. The man had started his adventuring career as a conman, a Grifter, and a good one. They'd had a run in with him in Upper Derope, when he tried to talk Sabi out of her pants... in both ways, as after he'd enjoyed a night with her, he'd tried to abscond with her enchanted trousers. Melos and the rest had woken to the smell of burning, an irate innkeeper, and a very chastened and nude Graham, quite sorry for the whole affair.

Sabi had dragged him along as a translator to help pay off his debt to the innkeeper, and the man had eventually matured, expanding his horizons. Like Melos had, he'd given up an empty and... unsavory... existence in order for a life of adventure and heroics.

And along the way he'd become an Archer. Then, when he got high enough level to accidentally unlock it, he had become a Gambler.

Which, when combined with a Grifter's trick of Silent Activation, made for some nasty times.

The trick with Gamblers, Melos had worked out, was to not give them time to fire off their big skills. Get them focusing less on the things that could wipe out your party, and more on defending themselves.

And also, since the bastards were so hard to hit, to target pools that weren't so well-defended as their hit points and agility.

"I'm **Challenge**-ing you, Graham. **Aura of Fear. Staredown.**" He said, advancing as Graham backpedaled and groaned as a green '67' ripped loose from his skull. That was sixty-seven points of Moxie he WOULDN'T have for Silent Activations. Melos stomped after him, chasing him around the gothic cathedral that capped the tower, ignoring his friends fighting the vampire behind him. His wife had Emmet, and Emmet was enough. The fight would be there when Melos was done. He trusted everyone at his back... hell, he trusted Graham, too. At least when the man was in his right mind, anyway.

Normally Graham was unflappable. That was the name of the class feature that boosted his cool, anyway. But that aura ate into his defense, rendered his normal cocky self-assuredness much reduced.

Still, the Gambler hadn't gotten this far by being a pushover.

"Good thing I've got an **Ace in the Hole!**" Graham said, snapping a handful of glowing cards out of nowhere. **"Razor Cards! Crippling Shot! Rapid Fire!"** The handful of cards blurred, as Graham edged away, backing around, throwing cards into Melos, cards that sliced into his shield and armor, making them bleed and scream.

The daemons within the armor took the hits, took the pain, and Melos didn't. **"Mend,"** Melos chanted, as he weathered the storm of cards, ignoring it as best he could, ignoring the one that split his helm and came half an inch to cleaving through his eyes. **"Mend. Mend."** He said over and over again.

Graham was nimble. Graham was lightly armored.

And Graham didn't look out behind him.

"Dispel Magic!" Rezzak shouted, as soon as Graham was within range. Graham froze, eyes open. "Got him!" Rezzak confirmed.

"Welcome back," Melos said. "Next time put your damned earplugs in."

"You're the last person to advise anyone on damned anything," Graham snarked and ran back toward the Count and the rest of the fight.

"I think he means thank you," Rezzak said.

"You're very welcome, Graham," Melos smiled, then moved up to take some of the heat off Emmet. The Count had reached one of his final forms already and was busy leaping around the room and breathing vaguely-daemonic fire at the Seven.

"Hey, snaggletooth!" Melos yelled, as the maws on his armor yawned open and glowed with their own flame, and he ran faster... "You're doing it wrong!"

Finally, it was all over. The Count fell, as he had several times before to the most skilled of adventuring groups, and collapsed into a heap of ashes with loot items sticking out.

"Appraise," Amelia snapped. "No curses. Jane?"

Their ninja, Just Jane, materialized out of the darkness. After a few experiences squabbling over loot and dealing with respawning bosses, they'd all agreed it was best to let the Ninja grab the loot. She would anyway.

"Snaggletooth?" Amelia said, moving over and giving Melos a look.

"Best I could do in the heat of the moment."

"Come on, you've got more charisma than that."

"Well, this is the third time I've dusted the Count. Motivation tends to fade once you've got it down to a science. Speaking of which..." Melos glanced around. "Spread out! Look for the glow! You know the drill, people."

It was Graham who found it, ironically. The patch of green under a thoroughly desecrated altar. Emmet got to work shoving it aside, a task that took even the mighty golem's full strength. One by one, the Seven stepped into the portal, emerging into the Dungeon Core Chamber.

Melos was the last, and as he took one last glance around the room, a flicker of movement caught his eye by the door. A small brown-haired girl, wearing a purple-and-green head scarf. Clearly one of the

Bloodsuckah Urchins they'd cleared out in the orphanage level. She'd strayed far.

"Run, little girl," he commanded, whispering **"Staredown"** behind his visor as he glared.

A green '207' burst out from her, and she screamed, dropped the tea service she was carrying, spilled cups of blood over the floor, and fled for her life.

"Still got it," Melos chuckled, as he stepped into the place where logic went to die. Not that he minded... his former life had been good training for places like these.

He joined the rest of the party, as they wove their way through the green pillars, past midbosses and mobs and piles of loot, so many piles of loot. Count Joculah's Castle had been going for years, and so many adventurers had perished here.

And by the time he caught up with his wife, she was standing in front of the Dungeon Master's column, wands ready, Emmet by her side, and the rest of the Seven around the rather disturbed-looking undead. His face was green in the light, and he was older, paunchier than his projection had been.

"You would have gotten away with it, you know," Amelia spoke. The Count stared at her, through the column, saying nothing. He couldn't, as far as Melos could tell. Nobody in the light could talk.

"You could have stayed hidden here, stayed safe. But you let your monsters out to play, and they came out of the catacombs and murdered people above." Amelia shook her head. "Was that vampiric hunger? Driving you and your spawn to seek out flesh blood? Or was it vampiric pride, the colossal arrogance that made you think we wouldn't come for you, once we found your lair?"

Slowly, and with a shaking hand, the Count raised a fist and extended one brown middle finger.

"Oh. So you were just an asshole." Amelia snorted. "Goodbye, Joculah."

Emmet punched into the light, grabbed the Count, and hauled him out. The vampire fought the whole way, but he was weaker, so much weaker than his ideal form had been.

Reality rippled around them as they dusted the vampire.

"Get ready!" Amelia shouted, with ten seconds left on the clock. "Rezzak?"

"On it!" The Invoker slammed a hand to the floor, the second they came back into reality. **"This Hallowed Ground! Circle of Protection!"** Light flared around them, resolved into a six-pointed star in a circle, and Melos winced, as his daemon-infested armor and weapons screamed in unison. He hastily banished them before the metal ruptured entirely, leaving his armor black and dull again.

"Ward against Undead!" Amelia yelled, slamming a vial on the ground. Green dust puffed up and fell into patterns…

…and not a moment too soon, as shrieking vampires, skeletons, ghouls, and worse faded in to the large catacomb chamber that the dungeon had vacated.

There was a pause, as the dungeon creatures looked at each other.

Then at the Seven.

Then down to the floor, emblazoned and glowing with holy symbols.

And with a scream, they burst into flames as the heroes sat back and watched their spells do the work for a change.

At the end of it, Melos was the one to find it. A purple crystal, the size of a small apple, flickering with green numbers. "Such a small thing, to cause so much trouble," he sighed. Then Jane was glaring over his shoulder. "What? I was going to give it to you." He handed it back to the ninja. "Good day, good work," the demon knight said, straightening up. "Waffles?"

"Waffles!" Graham yelled.

And so the mightiest heroes of the realm went and had waffles. And Melos and Amelia went and paid their babysitter, rocked their girl to sleep, and made love sweetly once she was out.

"That's another one down," Amelia whispered, clutching him tight, resting in the afterglow.

"Mm." Melos said, laying still as her fingers traced through his beard. "And how many more will we find next month? I swear, for every one we seal, three more spring up."

Her arms tightened around him. "It'll work out. We'll find a solution."

"Maybe." Melos puffed, feeling his sweat dry on his bare skin. "We've lost so many people. So many promising young adventurers gone to these things. I don't know if there'll be much of a country left if we don't."

"We will," Amelia promised, kissing him.

And a few days later, they did.

*****

"To sum it up, Cylvania will shatter in a matter of years if this keeps going," King Garamundi said, leaning over the table, his gut spreading out around the edge. Eyes harder than flint flicked around the seven spaces of the table, and as they passed over Melos, the King's lips twisted in the way they always did.

The son of a bitch still doesn't trust me. Never will, Melos smiled back, keeping cool, keeping cool. Unconsciously he reached out, rubbed Amelia between the shoulderblades. His wife leaned back into it, but flicked her eyes his way, with what he called her 'srs bznss' look.

And yes, it was, but whatever. The Seven gathered at this table had overcome every difficulty thrown their way. This one would be no different.

Garamundi pointed at the map, moving his finger from the foothills in the north, to the spine of the Wintersgate Mountains curving it to the south as he went. "We're mostly stable along the axis, here. We've got Taylor's Delve holding the Thundering Pass, against the worst of the orc incursions. And the more ambitious Canites, for that matter. Balmor's anchored the north. We've got the center, but..." he gestured to the Raxin plains and drew his finger east. Past Brokeshale Valley, past the steppes, and out all the way to Bharstool. "They're coming west," the King sighed. "They've cracked the riddle of guilds; they're not sharing, and they're coming west, armies spearheaded by loyal troops whom no one else in Disland can match."

"Even so, even with various movement buffs, they're still decades off," Graham said. "Why are you saying years?" Graham was handsome. Graham dressed immaculately. Graham's silver tongue had talked the Seven out of many an unwinnable crisis over the course of their adventures. Graham's charisma was very high...

...but Graham, sadly, had never bothered grinding his intelligence, much. Melos shot Amelia a glance, and she rolled her eyes in response, then glanced back to the King. "Sire? Care to explain it?"

Garamundi shook his head and drew his finger west, naming each land his finger crossed. "Nevergreen. Lower Derope. Canticle. Kai-tan, the Wicked City. And that's BEFORE you get into the Brokecrown Borderlands. None of them can stand against Bharstool without a miracle. They WON'T work together, and all the refugees and fleeing monsters from those nations are going to come west. We're the gate between eastern and western Disland. Us. They're going to flood through the passes, and we don't have the numbers to stop them."

"I'm not so sure I like this talk about stopping refugees," Rezzak spoke up, the angelic-sealed rings on his hands glittering as he gestured. The man was partially deaf so whenever he spoke, his hands did too. Initially, it had annoyed the hell out of Melos, along with his sanctimonious attitude... but the man walked the walk and held himself to the same standards as he did the rest of the world. Melos could respect that.

Hell, it's not like he was a *Nurphite*.

Garamundi leaned back, folded his hands across his ample belly. "The refugees, per se, aren't the problem. Any ruler with brains enough to blow their nose sees the opportunity there. They come bearing wealth, looking for work, and desperate enough to settle in bad areas. Refugees are GOOD. But along with them, come the things that prey on them. Bandits. Warlords. Folks who survived the Bharstool battles and now might see our land as easy pickings... which it is." He sighed and started pointing to the smaller settlements. "The harvestlands to the east and west of Cylvania City *are* easy pickings. We're already having problems enough keeping goblins and roaming monsters out. And once they\ smaller settlements go, it doesn't matter how high the walls along our larger settlements, because we won't have the food to survive at a size large enough to stand against conquerors. And then there's the monsters. Jane?"

The group looked to its most silent member. Hair jagged and black as her body suit, eyes narrowed, Just Jane stared back for a few seconds, before the assassin-turned-ninja found her voice.

Privately, Melos thought it was cute and squeaky. Not that he'd ever tell her that. She was moody and sensitive and had this trick with pressure points that hurt quite a lot.

"The Agents of the Nevergreen told me that the Bharstoi are pillaging every dungeon in every conquered land... and sealing them. They often do not bother to slay the monsters they evict, instead driving them from their lands."

"And since all lands east of them are THEIR lands, that means the monsters go west. And they have a trail of refugees to follow and eat, right up until they'll get to our doorstep. So yes. Years," King Garamundi said, mopping his forehead with a royal handkerchief. "I'm hoping, I'm really hoping, that you can help me come up with a solution. Now, not years down the road, because when the first waves hit? They'll only get bigger, and we'll have less and less time to do anything but deal with them."

The eight of them stared at the map.

"Do the dwarves know what is to come?" Sabi said, the silks of her headdress twisting as she looked from the map to their King. The ribbons woven through her hair gleamed bright red against her dusky skin. She'd come to Cylvania as a refugee herself, dragged along by parents fleeing the echoes of a nasty religious war. Melos had initially had a thing with her, but it hadn't worked out. Date a fire elementalist, get burned, he thought to himself with a chuckle. Then Amelia rubbed his shoulder and he let the old mix of regret and shame go. If it hadn't ended so badly then, he wouldn't have it so good now.

"The dwarves do, actually," came a calm voice from the end of the table. The entire group turned to stare as Grissle rose, his gaunt and withered frame creaking as he leaned on his cane. "I've been in touch with their Delvers society."

"The Delvers. Those rabble rousers?" Garamundi frowned.

"An undeserved reputation. Some rail against the King, it's true. But the wiser among them have been researching the... changeover, as have I." Grissle's white hair was plastered to his scalp with sweat. Some diseases, not even oracles can cure, Melos knew. It ate at his guts, caused Grissle pain every minute of the day. Which was why the man had stepped back from active duty with the Seven and taken on the responsibility of supporting them. He'd made most of their magical gear, including the black iron armor Melos wore at this very minute. The wizard and enchanter pointed with a shaking hand. "They've closed Badgerdoom."

"Really?" Amelia leaned forward. "They finally got around to doing something about the badger swarms?"

"Oh yes. And they have been experimenting with the dungeon core." Grissle's wet small, tongue licked out and moistened his lips. "Their findings match my own. The arrays, the sorting, we're seeing the same patterns. The universe, laid out in a numerical code, the very secrets the gods once kept from us laid bare before—"

"Is this getting to a point?" Melos said. Grissle had a tendency to go on, until he reached jargon levels that could put the most patient of men to sleep. And Melos had never been very patient to start with.

Watery brown eyes found his own. For a second Melos toyed with turning on his fear aura, shot down the idea as soon as it crossed his mind. "Yes," Grissle said. "I think I can use the dungeon cores to protect us from the incoming waves."

"So the damn things would actually have a use?" Amelia said. "That's good. I'd hate to think we've been collecting them just to take them out of circulation."

Melos' wife was an enchanter herself. She'd tried to teach him the art, but he found it boring.

"Oh, they've got a use, all right. Come and see!"

"What?"

"We've got one set up in the lab right now."

"We?" Melos asked.

"Oh yes! Once we realized we were getting the same information, we decided to pool our resource. The three most promising apprentices from the Delver Society are my guests at the minute. And yesterday we made a huge breakthrough."

"So that's what those little bastards are about!" King Garamundi laughed. "I wondered why there were dwarves wandering around my castle and eating my food."

"Gris?" Amelia asked, looking pensively at the old wizard, "exactly what is it you've got in the labs, right now?"

"If I'm right?" Grissle beamed a thin-lipped smile, "The key to protecting our homeland. Forever!"

*****

"I'm sorry, what's that word you just said?" Melos asked, blinking down at the small, incredibly well-dressed dwarf.

"I'm a Pygmalion," she said, tossing her elegantly-braided hair.

And beside her, five stone statues of her did the exact same thing. Which was disconcerting, because their hair was carved from something that really wasn't supposed to be that flexible.

"It's an animator and model blend," Amelia said, smiling down at her. "I'm surprised. Most dwarves don't go in for the model job."

"Yeah, well, it's that diet thing that does most of them in. And a lot of my kin think it's foolish and wasteful." She snorted and leaned back in her chair, crossing one perfectly-shaven stumpy leg. "It's their own fault if they don't want in on these buffs."

"No kidding," Graham said, running an appreciative eye up and down her miniskirted figure.

"Rein it in. Remember, you're no Bard," Grissle joked. Then he pointed at the apparatus spread out around the room. "She's the key to this whole affair."

"What affair?" Melos asked.

"All my copies act and think as I do," Brin the Pygmalion explained. "So if you stick one of them in a dungeon master's slot, it will act like I would and run a dungeon like I would."

Grissle nodded. "There are flaws. The uplink—"

"The what now?" Rezzak asked.

"The green pillar prevents her from communicating with her copies like she normally could."

"So they're on their own initiative. But since I'm all for helping you guys, that's all well and good." Brin smiled up at the humans surrounding her.

"And your friends?" Melos glanced over at the other two dwarves. One younger male in a blue robe, who spent most of his time gawping at them, and blinking behind his beard. And an elderly one, wearing light plate mail, who glared at Melos with disgust.

There's always one of those bastards, Melos thought.

"I'm er, I'm Ragnor." Said the younger one. "I'm a wizard, here to study the, er, the artifacts—"

"The cores," The older one said. "Which I've provided from my personal collection."

His voice... "You're Ambersand," Melos realized.

"You are serious?" Sabi said, eyes widening over her veil. "The Ambersand? Savior of Gerdland? Ravager of the Gnolls and the Voids?"

The dwarf's gaze softened as he looked upon her. "Aye. Though that was a bit ago." He coughed. "Before the... changeover."

"Old school. Whoa." Graham said. "So what was that whole thaco thing about, anyway?"

Ambersand chuckled. "Well, y'see, it was this backwards scale, where plate was a three, and leather was a nine, and you had to—"

"Oh don't get him started," Brin said. "Or he'll be going on about saving rods, staves, and wands."

"Throws, ya wax-legged wastrel! Ye saved yer throws!" Ambersand yelled.

"Please..." Grissle said, lifting a finger.

"Sorry." The elderly dwarf cleared his throat.

"Anyway... look. It's easier if I show you," Grissle said, moving to what looked all the world like a throne, emblazoned with arcane sigils, that matched the metal pillars around the laboratory. Copper tubes trailed from the throne, stretching out to wrap around the various pillars. "Brin? Column one, if you please."

Smiling, the little Pygmalion went over to the metal column, and put her hand on the pillar. Purple and green light glittered as she cupped the hollow top of it.

"That's the Dungeon Core," Jane rasped. "From Joculah's."

"Yes. And with some alignment..." Grissle shifted levers, adjusted sliders, and stabbed a finger down onto the throne's buttons. "There."

The remaining six of the Seven tensed, as darkness surrounded them, with green numbers flashing above. Sound faded away, and once more they were in that darkling place between the worlds. The dwarves watched, the younger in awe, taking notes on a parchment, and the elder with wary caution.

Brin, for her part, was enclosed within seconds by a green column.

The metal pillar vanished, and she stood there, a beatific look on her face.

All save for one patch of white light, that coalesced to reveal the laboratory. "The entire room is now enclosed, the space replaced by our dungeon," Grissle happily pointed out. "It's filling the entire lower level of the castle, all of my labs. Although... it needn't." He adjusted spinners and sliders, and as they watched, the perspective through the doorway out shrunk, until the space grew thinner, distorted. "A person could easily step outside and get back to the real world. The dungeon's a mere few inches thick right now. But we won't send a person out, no." He waved to one of Brin's statues. "The number two, please."

The statue roused itself, and walked out through the doorway, its own form distorting briefly, then it was through.

"Once she's got her hands on the second core and wills it to activation..." Grissle smiled. "Ah yes, there we go!" A rune on the throne lit up, and he threw a lever.

Abruptly, the light from the exit changed. He fiddled with the dials and sliders again, and space straightened out...

...revealing the laboratory beyond, and a door in the middle of it, showing a flickering green space.

Wonder stirred in Melos' mind. "You've found a way to nest a dungeon within a dungeon."

"Oh yes. And by itself that'd be a century or three of study," Grissle's voice was smug. "But it's the ability to adjust and shape the amount of space that the dungeon occupies that makes it useful for the King's purposes."

"Explain." Amelia said.

"Dungeons always have one entrance, don't they?" Grissle's tongue wet his lips. "And they block off all the space they occupy... absolutely no way to enter it, save through the entrance. So what if... what if we surrounded our land with a wall of dungeons?"

"You'd need a lot of dungeons," Amelia shook her head. "And what's to stop our enemies from entering them and closing them..." her eyes went wide. "...except that you can put the entrance to each dungeon inside another dungeon!"

"Inside the main one," Grissle smiled. "And thanks to your retrieval of a Rank five dungeon core, it's just big enough that I can stretch it out to cover the entire Kingdom."

"Wait, whoa, you'd turn our land into a dungeon?" Graham said. "Not sure if that's a good idea."

"A dungeon with nothing in its own main pillars!" Grissle snapped. "No bosses, no mobs, nothing spawning." He grimaced. "Which is good, because as diffused as it would be, it would be a dungeon in name only. The pillars would react... weirdly. No, the master dungeon would just be there to control the others, allow them to be nested. And once nested..." He grinned and manipulated dials. And through the doorway into the lab that was now a dungeon, the space in the OTHER doorway distorted. "I can spread THEM out, too. Shape them into a barrier."

Rezzak rubbed his chin. "How many. How many cores, all told?"

"It varies. Seventeen's optimal. You could do it with one, but there would be... side effects." Grissle sighed.

"What are the downsides?" Melos asked.

"Mm. well... The problem arises that it's a little hard on the slaved cores. They're not meant to be used this way. So they'd need replacing on a regular basis. But since we're not planning to keep the dungeon wall up permanently, this isn't a real issue. Just shut down the cores in sequence, swap out any damaged ones, and off we go." He chuckled, and pointed at the loot pillars spread throughout the room. "I've placed the core pylons in synched locations to the loot pillars. If one blew, in a pinch, it'd be the simplest of matters to go and swap one out. Even a monkey could do it. That'd be a little rough on the control throne, though, so you don't want to do it too often."

"This is good," Amelia nodded. "The King needs to see this."

"I'm glad we agree," Grissle rasped, the smile stretching his face. "As legacies go, it'll be a good one for me to leave to the kingdom..."

INTERLUDE 3: KING'S LOSS

"Number seventeen." Melos smiled, as he handed the orange crystal over. "We had to run down to Caneland for this one, so I hope you appreciate it. It was a swamp dungeon, with Gribbits everywhere. You would not believe how many of us saw the inside of giant froggy stomachs."

"That?" Grissle said, taking the core with a rictus grin, "that is why I don't mind retiring from the field so much."

"So what now?"

"Now?" Grissle looked toward the throne, powered down, and looming, all angles and runes and spiraling copper tubes. At the pillars, each of which bore a gem at their peak. "Nothing. It's the middle of the night and Brin's asleep. It takes a lot to make seventeen Pygmalion copies, as it turns out. A lot of materials, a lot of crafting, some of which has to be done the old fashioned way."

"Ouch." Melos frowned. "I can't imagine the patience that would take."

"Which is why it's good she's a dwarf. They're not as bad as elves, but they'd rather spend a few years working on something rather than admit it has some minor flaws." Grissle glanced toward the throne. "Unlike me." The old wizard's face grew pensive.

"What is it?"

"No... I'm sure it'll be fine. Nothing." Grissle shook his head.

Melos put his arm around his oldest friend, the man who'd given him a chance, who'd looked past the cultist to see the hero within. "Gris, talk to me here. We're dealing with forces that daemons tread cautiously around. And you're..." *dying,* "...you've been busy, and under a lot of stress. Talk to me here."

Grissle sighed and sat in the throne, staring down at his slippered feet. "There are some issues with feedback. There's been a side effect to nesting the dungeons... it puts pressure on the central dungeon master's column. I've been able to rig an emergency shunt to the throne, but I can't cancel the bleed-out entirely. "

"Pressure. What kind of pressure?"

"Mental pressure. It..." Grissle mopped his face. The man was sweating far more than normal, his voice dull. "All pillars do it, they fray at the sanity of those within it. But in most, as far as I can tell, it's gradual. When you're nesting seventeen dungeons at once? It goes quickly."

Melos rubbed his beard. "Mana potions?"

"Good when I'm on the throne. Non-functional in the main pillars. You don't regain any pooled energy in there, not sanity, not Moxie, not anything. Drinking doesn't work. Sleeping does, a bit, but it's deuced uncomfortable."

"You've been trying this on yourself."

"And who else could I ask?" Grissle raised his hands. "King Grundi's found out that the Delvers are messing around with dungeon cores and taken it hard. If a dwarf dies here, it'll be the end of their society."

"Wait. Dies?" Melos said, crossing to the throne and leaning on it, scrutinizing the old wizard closely.

"A small chance." Grissle licked his lips. "But there."

"You're experimenting on yourself, with something that could kill a DWARF."

Grissle sighed. "They don't have my contingency plan."

"Gris..."

"I know. I know I said I was done with necromancy. But..."

"You know how the King is going to take this."

"The King doesn't know. Nor will he, unless the worst happens, in which case I fix it and go to my eternal rest." Grissle stared up at him, with watery, desperate eyes. "Unless you tell him."

Melos closed his eyes.

A breath. Two. Three. "You're bound and determined on this."

"This is only the first iteration. Every day, I'm learning what I did wrong with this control throne. Every day I'm another step to understanding. Understanding why."

There were four tier one jobs that granted access to a form of the experimentation skill, at twenty-fifth level. Grissle had all four, had ground them obsessively, seeking answers. Answers for the changeover. Answers for why the cure disease spell had been stripped from every cleric in the land, well before his own illness surfaced.

Some people had determination. Grissle *was* determination.

"You've unlocked that job, haven't you," Melos opened his eyes, staring into Grissle's brown, tired orbs. "The thing you said you gave up searching for, years ago."

"I have," Grissle whispered. "And the fact I'm here, in the pain I am, proves that I won't take it unless Cylvania itself is on the line."

"I've fought enough undead, destroyed enough undead, to know that it changes even the strongest..." Melos looked away. "It'll change you. You... I trust you. I don't trust what you might make of yourself."

"Melos. I gave you a chance. A chance for redemption."

"No. No, that was different."

"I didn't tell them about the children."

Melos inhaled.

"So it's like that, is it?" he said, as the old shame came back to haunt him.

"No. It doesn't have to be."

"They..." Melos shut his eyes. "It was the final test of loyalty. They would have killed me if I refused."

"And so you cast three innocent babes into Cron's flames."

"I avenged them!" Melos roared, stomping away and clenching a fist. "When I saw the truth I went back and slaughtered every last one of those evil shits!"

"And yet one of the guilty remains."

Melos punched the stone wall. Punched it again, felt his gauntlet flex and dent. Punched it a third time, felt his fingers nova into pain, and then the tears were coming now, tears of shame. Tears of weakness.

"I will spend the rest of my life atoning for what I've done." Melos said. "I have. I've restricted... there's entire skills I've given up; things I don't use, will never use again. And you've trusted me to do that."

"Yes. And I still do." Grissle said. "All I'm asking is for the sort of trust I've given you, over a thing I haven't even done yet. A thing that pales by comparison, to be honest."

Melos clenched his eyes shut, willed the weakness out of his voice. There was still a quaver. "And if I don't, you'll tell them. Tell my wife."

"No."

"No?" He turned, shocked, eyes red and warm and still blurry.

"No. If you tell them what I plan, I'll say nothing on the matter. But..." he turned his head, looked around at the room. "But there is no contingency plan if I die with this uncompleted. Amelia can't match me. Rezzak was never arcanely-inclined. The Dwarves won't touch the plan, not with their King agitating against it. Who else could we trust?" The old necromancer said to the ex-cultist. "Who could we trust with this responsibility?"

"It's power," Melos agreed, peeling his gauntlet off with a hiss of pain and mopping his face with his throbbing hand. "And I know what power does. Just..." he sighed, feeling the fire drain from him, feeling old. "Promise me you won't get dumb over this."

"I won't. Didn't get this far by being stupid." Grissle looked around. "This really is my legacy," he said, gesturing at the cluttered workshop, and the apparatus he'd spent months building, perfecting, while the Seven hunted down cores to finish it. "I don't want it tarnished by my weakness."

"You're not weak," Melos said, smiling, though his eyes were still hot and his head throbbed. "You're the second strongest person I know."

"Amelia's the first, I'll wager?" Grissle smiled.

"You'd win that bet, if I was stupid enough to make it..."

*****

Cecelia cooed in his arms, and he rocked her as best he could with his armor in the way. He'd had special, non-spiky pauldrons made for expressly this purpose. The effect diminished the overall look he'd gone for, but... well, somehow, scaring people just wasn't as fulfilling as it had been, before he'd become a father.

Besides, he could still use his Demon Knight skills to help with intimidation when the need arose. The job was all about fear, but fear didn't have to dominate his life when he was off the clock, so to speak.

A noise at his back made him tense, and he shifted in the creaking wooden chair—

—but it was just a black kitten, creeping up onto the table, all pudgy belly and curious little face. It stared at the little girl, then Melos met its gaze. Little yellow eyes widened, and the cat was gone, disappearing so quickly that Melos almost doubted it was there in the first place. Up until he saw a quivering black tail behind one of the mantle plates.

"Oh come on, I wasn't even trying." Melos complained.

Which spooked the cat and sent the plate crashing to the floor as it fled the room entirely.

Cecelia wailed, frightened by the sound.

"Is everything all right?" Amelia called, from upstairs.

"It's fine," Melos said. "Fine, just... fine." He rocked Cecelia until her sobs subsided, then made his way to the shards of the plate. **"Mend,"** he whispered, and picked up the reconstructed dish.

When he looked up, Caradon was glaring down from the balcony at the top of the staircase.

"Your cat got a little clumsy," Melos explained, putting the plate back on the mantle.

Only to have it slip through his gauntleted fingers and hit the ground again. Cecelia wailed as it broke, and Melos felt his temper flare as the middle-aged man snorted in disgust.

"My cat. Sure," Caradon said. "You could use a few more animator levels, looks like. The dexterity would do you good."

"True," Melos said, raising his voice over the wailing infant. **"Mend."** The plate reassembled, and he put it on the table this time. "Although they're good in other ways. Animus Blade has got some interesting synergies with my Hellswords—"

"I don't want to hear that filth."

The air fell silent between them, save for the frightened infant's sobbing. Melos rocked her, shushing her, but his eyes never left his father-in-law's gaze.

Finally, Caradon turned away. "Are you done yet, Amelia?"

"Almost!" she called back. Her voice was very muffled. This house had thick walls, and for once, Melos was thankful for it. Around her, both he and Caradon pretended to be on polite terms. It was an unspoken agreement, really.

Caradon finally shook his head and pointed at the bassinet to the side of the fireplace.

Melos breathed hard, sighing with Cecelia as she finally subsided, and deposited his daughter into the baby bed, smoothing her frizzy little fringe of hair with one hand, all under Caradon's stare.

A stare that finally turned, as his daughter hugged Caradon from behind. He turned and she kissed him goodbye.

Melos held the door for Amelia when she bustled downstairs and ordered Emmet to follow.

"Remind me why we're here and not at the pass again?" Melos asked his wife.

"Besides a chance for Father to meet Cecelia? And Grissle needing us to check his calculations?" She grinned. "It's a chance to go hiking. There are some awesome views along here, and I want to show them to you."

"Did I mention that I'm more of a city guy? I'm really more of a city guy. We've got some awesome views back at home. Outside our window and all. Really, they could have sent Jane."

"Jane's got her own hands full in the North. With whatever the Earl of Balmoran has her doing."

"Is that where she is?"

"Oh yeah."

"She say anything about what was going on up there?"

Amelia snorted.

"Right, right, dumb question."

She led him through the hills, up a small mountain, and into a shielded valley. It was… good for his agility, at least. "You know, Jane could have totally done this with one of her ninja run thingies or whatever it's called," he griped to Amelia. "Just stuck her arms out to the back of her and charged headfirst through the thickest forests here, never eating a tree branch once."

"You're the one who insisted on wearing armor. Don't you have Always in Uniform?"

"Well yes, but Demonplate doesn't work with it."

"Probably good. There's no way I'm letting demons get into your pants. You're past those days," Amelia smirked.

"Har har de fucking har. Please tell me we're there."

"About." She stopped, stared up at a high mountain slope. "Now we wait."

"How'd you find this spot, anyway?"

"One of Dad's friends used to take me all up and down through these woods. Tried to convince me I needed to be a scout. Good guy but obsessed with the outdoors. All the time."

"Ah. So you told him—"

"Same thing I told you, when you wanted to sleep with the window open a few months ago. Fuck winter. Winter is for curling up inside with books." She smiled and leaned back against a tree. "And warm husbands."

"Can't object to that," he said, feeling himself stir as he looked at her, arms spread out, flush with life and heat from the walk.

She was beautiful.

"How much time do we have, do you think?" Melos said, bracing himself against the tree, looking down into her black eyes. She smiled, lips parting, as he moved in close, so close to her.

"Mmm. I like the way you think—"

The light shifted.

"None," she said, looking sharp, and pushing herself away from the tree. And him. "It's happening."

A flicker, then a CRACK, followed by a rolling rumble so loud that for a second Melos thought it was a storm. To the south the light above the mountains dimmed, then dimmed further. "Is that it?" he asked Amelia.

"Appraise." She squinted up the peak. "We need to get closer."

"Is it safe?"

She reached into a pocket, pulled out a mechanical bird. **"Animus."** It wound within seconds, key turning in it, then it fluttered up into the sky. **"Dollseye,"** Amelia said. Then she nodded. "It's there. It's... huh. I think it's stable."

"So he succeeded!"

"Maybe. We need a closer look. Come on, it'll only be up an hour."

"That's a pretty steep slope."

"Yeah, we'd probably better leave Emmet here. Agility isn't his forte."

"I was more worried about me. Agility isn't mine."

"Oh don't be a baby. C'mon. Animate your own armor if you get tired."

"Fine, fine."

They made it in about fifteen minutes. It was a rough climb, but Melos had spent so long building his constitution that it scarcely mattered. Amelia actually had it rougher than he did, and though wisdom had never been a priority, he was wise enough to keep his mouth shut as he gave her a hand up the last few feet.

And there it was... A rippling black curtain that filled the sky, filled the world, stretching up beyond sight and to both sides. It was, simply, nothing.

Amelia's animated bird sat on a boulder, observing it.

There wasn't much else up here, on this little plateau. A few trees, a few rocks, a small pond that wasn't much more than a collection of puddles with delusions of grandeur.

"Well, it's here." Melos scooped up a rock, hucked it into the big wall of nothing. It disappeared soundlessly.

Amelia scooped up the bird, hesitated. "I don't want to lose it. Let's see..." She dug in her pack, pulled out a little black bear. "Whoa no. No, you stay right here, Fluffy."

"Fluffy?"

"One of my old toys. Dad wanted to give her back to me."

"Fluffy."

"Shut up! I was like two!"

"I wasn't laughing. It's cute."

"Damn straight she's cute. Ah, here we go." Amelia pulled out a straw mannequin, tossed it to the ground. **"Animus. Dollseye."** She blinked a few times. "Always weird shifting sight from one to another. Okay, dolly. March!" The little toy went in, and Melos watched it vanish just like the rock had.

"Nothing. Nothing… whoa," Amelia gasped. "Numbers. Green numbers."

"Above you?"

"No, It's like it's in them, they're all around." She shut up for a second, then spoke again, her voice troubled. "The link is gone."

Melos looked at his party screen. Himself, Amelia, Emmet… "You invited the doll before you sent it in there, right?"

"Of course I did."

"Got any more of those?"

"Nope, but those trees have deadwood, and I've got Carpenter. Give me a few."

Every experiment ended the same way. The animi went in, and the ones who didn't encounter the numbers managed to return intact. The ones who did disappeared entirely.

"It's almost like it's moving, too. The numbers aren't always in the same place. And with no frame of reference, it's hard as hell to avoid running into them." Amelia shook her head. "Once you do, you've got like a split second to back off, but if you get in among them, you're gone. That's what it looks like to me, anyway. You want to give it a whirl?"

"I don't have Dollseye yet. It'd be pointless."

"Oh, right, right, we can work on that."

"Should we head back?"

"Mmm." Amelia debated, then shook her head. "It's only got about twenty minutes left. Let's wait to see what things look like when it goes down."

But it didn't go down. Not twenty minutes later, not an half an hour later, and not a full hour later.

"Something's wrong," Amelia said.

"We need to get back to the Castle," Melos said, feeling a premonition stir in the back of his mind. "And we need to go prepared for trouble."

She bit her lips. "Cecelia…"

"We can leave her with your Father."

"No. This is too close to the… whatever that is. If it shifts a few miles, it could take them." Her face set into hard lines. "We'll teleport to the townhouse. Drop Cecelia with Betsy, then go to the castle on foot. And hope that the others did the same…"

*****

Chaos reigned.

The city rotted, as dead things stalked the night, mist filled its streets, and sane people hid indoors to try and survive the nightmare.

And Melos and Amelia carved a path through it, braving the choking fog that filled the air, battering through the glazed-eyed zombie dwarves that filled the street, all wearing miniskirts and looking fabulous. Even while they were hunched around the bodies of the fallen, eating their brains, they somehow managed to do it with dignity and poise.

They were too late to save the people who'd died at the city gate, or in the market, or in the thoroughfare leading up to the castle.

But when Melos hammered his gauntlet against the siege door, his heart lifted when it opened, revealing a ring of pale palace guards... and a familiar figure. "Rezzak!"

"This is the gladdest I've ever been to see you," the Invoker said, hands full with a mug of something bubbly. "Everything's fucked."

"Can you be more concise?" Amelia entered, collecting her daggers from the air as the guards slammed the door behind her and barred it.

"I can't. He can," Rezzak pointed to a shivering dwarf in a torn blue robe.

"You're..." Melos squinted. He'd forgotten the dwarf's name.

"Ragnor. Sir." The dwarf stared past him, unseeing. Melos knew that look.

"It's all right, you're safe," Melos lied, kneeling down to look the little guy in the eyes. "Tell us what happened."

"I... it... Grissle, sir. We fired up the Throne; the dungeons integrated fine, then Brin collapsed. Grissle yelled at me to get her clear, and I did, then he shifted the column control to the main runic integration console, and, and, and..."

"He collapsed too," Melos said.

"Yes. But... he, he got... he..."

"He stood back up." Melos said. "But it wasn't him anymore, was it?"

"At first I thought it was all right," Ragnor babbled. "I thought ah, he's got this. And he did. He sat back down in the chair, and remodulated the arrays until they balanced. But he left them on. He just sat there, blue light glowing out his eyes, in the throne, looking at everything."

"What did you do then?"

"I tried to pull Brin toward the entrance. Get her some help, once I was sure things were stable. And he said no. I asked him why the hell not? He said he didn't want any interruptions until his research was done."

"Damn it all." Melos closed his eyes. "I warned him."

"I kept on dragging her, and he looked at me, and I thought he was blinking until the smoke goes up, and no, it's his eyes. His eyes are bubbling out of his head. Bubbling away until the only thing left there is the light, that blue light..."

"Oh gods," Amelia whispered. "Blue eyes. Hot blue eyes."

"The eyes of a lich," Melos said.

"I asked him when his research would be done," Ragnor whispered. "He said, a few decades, maybe. I said no, Brin wouldn't survive that long, she needed help now, and he said that was easy to fix." Ragnor swallowed. "He killed her. And told me to keep taking notes."

"You ran," Melos said.

"I'm sorry."

"No. You did the smart thing." Melos felt his guts clench. "Rezzak? Where are the others?"

"Combing the city, getting everyone inside." Rezzak took a long swallow of wine. "I'm only back because my pools are down. It's all zombies out there. To us they're nothing, but there's a lot of them."

"He animated her and put her in a mob pillar," Melos shook his head. "Just to buy himself time."

"There are dozens dead because of this." Amelia's face hardened. "How could he do this?"

"It's not them he cares about. It's us." Melos took a breath. "He's a creature of pure logic and pure obsession now. I warned him. I feared this. But not enough." He reached back, felt the hilts of the blades on his back. "We have to stop him. We have to make this right. And we have to save our kingdom, bring down this thing he's built without destroying everything. Ragnor? Do you know how to do that?"

"No. I'm sorry. No, I don't. I don't have the first clue how to undo this." The little wizard's bearded face scrunched up into a mask of sorrow.

Amelia squatted down next to him. "Will you come with us, then? Will you help fix this?"

Ragnor shook. "I can't. I can't go back there. I'm... no. I'm sorry. I'd be of no use to you."

"But I will." The heroes looked up as Ambersand entered through the castle door, axe bloody, shield battered, and armor gleaming in the light. "Halls are clear. For now."

The guards around them relaxed. "Thank you, sir. We'll get out there and secure the way down!" Their captain saluted, then got them moving.

"Welcome, then. Let's go save the world," Melos offered a gauntlet, and with some hesitation, Ambersand stowed his axe and gave it a shake.

"Just keep yer demons to yerself, lad. I'm lawful."

"I... am too?" Melos squinted.

"Pfft. Yer alignment's chaotic if I've ever seen it."

"Okay." Melos had no clue what the old dwarf meant, but at least he wasn't giving him dirty looks every damned minute.

"I'll call them in," Rezzak said. "I hate this, but we've got no other choice—"

Melos woke up.

Green light filled his vision, and he sobbed as the chamber, his own personal hell, swam back into view. Grissle's shattered husk on his broken throne, the shredded pipes leaking green zeroes and ones, and the columns, the columns full of burnt cores. Broken magic, broken artifacts, as broken as the numbers that swirled overhead, half of them vanishing or shattering when they hit the hole in the center, the hole that kept growing.

A mighty engine, a triumph, a proper wizard's legacy… all in ruins and threatening to take everything he had left into the void, should Melos falter. Should he ever be weak.

Like he had just a bit ago.

He'd slept, even though he hadn't planned to. Melos pushed his mind into his dungeon master's projection—

—and found himself inches away from his High Knight's pale, frightened face, as she scooted back in her chair, eyes wide with surprise and mouth open.

What did I do now? He pulled back from General Mastoya and looked down at himself. Still armored. Still clad. Sword sheathed. He was in… he was in the war room, he saw. The maps. He recognized the maps.

"Sir?" She whispered, and the uncertainty in her voice shook him. He needed her. Needed her trust. She was loyal; he'd tested her so often, and she was one of the last balances against… against Anise. Against his first mistake.

No, he thought, remembering the wails as the babes fell one by one into the fire, remembering how the children smelled as they cooked. Remembering how his cult leader had smiled. *Not my first mistake. Not by a long shot.*

"Did you understand me?" he said, gambling. "Tell me what I just said to you." He'd done this in similar situations in the past, and it worked about half the time, usually.

Some color returned to Mastoya's face. Green, naturally. "You ordered me to begin the assault, sir. Even though we've only got half the siege engines replaced and repaired. To… kill them all. Down to the last dwarven child."

"Then we understand each other," Melos said, turning his back and folding his hands behind him. He closed his eyes, as he let his face fall into a mask of sorrow. It hadn't been him. Hadn't been his orders.

Well. Maybe it wasn't too late. "That was, of course, a test."

"Sir?"

"If you'd objected, I would have thought you too weak to handle the assault. I don't want every child dead. We don't make war on children."

"No sir." Something in her voice caught his attention, but he was too tired to focus on it, to catch the hints. No, this was going well enough, she could have her doubts.

"Just win the war, so we can have our long-deserved peace, General." He said, smiling, turning to face her again. "That's all I ask."

The half-orc's face was unreadable, as she stood and saluted. "Sir. I'll see to that immediately."

And then she was gone, gone to the Waymark Station, down to collect her waystone and return to the front. Melos sagged into the chair in the war room and put his head in his hands.

"We can do this." He told himself. "It's not too late," he said. "There is a way to fix everything. We just need to hang on a little longer."

They were very pretty lies.

Perhaps if he kept saying them, he'd believe them.

CHAPTER 10: ON THE EVE OF BATTLE

"...there's not much else to tell," King Grundi finished, as his officials hammered out a contract with the giants and the troops withdrew back into the mountain. "Ragnor came back; Ambersand didn't, and the Seven fell taking down one of their own. All save for the demon knight."

The toys considered this. Threadbare raised his head. "Celia, did you know about any of this?"

"No! Well... that's not exactly right. I knew that Grissle turned on everyone else and used the Oblivion to try and gain power over the Kingdom. And that Mother died stopping Grissle. That's what I learned, but it's what everyone in the Cylvania learns."

"Yeah. No mention of dwahves or how exactly the Oblivion wahked," Madeline said. "Man, I remembah dwahf zombie night. That was really freaking weahd."

"I see," Threadbare said, looking up at King Grundi. "Why didn't you tell people about it?"

"Wouldn't have done any good." Grundi sighed. "I had a good talk about it with King Garamundi, before Melos pulled his coup. People knew all of the story they needed to know. Telling them about how dwarves had been involved would only make people blame dwarves. And telling them about how dungeon cores powered the Oblivion would just make people go and try to experiment with dungeon cores more. Which is how we got into this mess in the first place!"

"You're not wrong," Garon said. "But why exactly is the Oblivion still going? Grissle was defeated, right?"

"Aye. But..." Grundi shot a look over his shoulder, at the arguing ministers and the big blue giantess. "Ah, let's discuss this inside. Dealing with giants always pisses me off."

Once they got back to the tunnel leading back into the mountain, a cadre of his honor guard fell in around the small king. Working with long expertise, they pulled his blankets back and used tools to pop apart the stone plinth that the Kneelchair used as a skirt and uncoupled about half of the bulky machinery, until the king was down to just a small throne with wheels.

"Modular! Nice," Cecelia looked it over. "It'd have to be, to fit through these tunnels."

"Modju-what?" Graves asked.

"It's tinker talk. Means you can swap parts around. There's more to it, but..."

"It's a bit sleep-inducing for non-tinkers so we're best keeping it short," Grundi laughed. Two of his honor guard took the back of the throne and wheeled him forward. Threadbare and Cecelia kept pace with him as he rolled back to the hold.

"This sounds like a fixable problem, though," Threadbare said, still thinking about it. "If there's a magical machine, and you have notes on it, then why can't other wizards go in there and fix it?"

"We were trying to." Grundi sighed. "But Grissle was a genius. Smart as a whip before he started stacking jobs is what I hear. Then he went and got twenty-five levels in alchemist, twenty-five in enchanter, twenty-five in wizard... and twenty-five in necromancer, as it turns out. But we were trying to line up the people to handle it, when Melos started getting skittish. He controlled access to the dungeon core. The main dungeon's core, I mean. He was like a dog with a bone, suspicious and paranoid. And the daemon he brought in didn't help matters none."

"But wasn't King Garamundi in charge?" Graves asked.

"Mm. In charge." Grundi raised a withered hand, rubbed his beard. "It's a nice idea. Smart kings know they're only in charge so long as they can keep their vassals wrangled. Garamundi was smart enough to see Melos was on edge. One of his best friends had betrayed him, after all. Ordering him to stand down and stop guarding Grissle's work would have been like throwing fire at a mining charge. We thought we had time. We thought that things were stable, that eventually he'd come around." Grundi sighed. "Then Garamundi died; Melos took the throne and told us we wouldn't be touching the core device until he had enough skilled people of his own to ensure we wouldn't try any funny business." Grundi scowled. "About the same time, Ragnor went... missing." The dwarf spat the word. "Along with his notes. Then Balmoran rebelled against Melos, and there was no talking to the man after that. Not that there was much in the way of cooperation before that."

Grundi sighed again, ruffling his beard. "We figured it would end badly. We should have joined Balmoran when they begged us to. But we figured it was human affairs, and that they could sort it out themselves and there was no point in trying to fix things until they did. But here we are."

"The core device is the key to all of this." Threadbare said, thinking hard. "We need to go to Grissle's lab and see what's wrong with it."

"The old labs have been sealed for years," Graves said. "And to get there you'd have to get to the Capital City, go through Castle Cylvania, and hope that the entrance is somewhere down there in the sealed labs. With the most elite forces that the Crown has guarding it, including the king himself, and the Hand. Who are apparently the daemonic resurrections of the Seven?"

"The odds aren't good to begin with," Kayin said. "Then you have to figure out something that took a genius a hundred levels of the nerdiest jobs around to create. And hope that you have a way to fix it."

"Aye," said King Grundi. "We were grooming people for the task. Had a good start on it. Then Melos pulled his treachery, tried to kill one of our families, and we had to go to war. And between The Lurker and the war... we just don't have the people anymore." Grundi shook his head. "Dwarves aren't exactly inclined to wizardry to begin with. Now we're a shadow of what we were."

Threadbare looked around at his friends. "We don't really have any wizards," the little bear said. "But we've got a few enchanters. We need to try."

"And I think I know how we could do it," Cecelia said, rubbing her hair. "But it's not going to be easy."

"Oh, well, when have we ever taken the easy way on something?" Garon said. "I'm in."

"Psh, like any of us be out," Zuula snorted. "We come dis far kicking ass and taking names. Not about to stop now."

Threadbare smiled. "Thank you Zuula. Thank you everyone."

"Dude, don't mention it," Glub said. "This is kinda fun when it's not scary. And sometimes when it's scary. And at least I'm not stuck in some weird cult where I have to bang women all the time anymore."

"Wait, what?" King Grundi stared down at the little wooden fishman.

"Ah... nevermind. So here's the plan—" Cecelia started.

"Wait," King Grundi said. "Let's discuss this in more secure quarters. The Lurker might be dead for now, but there's no harm in being cautious."

The honor guard led them through the hold, to a large building they'd passed by last night, on their way to visit Beryl and Jarrik. Great foundries thundered in the halls surrounding the structure, hammers falling like raindrops as the din swelled and pulsed. This part of the dwarfhold never slept, forgefires burning hot, as ore was converted into metal, and stone was shaped to the needs of their society.

Hidon was waiting out front for them, frowning.

"What do we have?" King Grundi stopped, and his Honor guard fell in around him, reassembling his Kneelchair, snapping back together the heavy pieces of the stone plinth that they'd been hauling around for the better part of a mile.

"We found Montag's body sealed into the wall of his office. He's been there a while."

Grundi bowed his head. "I'll arrange his coin. This was war he died in. His family gets the adamant due."

"I was hoping you'd say that." Hidon led the way inside, through long, curving halls with heavy metal doors sealing off side passages. "Here," he said at last, opening the first wooden door any of them had seen in the place.

The office inside was covered in blood, with hooded dwarves in heavy leather garments scrubbing the floors and walls and sorting through the stained piles of papers scattered everywhere.

But the golems' eyes were drawn to the piles and heaps of gleaming yellow powder that lay scattered all over the place.

"Oh... my... goodness..." Madeline squeaked. "That's... that's easily wahth..."

"Shh," King Grundi said. "Don't remind me. Because I'm going to have to do something very undwarflike here in a bit."

"The Lurker bought out the market last night, working through intermediaries," Hidon shook his head. "Knew we'd find out sooner or later. Didn't care. Which means that the Crown is close to their endgame." Hidon sighed. "We had to disable some blasting charges to get in here. Oh, and we found those tinker parts you needed," Hidon nodded to Cecelia.

"Thank you!" Cecelia smiled. "Now I can get to work."

"Work fast," Hidon sighed. "We've got a week, maybe two. That's what our spies tell us. Then the Crown's forces are going to march."

"Oh. Oh no. I won't have time to montage anyone. This..." Cecelia shook her head. "This is bad."

"Actually it's good. They were almost all set to go days back, but someone sabotaged the tunnelers they needed to break into our networks." Hidon smiled under his beard. "Not sure who it was but they did us a good turn. Probably the Rangers, that's their sort of thing."

"Now you can tell me about your plan to fix the Oblivion," King Grundi said, while Hidon and his agents cleaned up the yellow reagent, bottling it in vials and stacking it in crates.

"Well first we need to go get a look at it," Cecelia said. "But I think I know how we can get inside the castle, at least, without having to fight our way to the city, then through the castle gates. Fort Bronze has a Greater Waymark inside it. There's a station where waystones are kept. If we can get one of them, we can pile into Madeline's pack and one of us can teleport right inside the Castle. Mind you, that chamber's guarded too, but it isn't set up to handle a merchant's pack full of golem adventurers."

"We had enough trouble getting into that place the first time around." Garon shook his horns. "I can't imagine they won't have upped the security."

"We can't go in the same way, obviously," Kayin said. "And they'll be on the lookout for little golems now, desu."

"Well, we'll just have to fight our way in, then," Threadbare said. "Because we're going to be helping the dwarves anyway."

The room fell silent.

"They turned us down," Cecelia said.

"Aye. About that..." King Grundi coughed, his lungs rattling. "The situation has changed a mite. Namely, The Lurker ain't here no more. So I don't have to pretend that I don't like your offer."

"You were lying about that?" Threadbare frowned.

"Mmmm... it wasn't so much lying, as it was... prevarication. We had an enemy agent around. Had to be careful, because anything we said would go back to Melos. Of COURSE I want three hundred golems marching alongside us! Which brings me back to that undwarflike thing I said I'd do." He waved a scrawny arm around to the crates of yellow powder. "Take it. Take all of it. Along with any other thing you need."

Every dwarf in the room stilled and looked toward their king, eyes wide open.

"What? Can't spend it if yer dead." Grundi shrugged. "And Melos is out for blood. Whoever he might have been once, whatever he did, he's in league with daemons now. There's no way this won't end with blood." He leaned forward, staring down at Cecelia. "Which brings me to one big question, here. He's your father. If it comes down to it, comes down to his life versus all of ours and probably everyone else's, what will you do?"

The rest of the dwarves looked to each other, slowing in their work as they tensed, and looked to Cecelia.

Cecelia looked down. "I..." she said, then stopped.

Threadbare took her hand in his paw, and she looked down at him, gazing into his button eyes. For a minute she stood there, thinking.

191

"I have to stop him. But I'm sorry, he's my father. I can't kill him," Cecelia told King Grundi. "I... if he won't surrender, I'll try to capture him."

"That answer..." King Grundi began, and Cecelia closed her eyes.

"...was completely correct!" The dwarf finished.

Cecelia opened her eyes."Wait. What?"

The tension in the room had eased. The other dwarves were nodding, as they cleaned.

"Lass, I don't care how undwarfy we're getting here by giving up valuable reagents, there's still a line. Asking family to kill family is just wrong." Grundi snorted. "As far as I can see, we're in this mess because hard men made hard decisions over and over again and look where that's got us. Fuck that noise. You reminded me of that with the giants," He said, looking down at Cecelia and Threadbare with a smile poking through the braids of his beard. "The only way we're going to win is by helping each other and saving lives. Not by doing MORE evil things, on top of what's already been done."

"I like you!" Fluffbear squeaked.

"Bahhahahahaha! Thanks, lass." Grundi nodded to his honor guard. "Now if you'll excuse me, I need to go figure out who to appoint as my replacement minister of dangerous and new devices." He sighed. "And talk with his family. That's not going to be fun."

"Sir," Garon shared a glance with Jarrik. "I have a recommendation, if you don't mind..."

*****

"I'm what?" Beryl said a day later, after the details had been hammered out.

"In charge of the department. Oh, and if you need more yellow reagent we're going to have a lot to spare," Threadbare said, his golden laurels gleaming in the light of the glowstones. "The Lurker went a little crazy trying to keep it out of our hands."

"Fuck me running with a pogo stick."

"I'm sorry, to begin with I can't do anything like that, besides it sounds really uncomfortable to try to run at the same time, and I really have no idea what that last thing is."

"This is what you were hiding from me?" The purple-haired dwarven girl turned to Jarrik. "This is why you wouldn't tell me what was going on? You, you, you..."

She grabbed his shirt, hauled him in and down, and locked her lips on his. "You wonderful boyfriend, you," she murmured, when they came up for air. "Holy shitcakes with fucknuggets on top."

"So that means you like it?" Threadbare guessed.

"Ohhh yeah." She grinned up at Jarrik, who shot her a goofy, toothy grin right back. "Ah... you need anything from me, Threadbare?"

"No. Not really. Nothing that we can't figure out later. We have some time yet."

"Good. Me and Jarry are gonna go find my new office and break it in." She ran out of the room, giggling, with Jarrik chasing after her.

Threadbare rubbed his head and wandered out the door, back into the heart of the foundry district. The rhythm of the hammers had changed overnight, and the streets were full of dwarves and carts full of ingots, shipping them frantically to the forges and machine shops and enchanters. The dwarven way of war relied on metal, on crafted objects, on having the best equipment and the most gear, and by golly, every last dwarf who lived in this place was finding ways to help however they could.

Threadbare was doing his part. And his sanity was low because of it. Recharging faster, thanks to the skill the golden laurels granted him, but the fact remained that golems took a lot of sanity to prepare and animate. And Zuula was busy shuttling around between the other members of the group, dreamquesting them to recharge their pools faster, so Threadbare, for the moment, had a rare hour or two to himself where he wasn't casting or sleeping.

Three streets down, he found the small chamber that Cecelia had requisitioned and knocked on the door. After a few minutes, a viewslot slid open, and he found himself staring into Kayin's glass eyes. The slot closed, and the door opened.

"Desu, boss," she greeted him with a thumped salute, fuzzy hand to her chest.

"Hello. Is everything alright?"

She glanced to the rear of the chamber, where tools rattled, and an old suit of plate armor shook as a doll-sized figure worked within its opened breastplate. "I guess? Cecelia! Bear's here!"

The rattling stopped. The plate shook. Cecelia's grease-smeared face poked out of the armor, hair bound up in a kerchief. "Oh! Hi."

"Hello. I wanted to see how you were doing."

"Good. Working in smaller scale is harder, but... well, I've got access to dwarven engineers. You just missed a couple of them. They're in here studying how I'm doing it. Since I've got them to handle the parts that require non-job tinkering, I can focus on just one part at a time and get it done quicker."

Threadbare nodded and stood there, feeling awkward for no reason he could tell. "That's good."

Cecelia considered him. **"Clean and Press,"** she said, and the smears vanished from her dress. She hopped down off the armor and gathered the little bear into her arms. "Your sanity is low, isn't it?"

"Yes." he hugged her back. "I'm sorry if I'm imposing."

"No, no, you're not. Don't even think of it. This..." Cecelia gestured around the workroom and all the tools and gears and items that Threadbare didn't know the names of. "This is all because of you. I'm here because of you. I'm alive because of you."

"Are you really alive?"

She nodded, her chin moving against the top of his head. "I think so. It's weirder than it used to be, but I'm still me. You saved me, and I'll never forget that. You'll never impose. You can always visit, always get a hug. I'll always have time for you."

The little bear leaned into her, buried his muzzle in the porcelain between her neck and shoulder. "Thank you."

And there they sat for a while. Kayin busied herself cleaning up other parts of the workshop, giving them peace.

Finally, Threadbare stirred. "I should let you get to it."

"Yeah. They'll need me on the battlefield. And I'll need the armor to do the most good."

"I'm a little surprised you aren't making it... well, bigger."

"I thought of that. But there's a lot of reasons not to do that. If I did, then the Hand would be after me. I'm a priority target that way, and I don't think I could survive with all three of their active members on me at once. And also, this will let me get into the fort and bring it into the core chamber. Then there's the fact it's going together quicker, and actually? I think, if I'm lucky, that the strength reduction won't be too bad. All of our calculations are indicating that. Though there are downsides. I'm going to burn through coal faster. No way around it."

"Madeline does have that merchant's pack," Threadbare pointed out.

"Ooooh, there's a thought. I'll talk to her and Graves later, see if we can rig something up..." She put him down and picked up a wrench. "Don't worry about me," she smiled over her shoulder as she turned back to the armor. "But you might check on the others, if you're looking for something to do. I've been at low sanity many times, and company always helped me get through that. I think it could do you some good as well."

"That's not a bad idea," Threadbare said, adjusting his laurels. His ears really weren't set up to hold them too well.

So the little bear went and found the corner where Kayin was sweeping, handling the bulky broom that was five times her size with easy dexterity and strength. "Hello. Are you alright?"

"Yeah. Why wouldn't I be?"

"Well, we've got that war coming up."

She snorted. "I've been training for years to fight that war. On the other side, mind you. Don't worry about me, I don't let things like that worry me. Do the job, get paid, move on."

"Oh. Should I pay you?"

"You already have!" She indicated her body with her furry hands. "This gets you my help until the Kingdom's saved. Afterwards... I don't know." She shrugged. "I like you guys, but we're all going to have to decide on our own individual 'afterwards'. I don't have any family to go back to; my old killers' guild is dead and gone, and I don't have many friends outside of work."

"I thought we were your friends."

"Oh. Uh... well, you are. I didn't mean anything bad by it." She wrapped her arms around the broom and leaned against it. "You're cool enough. Some of the others aren't the friends I would have chosen, but I guess it's fair to say mostly we're friends. But I don't know if I want to spend the rest of my life with you all. You know?"

"It is a pretty big decision," Threadbare agreed.

"Bottom line, don't worry about me. I look after myself, and I'll look after you and the rest." She shrugged. "Might want to check in with Graves, though. He's a little more invested in... well, everything."

"I can do that."

Threadbare found his way outside and went back to the temple of Yorgum. Back around to the side-entrance into the storeroom where rows and rows of plush toys had been laid out with glistening black soulstones resting in bundles of cloth next to them. Graves moved among them, chatting. Fluffbear kept him company, as she worked on the wooden toy bodies that some of the ex-cultists had requested.

"No, I don't think it's a bad notion," Graves said. "A bunny has some advantages over a bear, just in different areas-"

He broke off as he saw Threadbare. And about two hundred voices shouted out various greetings, as the soulstoned dead got into the act.

Threadbare greeted them back by name, one at a time, and chatted with them for a bit until about ten minutes later when Graves interrupted. "Sorry, I think we'll need a few minutes. Can I shut off the Speak with Dead for a bit, folks?"

Then it took another few minutes to get through all the goodbyes. Threadbare didn't mind. Everyone seemed happy, so that was good.

Graves, on the other hand, looked almost as haggard as he had back when he was still affected by Anise's kiss. "Let's walk, okay? I need to get out of here for a bit."

"Sure."

Fluffbear joined them as they walked out. "Breaktime is good."

"Very good." Graves sighed. Then he smiled. "I wonder if this is what it's like to have children."

"Well," Threadbare said, glancing to Fluffbear, "She's making their bodies so that makes her their mother, and we're giving them their souls, so that makes us... hum... no, it doesn't quite add up."

"Am I being a good mother?" Missus Fluffbear asked.

"The best." Graves smiled down at her.

"It really is a strange situation." Threadbare admitted.

"I wasn't meaning in the biological sense or even the creator's sense, like Caradon was with you lot. They're already existing people; we're just helping them transition from a bad state to a good one." Graves rubbed his forehead. "Though I'm worried that they're... well, they're coming to see you as more than a good samaritan. Me too, but I've been discouraging it. I think if there was a job based around worshiping you, they'd take it."

"What?" Threadbare would have blinked if he could have.

"Remember, these are people who let a charismatic cultist talk them into worshiping a dark power. You're very much not that; you saved them from him as far as they're concerned, and they've..." Graves shook his head. "They went for a good long time with a center to their lives. A faith, no matter how misguided. Then that faith got taken away. Now they're searching for a new one, whether or not they know it. And here you are."

"I'm not a dark power. I'm certainly not a god."

"No. But that's how they're coming to look at you."

"I don't know if that's right or wrong."

"I can ask Yorgum about it," Fluffbear offered, pointing to a stone bench off to the side of the Temple.

Threadbare looked to Graves. Graves shrugged. "Couldn't hurt."

The little bear clambered up on the bench, armor scraping on stone as she went, and knelt.

After a few minutes she looked up. "He said that if you don't like it, he'll take them."

Graves snorted. "Oh come on now..."

"He also said that you and Threadbare are the friends they need right now, but there's things you can't do for them, that will cause problems eventually. But he can do those things for them. And that in time if you survive and share responsibility, you will find a lot of friendly priests of Yorgum who will be willing to learn how to make golems and transfer souls, with rules about it to keep Nurph and Nebs and everyone happy."

"Huh. That's a good point, actually," Graves said, leaning against the wall, and pulling his goatee. "Right now it's dependent on us. This whole thing we've discovered. And it raises questions about eternal life, which no Nebite worth their salt would tolerate. I mean now, we're fixing the Kingdom and saving the world, but if we succeed, there's going to be a tomorrow." Graves' eyes lit up. "And if we can get the backing of the Church of Yorgum and turn it into a sect, a holy order... it'll be a lot easier to get it accepted by the populace. My gods."

"Just one," squeaked Fluffbear.

"I may have to join the faith. This guy is *savvy*." Graves grinned.

"Ooh! Ooh! You should join right away! Tomorrow is pastry day!" Fluffbear said. "Living people love those thingies!"

"I'll have a talk with the priest when we get back inside," Graves said, animated in ways that had nothing to do with necromancy. "Thank you!" Then he twitched and turned to Threadbare. "I'm sorry, what was it you wanted to talk about?"

Threadbare smiled. Graves didn't look haggard at all anymore. "Oh, nothing. Do you know where everyone else is? Ah, besides Celia and Kayin?"

"Glub and Zuula are down at the Sturdy Stout, doing dungeon triage. Garon is running the training dungeon. Pretty sure the cats are with them, though with Pulsivar, it's hard to tell. You know."

"I do." Now that his friend was a Misplacer Beast, it was amazing how little they saw of him anymore.

"Cool. Alright," Graves offered Fluffbear an arm up, and she hopped into his embrace. "Let's go talk about my sudden attack of faith."

"Yay!" Fluffbear said, as they went back inside. "My first convert!"

Threadbare smiled and headed down the street, to where the edge of the crafter's district turned into microbrewery lane. Copper vats started poking out of the walls, and the sound of gurgling water running over mash filled his ears, as yeasty scent filled his nose. He lingered for a few minutes by the meadhall, sniffing, as he always did.

But eventually he remembered his task, and found his way to the Sturdy Stout. A tavern that had fallen on harder times, due to the war and the death of a lot of its regulars, the owners had been happy to rent it out to the golems for training purposes.

After all, thanks to the giants, and King Grundi's negotiation skills, they had a dungeon core to play with, didn't they? And a whole lot of newly-made doll haunters who needed levels.

Downstairs, a strange melody played, as Glub squeezed an accordion and sang something soothing. Torn up teddy bears, with a brace of other toy types, sat at the tables and chatted, showing off loot and tending to their weapons. A few female-looking teddy bears leaned on the stage, gazing up at Glub with affection. And there, in the back corner, was Zuula. She sat there with a mug almost as big as she was, drinking it, then spitting it into a nearby spittoon.

"Is that fun?" Threadbare asked, pulling a chair up to the table. Dwarven chairs and tables were much more friendly to very small toys than human ones, he'd been relieved to find out.

"Is something to do," Zuula grumbled. "Garon not letting Zuula run de dungeon no more. Just because Zuula killed a few dudes. Pfft, not like it permanent or nothing."

"We're supposed to be making them stronger, not making them have to reset their levels with deaths."

"Bah! Is lesson! Next time fight better! Is... motivation." She pounded another gulp, then spat it out. "Now is all slow regeneration whenever dey come back hurt, or whoops, get in de soulstone." She gestured at the bag next to her. "At least Graves manage to get dem up to five-job stones. Which is more den most of dem need."

"Well..." Threadbare began, then realized the room had gone silent. Every toy in there was looking his way, and whispers were going around the small crowd. "I think it's good to have options," he finished, adjusting his laurels again.

Your Adorable skill is now level 36!
Your Adorable skill is now level 37!
Your Adorable skill is now level 38!
Your Adorable skill is now level 39!
You are now a level 11 Model!
AGI+3
CHA+3
PER+3
Checking timer...
Your Dietary Restrictions skill is now level 55!
Your Work it Baby skill is now level 55!

"Perhaps we could talk behind the bar?"Threadbare pointed at the room beyond.

"Sure. Beats barfing bad ale over and over."

"Why are you doing that anyway?" he asked, as he followed her into the back room.

"It is what you do in taverns. Besides pinch asses and start fights."

She sighed. "Not allowed to do dat even. Not dat it help. You punch one of de golems, dey say sorry. Dey..." she shook her head. "Too grateful."

"I had a talk with Graves and Fluffbear about that."

"Dey see problem too? Good." Zuula punched his shoulder. "Lot of faith dey got in you, Dreadbear. You better not let dem down."

"I'll try not to."

"You do fine." Zuula grinned. "Talking wit' Jarrik earlier. Beryl t'inking maybe we three, me, Garon, and Jarrik be first flier driver people."

"Really?"

"We all gots flight skill. Garon from when he trying to be dragon. Zuula from owl days. Jarrik because he actually survive first couple of tests. T'ree half-orcs be flying dose t'ings. Gonna call ourselves de Green Bear'uns because of you."

"Thank you."

Zuula leaned against a barrel. "You here because it starting to get to you, hm?"

"It is?"

"De fight. You not be liking fighting people. Not much for monsters, but dose is different. People, not so much. Not to you."

Threadbare nodded. "Yes. However this goes, people are going to get hurt. And a lot of them don't want to fight in the first place."

"Is war. Is why stupid gods got a goddess who only handles war. She do dat so people can deal wit' it." Zuula sighed. "Is gonna be hard on you."

"Yes. But I have to do this. Celia needs me to." Threadbare thought a moment, then looked back to the door. "They need me to. You need me to."

"Yes," Zuula said. "You saved us all. But when you save some'ting, you responsible for it, from dat point on. It only exist because of you. If it turn out bad or do bad, is because you save it. But..." Zuula punched his shoulder again, gentler this time. "It same t'ing if it turn out good. That is you good, too." She smiled, cloth lips stretching around wooden tusks. "And you done some good here. Never doubt dat."

"Thank you." He hugged her. And after tensing for a second, she hugged him back.

The door creaked behind him. "Hey man, I... oh, cuddle puddle? I'm in." Wooden arms reached around them both, and Glub grinned wide wooden jaws as he hugged them close.

"Yeah, Zuula go heal weakys up now," the half-orc said, disengaging herself. "Good talk." She punched them both in the shoulder and wandered outside.

"Ha ha! See, she's cool," Glub said, disengaging. "In a sorta spiky, might tear your head off randomly, kinda way."

"She's Zuula." Threadbare said.

"Yeah, that works. You doing okay, bossman?"

"I came to check on you all."

"I'm doin' okay." He shrugged. "Singin' to a good audience, chilling with peeps and old, uh, friends. Turns out they're pretty cool, now that I can talk to 'em all. I'm glad we're on good terms again. That whole cult thing was weird, in hindsight."

"I think that's how most of them are, from what Celia told me."

"Dude. Well, s'all right. I'm doin' okay. Just kind going with the flow. Y'know?"

"I think so."

"Never seen a war before. Don't have anything like that at home. Got a lot of cool stuff here we don't have at home." Glub filled his air bladders, let them sigh empty again. "Know what I'd like to do?"

"I don't know."

"I'd like to travel around some, after this is all done with and see everything. Then go home and tell stories and sing songs about it."

"Can you go home?" Threadbare asked. "Celia was pretty sure the Crown forces destroyed the gate."

"Eh, I'm pretty sure there's others around. And where there's gates there's cults to my old one. Just gotta find one." He shrugged. "I'm immortal unless someone kills me, right? I got time. And this explorer thing is pretty cool, so leveling it up is only gonna make it cooler."

"It really has helped us." Threadbare smiled. "And so have you."

"Thanks, man." Glub gave him a squeeze, then let him go. "Welp, gotta get back. Hand out waystones to groups going in, so they can teleport out if they get in over their heads."

"Okay." Threadbare nodded and waved. Then his laurels slipped, and he pushed them up on his forehead.

One last person to check with.

Given the choice between going into the dungeon and waiting with Zuula, he opted for the latter. He watched doll haunters in their new bodies enter the tavern, collect waystones from Glub, and head upstairs... usually staring at him the whole while or whispering to each other, with awestruck looks on their faces. His adorable skill chunked up a few more times, and he was pretty sure that he was getting model experience as well. To pass the time he put up buffs from that job.

Eventually, all the groups that went upstairs returned, coming back down the stairs or teleporting directly to Zuula, usually torn all to hell and back. And slowly they made their way out to let their pools recharge or perhaps just to experience moving around in bodies again. All told, it took a long time.

But golems are patient, and golems have no trouble with time. And after a couple of hours, Garon came down the stairs.

"We done yet?" Zuula growled.

"Almost. Figure it'll be morning soon, we can go hang with Jarrik. Oh hey, Threadbare!"

"Hello."

"Just in time. I wanted to talk with you."

"Zuula headin' back to de temple. Come get her when you done. Glub, you coming?"

"Sure, ma'am."

And then they were alone in the tavern.

"It's going well, before you ask," Garon said as he pulled up a chair. "We're letting them sort out their own jobs. We don't have a prayer at teaching them dwarven battle tactics before the big fight, so they're mainly going to be skirmishers. Skirmishers with seriously good endurance, who don't feel pain, and have a racial armor that stacks with the armor the dwarves are giving them. It should work out pretty well."

"That's good. How are you holding up?"

Garon tilted his head. "This is what I trained for, for most of my life. War. This isn't how I was expecting to come to it, but I'm excited to finally get to try out my lessons." He sighed. "And a little sad that I'm going to have to go up against my sister."

"So what did you want to talk about?"

Garon folded his hands. "It's about Mastoya, actually. I think I know how to reach her. But we're going to have to beat her first."

Threadbare nodded. "Okay."

"When we meet her on the field, if we meet her on the field, and I'm sure we will, I want you to follow my lead, okay? No matter what I say."

"Can you tell me what you're planning? So I know how to follow it?"

"That's the hard part. I can't, because it's all going to depend on the circumstances and how it plays out. But..." Garon spread his hands, slapped them on the table. "It's one last try. My last chance to save her. I... I need this. You know? And Mom needs this, even if she won't admit it."

"Zuula said something about you being in a flier."

"Then Wind's Whisper me when you come to her. You're staying on the ground, right?"

"Oh yes. I don't know how to fly."

"Then she'll come to you. I guarantee it. Stall her until I get there. Fight her, talk to her, whatever." Garon shook his head, tossing his horns. "Please. I need this."

Threadbare didn't look at Garon's face. Garon's face didn't move, save for his jaws. It wasn't like humans, whom he'd spent most of his life studying. Instead he studied Garon's posture, the way his fingers moved, the way he sat.

And Threadbare nodded. "Okay."

"Thanks. I owe you. Big time." Garon leaned back.

"Madeline." Threadbare slapped his forehead. "I forgot to talk with her."

"She was chilling on the roof of the temple, last I saw. Wanna walk there together? I can't leave Mom alone too long; she'll burn something down."

"I don't think she can. Most of this place is made out of stone."

"You don't know Mom like I do. She doesn't do well with boredom."

The two of them headed back, and sure enough, there was a flash of red on the temple roof as they approached. "There she is. Want a toss?"

"A what?"

"Some of the new guys invented this. The stronger ones just up and threw the weaker ones across a big chasm I put in their way. It bangs you up a little, but you've got mend." Garon laughed. "Here I was set to be the guy training *them*, and they're teaching *me.*"

"Sure, toss me." Threadbare held his arms out.

The dwarves on the street gaped as the little wooden minotaur whirled around a few times and threw the bear up to bounce off the steeple.

He flailed, caught ahold of the edge of the roof before he fell, and hoisted himself up.

Your Climb skill is now level 14!

"Hey," Madeline said.

Next to her, Pulsivar looked up and immediately hurried over. The Bear no longer smelled like him! This could not stand! Threadbare scrambled for footing, as Pulsivar rubbed his invisible face all over him, the image five feet away rubbing against air. The rank up had made the black cat *strong*.

Threadbare managed to find his voice. "Hello. I've been checking in with everyone."

"Why?"

"Cecelia suggested that I do it. And I want to make sure you're alright."

"Oh. Yeah, mostly." She put her head down, listened to Pulsivar purr as he groomed his bear.

"Mostly?"

"I've done a lot of things. Never done wah. Theah's a lot of stuff that could go wrong when the bacon hits the pan. I mean..." she flexed her wings, "We've gaht more chances of sahviving than most, so long as they don't take down you and Graves, but we really ah gonna be risking everyone in this. Nothing's fa shah."

"For sure?"

"That's what I said."

"I'm sorry. We have to do this."

"I know. Gotta beat the bad guys, win the Kingdom back. But aftah THAT, we gotta go take on the King, and maybe the Hand if we don't stomp 'em in the field. And he's a badass. And the people wahking for him are badasses. I'm..." She looked at Threadbare, and he'd never seen her like this. "I've lost so many people, you know? I've fahked up so many things. This heah, this is the best group of friends I've evah had, and I don't want to lose any of them, and I'm so godsdamned scahed—"

Threadbare pushed Pulsivar gently away, marched over and hugged Madeline.

CHA+1

She sagged into his arms, shaking, and he held her, rubbing her ridged spine. After a bit, Pulsivar came over and curled around them, because why not.

"Thanks," she said, pulling back from him, after a few minutes. "You give good hugs. I see why Cecelia keeps ya around."

"I do my best."

"I'll be fine." The dragon took a breath, let it out. "Will you?"

Threadbare thought about it.

"Yes," he said. "I think it will be hard, but we'll win. And I'll fight hard so none of us die."

The dragon smiled. "Then yoah fine."

"I should be animating more golems. But... I think they can spare me for a moment. Just a moment. If anyone asks please tell them I'm resting."

"You chose a good spot foah it," Madeline settled into Pulsivar's furry bulk.

And so, the little bear rested and prepared for what was to come.

Days fled as he animated golem after golem, gaining a level from his work. They managed to get every one of the soulstoned ex-cultists embodied and somewhat trained. Celia managed to get her Steam Knight armor up and running. And a myriad of other preparations with the leftover reagents helped gain Threadbare another two enchanter levels.

But even so, when the alarms rang through the hold, and the scouts returned saying the Crown's army was on the move, Threadbare did not feel prepared...

CHAPTER 11: DEATH FROM ABOVE

The Dwarven language has fifty-two words that all mean defense. They only have five for offense, and one of those five invokes both concepts. That word is "Lavasten," which means, "Cleaning the foe from a more defensible position, so that we can take it and dig in later."

Most human tacticians treat this as a joke, until and unless the time comes when they find themselves in conflict with dwarves.

When that happens, they usually don't find the word and its meaning funny anymore. Or anything else, really, unless they're tough enough to survive and smart enough to make sure the dwarves don't take the battle PERSONALLY.

Dwarves have fifty-two words for defense.

They have eighty-nine words for grudges.

And hoo boy, had Melos made it *personal*.

So when the Crown forces moved in, they moved in the way that years of losses had taught them to do.

Slowly.

From up on one of the foothills surrounding Brokeshale mountain, a massive part of the stone that had peeled away from it like bark falling from an old log, Threadbare watched them come. Well, as best he could. His perception was good, but they were very far away.

Cecelia was having an easier time of it.

"What is the word for that tube thing?" Threadbare asked, looking up at his little girl.

"It's called a telescope. A nation east of here invented these things, back before the Oblivion. Want a look?"

Threadbare took it carefully between his paws. It was heavier than he expected.

He nearly fell over when he looked through it, though. The teddy bear had NOT been expecting the extreme close-up.

But Threadbare adjusted and stared through the telescope, sweeping it around from one end of the valley to the other.

It didn't take long. The Valley was only perhaps fifteen miles across and just a bit wider from the Crown-controlled lines to the Mountain. He could tell the Crown's territory by the moats that they'd carved out in front of their observations posts, put there to help detect dwarven sappers. The dwarves were big on earth elementalism, along with traditional mining techniques and devices that humans just couldn't match. So the moats were an imperfect defense, but they'd kept the dwarves from breaking out and encircling them, which would have been the end of the war.

"What are those yellow bird things out in front?" Threadbare asked. "The ones with the riders."

"Wark Knights. It's not actually a job; they're just tamers who learned how to be decent fast cavalry and skirmishers. They're our first task, actually. They're sensitive to noises transmitted through the ground, so Mastoya's using them to find out which tunnels the dwarves are in right now."

"When you're fighting an army, first put out their eyes," Garon said.

"We don't have to do that, do we? That sounds rather cruel." Threadbare worried.

"No, it's just an expression," Cecelia reassured him. "All we really have to do is scatter them, then get down to the checkpoint."

"Then it's ah tahn," Madeline grinned, glancing back at the far end of the peak and the winged dolls climbing aboard Beryl's fliers. "So let's get this pahty stahted, huh?"

Cecelia took the telescope back and snapped it shut, handing it to Garon. "Here. You'll get more use out of this, maybe."

"Well, Kayin will. I'll be busy trying not to crash." The three toys walked toward the flying machines and the dwarves waiting beyond.

Garon peeled off, and Cecelia and Threadbare kept walking, back to the mouth of the tunnel, and the enormous steel barrel poking out of it. Dwarves called back and forth to each other, rolling spheres the size of tables along the ground. For all their size, they were light. They were, after all, mainly filled with cloth.

"You're the last," Beryl said. "And the heaviest. We can probably put you the most on target, but everyone else is going to have some variances, no help for it. So don't get fucking stupid all right? I don't care what dungeons you've done, you can't take on an army without help. Just... oh, just don't die."

"That's actually the decree I gave everyone." Threadbare smiled. "They liked that. They liked the quest more though, I think."

"Quest?" Beryl raised an eyebrow. "Shit, if you're just giving them away—"

"You have to be one of his subjects." Cecelia pointed out.

"Yeah, fuck that noise. Uh, sorry bear. Grundi's my king, that's not changing anytime soon. Hopefully." She coughed. "Just out of curiosity, what's the quest?"

"Win."

She laughed, braids bouncing. "Alright. Get in the ball. We're starting the sequence in five."

The dwarves nearest them cracked open the sphere of the bronze orb, showing layers and layers of cloth and padding, with twenty of the new teddies clustered around it. One waved and almost tumbled some of the padding out of the sphere until one of the dwarves cursed him out and tucked it back. "Stop moving! Time for that when you're all in."

Cecelia moved into the padding, nestling herself carefully. Threadbare piled in next to her, mend golem beads at the ready. Then darkness, tight darkness, as the dwarves sealed the orb... followed by movement as they rolled it upslope.

"Alright," Threadbare said, there, in the middle of the pile of golems. "Everyone hug, just like we practiced, please."

"Sir?" One of the smaller bears squeaked. "Can I say it's just an honor?"

"I think you just did. Oh, wait. Thank you!"

"He thanked me! Eeeeee!"

"We'll only be hearing this for the rest of her life," another bear grumbled.

"Ah, let her have it, Frenk, let her have it."

Rumbles from outside, clanking, metal scraping against bronze. "They're lowering us in," Cecelia said. "This won't take long."

"Right. First rule?" one of the bears spoke. "Nobody fart."

They all got a laugh out of that. Except Threadbare, he'd never really gotten why fart jokes were funny. It was just a thing humans did.

The minutes crawled by, in that dark, cramped space.

And then—

WHAM!

The impact pushed him back into the cloth, pushed them all against each other, with the Steam Knight armor at the very back, and the soft toys flattening out, all surrounding Cecelia's ceramic body in their center.

It would have broken bones in a normal person's body, but as it was...

Your Golem Body skill is now level 33!

"Woo!" Someone yelled. "Easy skill up!"

"Easy? Easy? Shit man, you're nuts!"

"Packed nuts!" Someone else yelled, and they all laughed again. The pressure eased, bit by bit, until the toys almost felt like they were drifting.

"We're falling now," Cecelia said. "This is going to be the hard part. Hug tight!"

Beryl had listened with wide eyes when Cecelia told her of how they'd escaped Fort Bronze.

Then she'd started sketching and doing math.

The dwarves had steam cannons; they'd been developed early on as counters to Fort Bronze's armaments. But the steam cannons had never been able to get the range they needed to shell enemy territory.

However, super-light shot, filled with stuffed animals and other toy golems, packed into a wooden shell that broke away and allowed the round to fire without disintegrating... well, that was different.

And when you threw Zuula into the mix, Zuula who'd recently re-learned her twentieth level skill that let her call winds... well, things got INTERESTING.

It took far less time than it seemed.

CRUNCH!

Red numbers drifted up, golems screamed-

-and golden light flared, as their innocent embraces fired off, a massive flare of golden light that drowned out the sunlight now flooding in from the broken shell around them. Padding exploded outward, as did teddy bears.

And Cecelia, who tumbled across the ground, coming to a rest with Threadbare grimly hanging onto her hands, digging his heels in to slow and stop her.

"Are you alright?"

"I think so. **Status.**" She nodded. "Only down a bit- uh oh."

"Hum," Threadbare said, as he looked up at the big, yellow birds and their armored riders staring down at him.

Down and past him, to where golden feathers fluttered to the ground, and a pair of big bird legs twitched under the mass of the broken bronze ball that they'd used to traverse the battlefield.

The dwarves had put the shot a little TOO close to the targets.

"Keep them busy!" Cecelia hissed in his ear and made a dive for the cannonball... and her armor, still packed securely within.

Threadbare looked up at the vanguard of the Wark Knights and waved.

Your Adorable skill is now level 44!
Your Adorable skill is now level 45!
Your Adorable skill is now level 46!

"It's the bear! Get him!" An officer called from the rear, spurring his bird into a slow trot as he leveled his spear.

"Are you sure, sir? I mean, look at him! He's just standing there!"

"How the hell many teddy bears are there on this battlefield, you think? Fucking get him!" The bird loped into a canter now, the rider's spear coming straight toward Threadbare.

"It's funny you should ask that question..." Threadbare said, spreading his arms. **"Guard Stance."**

Your Guard Stance skill is now level 22!

And then the rest of the toys charged in, from all sides, from where they'd been scattered. No time to retrieve armor or weapons, none to organize, it was just a score of fuzzy, tiny growling targets, panicking Warks, and yelling riders.

The officer managed to regain control of his mount, wheeling around

—

—and staring goggle-eyed at the dapperly-dressed teddy bear hanging by one paw from his spear.

"...there's quite a lot of us now, you see," Threadbare finished.

And then he launched himself at the rider, claws out and swiping.

CRUNCH!

Another bronze orb hit the ground, a few hundred meters away.

WHUMP!

Another descended, thirty seconds later, as the bears fought and the air filled with golden feathers and bits of stuffing, and the Wark Knights fought desperately against a foe they'd neither trained against nor were prepared for in any way. The birds beaks were actually the most dangerous part of the whole thing, as the toys were mostly prey-sized, but the golems were far tougher than their usual meals. Threadbare managed to knock the officer sprawling, sent him running in one direction, then leaped off the bird as it ran the opposite way. Looking around the battlefield, he charged back to his troops, shouting mend spells as he went.

And then from the wreckage of the bronze orb, Cecelia's voice rose, triumphant and high.

"Cast in steam and steel, raise thy blade! All systems go!"

The bronze half-sphere flew upwards, and Kindness rose from the wreckage, cloth padding spraying loose as it ripped free.

Five feet tall, in enameled red armor, smokestacks churning white smoke from either pauldron, it had a backpack-like boiler about as big around as it was. Though the blade it bore was only four feet long, it was wide and large and heavy. More like a slab of iron than a sword...

The other arm held the best and heaviest shield that the dwarves could spare her. She'd used her own tinkering and smithing skill to add more armor, heedless of the weight. It probably wouldn't stop a cannonball, but anything less than that wouldn't do much.

At the sight of their foe, the surviving Wark Knights turned and fled. They knew that call. They knew what it signified. And even a midget Steam Knight was still a Steam Knight.

"Is everyone all right?" Threadbare called.

"Harb and Jeri are down!" One of the bears replied.

Threadbare ran over to their torn, still forms, and dug in their chests, searching for Graves' last gift to them... and after some rummaging, removed two intact soulstones. He sighed in relief, and put them into the backpack that one of the dwarves had been happy to turn into a Pack of Holding.

Then the bear's hat was suddenly gone from his head. He blinked at it, saw it lying there on the ground, with an arrow in it. Something flickered past him, and he snapped his head around to see that the front lines of the Crown forces had moved up while they were fighting the Wark Knights. They'd forsaken a slow march for a steady charge, and the first archers were just now ranging them.

"We should go. Now!" Threadbare said, waving, and the teddy bears fell in behind him.

"But their weapons and armor..." Cecelia turned to the shot they'd arrived in, where most of their gear was still stowed. "No, nevermind. No time to dig them out. Go! I'll hold the rear!" And she galloped after them, shield behind her, doing her best to run cover for the slower teddies.

The toys fled. And the pursuing army found out one of the truisms of fighting teddy bear golems.

That running them down, without supporting cavalry or some obstacle in the way, is pretty hard to do.

Golems start with a good endurance, and teddy bears get more on top of that. Actions that would stress or strain a human are barely noticeable to bears, and simple commands like "Oh hey run that way and don't stop," have resulted in golems crossing nations, descending into the depths of the sea, and occasionally coming out on the shores of other continents.

Mind you, these were intelligent golems, so they didn't have that particular issue, but the long and short of it was that the pursuit didn't go as well as their commanding officer expected.

But humans had longer legs, and their ire was up. And they'd been given very *specific* orders about teddy bears, so they persisted.

They didn't see the danger until it was too late.

The teddy bears were hard to see in the first place, given their size and the various rocks and scraggly grass strewn around the valley. The regular line troops hadn't been in a position to see that they'd crawled out of the bronze shot. To them, the various craters and bronze fragments they passed were just missed artillery shells.

So they were pretty well blindsided after the toys let them go past, then emerged from the craters and attacked them from behind.

And from the back, glancing into the rearview mirrors of her small mecha, Cecelia was in a good position to see this. "Hey!" she yelled to Threadbare, who was easily leading the pack.

"Yes?"

"Stop running!"

"Why?"

"We need to save our friends!"

Immediately the little bear swerved, kicked up dust, made a full turn and ran back toward the fight. Cecelia turned with him, sending up a spray of dirt and gravel, as she pointed her blade. **"Steam Scream!"**

REEEEEEEEEEEEEEEEEEEE!!!!

Green numbers swarmed from the heads of the Crown troops, as the miniature mecha charged. And Threadbare and eighteen other teddy bears followed in her wake, claws out and ready to fight!

Some of the Crown infantry broke right then and there. Caught between an ambush of living dolls, and something they knew they'd barely be able to scratch, a few of the less-disciplined troops routed. Rallying cries filled the air, as their officers hastily spent Moxie like water, restoring what order they could. As for Threadbare, he let Cecelia take the brunt of the charge and focused on moving around the battle, mending where he could, and inviting and kicking the golems in and out of his party to buff up the ones who needed it most at any given moment.

For all that...

For all that, it was a close one.

The Crown troops had levels on the townsfolk-turned-golems. They also had weapon skill and knight levels, which made them hard to hurt. Their officers blended in a mix of mercenary, mostly for the group buffs and the self-healing.

The golems, on the other hand, had a weird mix of levels among several classes, Knight and Archer being the most common, along with the ubiquitous Cultist levels, of course. But they also had skills boosted by repeated dungeon runs, in a semi-controllable situation. Some fought with small crossbows, other bore metal armor and tiny blades, and each one of them had strength far, far out of proportion to their forms.

It was bloody on both sides. For every two of the Crown troops that fell or fled, a golem was ripped asunder, or decapitated. At some point in there, Threadbare got an animator level. Not that he noticed, he was too busy helping his people survive and harvesting soulstones from the fallen.

In the end, three factors won the day for Threadbare's allies. The first was the small size of the golems. They had managed a successful ambush and were in among the foe, making it impossible for the Crown forces to hold any kind of line or bring the bulk of their force to bear against the, well, bears.

The second was the fact that the golems outnumbered the troops in this section of the line. Two hundred little bears and other soft plushie golems had been jammed into the shells and dropped on and around the biggest concentration of Wark Knights. A few had suffered destruction during the drop, but most had survived, armed up quietly, and found themselves in an ideal ambush spot.

The third thing in Threadbare's allies' favor was Kindness.

Cecelia's Steam Knight armor was an unstoppable engine of destruction, a man-sized machine stomping around the battlefield, hewing about her with the overlarge sword. She might not have had the knight levels she once did, but she had the defense she needed to tank pretty much anyone in the unit they were up against, and the raw strength to blow through any armor, whether it be with a steel-capped knee, her heavy blade, or a nasty headbutt when people tried to corps-a-corps her.

Finally, the soldiers fled...

...revealing a double line of archers beyond.

"Loose!" Their Captain ordered.

Four golems went down immediately, standing stupefied at the sudden danger. Their colleagues grabbed their bodies up, dropping weapons to do so.

"Run!" Cecelia yelled, and they fled again... and this time there was no pursuit. But there were arrows, so many arrows... and a droning, in the sky above them.

"What?" Cecelia yelled. "They're not supposed to be near us, they're supposed to go after the main battle lines!"

"What if the main lines came to us?" Threadbare called back, holding onto his hat, the arrow in it bouncing and jouncing with every hurried step. "I think we got their attention!"

"Oh sweet Nurph." Cecelia took an arrow in the boiler, slowed. **"Mend!"**

"Are you holding up alright?"

"I leveled, but my pools didn't recharge! Steam Knight problems."

Arrows fell, and golems staggered as some of them hit. "We can't escape in time. Take cover everyone!"

The golems hit the dirt, putting shields overhead where possible, keeping still and taking cover behind rocks where it wasn't.

Threadbare crawled up under Cecelia, as she stood there, shield overhead, arrows raining off of her. Red zeroes and ones flew up, mostly, but the occasional lucky crit tagged her for ten or twenty. "Let me," Threadbare said. **"Mend, mend, mend..."**

"Thanks. Oh. Oh boy. It IS the main force behind us. And they're using razor arrows on me, not good! We need to get to the rally point. Just another mile to go, but..."

The droning deepened, and both of them looked to the skies.

Three of Beryl's fliers hung in the skies above, wings wobbling, air blades or whatever they were in front of the contraptions, pulling them forward. And as they flew down from above, black specks came falling down from them, specks that grew and sprinkled over the archers and the troops behind them like pepper...

...and then the first wave of explosions rippled through the Crown forces.

"Gather the fallen!" Threadbare yelled and went to grab soulstones while the archers were disrupted. "Get the stones then run north! Keep going north!"

Now that the arrows weren't falling, he could see across the valley. The dwarves HAD made an appearance at some point, some point he hadn't noticed in the chaos. They had emerged from their tunnels to take on the forces to either side. But they'd left the center to the golems, and they were too hard-pressed to aid. Threadbare winced as he saw dwarven shields splinter under a full-sized Steam Knight's heavy foot... a Steam Knight that looked their way and started stomping over with a purposeful stride.

"Cecelia!"

She looked over. "Oh no. Inkidoo."

"That's a bad thing?"

"Not the worst but still lousy. Run!"

The golems didn't have to be told twice. They left the fliers to bomb the front lines and completely missed the Dragon Knights flying over to intercept them, and the wave of flying golems leaping off the fliers to harass and target the dragon riders.

But that's what happens when you're fleeing for your lives against something that can singlehandedly stomp you and all your friends into mush.

The problem was, Inkidoo's knight didn't seem inclined to give up.

And unlike the human troops, his machine didn't have muscles to tire. And it took really, really big steps.

"We're not going to make it!" Cecelia yelled. "Oh... fump it. Go. Keep a soulstone ready for me." Cecelia slowed and turned Kindness around, looking for a good spot and finding it on a field full of loose stones. "I'll buy you time."

Threadbare stopped. He looked at her, looked to the fleeing golems.

The fleeing golems who slowed and looked at him. "Go!" Threadbare said, offering his pack full of souls to the nearest one. "We'll buy you time."

The teddy bear looked down at Threadbare's offering and shook his head. "No one dies, remember?"

"Yeah!" Another one shouted, as she slowed down. "We're not leaving you, Lord!"

"Besides," a plush bunny in a matronly dress said, winding up her crossbow, "we almost beat a steam knight that one time, right? What are the odds this one has a fireproof blanky?"

Threadbare stood still, as an idea occurred to him. He remembered an unexpected ogre, and how Zuula had dealt with the thing...

"Can you hold him?" he asked Cecelia, as Inkidoo slowed, blade out, and moved in for the kill.

"For a little while!"

"Please do!"

Behind him, the golem archers started firing at the knight, and the cries of **"Razor Arrow!"** rose to the skies... as did the red numbers. The knight was a big target, and the archer skill bypassed some of his armor. Not much, really, but it was enough to turn zeroes and ones into twos and fours. With a groan, Inkidoo whipped its shield up toward them, raising its blade high, and bringing it down—

—to miss, as Kindness sped to the side. **"Animus Blade! Animus Blade! Animus Blade..."** Cecelia called six times over, and from compartments on Kindness, daggers whipped out and started their swirling assault. She tried to close in, caught Inkidoo's foot in her chestplate for her trouble, but the daggers whittled scratches into its leg while she got her footing.

But she didn't rebalance fast enough. Inkidoo's shield slammed down on her helm, crunching it, and Kindness fell. The shield rose and fell three more times, and Kindness only survived by getting its shield in the way, getting driven into the ground a little further with each savage strike. The Animus Blades carved away, but Inkidoo took the damage, as its rider mended it whenever it got noticeable. And when the tiny steam knight was good and planted, Inkidoo drew back its massive blade—

"Get him!" A tiny voice yelled.

And the golems attacked.

Swarming it from all directions, they piled on it, grabbing onto its legs and climbing upwards. Inkidoo paused, shook itself like a dog drying, and some golems fell, but the ones that dropped simply got back up and ran in for another try. Inkidoo swept about it with the sword, but the targets were so tiny and so mobile that the knight had trouble getting a bead on its prey.

So it planted the blade in the ground and used its free hand to brush the golems free.

Which worked, up until Threadbare grabbed its fingers and swung up to land on its helm and squirm his way right through the visor slit.

Startled, the knight inside drew a misericorde and tried to stab him—

"Disarm," Threadbare said and managed to smack it from his hand with a timely crit.

LUCK+1
Your Disarm skill is now level 2!

"I'm very sorry about this, and you should probably go get help right away," Threadbare rummaged in his apron and pulled out a bright red seed pod. **"Firestarter,"** he said and dropped it down in the workings under the cockpit before scrambling out.

Your Firestarter skill is now level 11!

When they'd made Cecelia's hair for her new form, they had gone through several types, before finding the bright red, glorious stuff that was blisterweed pod silk.

Normally scorned because it caused hideous rashes among most who came into contact with it, they'd managed to boil it until it was nontoxic to the touch. Which wasn't a problem for golems, but Threadbare thought that she might like to get her head petted by friendly people at some point and that it would be awful if they got bright red painful itchy rashes from doing that.

But he'd still had a blisterweed pod left over from making her hair.

Inkidoo's pilot froze, as red and black smoke filled the cockpit.

Then he turned and fled with a horrible coughing echoing in his wake as he made for the lines and the nearest cleric.

"Thanks," Cecelia said, clattering Kindness to its feet and swaying back and forth as the daggers coursed endlessly around her. "Er. Could you?"

"Certainly. **Mend, mend, mend...**"

WHUMP!

He jumped and looked over in amazement as Inkidoo fell. "Oh my."

"What did you DO to him?"

"I borrowed a trick from Zuula."

Cecelia stood, flexing Kindness' arms, and retrieving her sword from where it lay. "Well I just got two Steam Knight levels, so it was a pretty lethal trick."

Threadbare found himself feeling a bit bad about it. "Oh. I really didn't mean to kill him."

Threadbare, though he was intelligent, had no way of knowing that blisterweed was commonly used as an insecticide in small doses. Doses that were about the size of a twentieth of the pod he'd just set alight in an enclosed, poorly-ventilated space.

You are now a level 20 Golemist!
INT+5
WILL+5
You have unlocked the Armor Golem skill!
Your Armor Golem skill is now level 1!
You have unlocked the Flesh Golem skill!
Your Flesh Golem skill is now level 1!

"Two golems in one level?" Threadbare mused. "I need to read this. Are we safe?"

"I think so."

"Status."

"Whoa. Whoa no. No, we're not safe at all!" Kindness reached down and scooped up Threadbare, and Cecelia fled. "Come on! Let's go!" She called back to the other golems. "The tunnel's not far—"

"Hm? What?" Threadbare stirred, looking over her shoulder.

And right at the approaching form of Reason, its white bulk moving with purpose after Kindness. It shrieked as it came, that hissing screech that he'd heard once before, when Emmet killed it in the machine bay.

Emmet wasn't here now.

But two others *were*.

On its left flank and above the machine, a batlike daemon soared through the skies, with a black-robed figure on its back. To Reason's right, a woman on a red carpet sat in lotus position, surrounded by flames.

The Hand had come for a rematch.

And the fact that two of them were visible, meant that the ninja wasn't far behind.

But this was the last thing on Threadbare's mind right now, as he smiled back at Reason, and started Wind's Whispering, contacting the allies he could reach. "Cecelia?"

"What?"

"Whatever happens, no matter how bad it gets, we must NOT kill the daemon who's wearing your body..."

CHAPTER 12: MORE THAN A HANDFUL

Threadbare's golems had been tasked with breaking the Wark Riders, then falling back to regroup and get new instructions.

What neither they nor the dwarves had anticipated, was that the bulk of the army would pursue the golems.

As such, there was no way that the group of friends could make the rally point before the full force of the Hand (Minus The Lurker, who was hopefully still dead,) came down on them.

So to that end, Threadbare knew that they had to stand and fight, and they needed terrain that would let them hold out until the friends he'd contacted could carry out their part of the plan.

He also knew he wasn't trained in this. Not at all.

"Celia! Where should we fight?"

"I don't know!" She waved her sword around in an arc, pointing. "There's old half-collapsed tunnels all around, but the Cataclysm will cook us if we cluster. There's open ground, but Reason will stomp us flat! There's old building foundations, but the Legion will harry us with conjured daemons, and the Ninja will rip us to shreds bit by bit!"

"I can make Reason not a problem. Maybe all of them. I just need a boundary."

"How?"

"Wards."

"What's your skill?"

"Two."

"That thing will blitz right through it. I'll do it, that might work... no. No, wait, that'll drain me. Gah! Kindness is... it's good against the line troops but useless against the elites. I just don't have the levels."

"Then get out. Once we get to the place we're going to fight in."

"You think wards will hurt Reason?"

"Did that thing Emmet beat up look like a daemon to you?"

"Open ground it is... there!" She pointed with her blade towards a small hill, with the remnants of what had once been a low wall around half of it. "Best we're going to get."

They shouted directions to the golems, and in a matter of minutes, the toys were clambering over and through the rubble of the wall, taking up positions, and readying their crossbows. Cecelia, with Threadbare's help, shut down the Steam Knight suit and struggled out of it. "Reagents?" She asked.

He gave her a vial of green, and she slammed it against the ground. **"Ward against Daemons!"**

Patterns flashed into life, green and red energy swirled and spread out to wrap around the wall and stretch up the hill.

"I don't suppose you have any blue reagents?" Threadbare asked her. "I've got two. With a third one I could do something nifty." He looked to Kindness' still form.

"No, sorry."

"Bother." He turned, to stare at the oncoming daemons—

—and twenty feet from him something hissed. A red '12' flashed up in the air, and a blurry form darted away, shadows swirling as the Ninja pulled back from the boundary of the ward.

"Shoot her lots please!" Threadbare called to his troops, and they filled the air with bolts. A few grazed her, but then she was gone, bounding across the scree and over the hill, out of sight.

"Okay. We've got some advantages here," Cecelia said. "Oh, and can I have the laurels please?" Threadbare gave them to her, and she slumped behind a chunk of the wall, jammed the laurels awkwardly on her head, and said, **"Rest."**

"What advantages?" Threadbare asked.

"When we fought The Lurker he didn't use any Gambler or Archer tricks that I could tell. And Grifters are good at disguise, but they can't shapeshift like he did. So I'm pretty sure what we're dealing with here is daemons that have natural skills that are close enough to what the Seven did to fool people. We're not dealing with tier two jobs and high level tier ones. But we ARE dealing with dungeon shenanigans that are boosting them to midboss levels."

"I see," said Threadbare, peeking over the wall. The Cataclysm and the Legion had slowed, somewhat, and were spreading out around Reason. "They stopped moving so quickly. Do you think they're being cautious?"

"Either that or they know we can't escape them now. Or both."

Cecelia yawned. "Wow, this is nice." She adjusted the laurels.

"I don't think you'll have time to go back to full."

"Eh," She tapped her sheathed sword with one porcelain hand. "If it gets me in the neighborhood I'll be happy. So we've got a ward. What else can we do?"

Threadbare thought, then ran over to the golems. They moved along the wall, and most of the crossbow wielders went up the hill, spreading out as they went. "There. That should help against the Cataclysm."

"From what that ward did to her, I think the Ninja's kind of fragile. At least to spells. So they can spread out so long as they stay within the ward, hopefully without getting picked off too much. Good, good. How many do we have left?"

"About a hundred and fifty."

"Ouch."

Threadbare rubbed the straps of the pack full of soulstones. "I don't know if I got everyone. I hope so."

A yell up the hill, then a flash of golden light. Threadbare looked that way. "Is everyone all right?"

"Ninja threw a knife at Rafe! Jackie and he hugged it out."

"That's going to get annoying quick, but sooner or later she'll run out of knives. We don't have organs so one-shot kills are going to be hard. For her. Not so much for—"

SNAP!

They stared at the ballista bolt shrieking towards them from Reason's arbalest. "—Reason," Cecelia whispered, and then Threadbare hauled her up to his shoulders and ran.

A section of the wall ceased to be, and rocks sprayed as the heavy bolt burst through. "I can run!" Cecelia said.

Your Dodge skill is now level 18!

"Not while you're resting, it'll break the skill." Reason had stopped four hundred meters out, give or take. A few crossbow bolts licked out toward it, fell vastly short. "Save your fire!" Threadbare called.

"That's an intriguing notion," the Cataclysm called, standing up on her carpet. "I think I'll disregard that." She whipped her hands through the air, ripping fiery holes into it, and pulling out gobs of flame. Molding it into a big ball, she raised it up above her head and hurled it straight at Threadbare.

He hurled himself into cover, dove over Cecelia, and hoped.

Turning his eyes upward, he watched as the ball hit the wards... and shrank abruptly, down to basketball size.

But it still continued through. And the golems screamed as it exploded above them, raining down fire and light.

Threadbare took a breath…

…and let it out as a red '21' drifted up from his singed fur. He'd put fire resistant enchantments on a few of his armor pieces, as he'd had time and reagents to do so. Now it was paying off.

"Wards? Thought so," the Cataclysm sat down on her carpet. "Legion, your boys will be useless here. Make sure nobody interrupts our playtime."

"Don't fucking tell me what to do!" The daemon rider called, as he wheeled overhead. But he spread out nonetheless, and little rifts appeared in the air, as flying daemons squeezed out and scattered around the area surrounding the hill.

The battle still raged on around the toys, dwarves clashing with the Crown's forces, but the bulk of the army seemed content to let the Hand take care of the golems. Or perhaps they just wanted to stay as far away from them as possible? Threadbare didn't know.

Another yell from up the hill, another flash of golden light. "She got Vance!"

"Pull his body back," Threadbare said. "And keep a watch out." He couldn't tell them to harvest the soulstones. The way the Ninja operated, she'd surely break them if she knew.

Meanwhile, across the field, the Cataclysm was assessing the fortifications and finding them not to her liking. "It's your turn," she slapped Reason on the arm, and backed away. "Break the walls, drive them back from the cover. I'll take care of the rest."

"With pleasure," Cecelia's voice echoed from the daemon machine, and Threadbare felt a stir of anger rise up in him to hear it. That was his little girl's body in there!

Threadbare turned to HIS Cecelia. "May I have your daggers?"

"What? Why?"

"I have an idea."

"Here," Cecelia handed them over, barely moving. "And if you can, get Reason close. I'll see what I can do."

Threadbare stood, moved around to a gap in the wall. The Cataclysm's gaze snapped around to consider him, and she sent a wisp of flame teasingly his way. It shrunk when it hit the wards, but he swiped his hand through it, not bothering to dodge and ignoring the red '44' that rose from his singed paw. "So how exactly does this work?" Threadbare asked.

"Does what work?" The red-clothed thing wearing a dead woman's face asked, as she idly gathered up a bigger ball of flame. "You dying? I think you should know how that goes by now."

"No. The daemonic possession part," Threadbare said, ignoring

Reason as it stomped closer, arbalest trained on him.

"It's not possession," she smiled under her veil. "Your bodies are just meat puppets for us. The brains provide the memories, the hearts run the bodies so we don't have to. You're just our material components, more or less. Well not YOU, you little freak. No brains, no heart... and no luck, for your path has brought you here to stand in front of us." The ball grew in her hands.

"Interesting." Threadbare stepped out of the wards, and the onlooking golems cried out, called for him to come back, and started down the hill. But he waved them back and kept moving...

...straight toward Reason.

The corrupted suit hesitated, snapped its arbalest around to point straight at him.

But the arm was shaking.

"Because I have a lot of memories of Cecelia. And she has a lot of memories of me. Of tea parties, and nights with her whispering to me, and cuddling, and that time I brought her water, and when we all laughed together in Catamountain, when I was wearing my first clothes. Well, my second clothes, I suppose," Threadbare said, lifting his hat. "You gave this to me, remember?" he said, walking toward Reason as the great engine stood there and shook.

He'd remembered how Anise had shaken, there, when confronted by Fluffbear. And Anise was much, much older and stronger than Cecelia's daemon had been, he thought.

"I... know what you... do," Cecelia's voice, tight with emotion, sobbed from Reason. "Won't work. Inefficient. Pain... passes."

"Does it?" Threadbare asked. "Because those were very good memories. I loved Cecelia. And she loved me. And there's nothing you can do to take that away from us—"

The knife took him from behind, stabbing through his coat, stabbing through his chest—

—and he turned, caught the Ninja's arm with both paws, and dug his claws in, pulling her hand through him.

Your Claw Swipes skill is now level 47!

"Animus Blade, Animus Blade, Animus Blade, Animus Blade..."
Six times over he cast. Six times over the daggers he borrowed from Cecelia ripped free from his coat, where he'd hidden them. And driven with the strength of his will, boosted by his Creator's Guardians, they ripped into the Ninja.

The creature screamed and fled, and he heard the Cataclysm shouting behind him, but it didn't matter. He clung on for grim death as she shook him, tried to pry him off, and sent the daggers after her, after her face, slashing her chest and neck, sending red numbers spiraling up as blood flew.

Your Ride skill is now level 13!
Your Ride skill is now level 14!
STR+1

Stuffing flew to mingle with the blood, as she drew her knife and stabbed relentlessly, and he switched to mending himself, dumping everything he had into Mend Golem spells. She switched to attacking the animated blades instead, but it took her a few swings to drop each one, and every time she did, he'd just animate it again. And battered and nicked and worn, it reanimated and dug back into her.

In the end the outcome was inevitable, as she shrieked and scrambled and failed to dislodge him. She weakened by the second, and she just couldn't do enough damage to overcome his healing—

—and unfortunately, the Cataclysm saw that too.

His world became fire, and light, and the explosion hurled him through the air, to land to the side of the hill. He couldn't see, and he tried to feel his face with his paws, but his paws weren't working right.

Your Golem Body skill is now level 34!
Your Toughness skill is now level 25!
Max HP+2

He opened his mouth to speak, to heal himself, and nothing came out. There was something filling his mouth. He couldn't say what.

His nose smelled ash, ash and burnt fur, and Threadbare knew that smell was himself.

Your Scents and Sensibility skill is now level 23!

"Oops. Hm. Well, she'll be back," he heard the Cataclysm giggle. "Okay, newbie. It's a charred lump. Think you can finish THAT off now? Without wussing out on us?"

"Like heck!" Cecelia shouted, and he heard porcelain feet hit the stony ground. "Everyone let's go!"

No! Threadbare thought and tried to crawl toward her voice. A paw worked. Nothing else did. *Don't come!*

Reason's footfalls shook the ground... but there was another sound over that.

A droning. From above.

Almost! Get back to the wall! You're almost safe! He tried to yell but couldn't; his tongue was ash.

"Mend!" Cecelia shouted, from a distance away. Threadbare spat ash out. **"Mend!"** she shouted again, and vision abruptly reappeared as one of his burnt button eyes flowed back together, un-melting. Reason was fighting the golems, he saw, and winning handily, but they were buying time at the cost of their lives. **"Mend!"** Cecelia shouted, and the stump where his right paw was shuddered and reassembled into a proper arm.

"I can take it from here!" he called, as he reached into his coat, found the beads, and slammed three to the ground.

The healing rushed over and through him, and Threadbare stood up as Cecelia reached him, and the little bear spun around...

Just in time to see another massive fireball shrieking toward him.

Threadbare knelt, fast as lightning, and dragged his paw around them, slammed a vial of green reagent into the ground, and yelled **"Ward against Daemons!"**

Your Wards skill is now level 3!

The explosion blew them out of the circle, consumed it.

But the hasty, weak ward did its job. And when Threadbare picked himself up off the stony ground, he saw to his relief that they'd lost no limbs.

"Oh for the love of Cron!" The Cataclysm snarled, as Reason slew a golem with every stomp. "Just give up and die already! Legion, they're out of the wards, swarm them. Finish this sad..."

The droning rose, and she looked up, as the bombs fell down.

"Get back! Get clear!" Threadbare yelled to the golems, and they fled. Some of them even made it in time.

But not all, as the bombs exploded around Reason, and the Cataclysm steered her carpet in a frantic attempt to dodge the worst of it. Gunfire cracked down as well, and the fire daemon shrieked as bullets ripped into her. From that range it was a long shot, even for Jarrik, but the few that found her HURT.

And as Beryl's fliers passed overhead, drifts of flying toys headed down, spreading out to go after the Legion and his daemons. The fliers circled back as the toys harried him, as Jarrik and Kayin and Zuula got into the fight, hitting him with bullets and arrows and wind bursts repeatedly.

Not that the toys below had time to spare for the dogfight above them. Cecelia certainly didn't wait. While the bombs were still falling, she ran up to where Reason was down to one knee, sheltering its cockpit with its arms. Great holes had been blown in the armor, and inhuman flesh and gore spilled out, as the machine groaned and sobbed. Cecelia ignored that, ignored the teddy parts and stuffing strewn around, and ran to the back of the machine, lunging for the compartment that she knew was there, and jamming one hand through the hole. **"Animus!"** she shouted. **"Invite blanket!"**

Then she ran.

Reason shook.

Reason let out a confused burble.

Reason abruptly fell to the ground and started thrashing, digging around in itself, ripping armor plates off, trying to get at the shapeless, crawling THING that had been let loose in the equivalent of its nervous system.

Months ago, Cecelia had put a fireproof blanket into Reason, as a last-ditch system to keep herself from being cooked alive in her armor. If Reason caught afire, she thought, then she could always animate the blanket and have it crawl out, and go smother the fire. It had worked very well, the one time she had to use it.

But the compartment the blanket occupied was open to the inside as well.

And now the blanket squeezed its way inexorably up through the fleshy mass of the daemon engine, towards the thing inside.

Threadbare saw none of this as he ran, trying to close with the Cataclysm as she hurled fire into the sky, shrieking, fireballs exploding in midair and burning daemon and flier alike. He shoved the remaining mend golem beads in his mouth and ran. One of the fliers caught a fireball square on and disintegrated, hurtling toward the ground, and Threadbare could only hope his friends survived as he leaped…

…and caught ahold of the edge of the carpet.

The daemon snapped her face down to him, stomped down hard, trying to kick him off her ride.

Threadbare was having none of it. He ignored her, clung on with both paws. She wasn't his target. anyway.

"Disenchant," he told the carpet.

Your Disenchant skill is now level 24!

They fell to the ground, as blue reagents rained down, and she fell. He hit first, tumbled to his feet, and launched himself at her.

"Fool!" she shouted, clambering up, and then the world was fire… but he had beads left, and he waded in, slashing, ignoring the blindness as his eyes melted, ignoring his face turning to ash, just lunging in and striking. Whenever he felt his paws start to burn he bit down on the beads, triggering the healing, and staying on her.

And then the fire was gone. He bit down on the last bead, snapping it, and his eyes returned to him.

She lay crumpled, with enough crossbow bolts in her that she looked a bit like a porcupine. Turning, he saw the surviving golems behind him, reloading their crossbows.

But she still breathed, so with a final slash, he ended that.

You are now a level 14 Cave Bear!
CON+10

WIS+10
Armor+5
Endurance+5
Mental Fortitude +5

You are now a level 11 Duelist!
AGI+3
DEX+3
STR+3

You are now a level 14 Ruler!
CHA+3
WIS+3
LUCK+3

And while Threadbare rejoiced to see her fall, he felt bad that only fifty, barely fifty of the golems were still up. Reason and stray fire had left the bodies of their friends and families strewn across the rocky ground.

He spoke, found his mouth full of clay fragments, and spat out the remnants of the beads. "Soulstones. Retrieve the…"

Reason groaned, and he turned to see the great machine on the ground, tendrils flailing from its cracks, thrashing the earth. Its cockpit was open, gore gushing forth, dark blood staining the ground. A trail led from it to Cecelia. The little doll moved toward Threadbare grimly, tugging with all her might at a squirming, blanket-clad form, dragging it along in fits and starts.

"Got her," Cecelia said. "Alive. For now."

"Dreadbear!" he heard above him, and the bear and his girl looked up to see Zuula ghosting down on spirit owl wings with Kayin in her arms. "We need to go! Legion is too strong!"

A shadow rose over Threadbare. He turned to see the final daemon descending on its batlike mount. Around it the swarm of daemons swirled, four times the size it had been just minutes ago. "Is everyone in the fliers all right?"

"Madeline be out dere somewhere wit' Garon. Jarrik…" Zuula shook her head. "Don't know. We tore daemon asshole up good, but… no more fliers. Can't finish de job!" She caught ahold of the winds, threw them at the skies, and the swarm swirled, then recoalesced as the last member of the Hand headed straight for them, and the first imps started their descent. "Get to de tunnel!"

"No time," Threadbare said, softly. "Get to the wards—"

Light lanced through the sky.

Light pierced through the batlike daemon, and its rider. An arrow of light, leaving a contrail of shrieking ichor behind it as it tore through the cloud.

Followed immediately by six more.

"Rapid fire arrows of light," Zuula whispered. "Burnin' so much fortune…"

"Wards!" Threadbare shouted, and they ran, ran as the lesser daemons kept on coming, tearing at the golems. Threadbare jogged over to Cecelia, grabbed ahold of the blanket, and helped her pull it up to the edge of the wards… then stopped. "She'll die if we take her in here!"

"We'll die if we stay out here!" Cecelia pointed out.

"I need her alive!" Threadbare insisted, as imps tore and ripped at him, trying for his eyes, and he laid about with his scepter, scattering them. They couldn't do much damage, but there were a LOT of them.

"Alright, I can do this!" Cecelia decided. **"Pommel Strike! Pommel Strike! Pommel Strike!"** Drawing her sword, she smacked the blanket-clade form with the blunt end of her blade again and again. Yellow numbers flew as she beat the stamina out of her daemonic self, and Threadbare kept the imps off her as best he could. "There! She's unconscious!"

The two of them retreated behind the wards, and oh, Threadbare's heart broke to see the state of Cecelia's clothes and hair, and the long scratches down her face. **"Mend Golem,"** he told her, laying a paw on her, relieved as her injuries repaired. "I'm sorry. But we DO need her."

The imps swirled around them, breaking on the wards, daring it a bit and hissing as it burned them. A few of them worried at the blanket, and Threadbare swung his scepter across whenever they got organized about trying to open it.

The golems got into the act, shooting into the cloud, using the rest of their crossbow bolts on the screeching, birdlike daemons.

But as the minutes passed, the swarm shrank.

"They're disappearing," Threadbare said, watching as holes opened up in the air, and swallowed them. Back to someplace full of red light, someplace they did NOT want to go.

"He works like a conjurer. Lots of things, some of them pretty powerful, but they don't stick around for long," Cecelia sighed. "Is that reagent over there?"

"Yes!" Threadbare went and gathered up the scattered bits that were all that was left of the magic carpet. "Good. I can use this. Right away, actually. Well, once the daemons are gone."

"What I want to know," Kayin said, as the imps slackened, and the last of the swarm returned to whence they came, "is who shot those arrows."

"Funny ya should ask that," an old, familiar voice drawled.

Threadbare whirled, as from behind part of the wall, a gray-cloaked figure blurred into existence.

Save for that gray cloak, he wore brown from head to toe and stubble adorned his chin. His face was a mass of wrinkles, and what hair he had left was on the sides of his head, stark white and unruly.

"Ullo Mister bear. Been a while, yeah?" Mordecai said. Then he squinted at Cecelia. "Oh, ya got a little doll what looks like Celia now? S'cute."

"Mordecai..." Zuula whispered, stepping out from behind Cecelia.

And the old scout froze. His jaw worked up and down, and he stared at the little doll. "What?" he barked, hands trembling. "What is this! What kind of... no. Mad. It's the madness come 'gain." Mordecai dropped to his knees, burying his face in his hands, fingers white as he squeezed his skull. "Out! Na really there! Na really there!"

"No," Zuula said, trembling herself. "Is Zuula. Is..." She whispered, then fell silent. She looked to her spear, cast it aside. "Dreadbear. Loan her your club."

"It's... more of a scepter, really."

"Do it."

Wordlessly he passed her the bear-headed scepter.

And the golems watched in silence, as Zuula strode up to Mordecai's trembling form and bopped him, HARD, in the knee. He yelled in surprise, jumped up with wiry strength, and his bow was in his hands, nocked with an arrow drawn, head right in Zuula's face.

"You is late!" Zuula thundered.

Then she bit the arrowhead, twisted her neck to the side, wrestling it from his grasp. It hummed as it went past Threadbare, and he watched as she started wailing on her husband with all her might.

"Hey!" Kayin yelled, starting forward—

—but Cecelia whipped her arm out to block the wooden catgirl. "No! This might work!"

"What might work? What might work?"

And as Mordecai danced backward, running from his wife, a wondering grin filled his face. He pulled out his knife, and the golems around him raised their bows... only to lower them as Threadbare waved his troops down. "Just go and harvest the soulstones. That's more important. Let's, ah... let's give them some privacy."

"Yes. Best not to stick around for what follows," Cecelia said, looping her arm around Kayin's shoulders and walking her away.

"What follows?" the assassin asked.

Cecelia told her.

"Um. But she's... and he's... how?"

"I'm not actually sure, and I don't want to know," Cecelia said.

Kayin agreed with that on general principles.

So they concentrated on saving their dead.

A few had broken soulstones, and a quick speak with dead saved some of them... others had expired too long ago in the battle for it to make a difference. Threadbare mourned with each one that came up missing. They were lost for good. This was war, this was the cost of victory.

But the battle wasn't done, not by a long shot. Judicious use of Cecelia's telescope showed that the fray had shifted to the south. "The giants are down that way." Cecelia said, from the top of a nearby hill. "They're having a hard time of it, looks like— oh fump."

"What?" Threadbare asked.

"Emmet. He's down there. Along with a whole lot of troops."

"An' our daughter too," Mordecai said, walking over to Threadbare and the two doll haunters, cuddling Zuula in his arms.

The half-orc glared at them. "Not one word."

The trio nodded in unison.

"Graves and Missus Fluffbear were over with the giants," Threadbare said, worried.

"So are the rest a' the dwarves," Mordecai said. "But there's too many troops still up. Dwarves can't stop that lot if Emmet breaks past them giants."

Threadbare looked around at his team. Then he looked south. "I suppose we're not done yet, then. But before we do, Cecelia, you've got a choice to make."

"A choice?"

Threadbare walked over the blanket and pulled it free, revealing the white armor beneath and the unconscious daemon within. "It's very risky. It's also maybe a bad idea. But if it works, I think, just maybe, I can give you your body back..."

INTERLUDE 4: SPOILS OF WAR

Mastoya hated fighting giants.

The big sons-of-bitches (and daughters of bitches,) hit hard, took a lot of hits, and scared the shit out of troops that weren't expecting them.

Which was why, instead of beating ass, Mastoya was stuck behind the lines, charging Petunia up and down them, and yelling **"Rally Troops!"** to rally her soldiers.

Honestly, if she hadn't had Goliathan in her battlegroup when the blue bastards had popped up out of a suddenly-opening tunnel, she wouldn't have bothered. Just sounded the retreat, and moved north, turned the feint up that way into a real strike.

But no, the Steam Knight had reached the level where she was Named and Feared, and also the giant she'd battered to pulp with her enormous flail still lay there, crushed, in mute testament to her might. The giants had lost momentum then, fallen back and played keep away with it, tried to get at the troops behind Goliathan instead while a few of their smarter sisters barraged him with rocks.

That was one anchoring point.

The other was Emmet.

With Inquisitor Layd'i just behind him, Emmet marched across the battlefield, and things died. When the dwarves came out to support the giants, Emmet was there. When Goliathan faltered, caught between three axe-wielding giants at once, Emmet was there.

Whoops, no, Emmet was here, Mastoya realized, reigning Petunia in as the massive armored shell loomed out of the lines. The daemon followed in his wake, frowning. "Why are you taking prisoners?"

"Why are you not on the front lines?" Mastoya bellowed, waving her sword between the two of them. Anise stepped back, eyes opening wide as Mastoya continued. "This is my battle! Fucking get back in position!"

"This is against the King's direct wishes—"

"GET BACK TO IT!" Mastoya bellowed, riding directly up to the Inquisitor and rearing Petunia's hooves over her head.

Anise backed up quickly. Then she looked to Emmet.

Emmet who was moving back to the front lines.

"What?" and oh, the daemon's face was beautiful to see in its outrage.

"The General gave us orders," Emmet said, moving through the ranks of the archers, and Anise followed, complaining, her voice fading as she chastised the golem.

Not that Mastoya listened for long, she was already moving again. Explosions northeast meant mortars, and the advance was slowing there.

"Unyielding," Mastoya whispered, protecting herself against critical hits. She sheathed her sword. **"Lancer,"** she said, reaching into the air and pulling a steel spear out of nowhere, twirling it between her fingers before snapping it into place. **"Last Crusade!"** she yelled, passing through her front line, bellowing it, and hearing her troops roar as they followed her, straight towards the thin line of dwarves and the mortar teams behind them. **"CHARGE!"** she commanded, and Petunia sped up, sped as the bombs fell around her, as her troops crumpled from shrapnel and concussion, charged straight through the fire, leaped OVER the double-line of axemen, and landed amongst the first artillery nest.

She wanted to rage. She NEEDED to rage. It was there; it was hungry, and this was its feeding ground. Blood would sate it, she knew, more blood, even if it ripped through her like a glorious storm, even if her own blood spilled...

...but no. No, she had to keep to the plan or all was lost.

And in the split second before Mastoya landed, she sighed, fought her rage down, and said **"Pommel Strike."**

Her lance reversed with a quick flip, but she STILL knocked the poor bastard with the telescope back about fifty feet. Then swipes took down the rest, and before the axemen could turn, she was galloping hell for leather towards the next nest, and her troops were roaring, too close for the axemen to turn anyway, unless they wanted seventy-five riled up infantry up their asses.

Mastoya beat down the artillery crews or sent them running, running back toward the newly-opened holes that they'd come from.

Once it was done, she allowed herself a moment of respite, looked around. Took stock of her battle.

She'd started with a wide advance, putting the northern forces out in front. The Wark Knights made it look like a regular assault, like many she'd tried before. Then enough of the line troops that it looked like both fronts were even.

All this had been to mask the major push that she was with, the one moving up the southern front now. The plan had been to draw the bulk of the dwarves' forces north, retreat the northern front west, and push hard with the southern front through the diminished dwarven forces, and straight on to the mountain. Once there the siege engines could do the work.

But she hadn't counted on the Hand tearing north and leaving the forces they were supposed to support in the lurch. She hadn't counted on the dwarves having artillery that could reach that far or the loss of most of the Wark Knights. Hadn't counted on fliers, fucking fliers, with swarms of tiny monsters that had driven off the Dragon Knights she'd deployed to cover the northern flank's withdrawal.

So instead of pulling their forces north, then having her troops do a disciplined retreat back to threaten the dwarves and keep them from rejoining the battle in the south, she had been forced to put everything on the southern push, while the dwarven forces held firm to the east and were starting to tunnel in and drop off their troops from the north. The western rally point was full of injured soldiers and broken warriors. They were no threat to the dwarves, not anymore.

The dwarves were way off script. Fliers, long-range guns, and giants. Three wild cards she'd known nothing about. Combined with her own unreliable elites going off on a wild bear chase, the plan's chances of success were dropping by the minute. Too many more surprises, and she'd have to order a retreat. And then, if she was wrong, the Inquisitor would ensure she had a long, painful death.

One chance, Mastoya knew. Once chance to win this.

She looked back to the very rear, to the massive wagons, animated and driving along under their own power, the drills and cannon and catapults and the carts of explosives that would crack the mountain wide open, break open the dwarvenhold to the point where the dwarves would be forced to surrender. All they had to do was get them intact to the mountain. Five more miles, and they could do this.

She shook her head, threw a Greater Healing on herself and headed back south—

—only to be brought up short as a figure loomed out of the dust on the horizon.

Reason.

Battered, covered in seams, staggering, it moved with ponderous speed, smokestacks still for once. Its arbalest was a shattered mess, but the monstrous machine still gripped its sword in one hand.

Mastoya stared at it for a second, something niggled in the back of her mind, but… it was gone.

No time to think. She had a battle to run. "You alright in there, Ragandor?" Mastoya bellowed.

"I've been better," the heir spoke, her voice faint, barely audible. And again, something niggled at Mastoya's mind.

No. It was Cecelia's voice, or the voice of the thing pretending to be her, if Mastoya's suspicions were true. Either way, it was in no shape to take on giants. But… "Go guard the engines!" she shouted. "Protect them with your life!"

There, that should keep her happy. She spent the last couple of weeks fixing those damned things anyway; she's invested in them.

Without another word or thought, Mastoya turned and wheeled Petunia away, back to the lines.

The giants were in full rout, she was pleased to see. She was less pleased by the stream of casualties heading west. This is going to be close. And we haven't even hit the main dwarven force yet.

Their lines were just ahead. She could see them spilling out of the tunnels their elementalists had opened, see them dressing their musket lines, braced on the shields of the axemen in front of them. So few, compared to her troops, but that didn't matter. Each one was a veteran. Each one had been here from the start. She'd need to drown them in numbers to win, and she wasn't sure she had the numbers.

But she did have a Goliathan. And an Emmet.

Then the cannons started, from the cliffs above, and she winced as Goliathan rocked under heavy fire. It held its shield up and forged forward, and she bit her tongue. The giants had battered him up pretty badly already… and the damage hadn't all been mended. Was the pilot low on sanity?

She cast a look over to the Inquisitor, who was waving her hands, as Emmet's wounds healed.

Mastoya activated the voice enhancer in her helm. "Emmet! Front and center! Goliathan, fall back!"

Goliathan hesitated. The helm turned to her.

"THAT'S A FUCKING ORDER!"

Unlike Sir Grayson, the Steam Knight of Inkidoo, Goliathan's driver was a far more reasonable person. Less prone to outrunning her support, more willing to listen to orders. Which was always a tough one with Steam Knights, because they were charismatic enough to argue the point if they felt like it. Goliathan tipped the dwarves a jaunty salute with the handle of his flail and trudged backwards, soldiers scattering to let her by and reforming around the titan.

"I don't like this," Dame Genya spoke from Goliathan's visor as she passed Mastoya. "They'll need me."

"I don't give a flying fuck. Go back to the siege engines and get one of the menders to patch you up."

She spared a glance north, saw the force she'd led to swarm the artillery position on their way back, escorting battered dwarven prisoners with them. "Then get the latest bunch of captives back to the fort. Make sure nobody gets stupid."

"Yes ma'am!" Goliathan left.

The cannons rolled, the muskets fired, and Mastoya drove her troops forward, shields up. But even with the lines running Shield Saint, even with their heavy armor, the bullets still ripped through into the troops behind. Add in the cannonballs raining from above, and it was a slog just to get to the dwarves.

This was why their small numbers didn't matter. What mattered was what got across the field.

And Emmet, thankfully, was drawing the fire she hoped he would. He was half the size of the Steam Knight, a much smaller and faster target. Musket fire sheeted off of him, in rains of zeroes and ones as he stomped forward, Juggernaut powers active.

For her part, the Inquisitor was just as brave, give her that. She moved along behind, almost birdlike, shifting in microscopic increments, zig-zagging, dashing unpredictably. She kept her arms behind her.

"Incoming!" Sergeant Tane called, "Graves? Graves!"

"The fuck is a…"

Screaming, clinging for dear life to a cat the size of a great dane, a man in armor burst out of the dwarven lines, rode through her own, leaping over everything in his way. He was CLEARLY not in control of the great black cat.

The bizarre sight was immediately followed by a smaller, tan cat, with a very familiar little bear riding on it.

She slowed as they loped past her, stared… then her breath caught in her throat as she realized where they were going.

The Siege Engines!

"Fucking…" Then, to her amazement, she saw Sergeant Tane gesture to his squad, and start backwards. "TANE! KEEP IN LINE! REMEMBER YOUR ORDERS!"

The veteran knight yelled back, but she couldn't hear him—

—and then he was gone.

She blinked, looked to the side, found him on the ground, his shield in fragments, and the cannonball that had caught him rolling on the ground, glowing red.

He had Unyielding up. He didn't take the crit. His squad clustered around him, shielding him from musket fire, and then he moved and Mastoya wheeled.

The next part was the melee, and it'd be up to Emmet and her troops, now.

They'd win the fight.

She had to win the war.

Mastoya rode like mad, spurring Petunia on. An ordinary horse would have been exhausted long ago, but Favored Mount buffed her, and Horsemanship buffed her more. "Lancer," Mastoya said as she went, pulling a spear from the air. Then she grimaced, and dipped into her sanity and fortune. **"Ritaxis' blessing of strength upon me. Shield of Divinity. Holy Smite."** The lance developed a halo, was outlined by light.

And when she got within sight of the wagons, she arrived to a scene of madness.

Reason, broken and scarred Reason, was standing over the shattered form of Goliathan.

Beyond it, the Siege Engines were in full retreat. Three wrecked carts lay scattered nearby, cleaved in half by a massive blade. Overhead, a tiny dragon wheeled with a horned rider on its back. The catriders were, oddly enough, not heading toward the wagons. They were heading toward the battlefield where she'd broken the giants.

Mastoya reigned up. Had one of the giants survived and wrecked the wagons?

Then Reason brought its fist down to hover meters above Goliathan's helm. "Yield, Genya," Cecelia's small, muffled voice spoke. "I don't want to kill you."

It's silent, Mastoya realized. The engine's silent. *That's what was wrong with it!*

"I yield!" Genya called, from what was left of her cockpit, laying in the remnants of her green armor.

Reason turned then, back to the wagons as it lifted its blade and started moving forward...

I am betrayed, Mastoya realized. *The daemons have betrayed me!* She felt rage curdle in her heart...

But she knew how to fight this foe, now didn't she?

She spurred Petunia, and chanted as she went. **"Divine Conduit. Unyielding. Back You Fiend! Charge..."**

And the minute before she hit, **"Twisted Rage!"**

Oh, it felt good.

She snapped the lance in Reason's leg, making it stumble... and from aboard it, she heard screams. Many many screams. Oddly different from the last time she'd killed it, but she was too busy to think about it, too filled with the red anger, and she leaped from Petunia's back and drew her sword, beating the thing over and over again, hacking chunks of metal free, chopping without a heed for defense. The Divine Conduit healed the wounds she took as it struck back, draining her fortune to give her the smallest bit of power from her goddess.

But Reason was healing, too.

As fast as she chopped, it mended. And it wasn't burning.

Something inside was burning, smoke was leaking out, but the massive mecha itself remained unimpaired...

...and between hacks, as time dilated and stretched while adrenaline thundered through her, she saw the hatch in the back open and flaming teddy bears drop out.

The rage paused.

She stared, open mouthed.

And Reason backhanded her away. The teddy bears stopped burning, kept running. Someone was shouting. What were they shouting? The words blurred, the rage distorted them.

Mastoya fought it back, bottled it up.

"...go help Graves! Keep clear of her!"

A tiny red-headed doll, mildly burned, hopped out of the hatch. She was wearing a replica of Dame Ragandor's armor. And talking in her voice.

Mastoya blinked again. Then she grunted and dashed forward, hacking into Reason. The details didn't matter. The goal was the same. Protect the Siege Engines or lose.

Then her world turned to fire.

"Give it up Nasty Masty!" she heard from above. Garon? Then that means...

"I can't!" she said, taking Reason's sword on her shield and returning its strikes fourfold. Its healing was slowing; she WAS having some effect. But her fortune was draining so very fast...

"Stubborn girl!" she heard from behind her and froze.

Reason fell back.

"You... I killed you," she said, turning, the goddess' light filling her eyes and blazing forth.

"Yeah. Killed Zuula fair and square. But Zuula cheat," said the little half-orc doll, waving a spear at its wayward daughter. "Sorry."

"I'll kill you again!" Mastoya roared...

...and her heart skipped a beat, as the air rippled next to her mother, and Mordecai faded in.

"Dad?" she whispered.

He looked old.

"That'll be quite 'nuff out of ya, Mastoya Skunkthumper," said her father. "Yer on the wrong side, and yer beat fair an' square."

The Divine Conduit flickered. One of its conditions, one of its drawbacks, was that you had to align yourself, your being, your purpose with the work of the deity you called upon. And Ritaxis wanted only war.

Ritaxis did NOT do domestic disputes.

"I…" she said and willed the buff away. "I can't."

"Yes you can," Garon said, as his dragon beat its wings, hovering with unnatural wooden grace. "Look behind you."

She turned, whipping her shield up, expecting Reason to pummel her down—

—and saw blue forms chasing after the Siege Engines, loping along, snarling. The giants! But no, they weren't moving like giants. And a lot of them were wounded, bloody, and… undead.

"Even if you get through the armor golem, you won't get through the giants that Graves just animated. And all the while we'll be on your back, harassing you, hindering you, but NOT killing you," Garon continued. "And it'll be the whole family, save for Jarrik and Bak'shaz, against you. But hey, if you wanna go for a threefer and take down Dad, too, now's your chance. Bad odds. Wanna try it anyway?"

The sword fell from Mastoya's hands.

"I hate you, Mother," she told Zuula.

"She know… Zuula is…" The half-orc shook her head. "Sorry. Was stupid to beat you. Was bad to hurt you. Was… trying orc parenting on half-orc. Bad t'ing to do to little girl. Never did it again."

"I will never forgive you for it," Mastoya told the doll.

"Okay. Is fair."

Mastoya picked up her sword and sheathed it with a snap, reached up to the ring of beads around her neck, and ground one to dust between her metal-clad fingers. "Retreat," she said. "Surrender where retreat is impossible. We've lost. We're done." she spoke, and the enchantment whispered the command through six more officers. They had their own beads. The command would echo down, she knew. The General of the Crown's army bowed her head.

"Oh no." A strange voice said from behind her, and she turned to see a little bear, a sharply-dressed bear clambering out of Reason's hatch, pulling a charred form behind it. "No, no… I'm sorry Cecelia; I didn't even notice."

The form wore Dame Ragandor's armor, a full-sized version of it.

With sudden understanding, Mastoya dropped her buffs and clapped her hand over her mouth, eyes going wide. *The daemon princess had been in Reason, and I was fighting it with Back You Fiend up for... how long?* Long enough, evidently.

"Oh. Well. I guess that settles that," the doll-sized version of the princess said. "No going back to my old body now. If it was even possible."

"I didn't even notice she was dying. Everything smelled like burning, and I was healing Reason," the teddy bear said, staring forlornly down at the meaty lump.

"No. It's not your fault. And it was the right choice. Messing around with daemons at the last minute was how my father fumped everything up. Come on, it's better this way." The doll moved forward to hug the teddy bear.

And goddamned, if it wasn't as adorable as it was tragic.

Mastoya pulled her hand from her mouth. It still took two tries to wet her lips and whistle until Petunia returned. Then it was up, up and to the front lines, to get her troops in safe.

"See ya soon girl," Mordecai drawled and faded from view.

She got up to the lines to find one of Tane's subordinates leading the withdrawal. *Lana? Kara? No, Kara was the shorter one.* "Status?"

"Bad. The dwarves let us go, but... the golem..."

"They killed him? How?"

"Not them. The Inquisitor."

"What?"

"He was too thick in the fight to retreat. He surrendered. The Inquisitor looked furious. She... she punched right through him. Then she ripped his helm off, ripped it clean off. I don't know how!" The blonde woman shook as she recounted the betrayal.

Mastoya closed her eyes. *My last ally is dead. I told him to surrender if I ordered it, and he followed my orders into death.* "Back. We need to get back to Fort Bronze. The King needs to hear this. From your lips, right away."

It took two hours to get back to the gates of Fort Bronze.

They were closed.

And the Crown flag no longer flew from its towers.

"Told yer we'd see yer again," Mordecai said, fading in next to her. Without Zuula around this time, thankfully. Mastoya thought that if she had been, there would have been nothing on Heaven or Generica that would have stopped her from trying to kill her Mother. Again.

"How?" Mastoya whispered. "The garrison..."

"Fell ta Jericho and tha rest o' tha Rangers when ya were far enough away. Our fort now."

Mastoya looked at him. In front of her, her army stood, staring at the gates, not quite comprehending what was wrong yet. Lines of dwarven captives stood off to the side, staring silently. Staring at her.

"Ma'am?" Sir Renick asked, riding up, eyeing Mordecai. "Everything all right?"

"No." Mastoya said, and she drew her blade. The nearest soldiers called out in alarm, but she waved them down, as she eased off Petunia. She was tired, so tired, as she walked forward, walked to stand in front of the gates and whirled to face her troops.

"Soldiers of the Crown!" she said, using the final charge for the day on her helm's giant voice. "You fought well. You fought hard. You fought with honor. But you lost. We lost," she said, feeling her eyes burn, fighting the tears. "This war is over. We fight no more." She took a breath, turned to the gate again. "This war is over. I order all of you to stand down. I order every prisoner freed. And I surrender unconditionally."

We're done, Mastoya thought, bowing her head.

And may the victors be kinder to us, than we would have been to them.

CHAPTER 13: BREACHING

"Honestly I have no idea what she was trying to achieve," Emmet rumbled.

"Something to do with making a demonic version of you, we think," Threadbare said, looking down on the trudging, battered golem walking next to Reason. He and Cecelia were sitting atop the mecha-turned-lesser-armor-golem, trudging west. Below, the rest of their friends mingled with the dwarven army. King Grundi's Kneelchair, in its warwagon configuration, kept pace with them a few hundred feet away.

Emmet was with them and not with the other prisoners. The dwarves had objected to that, until Threadbare pointed out that if Emmet really was planning treachery, it wouldn't matter WHERE he was.

They finally backed down when Threadbare told them Emmet was his brother and that he'd take full responsibility for the guy.

"Yeah, making a daemon copy of you would be the most likely conclusion," Cecelia said. "The parts she tore out of you are— are the parts she ripped from me." The doll smiled. "If it's any consolation, when we mended you up, they probably vanished right from her hands. I like the idea of the frustration she must have felt from that."

"I did have a heart, but it was for show. The head was... damaging. I barely survived that," Emmet said.

"So she was able to hurt you that easily?" Threadbare asked. "That worries me."

"Not so easily!" Emmet sounded offended, just a touch. "I surrendered. I deactivated all skills and buffs. And then she commanded me not to resist her attacks."

"And you listened to her?" Cecelia said.

"I had no choice! She COMMANDED me. She used three scrolls to do so."

"Oh," Cecelia said, putting her hands to her mouth. "Oh gods she's got command golem scrolls."

"Oh no. Those again." Threadbare rubbed his head. "I'm to blame for her getting those."

"You? How?"

"I was very stupid when she gave you the quest to bring her the scrolls. And it was a public quest, so I got it as well. And..."

"Oh no."

"...yes. That was why you couldn't find me after we became scouts. I was out delivering them."

Cecelia was silent for a few minutes.

"I wish I hadn't," Threadbare said, "everything that followed was my fault. When they came for Caradon, you could have fought them off, Emmet—"

"No," Cecelia said. "No, he couldn't have. The house was a wreck, things were messed up, and my father had brought overwhelming force. Don't... don't beat yourself up over this. It wouldn't have made a difference in the end. It just would have meant more deaths. They would have found another way to get what they wanted."

"I do not understand what you are upset about," Emmet rumbled, "I do not know the details. But the current state of affairs is not displeasing to me. I have found a way to satisfy both my honor and my family, as General Mastoya suggested."

"Wait. What?"

"I spoke to her after the Inquisitor commanded me to do something I did not want to do. Together we found a workaround. And it has worked."

Cecelia looked at the bodies they were passing, then at the small train of human prisoners... which included four knights that hadn't stopped staring at her since they'd first laid eyes on her porcelain form. She gave Sergeant Tane a good hard look, then turned away. "What exactly are you saying? Mastoya wanted this to happen? I find that hard to believe."

"It is..." Emmet said, pausing. "It is not enough to do the good thing, or to have justice on your side. You must also be strong enough to win. To survive. Or else good and evil don't matter."

"I think," said Threadbare, glancing over to Garon and Zuula, where they were walking happily alongside Jarrik and Mordecai, "that we need to have a good talk with her when we catch up to her."

*****

They found Mastoya in the depths of the cells, guarded by two grey-cloaked women who muttered **"Scouter,"** as they approached, then nodded and faded back into the shadows. The half-orc looked rather ordinary out of her battle plate. Someone had taken the fingerbones out of her hair, and she was painstakingly braiding it back up into a knot.

For a good long second, Threadbare and Cecelia surveyed her, and she looked back at them.

"And?" the imprisoned general asked.

Cecelia spoke. "I didn't come back from Outsmouth. That wasn't me, these last couple of weeks."

"I know."

"Then why?"

"Why what?"

"Why did you…" Cecelia covered her face. "Did it make a difference to you, that I'd been replaced by a daemon? I thought you cared about your troops! I was under your command! Why didn't you…"

"Do what, precisely?" Mastoya said. "Tell the King that his daughter was a daemon? For all I knew he'd ordered it. If that was the case, then I'd be dead or out of command. And if it was the Inquisitor who'd just killed you? Then I MIGHT be able to tell him, but if he believed her over me, or she got wind of it, I'd be dead or out of command. Then what? Stage a coup? Go traitor?" Mastoya hawked and spat in a nearby chamber pot. "Fuck that noise. My troops wouldn't have followed me. My only worth, my only chance of doing anything was if I remained a General and gave you the chance that you needed. And I did."

"The chance that we needed?" Threadbare asked.

"Yes. You want to break the cycle, right? You want to claim the throne and stop the wars and get rid of the demons, right?"

Cecelia said nothing. But evidently it had been a rhetorical question, as Mastoya continued. "Five years we've been fighting this war. Five YEARS. The nation was invested. IS invested. This isn't just pride, it's the heart of who we are. Good, evil, it doesn't matter. We threw ourselves into it. Through orders, through drafts, or through volunteering, it's Cylvania's war. And if you hadn't won? Then there's no way you could achieve a lasting peace, later. You had to decisively beat the Crown. And you had to do it in a way that SHOWED my troops they were beat. And you did. You've won." She lay back on her cot, staring up at the ceiling. "Deposing the King? Taking the castle? That's just the finishing blow. Won't be an easy one, but it's inevitable, now."

"If only that were true," Cecelia whispered. "The final struggle's just starting."

"What?"

"Did you know that all of Cylvania is inside a massive dungeon?" Threadbare asked.

The half-orc sat up and stared. "What the fuck are you talking about?"

They explained, and she listened, eyes getting wider and wider.

"This... this explains so much." She clenched her hands on the cell's bars. "Why he's like two different people, depending on his mood. He..." She looked down at Cecelia "He ordered me to kill the dwarves. All of them. No mercy, no surrender."

"You disobeyed that order?"

"I told him to his face to get a different general. He was over me, roaring with fury, and then it just— cut out." Mastoya's face turned ashen. "He pretended it had been a test and commended me for not fighting him on those orders. When I'd just refused them seconds ago. I thought he was mad. Now you're telling me he's a dungeon monster."

"Yes."

"Okay. This makes me feel better. I wasn't betraying the king I'd sworn to serve, then. I've been working against a monster who's usurped his place, more or less." She sighed, smiling. "That makes me feel better."

"I don't really care about your feelings," Threadbare told Mastoya.

"Threadbare!" Cecelia gasped.

"I don't. It doesn't matter why you did things. It only matters what you do." Threadbare pointed up at her. "And a whole lot of people died today because you decided to put your code of honor before them."

"You know nothing of it!" Mastoya yelled. "My code of honor is THEIR code of honor! I couldn't ask them to compromise themselves, just because—"

"Because you thought you were following a mad king into oblivion. So you didn't tell them. You chose for them." Threadbare continued.

"That's what Generals... that's what Generals DO." Mastoya said, staring at them. "Don't you understand? How could you not understand?"

"I understand," said Cecelia. "You coward."

Mastoya flinched back. "What?"

"You didn't trust them. You didn't trust them to make the right choice. You thought he was MAD, and you went 'Oh well, guess we'll keep on with the plan, just do things a little more nicely,' You didn't tell them because you didn't trust them with the decision. And the dead? They're on you. Meanwhile you're in here trying to sort out your FEELINGS."

"I'm in here because the rangers fucking put me in here, you little dolly dummy!" Mastoya roared.

"No, you're in here because you looked at evil, and you looked at good, and you thought 'Meh I don't care, so I'll go with whoever's stronger!' Cecelia stalked up to the bars, shaking her ceramic finger. "You didn't CARE! You put yourself in here! You chose POORLY. You are a HORRIBLE person."

Mastoya closed her eyes and sat on the cot. "I know," she whispered. "Knew that all my life." Tears leaked from under her eyelids. "Never had a chance, I guess. Tried. Never found a place where I could do some good."

The little bear squeezed through the bars and moved up to her. "Then maybe it's time to change that."

She opened her eyes and stared down at him. "How?"

"Three chances. Garon tells me that's how many you should give family. You aren't my family, but Garon's very much a friend, so I think three is fair. You've used two of them. One when you turned down Garon's offer the last time we were here. The other when you fought a war that you didn't need to. But we have one more chance for you."

Mastoya spread her hands. "Alright. What do you want from me?"

Threadbare shook his head. "No. It's not for me to say."

"Then who?"

"Your family. All of them. Garon and Jarrik and Mordecai and Bak'shaz and yes, even Zuula."

"I will never forgive her."

"I don't care if you forgive her or not, but you have to talk to her. Because without her blessing you won't get that third chance. And we'll do what we're planning, without your help, and more people will die and maybe everyone. So if you must blame her, AFTER her death, AFTER you settled your troubles with her in blood, then you aren't the person we need for this after all."

"Wait." Mastoya blinked. "Jarrik? Bakky? They're alive?"

"Bak'shaz went to the Rangers when they rose up. We just found out he was here today," Cecelia smiled. "He's so grown up now." Then her smile disappeared. "Jarrik went to the dwarves, and the Hand's daemons almost killed him. Because of this battle that nobody needed to fight."

Mastoya set her jaw, glared... and the glare faded, as she looked away. "I... don't know if I can face them."

"Up to you," Cecelia said. "They're all outside. Waiting to talk to you. They want to talk to you. And what they decide, after that, determines whether or not you help us or not. So it's up to you, General."

Threadbare walked out of the cell, offered Cecelia his arm. She took it, and together the two toys left the cellblock.

"Well?" Bak'shaz asked, as they came out. He was taller than Jarrik now, a gangly youth just out of puberty, with a turtle-shell helmet and boar's leather armor wrapped around his lanky frame. "What do ya think?"

"I think we need to get ready to move, with or without her. This will go easier if she's on board, but… she's a mess," Cecelia sighed. "If we can't get her along willingly then we're better off without her."

"Well. Thanks for tryin', anyway." Bak'shaz shrugged. "On us, now." He headed down to the guardroom to round up the rest of his family. Threadbare and Cecelia headed upstairs and found themselves joined by Madeline, Fluffbear, Glub, and Emmet on the walk up.

"I have never had a sister before. I am still ascertaining how I feel about having a brother." Emmet told the little black bear currently perched on his shoulder.

"It's great! Do you like kitties?" Fluffbear said, bouncing up and down a bit.

"I do not know. I have never been permitted to have a pet."

"Oh no! That's horrible! You can share mine and see if you like her. If you do we can get you one of your own!"

"Okay."

"There's something different about you, Missus Fluffbear," Threadbare said. "Have you gotten a bit bigger?"

"I'm a grizzly now!"

"Oh! That would explain it."

"A grizzly bear?" Cecelia scrutinized her. She was perhaps two inches taller then she had been before. "I'm not seeing it."

"I can hug really, really hard now. It's awesome! I've got good hugs for good guys and bad hugs for bad guys! I am the decider of the embraces! Hee hee!"

"Never change, okay?"

"Oh that's an easy promise for golems to make," Fluffbear said.

"It is, isn't it?" Cecelia said. "And that's what we are now, more or less. There's no going back, is there? This is it, isn't it?"

"Stahting to sink in, huh?" Madeline said, bumping her sympathetically with the side of her muzzle.

"It didn't until my body was dead. If it was my body at all, and not just… mostly daemonflesh." Cecelia sighed. "I've been trying to sort out how I feel about it."

"I'm still very sorry about that," Threadbare said. "I forgot she was being affected by Mastoya's spell."

"Oh Threadbare…" She reached over and rubbed the back of his head, where the hat didn't cover. He leaned into it. "No. It's fine. Daemons are nothing but trouble. I'm pretty sure it wouldn't have worked out, and... well, I wouldn't really be alive, either. Just trading one shell for another."

"You got a pretty good shell now," Glub said, as they reached the top of the stairs and started down a long hall, past a pair of dwarven guards.

"Thanks Glub." She smiled. "Well. There's no point in feeling sorry for myself. We just saw an abject example of that, and I'll be hanged before I go that route. One more thing to do, one more thing to get through, then we can figure out life, the universe, and everything."

"There you are!" Kayin said, waving to them from next to a pair of large, oaken doors. "You're late, desu."

Emmet moved forward and pushed the oaken doors open, revealing one of the mess halls of Fort Bronze. It was vast, and it was empty... save for King Grundi, his honor guard, Hidon Fingers, and a stubble-bearded human clad all in gray. The stranger studied them for a long moment as they came in.

Your Adorable skill is now level 47!

"So you're Caradon's legacy..." The man murmured, walking over and kneeling down, offering a hand.

"One of them. I'm Threadbare. He's Emmet. She's Missus Fluffbear. And these are our friends." Threadbare put his paw in the man's hand and shook.

"I'm Jericho." He turned blue eyes to Cecelia. "I'm sorry for the circumstances, milady."

She shook her head. "It's all right. I'm very glad Mordecai found his way to you."

"You made Bak'shaz very, very happy, when he told him how you'd saved him." Jericho smiled. "I'm glad you made the right choice."

"Believe me, so am I." She shook hands with him as well, and he escorted the toys to the table.

"Now that's all well and done we've still got a Kingdom to save," King Grundi said. "But before that, I'd like to make sure we're all on the same page. So as to prevent trouble afterwards and all."

"Trouble?" Cecelia asked.

"Aye." Grundi shared a glance with Jericho. "I'm just going to hammer it straight, here. We don't think you can be queen."

"Okay," Cecelia said. "Who gets it then?"

"I mean, there's a number of reasons why, and it's not a dig against YOU—" Grundi caught himself. "Okay? That's all you have to say?"

"I never wanted to be a queen in the first place. It was just the duty I thought I had to do. But I'm not the heir anymore, now am I? Not by dwarven law."

"It's more the undead thing for the people of the North," Jericho said. "Well, the immortality thing in general. We don't want immortal rulers on Cylvania's throne."

"But it's that last part we're having some disagreement on," Grundi said. "Cylvania's throne."

"We're hoping you can help break it."

"Me?" Cecelia asked.

"Well, all of you," Grundi said. "You may not be good candidates for ruling, but let's face it, we have no prayer of victory without you, we've only got this far because of your help, and if you can handle Melos and save us all, then I really don't want to have to fight you if you disagree with us THEN. So I'd like to hear your thoughts on the matter NOW."

"What's the disagreement?" Threadbare asked.

"For years we've fought because we've dreamed of a Cylvania at peace," Jericho said, flexing his gloved fingers in nervous habit. "The survivors of Balmoran, and we who joined them, I mean. Driven into the woods, forced to a nomadic existence, down to a tenth of the population we once were. The dream has been to reunite the country with the Tyrant's fall."

"And I'm saying that there ain't no country left," Grundi's voice was uncharacteristically soft. "You got the west, that's what, four villages? Then a few villages in the East. South's gone, lad. Taylor's Delve and Grubholm and Outsmouth were the last holding it. They're gone. There's no point in having a Cylvania anymore."

"Grubholm's still there, but it's all Gribbits now," Cecelia spoke up.

"Gribbits? The frog monsters? That's no good," Jericho said, frowning. "We'll have to clear them out once—"

"No!" Fluffbear jumped up. "They're nice froggy people! They helped us sneak in here!"

"What? What d'ya mean?" Grundi asked, leaning forward in his Kneelchair.

"She's sayin' that theah actually decent folks. Just a bit territorial," Madeline said. "Which maybe brings up a point. Might not be many human settlements left, but theah's some groups of monstahs out theah that might be on boahd with being all civilized and the like. Or at least not having to fight humans. Er, and dwahves, too."

"Like raccants!" Fluffbear spoke up. "They'd love to help humans! They're just... kinda bad at it," she admitted.

"That's a point," Cecelia said. "Leaving out goblins and ogres and the other things that can only be trusted to be malicious, there's creatures living here now that might be up for... something. We can't have the old

Cylvania back, but we can maybe make a new one."

"We might be able to help with that," Threadbare said. "A lot of monsters seemed to react better to us than they did to humans. Perhaps we could travel around and see if they're interested in... what, exactly?"

"In a council," Grundi said, steepling his fingers. "Aye. That would work. Better than the dwarves having to take over the whole damn thing. My folk have tried ruling over humans before, never goes well. Never ever."

"I'm honestly not sure if it would work, but..." Jericho rubbed his stubbled chin. "So long as neither of you are planning on seizing the throne once this is all said and done, we can focus on DOING it, rather than trying to maneuver for the spoils afterward. All right. I'll agree to this. We'll give a council a whirl and sort out the details afterward."

Grundi nodded, and snapped his fingers. Hidon pulled out a mass of parchment, ripped entire sections of words out, taped a few new sheets in, scrawled quickly, and handed it up to his King. The King read it over, nodded, signed, and slid it to the rest of them.

And with a few strokes of a pen, Cecelia signed away any claim she might have on the throne. The rebel leader signed his part, and Grundi nodded with satisfaction as he stuffed it into one of the compartments of his armrests. "Now that that's done, how are we going to take down Melos? Without killing everyone, I mean?"

"You told Jericho about the dungeon situation we're in?" Threadbare asked.

"Aye."

"We've suspected something like this was going on for a while. The Hand show up as midbosses, it's plain as day on their statuses. Speaking of which, we've got maybe a week before they respawn. Possibly less."

"Less than that," Threadbare said. "The daemons are our real foe. Anise lost here, and right now she doesn't know the fort has been taken. But once word of that gets out, we'll lose our backdoor into the castle."

"Backdoor?" Jericho asked.

"The Waystone chamber," Cecelia said.

"That's a deathtrap." Jericho shook his head. "The security on there is ludicrous. We've considered and rejected it. Even if we had the passcodes, it would be almost impossible to survive, let alone get through with a force that could storm the castle."

"Ah, but when you throw a mastah merchant into the mix..." Madeline leaned in.

"I see what you're thinking, but it won't work. The very first thing that happens when you teleport through, is a battery of dispel magics, from the wizards on duty. So merchants' packs explode, the invasion forces in them are revealed, then the room seals and…" he trailed off, as he realized.

"The room seals and fills with poison gas," Cecelia finished. Then with a grin, she reached up and tapped her nose.

"Okay, so you don't care about that. But there's the other traps to consider, and the guards beyond. And that helps your lot, but I'm sorry to say that I don't think you can do it alone. You'll need us for backup, and even if you can, I don't know, *golem* through all the traps, we can't."

Cecelia nodded. "Which is why I've got a plan. And in an hour I might just have someone to help with the initial breach…"

It took five hours, actually, before Mastoya caved in and agreed to help. But that was more than enough time, for the golems to wrap up their dreamquests, refill their pools, and ready themselves for what lay ahead.

They said their goodbyes, and took one last look around Fort Bronze.

One way or another, they wouldn't be coming back.

*****

Waystone duty was boring. The guards on shift hated it, the four wizards encircling the chamber and watching through windows above hated it, and the alchemists in the slaughterpits below hated it.

That changed the second that the bell tolled. The guards went from numb boredom to wide-awake adrenaline.

This was an unscheduled incoming arrival.

"Dispel Magic! Dispel Magic! Dispel Magic! Dispel Magic!" The wizards did their thing. Nothing exploded, so the guards relaxed. A bit, just a bit.

"You have ten seconds to utter the passcode! Fail and you die!" The sergeant on duty called through the grated door. "Ten nine eight seven —"

"The password is Gladius Piscine!" Mastoya snapped. "Fort Bronze has fallen. Get ready to shatter the waymark!"

The guards paled and stared beyond her, at the pillar in the center of the room. For twenty years it had stood, emblazoned with glowing glyphs, allowing easy transit from the center of the Realm to the Eastern and Western edges. "Ma'am? I…" The sergeant stuttered. This was way, *way* above his paygrade.

"FUCKING DO IT!" Mastoya yelled, slamming her gauntlet against the door. "AND GET ME OUT OF HERE BEFORE THEY STONE

IN!"

"I... I..." The sergeant said, after she was past the barriers and traps. "Yes Ma'am. Will you, will you sign the logs at least?"

Mastoya looked at the book. She picked it up and ripped it in half, with such force that the wooden toy on her belt jiggled and rattled. "I'm calling in Damocles protocols, and you want me to sign the fucking book that is irrelevant after today?" she snarled.

The sergeant swallowed and turned gray.

"Do it, before—"

The bell tolled. The wizards doled out dispel magics, and were answered by arrows. LOTS of arrows. **"Rapid Fire! Razor Shot!"** Mordecai and Jericho bellowed in unison, and mages screamed as glass shattered.

"Damocles!" The sergeant bellowed, running for the door. "I declare and authorize Damocles! Blow the room!"

Mastoya snarled and pushed her way through the mob of guards. Behind her, the gas rolled in, the explosions started to shake the room...

...and unnoticed in the chaos and fury, two rangers used temporary waystones to return back whence they came.

Five minutes later, as guards rushed past her, she turned a corner, opened a door, and walked into guest chambers that hadn't been used in months.

"Alright," she cleared her throat. "We're safe."

"Dude," Glub said, untying himself from her belt. "That was intense. **Waymark!**" he said, as he touched the floor. "You got the thingy?"

She handed him the Greater Waystone, and without a word, he took it, and faded, disappearing from Castle Cylvania...

...and reappearing back at Fort Bronze.

With a sigh, Mastoya sat on the bed, and looked in the mirror. Soon the little fishman golem would be making waystones and handing them to the invasion parties. Soon the room would be full of invaders. And the last one to arrive would bring her the waystone that would take her back to her cell.

Her part in this was done.

And though she'd never admit it, for the first time in years, she was very, very relieved she wouldn't be around for what came next.

CHAPTER 14: THE SINS OF THE FATHERS

"Theah!" Madeline said, as Emmet's massive hand reached into the pack. "It's go time!"

"Makeup. Parry," Threadbare said, smearing his face with paint and feeling it shift into the patterns that resembled a grinning, cocky face with a sweet goatee. He moved to the front, grabbed his brother's gauntlet, and rode it out.

He arrived to a large bedroom full of dwarves, hopped out of Emmet's grip, and started looking around until he saw the familiar form of Kindness. Feeling relief, he moved over to it and tapped on its knee with his scepter. "Are you okay in there?"

"Just waiting for the signal," Cecelia said. "Activation is loud. I can't risk doing it until-"

The room shuddered. A gong rang outside, echoing through the castle.

"Yeah, there we go. **Stoker Feed Activated!**" Cecelia shouted, and the miniature steam knight shuddered as metal ground on metal.

Threadbare turned, looked back to Emmet, who had gotten through most of the golems and was working on drawing out his mortal friends. Pulsivar came out, scrambling, as his form blurred and shuddered around Emmet's arms. Then the golem let the Misplacer Beast go, and the great black cat hopped up onto a bed and started grooming himself with an aggravated air.

He calmed down once Threadbare clambered up next to him, and Pulsivar did that air grooming thing, tongue rasping against the little bear even though he was visibly several feet away.

Then the dwarven commander shouted. "Alright lads and lasses! Through that door! Hold the halls! GRUNDI AND BROKESHALE!"

"GRUNDI AND BROKESHALE!" The dwarves roared and burst out of the door, shields ready and axes high.

"Boiler Shunt is Go!" Kindness screamed steam, and Pulsivar flattened his ears. Mopsy, who'd just emerged, tried to clamber back into the pack until Fluffbear grabbed her by the hind legs and wrestled her back.

The dwarves rushed out, as fast as their commanders could haul them out of the plus-sized backpacks that they'd been shoved in. They hadn't lacked for merchants among their own ranks, even if their packs of holding couldn't fit quite as many people in as the plush golems had.

Beryl and Jarrik were two of the last to clamber out, and with a grin, Garon waved them over. "Family party's over here, bro. Sis."

"Technically I'm not your sister," Beryl said, adjusting her long-disused chainmail.

"Neither's Sloopy," Bak'shaz pointed to the enormous serpent coiled in a corner. "But she's close enough."

"Gee. Thanks."

"Clockwork Engaged!" Cecelia bellowed. Clattering ticks and tocks chimed out from Kindnes, a rattle at first, then turning to a solid, drawn out hum.

It's about time, Threadbare knew. So he put up all the buffs he could while he waited. **"Bodyguard Pulsivar. Organize Minions to Stop Melos. Flex. Self-esteem. Strong Pose. Deathsight. Guard Stance. Harden."**

"Is Cecelia going to be much longer?" Graves asked.

"No," Kayin said, clambering up above the doorframe. "Just cover her for like another minute."

Emmet kept pulling more and more of the golem army from the bag. The forty surviving teddies and plush toys were joined with about fifty more who hadn't been part of the assault on the Wark Riders. They spread out, filling the room now that the dwarves had vacated, readying their weapons, putting up buffs, and staring at the door with button-eyed intensity.

"Linkages Aligned!" Cecelia yelled, and Kindness straightened up, flexed its arms, and drew its sword and shield from the magnetized holders on its back and side.

"You be safe Gar, awright?" Madeline went over and thumped her head gently into Garon's. "We got a lot to talk about aftah this is done."

"Wouldn't miss it for the world." Garon hugged her neck. Then he shot Zuula a look.

Zuula didn't see it. She was too busy kissing Mordecai.

"I'd say get a room, but she'd take me literally." Jarrik elbowed

Bak'shaz.

"Cast in Steam and Steel, Raise Thy Blade! All Systems Go!"
Cecelia finished. "Let's go finish this!"

The plan had hinged upon Glub.

He'd been carried in by Mastoya and established a lesser waymark in an out-of-the-way place that was centrally-located enough to be a good staging area. Then he'd used one of the Fort Bronze greater waystones to return to the waymark there.

Once there, he started creating lesser waystones and handing them out to the leaders of the assault teams, each of whom was carrying a merchant's pack of holding full of their people.

Lesser Waystone used fortune. Glub had about enough fortune left in his pool after casting the waymark that he could make twenty waystones.

The first wave of people through had been six rangers, each carrying a pack of about five to six more. They'd spread out in advance, using their superior infiltration skills to roam unnoticed and get to critical points of the castle.

The next wave of people through had been thirteen dwarves, clerics, officers, elementalists, and other skilled veterans. Each of them had borne a pack holding about four more dwarves and some assorted gear. Their job was to wait for the signal, then spread out and secure the halls, advancing forward bit by bit and leaving a rearguard at every junction.

Emmet had been the last one through. And he'd had the honor of carrying not only Threadbare and his friends, but all the doll haunters they could cram into Madeline's packspace... which was by now up to a pretty good-sized sitting room. It had been a tight, tight fit, and air had been a bit limited for the living ones, but they hadn't had to wait long. It was done in a matter of minutes, and now they followed behind the dwarves, looking for their objectives.

They only had two.

And it was only a matter of minutes, before one of them surfaced.

Threadbare straightened up on Pulsivar's back. "He's in the inner courtyard!" he called. "Where is that?"

"Follow me!" Cecelia turned and metal slammed on stone as Kindness charged past them, with Emmet in hot pursuit. The squads of toys behind made space, waiting for Threadbare's team and Garon's team to catch up to her.

"Remember," Threadbare told the doll haunters as he passed, "He's very dangerous. Leave him to us, just keep a perimeter and stop the guards from intervening."

They emerged onto a scene of slaughter.

Guards lay strewn about the courtyard, bleeding and dying, filling the air with their screams. Dwarven bodies lay among them... not as many, but enough to show that a mighty battle had taken place here.

The battle still raged on.

Up on the battlements, gray-cloaked men and women clashed blade to blade with a huge man in black-armor swirling with red demonic faces. Six blades scythed around him, driving his foes back as he clashed the largest sword, the one in his left hand, against his shield. Everything that was metal on him roiled with demonic features, eyes and arms and claws and maws, gaping and hissing and shrieking. And in the split-second that passed as Threadbare took it in, the figure called **"Entropic Strike!"** and brought his blade crashing THROUGH one of his opponent's, and into the man below. Black light flared, and the ranger fell, flesh crumbling to dust, clothes fading and falling to bits, until what hit the ground below the battlements was old bones that shattered on impact.

"Father!" Cecelia's voice rang out from Kindness.

And King Melos, first of his name, turned.

The surviving rangers fell back, escaping the flashing blades.

"His blades leave wounds that don't heal," Jericho whispered in his ear, faint as the wind. "We'll support you as we can. Good luck!"

"So this is what they've made of you," the King's voice was as deep as Threadbare remembered it. With a mighty leap, the monarch hurled himself over the battlements. Red, blazing batlike wings stretched from the back of his armor and flapped, as he glided to the ground below, alighting with a crash of metal. "He's turned you into a slave, a hollow suit of armor."

"Father, Anise has been playing you from the beginning to the end of this. You have to—"

"I know," he said.

The courtyard fell silent.

"Then..." Cecelia said, voice tight and trembling, "then why?"

"I have no choice. Never did. I needed allies, to contact the King, to keep things under control. I turned the strongest-willed woman I knew, used her as a host. I knew she'd become corrupted in time. But I hoped that her love for me would buy me the time we needed. Time to find a solution." The King's voice wavered. "But there wasn't any solution. No way to fix things before it all fell apart. And I've been here ever since, trying to stall, hoping that time would present a solution. But it hasn't, and everyone's betrayed me. As I knew they would."

"You had a choice every step of the way," Threadbare said. "And you chose to trust daemons over everyone else. And it's gotten you here."

Melos' helm turned, turned to look at the little bear sitting on the big black cat. "And so my daughter's enslaver shows himself."

"I've enslaved no one," Threadbare said. "Betrayed no one... well, not really," he shot a look at Madeline, who shrugged. "And I'm here to stop you from killing this country and everyone in it."

"*We're* here to stop you!" squeaked Fluffbear.

Melos laughed, loud and long. "Two parties? Two parties of rabble, toys and half-breeds and traitors? What hope do you have? Come then. This won't be the first assassination attempt that I've destroyed."

"Assassination attempt?" Garon snorted. "Oh no, buddy. This is a **Raid!**"

And with that, the two parties charged the demon king.

Garon's new job had many drawbacks, thanks to Cylvania's weird situation. You couldn't form a guild in a dungeon, it was that simple. And since the entire land was a dungeon, that meant no guilds, no way, no how.

They'd even tried forming a guild in Madeline's pack, just to see if that was possible. But evidently you couldn't form a guild in an extra-dimensional space, either. Jarrik had even led Garon a few steps into the Oblivion, to see if it was possible to do it there, but no, that still counted as a dungeon. Which left Garon with four out of five skills that he couldn't use, since three of the rest of them dealt with Guild functions.

But the fifth one? The fifth one made up for that.

Because now all parties involved were linked in a raid, a coordinated attack that let them talk at the speed of thought and be heard by everyone on the same mission. "Our healing is useless," Threadbare told the others. "The strikes from him don't heal, Jericho told me that. Zuula, Fluffbear, can you switch to damage?"

"Sure, she do dat."

"Okay!"

Threadbare continued. "I can tank him—"

"No! Let me! **Boosters!**" Cecelia said, speeding ahead of him. "He thinks I'm Kindness. He might pull his punches."

And then they were on him, and his corona of blades screamed as they came, lashing out at Cecelia, slicing towards Fluffbear.

"**Rapid Fire!**" Mordecai shouted, and five arrows slashed a blade out of the air.

"**Rapid Fire!**" Jarrik echoed, and gunshots cracked out, and another blade dropped and shattered.

"**Dolorous Strike!**" Cecelia lashed out—

—and her sword rebounded from Melos' shield. The daemons inside shrieked, as it carved a chunk free from the steel. Then she was backpedaling, as Melos lashed out at her with all four of his blades, whittling her down. "**Entropic Strike!**" choked out the demon king, beating her back, as red numbers ground from Kindness with every strike.

Green numbers did as well. Only ten or twelve at a time, but they slid from her as she gasped and fell back. Mopsy and Fluffbear, who were moving around to the side, striking at his blades, shuddered as well. "What is this?" Fluffbear shrieked.

"Fear. It's fear!" Threadbare realized. "But that's all right. I can use an **Emboldening Speech, because you're all very brave! We can survive this. Keep fighting! I believe in you!**"

Melos' helm whipped up to study him. "A ruler? Oh no no no, this nonsense ends NOW!"

Quick as a wink he tossed his sword up into the air. **"Animus Blade!"** Before Cecelia could react, he slammed his hand onto her helm, grasped it by the visor. "You will never know how sorry I am for this, my dear. **All is Dust."**

And Kindness melted away into a cloud of rust. Melos was already moving past her, snatching his sword out of the air again, and missed seeing the little armored porcelain doll poke her head out of the rust pile and draw her sword.

"Stay back Cecelia!" Threadbare said through the raid chat. "Let me tank! Find things to animate! Melos, I **challenge** you!"

Your Challenge skill is now level 12!

Even with the boosted speed of raid speech, he barely had time to get that out before Melos was on him.

But as the King closed, Mordecai and Jarrik shot down the last of the animated swords, and the rest of the melee team encircled Melos. Bak'shaz fought side by side with Sloopy the snake, borrowing his minion's venom, manifesting it through paired knives. Fluffbear smote into Melos with lashes from her whip that left long, smoking wounds in the demon-infused steel of his armor. Garon struck out with his hatchet, reforged by the dwarves into a proper weapon, while Madeline chomped bites into his shield, keeping that side of him busy. Zuula dove and harried him from above, spear flashing as she tried for his eyes. And Kayin, tiny Kayin, leaped on his legs and did her best to stab him through the chainmail protecting his knee joints.

For his part, Threadbare focused on staying alive. He'd put up all his buffs and guard stance back in the room while he was waiting for his friends to prepare, and he was very, very glad that he had. Even with his blades gone, Melos was an unrelenting foe.

But for all that, even the King couldn't land a solid strike on the teddy bear. Pulsivar was a Misplacer Beast now, and Zuula had spoken with him, hammered his part in their plan home. He dodged for all he was worth and between that and his image displacement, Threadbare was everywhere the King's blade wasn't.

But Melos had more than one way to grind his foes to dust.

"I know the weakness of emboldening speeches, little bear," he hissed, as Threadbare parried a blow that came far, far too close.

Your Parry skill is now level 23!

"They don't affect the ruler who gives them! **Staredown!**" Melos called, and his eyes burned red from under his visor, boring into Threadbare's own.

Within Melos' aura of fear, Threadbare's cool was stretched thin already. The eyes blazed into his own, and the little bear gasped as Moxie fled him. He knew fear, for the first time ever, and he quailed, even as he ducked another strike.

And then Garon spoke. **"Emboldening Speech. Come on Threadbare, you've got this!"**

Melos' red eyes widened, and he slowed, just for a second. "What? You're... two rulers?" He gasped. "How? WHY?"

"It's amazing the things you can do when you're not insane with paranoia," Threadbare told him, recovering himself a bit. "Plan snekshot, please!" he called.

Zuula snarled, a long wordless howl in feline, and Pulsivar leaped away. The team hacking away slowly at Melos' hit points cleared out... all save for Sloopy, who coiled around the King at Bak'shaz' command. "Hang on Sloopy! Sloopy, hang on!"

Melos snorted, released his sword, and the blade hacked mercilessly into the serpent, who tightened his grasp—

—until Emmet spoke, in a voice like crashing metal. **"Rapid Fire. Razor Shot. Concussion Shells."**

Emmet's hand split open and rolled back, revealing the cannon behind it.

And he put his grenadier levels to good use.

"Call Beast!" Bak'shaz shouted, and in a heartbeat Sloopy dematerialized from Melos and returned to his side, as the lanky half-orc beat feet... along with everyone else who had been hacking at the King a second ago.

The bombs exploded, sending Melos staggering back. His shield warped under the pressure, and with a shriek, the demons inside burst, dripping from the cracks as red goo.

With a shout, Jarrik and Mordecai unleashed arrows and bullets on him, rocking him back and forth...

...and from the battlements, gray-cloaked figures rose and added their own arrows, arrows of pure light, ripping into his armor.

Cobblestones flew from the misses and explosions; the two ground teams backed up, and smoke and dust swirled through the area in clouds... clouds that dissipated, as Zuula shouted **"Call Winds!"** and whisked them away...

...to reveal Melos standing, helm cracked, revealing his lower face, and the spreading grin across it. His shield was a wreck and he tossed it aside... then drew six more blades from his sheaths, one by one, energy flickering as they produced swords from thin air. **"Animus all,"** he said, and they snapped into position around him. **"Hellblades!"** he cried, and the black steel bubbled and burst with red light that resolved into demonic faces. Melos spat and pointed his sword at Threadbare. "You face a **Champion of Entropy!**" he yelled, and wrecked shards of cobblestone rose up around him. "Who will **Fight Beyond Reason,** offering **No Mercy!**" he roared. "I will not yield! I am **Unyielding!** Now come, my **Hellsteed.**" he said, and a fiery horse ripped out of a hole in the air and screamed, as he mounted it in a swift motion. "Prepare to Charge—"

"Dispel Magic!"

Beryl had been lurking on the sidelines, for the most part. With mediocre close combat skills, and no way to heal the wounded thanks to Melos' entropic strikes, she'd been feeling useless. But now, now she was very grateful that she'd fought so hard, and adventured so hard in the last few years, and ground Cleric up to twenty-five. Because watching that bastard fall to the ground as the horse disappeared out from under him? That was pretty fucking awesome.

Then he rose and ran for her, and it was a hell of a lot less awesome, as she fled and kept throwing dispels back at him—

—and then Threadbare and Emmet were in the way, Threadbare clawing at him, and Emmet smashing down on his former liege with heavy metal fists, and Melos was backing up. Again the melee teams closed in, and again Mordecai and Jarrik sniped his blades from the air.

Melos fought hard. Melos fought brutally. Melos fought with all the strength of a high-level adventurer, amplified by his status as a dungeon master's projection.

But Melos fought alone.

And with the superior communication coordinating all the groups, Melos could not win.

He still fought. His blade crashed down on Emmet again and again and managed to connect with Threadbare a time or two, but they persisted. They had the hit points and armor to stand against him, and whenever he tried to turn back to take care of one of the smaller fry tormenting him, they'd back away while the others pressed harder. It was like a great lion fighting a wolf pack, and the outcome was inevitable.

But it was Cecelia who finished it.

"Drive him towards the gate!" Cecelia said through the raid chat.

"What? Why?" Garon snapped.

"Do it!"

Threadbare snapped his head around, almost lost it, as he saw that the portcullis was up and the gate was half-open.

"Okay," he said through the raid chat. "I'm going to try to trick him." Then he spoke, pointing. "No! They've got the gate up! Don't let Melos escape!"

CHA+1

Immediately, the King turned and bolted, backhanding golems out of the way as he did. His armor a wreck, green patches glowing from gaping holes, he darted with all of his agility—

"Command Animus! Shut!" Cecelia shouted.

—and as he passed under the portcullis, a solid ton of animated steel snapped down, crashing into him and pinning him to the ground like a butterfly.

"Now! Hit him with everything!" Threadbare called.

And this time, when the smoke cleared, Melos did not stand.

Melos merely turned his head as Threadbare and the others approached, spitting out blood. He gazed at them with weary eyes. "Knew... it would... end this way."

"It doesn't have to," Threadbare said. "Dismiss Anise. Dismiss the other daemons. We'll come to you, and we'll figure out a way to fix the Oblivion."

"No," Melos said, closing his eyes. "Better this way. Find me. Kill me. The things I've done..."

"No Father," Cecelia said, moving to stand next to Threadbare. "You'll get a trial. And then you'll be executed or imprisoned for life, maybe. We're not going to commit regicide. Not today. Besides, this isn't you, anyway. If we killed it, you'd just reform it. You're going to stay here pinned while we find the core chamber entrance, and—"

Melos screamed, long and hard, and reality flickered. And when it stopped flickering, he was gone.

And Threadbare stared, as words flashed pass his view

Royal Quest Stop Melos failed!

Target is dead.

"What the hell?" Garon barked. "Who—"

"Anise." Cecelia said, pointing upward.

The sky was turning red. Clouds like bloody clots grew and rose in front of the sun. "She killed him," Cecelia whispered. "She killed him and took his place."

"Aw shit!" Madeline said, as the castle shook, twisted. Spikes burst from the walls, bloody protrusions, and demonic sigils rippled and formed patterns in the walls. "This is BAD."

"We didn't level. We spent so many resources and we didn't level to recharge any of it," Kayin said. "How the hell are we supposed to deal with THIS?"

"No," Threadbare said. "We don't have to deal with this. We have to get to where she is, and stop this. Jericho?"

"I'm here."

"Go to the labs; we'll be right behind. Tell the dwarves to secure the way. Find a place full of flashing green light and guide us to it. Quickly!"

"On it! You heard the bear! Move, people!" Jericho waved, and the rangers faded out one by one, save for the last couple, who simply hopped down from the spiky wall and ran.

"Let's go!" Threadbare said, riding fast after them.

"She pretty much almost annihilated us the last time we fought her," Graves said, falling in behind him, riding a skeletal horse he'd gotten from somewhere. "How are we going to deal with her AND the Hand at the same time?"

"I'm working on that right now," Threadbare told him.

"And what of us, Lord?" said one of the teddy bears, as the golem army fell in behind him.

"I have part of a plan," Threadbare said, mopping the makeup from his face. "Once we get down there I'll need every one of you to get naked..."

CHAPTER 15: INFERNAL RECKONING

The castle groaned under the weight of demonflesh, spikes protruding from the walls and buzzing swarms of flies and stranger insects seeping forth from gore-dripping holes between the cracks. It was strongest down here in the labs, and the allies fought with all their might against the twisted things that lunged at them out of the darkness.

But the rangers had spent years honing their craft; the dwarves were sturdy and unimpressed, and the golems ran interference for Threadbare and his friends with all the fanaticism that a former-fish-cult-turned-immortal-warriors could bring to the matter. Bleeding and spiky walls? Unspeakable horrors? Pfft, wasn't a big deal. The worst they could do was KILL you, and eh, they'd been through that already.

"We're here," Garon said from ahead, and Threadbare and Cecelia moved through the shattered doors, It was an open laboratory, with a curtain of green light shifting back and forth inside a doorless cabinet.

"Looks kind a' like a wardrobe," Jarrik said, hands flickering nervously as he checked each pistol in his harness.

"Well, we know theah's a witch inside." Madeline said. "Not too shoah about a lion, though."

"Give me time," interrupted one of the plush toys, brushing his mane back, and the group shared a nervous chuckle.

"Is everyone ready?" Threadbare asked, dismounting from Pulsivar. The big cat nudged at him, but Zuula hopped down from Mordecai's arms and snarled in his own language. Pulsivar moved back to Mopsy, sulking. "Everyone healed up?" Melos' entropic effect had worn off a few minutes back, thankfully. Healing worked again. They would have been pretty bad off if it hadn't.

"Ready!" Chorused every teddy bear in the group. Like Threadbare, they'd stripped down to their fur, leaving their gear in piles outside the doorway. All save for Missus Fluffbear, who had a different task entirely.

"Right," Madeline said, positioning herself next to the wardrobe. "Glub, give us a song. Fluffbeah, do the clarity."

"Clarifying Song! Whoa oh. Gonna keep it going long, whoa-oh…"

"Aura of Clarity!"

With her sanity regeneration bolstered, Madeline started handing out Endure Fire spells.

Threadbare nodded. "I suppose it's my turn. This is your **King's Quest. Kill all the daemons.**"

"Kill all the daemons!" roared the golems.

"And I'll **Organize Minions** even though that's not a nice name for you, so I'm sorry."

"We don't mind being minions!" roared the golems.

"You're really my friends, to be honest, it's just the name of the skill."

"We love being your friends!" roared the golems.

Threadbare smiled and picked up the bag full of soulstones left over from the Brokeshale battle. "Remember! If she shatters your stone, find the bag! Nobody dies permanently!"

Garon interrupted before they could cheer. "All right! Party captains, like we rehearsed… **Do the Job! Fight the Battles!**"

Their roars shook the ceiling. As did those of the dwarves. The rangers, at least, were a little more quiet.

Threadbare turned back to his friends…

And stopped, staring at a dreadlocked green teddy bear with tusks. "Um…"

"Beast shape not work way Zuula think it do," the shaman told him. "It be fine."

"Got the fahst wave done," Madeline said, resting and regaining her sanity. "I'll be in with the last. If you kill Anise quick I don't mind." Threadbare handed her her laurels, and she grinned. "Thanks."

"You saved me family, Mister Bear." Mordecai told him, kneeling down. "And Celia girl saved me. We'll back yer up. Just survive, remember what I taught yer."

"I'm looking forward to the rematch," Graves said, locking his visor in place. His new dwarven helm completely covered his mouth, but they got the gist of his muffled words.

"Bitch is going down," Kayin drew her thumb across her throat. "And I'm not desu to say that."

"It's smiting time!" Missus Fluffbear squeaked, bouncing up and down on Mopsy.

Glub just kept singing his song, but he shot them a thumbs up.

"Yeah, let's go fuck her up," Beryl grinned wide. "I owe her some pain."

Pulsivar just slurped his crotch. It seemed like as good a time to groom as any.

Emmet offered a hand. Threadbare shook it. "We will fight well, just as we were made to do," his big brother rumbled.

"He's not wrong. One more fight, Threadbare." Garon hugged Threadbare and got a hug right back. "We've got this. Now let's go **Raid!**"

And so, the first wave of teddy bears charged through into the green-lit darkness beyond. **"Camouflage,"** Threadbare whispered and followed them.

Your Camouflage skill is now level 14!

It was different from the raccant dungeon, Threadbare realized on the way in. The dark space between this world and the next wasn't unbroken blackness. There were four green discs spinning, weird distorted, uneven things, that drew the eye—

—and then the world turned to fire.

But Madeline had buffed him before he went in, buffed him like everyone in this wave, and half of the damage simply evaporated. He didn't burn; he merely smoldered, and then he was out and through the wall of fire and running faster.

"Command Golem! Destroy all golems!" he heard Anise shouting from ahead. The scrolls, of course. If he'd walked through the portal alone, she would have targeted him with it. But lost in a crowd of forty others who looked very much like him? She didn't have the luck to hit him with it straight off the bat. Even if she had a way to see through his camouflage, which he doubted.

Anise was on his to-do list, but he had a few things before that. Threadbare looked around.

Black nothing, most of it, a floor that felt like stone but wasn't. A wall of fire in front of the portal, blocking the way, burning with oily smoke. Green pillars, far more than had been in the raccants' dungeon, some small, some large. And in the center of it, a throne, with an old man's corpse on it, his eyesockets burnt out. His body was broken, many times over. As was the throne, the tinker-like gadgets on it and the pipes running from it shattered and sparking green energy. The pipes ran to pylons, columns of green light... and four of those held gems, he thought, glittering on their podiums. The rest held what looked like lumps of charcoal.

Bodies lay about the largest column. In it floated a handsome, nude man... The Lurker, Threadbare realized. His eyes were shut, and he had his hands clapped to his ears.

The rest of the Hand and Anise moved among the columns, battering down the teddy bears. Threadbare searched until he saw the Legion, flanked by a pair of enormous red dogs that breathed fire. He wasn't calling in swarms, so Threadbare mentally crossed him off his list, for now. Limited pools meant that the summoning daemon wasn't the immediate concern.

The blackness above flashed with green light, and Threadbare looked up and gasped. The sky was crammed full of numbers. Flickering, reeling drunkenly in long strings, like a woven tapestry of ones and zeroes and other digits... but this was a tapestry full of holes. Black spots writhed and danced among them, like slimes quivering and trying to engulf prey. And where the void touched the numbers broke and dissolved.

It looked *wrong*.

But enough was enough. Now that he had a sense of what he was up against, it was time to fulfill his part of the plan.

Threadbare dropped the pack of soulstones behind a column, rummaged in a pocket, and pulled out a vial of green reagent. **"Ward against daemons!"**

Error! Coordinates for Ward_0125123 not found!

The reagent didn't flow into a ward, and Anise's mocking laughter rose above the din of the battle. "Fool! This is far outside of what you think is reality! Wards don't WORK here."

Her voice was approaching, and Threadbare muttered **"Camouflage,"** before slipping back into the darkness, running for the nearest knot of teddies.

Not three seconds later she rounded the column, stared at the nearest bunch of teddies, and whipped a scroll out from her pocket. **"Command Golem! Destroy all golems!"**

The scroll turned to black ash, and she snarled. Then she leaped in among them, landing with her legs in a perfect split, hands flashing as she dealt out a flurry of furious fists. Her hands hit and tore, and two of the teddies died in a heartbeat.

And from the side, Threadbare crept closer, eyes fixed on the scrolls poking out of her pocket. This would be a risk, but...

"Firestarter," he whispered, stretching out a paw.

Your Firestarter skill is now level 12!

At the sound, Anise slammed her hands into the ground and whipped her feet around, like a scythe cutting grain. Caught square on, Threadbare went flying back, out into the darkness. Anise backflipped to her feet, kicked the last couple of golems left, and looked around.

"There you are!" she said, striding right for Threadbare.

"I suppose I am," he said. **"Call Outfit."**

Your Call Outfit skill is now level 6!

His clothes materialized around him, and instantly, he felt much better.

"I'm going to enjoy this," she said, reaching toward her pocket...

...and shrieking in surprise as her hand hit fire. With a look of disbelief she dug into her pocket, cursing, whipping out the wad of burning paper. "You worthless little toy!" she snarled, casting the ruined scrolls aside, as fire burned and arcane sparks flew off in all colors.

Threadbare used the opportunity to break and run for it, whispering **"Camouflage,"** as he went.

"You only delay the inevitable!" Anise screamed. Behind her the last of the teddy bears fell, as hellhounds tore it to shreds. The three figures rushed to join her, spreading out at her command, searching for the little toy.

And not finding it.

Your Stealth skill is now level 18!

"A few dozen teddy bears. Really, what did you hope to achieve?" Anise said, flicking her gaze over to the Cataclysm. "Renew the wall."

Wordlessly, the beautiful brown-skinned woman did so.

"Did you think to soften us up? Did you think to weaken us?" Anise laughed. "It was no trouble at all to deal with you. I lost a few scrolls, so what? We're barely wounded. And every second that the one you call The Lurker is in there, more of your puny little kingdom dies. People, animals, even the crops... every tragedy you can imagine, he's inflicting on Cylvania right now. Every nightmare Melos had ever hoped to prevent, happening at once. And everyone will die in torment." She stalked around the pillars, looking for the little bear. "Why?" She said. "Why bother coming here? You've LOST."

Threadbare weighed his options and sent along a Wind's Whisper. "I wonder," Threadbare's voice whispered in her ear, "Why you didn't do this sooner, if this is what you wanted. Everyone dead, I mean."

Your Wind's Whisper skill is now level 20!

She smirked. "It was funnier to make Melos and the rest of you fools do it to yourselves. But in a pinch, this'll do."

"And I wonder," Threadbare continued, "if you know how to work this dungeon at all." He paused, then sent a third whisper. "Or if you're just playing it by ear and hoping it works the way you think it does."

Your Wind's Whisper skill is now level 21!

Anise laughed smugly, as she moved past the throne, eyes peeled, looking for him. "Are you looking for the part where I tell you how to fix this mess? Forget it. I know what you're trying to do, and it's already hopeless. I just killed the only one who might help you with that," She grinned over at Melos' slumped corpse, lying in a puddle of blood, his head gone.

"Oh, he's dead? That's all?" Threadbare whispered. "Well, that part's easy. **Speak with Dead**" said the little bear, stepping out from behind the throne.

Your Speak with Dead skill is now level 25!

Melos rose from his corpse, whole again, in ghostly form, staring about him.

But Threadbare didn't have much time to examine the dead King. Instantly, Anise was on him, foot catching Threadbare and sending him flying. He bounced off a pillar, rolled a few times in a shower of green sparks, and scurried to his feet. "Fry him!" Anise shrieked.

The Cataclysm hurled a bolt of smoking flame—

"Manipulate Faia!"

—only to see it turn aside.

The daemons froze.

The daemons turned to look at the entryway.

And at the wall of fire that had been quietly been pushed out of the way with elemental magic, and reshaped into an enormous fist, with the middle finger fully extended.

"Good distrahction, boss!" Madeline said, ripping the golden laurels from her head. "We'll take it from heah!"

"Get'em!" Garon yelled, and the second wave of toy golems charged.

"Mend Golem, Mend Golem," Threadbare said, putting himself back together, before slipping away again. **"Camouflage,"** he whispered, fading away, moving toward Melos, who turned to meet him with a sorrowful gaze.

Behind him, the daemons started up a dark chant, hailing Cron and Vhand…

"Dispel Magic!"

…but Beryl was having none of that.

Threadbare did his best to ignore the fighting at his back. He didn't have the sanity to heal, like he normally did in these fights, and Anise would shred him if he tried to tank. No, he had to trust his friends to handle them and focus on the third task in his checklist.

"We don't have much time," Threadbare whispered, drawing close to Melos. "How do we fix the Oblivion?"

"If I knew that I would have done it!" Melos raised his hands. "Do you think I wanted this?"

"Well, what have you tried?" Threadbare asked.

"I… I've been trying to get enough wizards and enchanters skilled enough to take a look at the damn thing, but… I think she's been killing them," Melos muttered, glaring at Anise. "So I haven't tried a hell of a lot. I'm in over my head, here. I was." He sighed. "Cron's balls I've made a mess of things."

"Self-pity later, please," Threadbare asked, shooting a glance back. Graves and Fluffbear were leading a line of wooden toys against Anise. It wasn't going well. Meanwhile, the other half of the strike force was focusing on the Ninja, while Madeline countered the Cataclysm and dealt with the hellhounds' fiery breath. That was going a bit better but still not well. "I need helpful suggestions. What happens if the dungeon is sealed?"

"The other ones forming the barrier will still be open. Everyone dies," Melos said, shaking his head. "The Oblivion sweeps inward and everyone will go into the numbers. No one comes back from them."

"Okay, how do we close the other dungeons?"

"You can't." Melos pointed at the green, warped discs between the core chamber and the rest of reality. "The throne adjusts the space in the dungeons. They're… stretched out, to form the Oblivion. And the throne is wrecked! There's no way to un-stretch them! They're stuck at WIDE. If they were returned to normal, you could enter them, one by one, and kill the pygamlion animus that's holding each one open. But with space distorted? Nothing would survive that. Not even you, little golem."

Threadbare looked at the Throne. **"Mend."**

Invalid target! Unidentified item.

Melos laughed, ruefully. "Don't you think that's the first thing I tried? It's too complicated, it's an artifact, minor magic won't work on it. You can't mend the throne, you can't mend the exhausted cores. It just doesn't work."

"The active cores. Is there something we can do with those?" Threadbare pointed at the glittering gems.

"No!" Melos shouted, covering his mouth in horror. "I had that idea too. I threw a Dark Augury for that one," Melos said, pointing at a pile of gore and guts assembled into a blasphemous pattern. "The vision was horrible but true. If the throne were intact, it might work. But if the cores are removed BEFORE this dungeon is sealed, even a split-second sooner, then the part of the Oblivion they make up EXPLODES instead of IMPLODING. You'd wipe out an entire region, for each one you removed, and then the other three would be stressed harder to compensate, and the Oblivion would snap around into a smaller space..."

Threadbare shook his head. He looked back at the battle, saw Emmet manage to get his hand around the Ninja's leg, and get shanked repeatedly for the trouble. His brother staggered, guarding his helm and eyes, as red numbers leaked from the cracks in his armored shell. And then the Legion was on him, summoning up another giant hellhound to replace a fallen one, as his friends worked like mad to keep him at bay.

This isn't going well.

He looked around the room. Looked up. "What are those?" he said, pointing up at the sky, at the shattered numbers and the voids.

"I... don't know," Melos said. "I think it happened after we broke the throne. It's been getting worse ever since. Like cloth wearing down. Losing threads, losing thickness. Getting thinner." Melos shuddered. "I fear it. I fear what it means, when those holes join, and everything ruptures. Like space itself is... threadbare, I suppose. Just waiting to rip away completely."

"So it's broken," Threadbare said, staring up at it.

"I... suppose? But not in any sense that could be..."

"Mend," said the little bear, stretching up a paw.

And one of the holes shrank.

"...what." Melos said.

"Look!" Threadbare said, pointing at the entryway. One of the warped disks was noticeably LESS warped now. And less like a disc. There were shifting colors on it now, there was just a hint of depth.

"My gods," Melos said, looking like he might cry. "You can't tell me it was that simple."

"Celia!" Threadbare whispered, through the wind. "Look up! Mend the holes in the sky!"

A second, while he wondered if she'd gotten the message. Two. Five. And then...

Then, as he watched, the holes started shrinking. Green numbers filled the gaps in between them, flowing now, moving with more vigor.

The battle slowed, as both sides noticed the changing light. "Everyone," Threadbare shouted. "Everyone who can mend, mend those holes in the sky!"

"No you don't!" Anise shrieked and went straight for Cecelia...

Only to be forced back, dodging, as Jarrik emptied all his guns at her.

"Mend!" shouted Cecelia.

"Mend!" Graves muttered, behind the muffling visor he wore to keep Anise from kissing him again.

"Godspell Mend!" squeaked Missus Fluffbear, as she moved Mopsy out of the fight, much to the cougar's relief.

And the holes shrank. The discs in the entryway flexed and gained shape... until they were portals again. "Keep her busy," Threadbare whispered to Garon, spending five more points of his dwindling sanity. "I'll go sort this out!"

"Not alone you're not!" Garon said. "Kayin, go with him!"

Threadbare bolted for the first portal, and Kayin hurried in behind him, keen eyes piercing his camouflage.

With a ripple they were through, into another darkling plain... this one tiny. Only a few columns gleamed green here, and in the central one, stood the statue of a beautiful dwarven woman, motionless, staring out at the world.

Then a flicker behind him, and Threadbare glanced back in time to see the Ninja cartwheel through the portal, hurling shuriken straight at him.

"I don't know how to fix this! But I can fix her!" Kayin yelled. "Go! I've got this!" The catgirl growled and launched herself at the black-clad figure, and knives flashed and flew between them as they moved, almost too fast for the eye to follow.

Threadbare ran straight up to the column. "Get out! Please get out!" he said, but the statue didn't move.

He poked the green light around it, found the light no barrier, and smacked the statue on the leg with his scepter. "Hey there! Please come out!"

The Pygmalion statue charged out and tried to stomp on him. Threadbare danced back and weighed his options.

Well. It WAS some sort of construct, wasn't it? **"Eye for Detail."**

Behind him, Kayin shrieked. There was a sound of tearing cloth. But the spell told Threadbare what he needed to know, as he dodged away. **"Command Animus, accept my invitation!"**

And he invited the statue into his party. It stopped trying to stomp him, turned, and charged the Ninja.

Reality flickered, as numbers appeared in the sky. Threadbare ran back, pausing to grab up Kayin's torn body as he went. "Are you alive?"

"That's a good question," she coughed. "But yeah, just lost another life." The ninja had cut her clean in half.

He shoved Kayin in his pocket for now.

Behind him, stone shattered, but that didn't matter, because he was back through the portal. "Zuula! Vines!" he called. "Block the portal!"

But it was Bak'shaz who reacted, reaching into his pack and throwing a flowerpot down in front of it. It broke, plants and dirt went everywhere...

"Call Vines!" Zuula said, and then there was a wall of plant matter, that rippled and churned. Something behind it struggled, writhed, trying to get out...

...too late.

A scream echoed, trailing off, as the vines pushed inward to the empty space where the dungeon had been. The ninja was gone.

On the loot pedestal, one of the glittering gems churned for a bit, then popped, like an overheated glowstone. "One down!" bellowed Melos' ghost. "It's working! Keep at it!"

"Go!" roared Anise, and across the field of shattered toys, the Cataclysm roared towards Threadbare as he ran for the next portal. Then he was through, and already, already he could hear the air burning at his back—

—and turning from him. **"Manipulate Faia!"** Madeline yelled, swooping in behind the Cataclysm.

"How many of those do you have left, little dragon?" whispered the daemon, as fire traced arcane patterns on the black ground below her, and flaming tentacles rose up. "And can you withstand a magma kraken, I wonder?"

But then Threadbare was smacking the statue and backing up as it came out kicking. **"Command Animus, accept my invitation!"** The statue hesitated, then arrowed straight for the Cataclysm.

"Yeah, I ain't fighting that thing, sweethaht," said Madeline, swooping over and grabbing up Threadbare, then beating wings back to the portal. "Seeya!"

"Get her—" The Pygmalion statue tackled the Cataclysm, and the daemon shrieked. "Get this off of me!"

Then they were through the portal. As soon as they were, the vines went up again. "Out of sanity!" Madeline whispered in his ear as she put him down. "What do you want me ta do?"

"Go tell the dwarves that it's their turn," Threadbare said, glancing around. That was two daemons down. But Legion was calling in armored fiends now, Anise was still going strong, and his friends were flagging. Pulsivar was down, Threadbare saw with horror, but he couldn't tell how bad it was. Sloopy the Snake was dead, torn into bits. As were most of the toys who'd followed them in.

No time! He raced through the next portal...

...and a brace of the armored fiends followed, pushing past Mordecai and his family, taking the hits, to race in after the little bear.

He was faster though, and he reached the control pillar with time to spare, smacking the statue and dodging its return strike, luring it out of the pillar. **"Command Animus, accept my invitation!"**

Threadbare sent it towards the daemons...

…who weren't advancing. They were guarding the exit, spears and blades out in a phalanx.

They're not trying to stop me from sealing it, they're trying to keep me here until it closes!

Threadbare ran forward, trying to pass, but their spears knocked him back every time. The damage wasn't much, but they had weight over him, and his thoughts were scrambled. He was low on sanity, with no clever ideas, no tricks to pull—

And then Emmet was there.

Emmet had no clever ideas. Emmet had no tricks to pull. Emmet just had his fists, and a whole lot of daemon butt to kick.

And it was enough.

The phalanx broke, Threadbare leaped through, and Emmet caught him, backing off just as the portal wavered and disappeared.

"One more! Get it quickly!" Melos commanded.

"No! No you don't!" Anise screamed. "Vevintarego? OUT!"

Grinning, The Lurker stepped out of the central control pillar, pulled knives, and came forward to join the battle…

…and the main dungeon rippled.

Reality groaned.

"Get to the pillar! Get someone in there!" Melos yelled.

"Not a chance!" roared Legion, and he ripped his hands through the air and shuddering walls of daemonflesh rose to bar the way, as Anise laughed and laughed. "Close, but no victory for you!" she called. "Well, at least you'll all die quickly!"

"Melos!" Graves yelled. "Get in there!"

"What?" the dead king stared at him. "What can I do? I'm dead!"

"Yes! You're temporarily a ghost. A disembodied soul." Graves yelled back. "And daemons can't do shit with souls!"

The battle stopped.

Anise looked at him, leaped over to Melos, and put her hand through his head so fast that her sleeves snapped in the air.

Melos stared back at her, unhurt. Then he grinned and blew her a kiss.

Reality flickered again, and when it returned the former King was disappearing through the flesh of the daemonic walls, hindered not one bit by their physical forms. In a matter of seconds the flickering stopped.

"No!" Anise shrieked…

"Yes," said Threadbare, emerging from the last portal with a statue following him. "You've lost." Then he shifted back out of the way, as a double column of dwarves rushed in, taking up positions around the entryway, shields held high.

He pulled Kayin from his pocket, as gently as he could. **"Mend**

Golem," he told her, using most of his remaining sanity. She gasped as her lower half reappeared and hopped to the ground.

Anise drew herself up, smiling. **"Focus Chi to hands. Focus Chi to hands. Focus Chi to hands. Offensive Stance,"** she said, as her arms disappeared into glowing, pulsing spheres of energy, roiling red and gold. The succubus sneered. "You saved your land. Bravo. But you really can't stop me from killing my way through every last one of your friends, before I get to you. Twenty dwarves? Bah. Speedbumps. I've still got enough energy left to—"

"NOW!" yelled the dwarven captain.

Twenty shields hit the floor.

Twenty pairs of dwarven arms shifted to the wide-barreled blunderbusses hanging from their backs and pulled them over their shoulder with a smooth motion.

"DOWN!" Garon bellowed, and the toys and their friends dropped.

And thunder came to the darkened realm between worlds.

Martial artists had phenomenal agility.

But blunderbusses, designed to throw clouds of shot at short range, really didn't care too much about agility. The daemons ate a full cloud of shot.

Legion rocked back, slicked with blood. One of his Hellhounds disintegrated. The Lurker vanished, then reappeared, holes punched straight through him as he dropped.

But Anise was made of sterner stuff. Bloodied, screaming in incoherent fury, she leaped into the dwarves, sending them down in crumpled heaps as her arms rose and fell, threshing, smiting them down, until—

"Corps a Corps!" yelled Cecelia, parrying her, staring up at her murderer with loathing in her painted eyes. Her blade locked firm to Anise's fist, as the chi pulsed around them both, rippling and making Cecelia's hair rise.

Sneering, Anise drew back her other fist—

"Corps a Corps!" shouted a squeaky voice, and suddenly tiny black paws were wrapped around the daemon's free hand. Anise froze, staring down at the little black-furred armored bear, snugged tight, dangling from her wrist.

"You?" she whispered in disbelief.

"Me. **Bear Hug! Innocent Embrace!**" And Missus Fluffbear SQUEEZED.

A red '320' burst up from Anise, as she shrieked, her bones cracking and her flesh melting to ash. Missus Fluffbear had put up Heavensblade and Holy Smite earlier in the fight, and they added in here as well. The succubus fell to her knees, as Fluffbear leaped from the ashen, crumbling remnants of her arm, wrapping her arms around her neck. "One more time for Yorgum! **Bear Hug! Innocent Embrace!**"

Anise fell. Cecelia sheathed her sword and turned her back on the crumbling ashes, slowly walking away from the daemon's remains.

The Legion gasped, turned to run—

"Rammit!"

—and got promptly knocked to the ground as Garon put his horns into the back of his knee. Zuula and Bak'shaz and Madeline fell on him, while the others tackled the last hellhound. In a hot minute it was done, and the daemonic walls withered to dust the second their summoner was dead.

In the silence, in the gasping of the dying dwarves, Beryl and Fluffbear and Zuula moved around the fallen, distributing healing while the toys checked each other, looked to make sure they were all alive.

The doll haunters, the ex-cultists had fallen to a man (and woman for that matter,) and Threadbare and Graves moved among them, collecting soulstones from the bodies. Graves made more whenever they found a broken one, and the ghosts that had been waiting on the fringes, staying out of the way, rushed in to fill them.

And then, Threadbare's vision filled with words.

You are now a level 17 Toy Golem!
+2 to all attributes!

You are now a level 15 Ruler!
CHA+3
LUCK+3
WIS+3
You have unlocked the Kingsguard skill!
Your Kingsguard skill is now level 1!
You have unlocked the Proclaim Treaty skill!

You are now a level 16 Ruler!
CHA+3
LUCK+3
WIS+3

You are now a level 9 Scout!
AGI+3
PER+3
WIS+3

You are now a level 10 Scout!
AGI+3
PER+3
WIS+3
You have unlocked the Scouter skill!
Your Scouter skill is now level 1!
You have unlocked the Wakeful Wandering skill!
Your Wakeful Wandering skill is now level 1!

You are now a level 12 Duelist!
AGI+3
DEX+3
STR+3

You are now a level 13 Duelist!
AGI+3
DEX+3
STR+3

You are now a level 14 Duelist!
AGI+3
DEX+3
STR+3

You are now a level 15 Animator!
DEX+3
INT+3
WILL+3
You have unlocked the Deanimate skill!
Your Deanimate skill is now level 1!
You have unlocked the Distant Animus skill!
Your Distant Animus skill is now level 1!

You are now a level 16 Animator!
DEX+3
INT+3
WILL+3

You are now a level 21 Golemist!
INT+5
WILL+5

You are now a level 22 Golemist!
INT+5
WILL+5

You are now a level 23 Golemist!
INT+5
WILL+5

You are now a level 24 Golemist!
INT+5
WILL+5

You are now a level 25 Golemist!
INT+5
WILL+5
You have Unlocked the Greater Golem Upgrade skill!
Your Greater Golem Upgrade skill is now level 1!

The levels tore through him, refilling his energy and expanding his mind. Threadbare felt things snap into clarity, felt everything crystallize. "So much," he whispered, then turned to Garon. "The raid skill you used. The experience gets split a little more evenly among the survivors, doesn't it?"

"Yeah. Even though Fluffbear got the killing blow, it spreads it out among all parties involved." Garon said, shaking his head. "My gods. She was…"

"Significant events, too, don't forget that," Cecelia said. "We just saved everyone. We just… oh gods. Didn't we?"

"Yes," Threadbare said, his high-powered intelligence running through the ramifications. "Without the dungeons that make up the outer wall, this is just an ordinary dungeon, now. Under the control of a strong-willed ghost." He stared at the dungeon master's column, and the see-through form of Melos, who looked back.

And for a second, Threadbare worried.

"Father," Cecelia said, moving up to the pillar. "Come out. Please," she said, beckoning. "Let's end this."

Melos looked down. He put his hand over his face, rubbed it. Then he stepped out.

And as reality flickered, he knelt, staring at his daughter. "I'm so very, very sorry."

"I know." Cecelia looked up at him, reached out a hand. He reached out to touch it, sighed as his hand passed through hers.

Cecelia stared at him, holding his gaze. "You remember, how you came to take me away from all childish things?"

"I do," said Melos, fading with the dungeon.

Cecelia looked around and smiled. "Be really fumping glad my childish things came to get me back."

The dead king laughed then, the first honest laugh he'd had in over a decade.

And with that, he and the dungeon were gone.

The toys and their living friends looked around at the darkened labs. Old, dusty, dirty, strewn with broken equipment...

...and lit by purple and green light, as a violet crystal appeared with a snap in midair, trembling. They held their breath, all of them did...

...before it shattered, into millions of shards and fell to the floor, green numbers wisping away, and gone.

"Well," Threadbare said, in the silence, as he hunted around and found his backpack full of soulstones. "It's over. Let's go home."

Pulsivar nudged him, purring, and Threadbare mounted up and led the way upstairs.

And with a mighty cheer, they all left the darkness and ruins of the past behind and walked out into the sunlight.

CHAPTER 16: LOOSE ENDS

"I feel silly."

"You look fine."

"I know I look fine, I still feel silly."

"You can still back out. Garon's going to be right there. He can give you Scout back."

"No... no, no, I said I'd go through with this." Cecelia sighed and tugged her clothes more firmly about her. A rich, grape-colored purple dress, draped with emeralds, it covered her modestly, and directed attention upwards to her hair, which had been stuck in place with a box full of golden pins.

"I don't think you'll regret it. It IS a very good job, particularly for someone who's going to be doing a lot of negotiating. And the buffs ARE nice."

"It... I'm wearing clothes that I made myself. It just feels... no, it's silly for me to be arguing about this. I know, I know, most of the kingdom gets by like this. It's just that until now, clothes were things that came from other people. I feel like my work is going to be tested, and I know it's a stupid thing to worry about but if I'm worrying about this I'm not worrying about the news or how to sell our idea to the others."

"It's a good idea." Threadbare said. He wore a matching purple suit, in lieu of his normal clothing. Though he'd kept the Toy Top Hat. The Gribbit envoy would be very disappointed if he didn't.

"Yes, it's a good idea, but that doesn't mean much when it comes to politics. Father taught me that."

"I'm not entirely sure he was the best one to follow when it comes to political advice."

"True, but I don't really have many other role models to go by, here."

"Well you're going to be your own model soon, then you can roll however you please."

"Threadbare! That's not what I—" Cecelia stopped when she saw his smile and laughed. "You're right. I'm worrying about nothing."

"Probably." He looked up at the double doors they'd come to and knocked gently with his scepter. After a minute, Emmet opened them.

Threadbare had made the armor golem's suit himself, and with a silent sigh he took in the rips, tears, and scuffs the giant metal golem had inflicted upon it. And the stain in the crook of its arm, where a tiny, fluffy dog dozed guiltlessly.

"Welcome," Emmet said, then turned and announced in his brassy voice; "Councilor Gearhart of Central Cylvania! Councilor Threadbare of Central Cylvania!"

"There y'are!" called King Grundi. "Come on over! We were just talkin' about Taylor's Delve."

"Oh? How's the expedition going?" Threadbare and Cecelia found their seats at the large, round table. It took some time to clamber up the chairs provided for them.

No one was quite comfy here. At the other end, Jarl Greta Sumvonesdottir sat on a pillow the size of a King-sized bed, her blue knees well above the table's edge. King Grundi and Bazdra Coaler stood to one side of her, with Jericho the ranger next to Grundi. Hidon Fingers and Beryl Wirebeard took the flank on the other side of her, with Garon sitting next to Beryl. Next to the little wooden minotaur, Longcroak the Gribbit Envoy nodded, his own top hat flopping as he spoke. "Well, goes well. Many carts, much traffic through Outsmouth. Much trade. Golems very happy. We are very happy."

"There's no trouble with the eggs, right?" Cecelia said. The first time they'd encountered the frog monsters weighed on her mind. No matter how reasonable Gribbits were at the council table, they couldn't shake the age-old instincts that drove them to aggression whenever predators neared their eggs.

"Trouble? No trouble. Don't have spawning grounds in Outsmouth or near Outsmouth where landsfolks can reach. Outsmouth is just... commute. For wu-rk," Longcroak belched the last word. The Gribbits were still adjusting to the new ideas.

"And there's enough fish for you and everyone else?" Threadbare asked.

"Oh yes. Big lake. Take only what we need. Golems don't eat. Plenty of fish to sell across land."

"Which is seriously helping with the expedition," Garon said. "We're clearing the area in record time, between the folks you loaned us," he nodded to Jericho, "and those of us who are golems. We don't have to sleep, and the living folks have plenty to eat... so long as they like dried fish, anyway. We... do have a request, though."

"Oh?" Threadbare asked.

"The Oblivion's gone, and the Thundering Pass is reachable from the Delve again. That's the only way in or out. We'd like a garrison..." Garon took a breath. "And we'd like Mastoya to lead it."

"Out a the question," King Grundi said, folding his frail arms.

"Mastoya? De vun who beat us?" Greta rubbed her chin. "Vhy is she out of der question?"

"Putting her in charge of anything military is risking a coup," Hidon scowled, tugging on his beard. The covert ops dwarf stared over at Cecelia. "We're already hearing rumors of unrest in the Central region, folks wanting the 'good old days' back."

"That's very much a minority," Cecelia said. "Mostly older folks who never fought in the wars and minor nobles who profited from them. More talk than anything else."

"Putting up a stone statue of Melos in the middle of the town square is a bit more than talk," Jericho said. Then his eyes crinkled. "Even if it did vanish overnight. Leaving tracks that looked like it walked off its own plinth and just kept going."

"I'm sure I don't know anything about that," Cecelia shrugged.

Threadbare knew plenty about that and was wise enough to keep that to himself.

Cecelia continued. "In any case they didn't ask my permission before putting it up, and it was in violation of public land usage regulations. Baroness Rhoda found the fine lighter than the public humiliation of being served papers at the unveiling ceremony she planned. That turned out to be an empty plinth, anyway."

"That's good and well. But there's always going to be a sentiment, a segment of grumblers," Bazdra said, toying with the silver hourglass hanging from her neck. "It's the cycle. Time and again it'll happen."

"Right. The grumbling will be there regardless," Garon said. "Which is why putting Mastoya in charge of the vital garrison for the pass is a good move, because she'll do the job regardless of politics or attempts to coerce her."

Grundi scowled. "There's nothing you can say to convince me that letting General Mastoya anywhere near a group of impressionable troops is a good idea!"

"Who said anything about General Mastoya?" Garon and Beryl shared a grin.

"What are you playing at, then?" Grundi scowled harder.

"I think SERGEANT Mastoya would do a fine job down there."

A pause.

Then Grundi laughed. "Oh, she'll hate that!"

"Yep. It'll be a training facility for the volunteer army. She'll be responsible for troops in a way she's never been before. And she'll answer to the best officers that you can provide." Garon moved his gaze from Grundi to Jericho.

Grundi nodded, grudgingly. "She'd be good for that. Decent with troops, just... too big on following orders to be a General. So long as she's never an officer again we'll allow it."

The ranger filled a pipe and nodded as he lit it. "**Firestarter.** We can give that a try. We'll be watching her, of course."

"Of course. Speaking of watching..."

"I suppose it's my turn," Jericho said, and stood, pulling out a map, giant-sized for the Jarl's benefit. He unfolded it, and the toys hopped up on the table to get a better look.

The map showed all of Cylvania, and a few days travel beyond. "There's nothing," Jericho said simply. "Old roads, foundations where homes and villages used to be, empty ruins for the most part. Monster tribes in a few cases, none of the peaceful ones, either. Nothing we couldn't handle, but..."

"Basically, we're surrounded by wilderness in all directions," Cecelia said.

Jericho shot her a sardonic look. "Mordecai talked to you, I expect?"

"Briefly. With everyone visiting the castle, I got a few minutes with him at most."

"Mm. Well, that's the truth of it. Best guess is that when we Oblivioned out, the nearby settlements that depended on our trade routes and proximity folded or got overrun. There's no sign of the invading army that King Garamundi was so worried about or that they even reached this far. Which doesn't mean they're not a week to the East, dealing with other business now, but... it seems unlikely. If they conquered the area a few years ago, I can't see that they wouldn't have a watch post set up, at least."

"We don't know what's out there," Threadbare said. "And we need to change that. I have an idea."

"We have an idea," Cecelia nudged him with her ceramic elbow.

"Sorry. Yes." Threadbare rubbed his head. "We'd like to send out explorers. Not just people with the Explorer job, either but people who want to go have a look around. Then come back and tell what they've seen."

"Scouts, basically," Jericho said.

"More than that. That's the thing, really. We want varied skills and jobs. We want adventurers. Young ones."

"My rangers can easily do that job." Jericho frowned over his pipe.

"True, but how many of you are there? And all of you are very high level. Some of the highest we've got." Threadbare shook his head.

"Which is the problem," Cecelia said. "You're already the peacekeeping force in the North and West, and you're spread thin throughout Cylvania, spying on things so that the hotheads don't turn unrest into rebellion. And that's not getting into the fact that in the event of a threat, we'll need you at home."

"There's the greater waystones, but they all go to Fort Bronze, since the central one's broken," Grundi shrugged. "And there's only about ten waystones left, all told."

"And they're not getting replaced until we get an Explorer up to twenty-fifth level," Cecelia said. "Which will happen faster if we send out EXPLORERS."

"Mm. To tell the truth I'm having trouble holding some of my people back," Jericho said. "Not the rangers, the young ones, the survivors of Balmoran. They've been living nomadically so long that they want to go exploring. What exactly are you proposing?"

"That we set up a sort of club to go exploring, to go see what's out there and reclaim it, if that's the right thing to do," Threadbare said. "I was thinking it could be called the Reclamation Association of Generica."

"Rag," Beryl snorted. "Cute."

Cecelia nodded. "Yes. We'll set up lodges along each of the routes out of Cylvania, to make sure people heading out get the best training and support we can give. It'll cost some money and resources, but in the long run, it'll benefit us immeasurably."

Grundi looked to Bazdra and Hidon. "How much money?" he asked.

Twenty minutes later, Jarl Sumvonesdottir was snoring with her head and most of her torso on the table, so loudly that everyone had to shout to make themselves heard over her. Forty minutes later they reached a settlement.

"Good," Cecelia smiled, as Hidon passed around the contract, and every leader signed it. Even the giant, when they managed to wake her up. "There's just one more thing."

Hidon threw his hands up. "You literally could have said that before we all signed!"

"No," Threadbare said. "This is more of an informal agreement. I've been thinking about it a lot. And talking it over with Cecelia and Beryl."

Eyes moved to Beryl, who shrugged, and tapped the newly-minted symbol of Yorgum on her chest. "What? I'm his confessor." It had been an amiable parting when she left Aeterna's service for the god of builders, thankfully.

"Anyway," Threadbare said, "I would like golems to be in as many of the exploration parties as possible. And for those living folks who want to do it to carry soulstones."

The councilors turned to look at Bazdra.

"You're putting me in a spot here," the dwarven cleric said, steepling her fingers. "I told you the problems that would arise, given enough time. My position on those haven't changed. Undead that can hop bodies and persist eternally are going to cause us problems, both with the mortal followers of the gods and the gods in general."

"Actually I'm not putting you in a spot," The little bear said, spreading his paws. "It would be in the contract if I was. I'm giving you the chance to say yes or no, and the society will abide by your decisions, without reservation."

"What?" Bazdra blinked.

Beryl spoke. "We're still trying to draw up rules for how to do the golem body-hopping shit without pissing off Aeterna or Nebs. NOBODY's dumb enough to want a beef with the Goddess of Time or the Goddess of Death," Beryl spread her hands. "So we're giving you the shot to stop it cold turkey. But at a cost."

"That cost being, a greater chance of permanent fatality among the explorers," Cecelia said, into the silence. "At a time when we're low on people already."

Bazdra rubbed her eyes. "We don't know what's out there, do we?" she asked.

"Could be entire peaceful nations beyond the wilderness," Jericho shrugged. "Could be hordes of dragons just outside our scouting range. We're running blind."

"I'm just worried that this will be a compromising decision," Bazdra shook her head. "Trading the moral implications for extra security. This land tried that already and look how THAT turned out."

"It's a good worry," said Cecelia. "And I'm glad you're concerned. But... well, doll haunters already make up a hundredth of Cylvania's population. We're already compromised. Short of going out and killing all of them, myself included—"

"No one's suggesting that!" Bazdra raised her hands.

"—I know, I'm just saying, the die has already been cast. Right now there are only two, possibly three sources for golems in the kingdom. But eventually more people will learn the unlock for Golemist, even if Threadbare and the others never teach anyone else. And necromancer's an easy unlock that anyone can get from interacting with, oh, doll haunters or other undead." Cecelia sighed. "They're our people. We have nothing to gain and everything to lose if we treat them differently. They're not going away, barring a major disaster. So we need to look at ways going forward. Which is why we want them represented in the RAGs."

"How would putting them in every team help us with that?" Bazdra asked.

"Because," Threadbare said, leaning forward, "this will let us test and see how the rest of the world reacts to the notion of sentient golems. And by seeding them in among the people most likely to run into the rest of the world, we get to find out how various nations, groups, and other sorts react to our discovery BEFORE they're on our doorstep with armies."

The Council considered that for a long moment. Then the dwarves were nodding. "When you put it that way... I can see the wisdom in it," Bazdra said. "Alright. I have no objections. Anyone else?"

"I got vun."

Surprised, the rest of the Council looked up to the grumpy giant. "We gots to do der north first. Exploring it, I mean."

"What? Why?"

"Ve're out of de Sunfire mead. And de only brewery what makes it vas up dere, last ve knew, so ve gots ter go north first."

"What?" Grundi shrieked. "I told you to nurse that stuff!"

"Ve did!"

"It ain't even been four months!"

"Yah, and it vas only t'ree kegs! Ve ain't made of stone, dammit! It's SUNFIRE!" Her bellow rattled the table.

About an hour later, after placating the surly Jarl, the Council resolved a few other minor issues and broke up.

"Did you get it?" Threadbare asked, on their way out the door.

"Hm? Get what?"

"Model."

"Oh yeah." she grinned. "I read the skill descriptions during the dull parts of that meeting." She sighed. "We're going to be having one of these every few months for the rest of our existences."

"Or until we are destroyed," Emmet said, falling in behind them. The small dog in his arms snapped awake at the motion and barked a few times, on general principle. Emmet scratched it with the tips of his fingers until it thumped its tail against his chest and settled.

"You really shouldn't let him pee on you," Threadbare said.

"Did he?" Emmet looked down. "Oh. My skin is not so sensitive to that."

"It's all right. **Clean and Press,**" Threadbare looked him over and threw in **"Mend,"** on the big golem's torn jacket for good measure.

"But yeah. Council meetings for the rest of our lives..." Cecelia said. "Or maybe not. When the time comes we can hand off the reins to someone else. Once things are a little more settled."

"Reason might be a good candidate. She's taking her name seriously," Threadbare said. "She likes books and debating things."

"She's coming along well, then?" Cecelia shot him a concerned look.

"Oh yes. We had Zuula and Fluffbear on hand for the luck buffs before I gave her the greater upgrade. Armor golems don't get any better mental stats, so it's a good thing we did. Also a good thing we were in the middle of nowhere." Threadbare frowned. "I'm still not sure where those maxicores came from. Anyway, she's got six adventuring jobs and three crafting ones. I think that's the best I can do right now, but I'll keep working on it. I might be able to get that number higher for future greater golems." He stirred, as he remembered a detail. "For her first job she wants to be a knight just like her mother."

"Her mother? Who— oh." Cecelia clapped her hand to her mouth. "You told her I was..."

"No. Not to begin with. She remembers you, vaguely."

"Much like I remembered you?" Emmet asked, "from before I had thoughts?"

"We think so. I told her of you after she brought it up and started asking who you were." Threadbare smiled up at Cecelia. "Would you like to meet her?"

"I would. She's... where, exactly?"

"About a day to the north." Threadbare sighed. "In a pretty burnt patch of forest. I think... that I need to talk to Jarl Greta about renting her dungeon core for a while. I could use it to make a controlled safe space for Greater Golems to grow up in and get their luck up before they go out to the outside world."

"So long as that's the only experimenting you're doing with dungeon cores, I'm fine with that," Cecelia said. "Yes. I would like to meet her. Maybe tomorrow, though? It's been a very long day."

"It has. Shall we retire?"

"Yes. Once I get out of these clothes."

Minutes later, Cecelia sat in her bedroom, dressed in her nightgown and brushing her hair. She didn't need to wear the one or do the other, not anymore, but it comforted her. Pulsivar curled up next to her, hogging most of the bed, even though he appeared to be on the edge of it. Even in sleep, his Misplacement effect continued.

And hanging his hat on the rack, clad in only his fur, her teddy bear joined them, hopping up on the small bed and waiting until Cecelia hugged him tight. She was smaller now, and her arms and body were much harder, but it was close enough for him. She was still his little girl.

She settled back in bed, next to the warmth of Pulsivar's invisible fur, and smiled. "Ready."

"Dreamquest," Threadbare told her. With Garon's help, he had swapped out Scout, then montaged and taken Shaman, and ground it up as fast as he could. It was nice to be able to talk to Pulsivar, and some of the skills were handy. But mostly he'd just got it so that Cecelia could sleep and dream whenever she wished.

And for now, for a little while at least, his girl's eyes closed, and Threadbare snuggled in against her, while she slept.

For this, for her, he had cast down a tyrant, defied daemons, and saved a kingdom.

And it had all been worth it.

*****

Madeline was waiting for Garon outside the conference chamber. "Is the boring stuff done?" the red-painted dragon demanded, grinning at him.

"Oh yeah. Is the fam behaving?"

"Mostly. They won't miss us foah a bit."

"Cool. Shall we?"

It was a few flights of stairs up to the battlements, then a quick hop on her back, and Madeline roared, before launching herself into the air. Garon clutched her neck tightly for a second, then relaxed as she took off, flapping.

"I didn't hear a scaly wings in there! Had me worried for a second."

"I roared it. Tahns out dragons can do that. Just roar out any skill they want, and it counts as commanding it. It's paht of that Draconic Tongue skill."

"Any skill? Not just the dragon ones?"

"Any skill." She beat her wings as they soared over the city, and Garon rode in silence for a bit, checking out the streets below. They were distressingly empty.

"We could use a few more dragons," he said, as his mind turned over the numbers he'd been privy to in the last council meeting. Four hundred doll haunters, give or take, among barely forty thousand other people in Cylvania's population. True that wasn't counting the dwarves, but even adding them in, they were only like two thousand more, at most. Cylvania was down way, way too many people for the territory they were claiming.

"Moah dragons? It's not gahnna be a hahd sell," Madeline said. "Mind you, that faia elementalist thing is paht of it too, unless you want people blowing themselves up."

"There's gotta be something in higher levels for that." Garon shook his head. "You're only level four. Maybe next level, I don't know."

"Guess I'll find out." Madeline grinned, as her spine twisted under him. She curved around the edge of the city, circled back, spooking pigeons and crows as they went. "Ya know, I never did ask. Why a minotaur?"

"Eh. More of a matter of why NOT a minotaur. Big, strong, not too obviously dumb, no real weaknesses or surprises. Well, beyond that Maze-ing Grace skill, but that's more of a weird boon than anything else. And no rage, that's a big deal."

Madeline laughed. "Don't have to tell me twice. It was pretty bad to watch, those yeahs I had to keep you tied up. Wait, shit. Soahry? Too soon? I didn't mean to…" She shut up.

"No. No, it's fine. You were a vampire, back then, and that's what vampires do. Did, anyway. Figure death has buried that, you know? We're free to be who we want now, and I figure the you that hurt me is dead, and the me that betrayed you in the end is dead, too. I'm Garon and you're Madeline, and we're free to be awesome together."

"Togethah." She beat her wings again. "Not the way I'd envisioned it, but it ain't so bad. Though it does make me curious. Zuula and yoah old man, what do you think they… I mean how do they… in bed, and all?"

"You know, you could ask her that, and she'd tell you in graphic detail."

"Why do you think I ain't asked her?" Madeline shuddered underneath him.

"Heh!" Garon snorted. His muzzle was good for that. "They sleep together, that's all I know. Whether or not they do anything uh, beyond that, I couldn't say. They're happy. That's all that matters. Personally…" He freed up a hand and rubbed his chin. "I think it's the intimacy. That's what makes it love. They can be alone together, and whatever they do is just icing on top, you know? The core of it is you've got two people alone, who trust each other and just enjoy each other's company."

"Sounds kind of like what weah doing now," Madeline said, flapping her wings to get over a tower.

"Yeah," Garon said, resting his hand back at the base of her neck. "It does."

"Think it's the same for mistah beah and his princess?"

Garon shook his head. "No. He's her bear, and she's his little girl. Wouldn't be right otherwise, and they know it. But us? Well. That's different, isn't it?"

They flew in silence for a bit longer. But not awkward silence. It was more of a warm silence, an answer given to a question that had never been asked and a satisfaction that grew as they considered it.

They stayed out much longer than they'd planned, but it was worth it.

Zuula was waiting for them when they returned, standing on the battlements and throwing pebbles down at the guards below.

"Mom! Stop that."

"No, it fine. Dey got helmets." She lifted up a rock the size of her head.

"No."

"Tch. Talkin' to you mother dat way..." But she put the rock down. "You got de t'ing you say earlier?"

"Yeah. You ready?"

"No, let her go be human and fart around and angst for an hour... OF COURSE ZUULA READY!"

Garon nodded and reached out a hand, smiling as she grabbed it like she was drowning. **"Shaman Promotion Fifty!"**

And Zuula's mouth fell open into a huge, tusky grin as she declared, "Level twenty-six!"

"Twenty-four more to go." Garon grinned. "Maybe by then I'll have unlocked another promotion skill."

"You bust butt on dat. Zuula ain't slowin' down. Er... maybe good time to mention dat." She said, nodding toward the trapdoor and the ladder leading down.

"Not slowing down?" Garon said.

"We... gonna go. Mordecai and me. Go sout', go on one last adventure." She sighed. "He... not in good way. Forgets t'ings. Slowing down."

"Oh jeeze. Mom, look, I... you're not going off to die, are you?"

"Pfft, no. Not our way. Don't be stupid. But if it happen, it happen. He not soulstoning. Not gonna come back dat way."

They descended the ladder as Garon considered.

Madeline spoke up. "Yoah coming back, though, right?"

"What? Yes. Or maybe we both come back. This one last chance to see world outside, while Mordecai can still get around." Zuula said. "Once we see enough of it, we make decision den."

"You'd better. I mean, we're not going to have kids, but there's still hope for Jarrik and Beryl. And Bakky too, maybe, I don't know what his situation is. Regardless, I really want my cousins to meet their grandmother AND their grandfather, if at all possible."

Zuula glared at him. "Fighting dirty." Then the glare softened. "So proud of you! Proper orky tactic!"

"I learned from the best." He hugged her, and she hugged him back, biting at his shoulder affectionately.

"So when are you going?"

"As soon as you promote Mordecai. He got some jobs to level up!"

"Yeah, he's at the top of the list. It takes a good chunk of fortune or else I'd do all the rangers at once." Garon rubbed his head. "Tell him I'll stop by tonight, okay? He's... doing well?"

"He sane. It worst in de mornings." She glanced up toward the sun, scowled at the ceiling. "Zuula be glad to be out of here, soon. When we waystoning back, anyway?"

"Tomorrow, I'm thinking," Madeline said. "Time enough foah another flight or two round the city." She nudged Garon with her tail, and he jumped. "See ya around, Gar." She sauntered off, smiling.

"Dat one a keeper," Zuula nudged him.

"Yeah." Garon nodded, watching a draconic tail give one last wiggle as it disappeared around a corner. "She is."

*****

"Nah. It's back to Brokeshale for us, bro," Jarrik said, draining the last of his beer. "Too much light out here. Too much space."

"That's kind of ironic, given how much I remember you being into the outdoors and exploring the hell out of things when we were kids." Garon said over his mug. It was full of water, but he drained a sip into the compartment in his chest whenever Jarrik took a pull of his own. It was good dwarven manners, that's all.

"Yeah, well... I think I found what I was looking for." Jarrik reached over to ruffle Beryl's hair and got his arm punched, for his trouble. He gasped but managed to avoid spilling his drink. "Ass," he muttered.

"Dick." Beryl responded. Then she smiled at Garon. "Yeah, we've been here long enough. I've got a whole ministry to run, and now that I've got all the shipments arranged, I'll have the supplies to keep us playing with all new weapons for a few years. After that, we'll see."

"So you're not losing business? Now that the war's done, I mean?"

"We're dwarves," Beryl said, refilling her mug. "There's always another war coming. And new weapons are going to be useful when it does."

"Yeah. And I'll be there to see it, too." Garon sighed. "Grundi's your guildmaster, so you're good there. But I'll have to stay here and stay safe until I've got some successors trained up. That's going to take time. Even after that, I don't know." Garon stared at his water. "It depends on what the RAGs find, I guess."

"Yeah. 'bout that," Bak'shaz spoke for the first time that afternoon, and everyone looked at him. "You got a spot open?"

"Of course!" Garon said, putting his mug down. **"Invite Adventurer,"** he told Bak'shaz. "We're still working out the rules and all, but welcome aboard."

Bak'shaz has joined your guild!

"Thanks bro." Bak'shaz smiled and fiddled with his helmet. "I'm thinkin' I don't want to explore much yet. But I wanna help set up the lodges an' stuff. I'm thinkin' that maybe it's a way around th' tamer problem."

"Tamer problem?" Jarrik killed his beer.

"It's hard as hell to keep more'n one critter tamed. Might be that changes in later levels, I dunno, but I'm thinkin' we can have like pens and paddocks set up at the lodges, so the RAGs can bring in more animals, stuff you don't find in these parts, and leave them between missions…"

Garon smiled, as the words flowed from Bak'shaz, starting hesitant and speeding up. That was the brother he remembered, normally curt but enthusiastic when he got talking. He'd been worried for him, after his snake died in the battle against the daemons. But now? Now Garon thought his little brother would be okay.

Putting his mug down, he leaned in, and the Skunkstomper boys (and significant other,) started talking about the logistics they needed to run a proper guild…

*****

"Me? No, I've got everything I need, to be honest," Graves said, looking up from the latest batch of golem bodies. "While I'll be assisting the Guild as needed, right now I need to see about making soulstoning and doll haunting socially and morally acceptable. Because if people HERE have problems, then the people we'll run into out THERE will have problems, too. It's better to settle the problem here first, so we have a united solution to present to the doubters out THERE."

"Alright, if you're sure. You're one of our members now regardless, so if there's ever anything, you let me know?" Garon held his hands up in a placating manner.

"Sorry. Was that too harsh?" Graves rubbed his face. "I'm used to having a lot more charisma than this. Twenty-two knight levels gone, that's sixty-six points right out the window. And I wasn't much of a charmer before I was a knight."

"Eh, look at it this way," Kayin said, walking among the golem bodies and plopping down right in the middle of his work. "It's easier to grind your charisma the normal way now."

"No, it wasn't too harsh." Garon shrugged. "You've got a ways to go before you piss off a half-orc. Even one who's had a race-change, I guess."

"And doesn't that open up some big questions?" Kayin asked. "Like, oh, how do you think actual high dragons are going to feel about toy dragons horning in on their dragonity? Is a dwarf still a dwarf if he's a golem and in another shape?"

"Well, the dwarves have that 'undead are no longer who they were when they were dwarves' rule, so that part's easy for them at least," Graves said.

Kayin nodded. "Yeah, but it's more complicated for other folks. Giants just flat-out don't like the notion, but they don't care if other people do it. The Gribbits are politely uninterested. And what about elves? They're out there somewhere, probably. What happens when we run into someone who wants to be an elf?"

Graves cleared his throat. "Actually..."

"You've already had someone, haven't you?" Garon asked.

"Yes. She wants to be a dark elf, actually."

"Oh. Shit." Garon was glad he didn't have skin to go pale anymore.

"Would that even work?" Kayin asked, the marbles in her eyesockets glittering.

"I have no idea, but we've got no good excuse to turn her down, so we're going to give it a whirl." Graves held up a pale, stuffed plushie, clad in spidery robes, with a cruel sneer on its face and black, pupiless eyes. Pointed ears jutted out from silvery hair.

"Who in their right mind would... you know what, never mind," Garon rubbed his horns. "Yeah, that'll go over well if we run into any elves out there."

"Do you even know what their beef with dark elves is?" Kayin glanced over to him.

"Not a clue. I think only other elves get to learn about that."

Graves shrugged. "I'm reasonably sure this is just asking for trouble, but whatever. **Speak with Dead.**"

"Oh wait, she's here? Now?" Garon said.

"Yes, I am. And it's my choice!" One of the soulstones pulsed.

"Are you ready, Janice?"

"Go for it, Mister Graves!"

"Toy Golem!" He poured yellow reagent out of a vial, and it dissipated into the plush elf, as did the soulstone in his other hand. **"Golem Animus!"**

They watched... and gasped, as the elf doll's skin turned from sheer pale white, to a regular flesh color. The black eyes rippled, then turned into white patches of cloth with pupils.

"What's wrong?" Janice said, staring at them. "Status." She frowned. "Hey! I wanted a dark elf, not an elf!"

"Ah. Er..." Graves sat down. "Oh dear. I think I see why the elves don't talk about it much."

"Why's that?" Kayin asked.

"This sort of thing only happens when somebody gets a ranked up body. The rank won't transfer, so the body defaults to the lowest possible rank of the form. Dire bears turn into regular bears. Misplacer beasts turn into cats. So that means that dark elves..."

"So can I be one or not?" Janice asked, thoroughly lost.

"Yeeess, but you'll have to get enough elf levels to unlock the choice. And figure out the race unlock," Graves said, massaging his eyes. "And for the love of Yorgum we need to keep this quiet. This is something elves would probably kill us to keep quiet and feel not a bit of guilt over."

"What?" Janice said.

"Please," Graves said. "I'll explain it to you later, but I'll need your promise to keep this secret."

"Okay. You are one of the makers. If you want me to, I'll promise."

"I do."

She did, then headed out, still relatively happy, off to show her friends her new body.

"We're going to hit more stuff like that, won't we?" Garon asked, as he stared after her. "Weird little secrets, stuff that we can't forbid, because then people will want to do it more. Stuff we can't predict."

"Yes," Graves said. "Which is why I need to stay here and sort it out as it comes."

"And I'll stay here and guard him," Kayin said. "Because he's one of the keys to our kingdom, and this whole thing we've got, and he and Threadbare are central to the whole operation. And that lady over in the dwarfhold. What's her name?"

"Irga. We're staying in touch. I already cleared it with Grundi; we've got golem birds dedicated for that."

"Yeah." Kayin smiled. "Because this?" She gestured at the tables full of golems, "This is something I can't help with. But keeping my shield buddy alive is. Lots of assassins will be coming his way if we keep doing this."

Graves reached down and scratched between her ears, and she leaned back into it, purring for a second. Then her eyes snapped open, and she glared at Garon. "Not a word."

Garon held up his hands and shrugged.

"Well. At any rate..." Graves said, turning back to his work.

Smiling, Garon found his own way out... and nearly tripped over Glub as he did. The little fishman had a pack on his back and a grin on his face. "So when we going?"

"We're going?"

"To set up the lodges."

"Oh. Ah, it'll take a while. The first one will be in the South; we're thinking."

"Right, that's where you're going back to, right dude?"

"Yeah, in a day or two."

"Aw man." Glub looked down. "Eh, I guess it's cool if it's later."

"Why the hurry?"

"Eh... at first it was fun singing at the taverns, but..." he scratched his head. "The uh, the ladies from Outsmouth. They're like following me, man. And there's some... living women, and dudes, joining them. I think I'm being flirted with. Like lots."

"And you're not okay with this?"

"No man!" Glub clapped his hands over his mouth. "I mean, don't get me wrong, most people here are pretty cool, but aside from those bomb-ass Gribbits, ain't nobody's got a booty worth slamming to me! And even if I was still inclined to that I'm a toy now! Got no urges or equipment to work with that'd do anything for me. No, uh, I think I'd kinda like to hit the road. Fast. And maybe let the... heat die down some."

Garon laughed and put his arm around the guy. "See, this isn't usually a problem that most bards care about. But I get where you're coming from. Hey, is Missus Fluffbear still around?"

"No. She's sorting out the troops. And getting used to her promotion. So you probably shouldn't call her Missus anymore."

"Right, right... General Fluffbear. Gonna take a while for me to get used to saying that," Garon shook his head. "Go help her. Run errands and stuff. That should keep you busy, I think."

"Worth a shot. Don't leave without me though, okay?"

"Promise."

Garon watched him go and headed back upstairs.

There was a hell of a lot to do. Cylvania was a shadow of what it had been, but they had a way ahead. It wasn't without problems, but he had his friends, and he had plans and options and a guild hundreds strong, now.

He couldn't say what the next year, or even the next month or day would bring, but he'd meet it with a smile.

A smile or a really big axe, as the occasion required...

*****

Arusheluxem floated in the inky sea, in the nothing, surrounded by endless rows of her own kind. Peaceful. Silent. Empty. They lurked there, enjoying the purity that filled the space that was Var Rhun.

But the daemon could not be still. Could not relax. Could not simply let go.

Fifteen years, she had striven to build a legacy. Fifteen years she had endured, battling to subsume her host, who had the strongest will she'd ever encountered, working to subvert and weaken that pathetic King and those who would help him. Fifteen years spent turning that little flyspeck of a country into her own personal abattoir, a monument to mortal stupidity and weakness.

And then she'd been thwarted on the cusp of overwhelming victory, a victory that would have surely been enough of an achievement to advance her a full digit in Vhand's eyes.

Fifteen years of work undone in a matter of weeks by one little living toy.

No, she finally decided; it wasn't good enough. She wouldn't let it end here. Sooner or later she would be summoned once more, sooner or later the lot would fall to the daemon who had once been Anise Layd'i. And then she would work tirelessly to get free, work until she was in a spot again to return to Cylvania, or whatever its descendants or conquerors called it. And then she would have her vengeance, on the golem, or the brat, or whoever else was around.

Because now? Now it was personal. Even for something that prided itself on being an eternal force of entropy, there were limits.

The summons came sooner than Arusheluxem expected, and if she'd had lips in this form she would've smiled. So soon? Oh, this was perfect!

All she had to do was deal with a mortal summoner, likely some desperate, sex-starved cultist, and then she could be off, finding her way back to Cylvania to strike them when they were weakened. All it would take was one slip, one flaw in the language of the pact, one of the traps that the progenitor daemons had seeded throughout mortal knowledge, and then she'd be able to turn everything around—

—Arusheluxem blinked, as she faded into the mortal body she'd been provided.

She wasn't in front of some scruffy, half-mad man in a black sheet. Nor was she in some dusty basement, or even a proper cave.

She was on a simple, flat metal table, covered with a mirrored glass case. Grilles in the side permitted the sound of the chant to pass through. There were multiple voices intoning this one, and her eyes widened. To do that, every Cultist there had to be level twenty, at least.

"Hello?" She asked, as she tested the pact in her mind. The usual backdoors, the treacherous areas of thought that were usually left open, were shut.

The chant finished, was replaced by silence.

"Hello? Please," she said, looking around. "I only want to serve you. Masters." Except no, no she didn't, because service wasn't part of the pact. That had been omitted.

Why?

The table shuddered under her, and the glass slid up, replaced by metal. Some mechanism churned below her. And she realized that she wasn't in a case, she was in a tube. She snapped her hands up, tried to stop the table from sliding, and nearly lost a finger. She yanked back her bloody hands before anything significant could got chopped off, and howled in frustration.

Level one again! I could have punched my way out of here easily if I still had...

Everything spun, and she hung on to the table below her for dear life. Then with a WHUMP, she landed, tilted somehow. The ceiling above her was now the ceiling in front of her, and she was standing on more metal.

Then the tube opened.

"Hello?"

No response. After a moment, the darkness in front of her lit up with glowstones. She followed the trail, down a short hall that ended in a grilled metal door. Next to it sat a chair, and a small desk, with a book, an inkwell, and a quill pen.

Hissing behind her, and Arusheluxem turned to see the doors of the tube she'd arrived through seal up, steam puffing out around them.

"Can you hear me?" a bored voice said from outside the door. It was muffled, blurred. She couldn't tell the species or even the gender of the speaker.

"Yes," she replied.

"State the time of your last summoning."

"I couldn't say— it was fifteen years, six months, and three days ago." She slapped her hand to her mouth.

She hadn't meant to say that. She'd had a number of prevarications lined up for precisely that question. Hastily she muttered the commands that let her review the pact... and found clauses woven in there, with such skill that she hadn't noticed them at first. She couldn't NOT answer. She couldn't lie or even omit information.

A creeping dread started to build in her gut. Who WERE these people?

"State the general location of your last summoning," continued her mysterious interrogator.

"Inside the altered dungeon located within the country of Cylvania."

"Cylvania?" Now the voice sounded interested. "Get back into the lift for archiving."

"What is this?" she asked. "Who are you?"

"That is none of your concern."

"Please. I'm..." She searched her mind for memories...

...and found it blank.

She'd been given a brain that had no memories of mortal life, beyond basic speech in whatever language she was speaking now, a rough knowledge of the date in about five different calendars, and a preference for orange as a favorite color. It felt... raw, around the edges. Someone had done this to her sacrificed host, for no other reason than to prevent her from knowing about her summoners.

The creeping dread in Arusheluxem's gut grew into shaking fear. She looked down at her nude, unremarkable form and realized that this would NOT be a standard summoning.

"Send me back. Please," she whispered.

"No. Not until you've given us a thorough accounting of everything you've experienced over... hm, what was the duration of your summoning?"

"Fifteen years, three months, and one day."

Silence for a bit. A muffled sound, voices talking.

"Well. No logbook for you, then." said the voice. "You're going directly to the inquisitors. Congratulations, you're now Intelligence Asset number three-hundred and sixty-two. We've been wanting information about that area for quite a long time. And you're going to tell us everything you know."

"And then you'll send me back?"

"Oh three-sixty-two," the voice sounded very amused, "how long have you been doing this? We make no promises."

"Just... tell me one thing." Arusheluxem begged, in a tone she hadn't used in a very long time. "Tell me that you mean them harm. That you'll hurt them. Conquer them, destroy them, I don't care," she knew she was being irrational, giving away too much, but she couldn't stop herself. She was level one again, and her willpower was a frail shadow of what it had been. "Just make them suffer."

"I don't owe you that answer. And I don't need to give it to you. But I'll tell you this much," her unseen interrogator chuckled. "I don't see any way that you telling us all about them will help them."

The doors to the tube hissed open again, and head held high, trying to salvage some dignity, Arusheluxem walked back into the metal-lined chamber. The doors sealed, and it rumbled, carrying her down, into darkness...

EPILOGUE

Once upon a time, there was a teddy bear who worked hard and hoped to live happily ever after. But nothing truly ends, and so, wrapped in the arms of his little girl, he lay awake at night and pondered what was to come next. And to be ready, he whispered **"Status,"** and this is what he saw:

Age: 5
Guild: Reclaimers Association of Generica

Jobs:
Greater Toy Golem Level 17
Cave Bear Level 14
Ruler Level 16
Tailor Level 11
Model Level 11
Necromancer Level 11
Duelist Level 14
Animator Level 16
Enchanter Level 12
Golemist Level 25
Smith Level 11
Sculptor Level 13
Shaman Level 5

Jobs stored in Guild Registry
Scout Level 11

Attributes	**Pools**	**Defenses**

Strength: 177 Constitution: 175 Hit Points: 352(462) Armor: 62(76)
Intelligence: 303 Wisdom: 233(240) Sanity: 536(712) Mental Fortitude: 52
Dexterity: 200(207) Agility: 137(144) Stamina: 347(471) Endurance: 72
Charisma: 139(168) Willpower: 289 Moxie: 428(567) Cool: 20(55)
Perception: 112 Luck: 125(132) Fortune: 237(354) Fate: 25(32)

Generic Skills
Brawling - Level 68 (+40)
Climb - Level 14
Clubs and Maces - Level 21
Dagger - Level 9
Dodge - Level 18
Fishing - Level 1
Magic Items - Resist Fire 29
Ride - Level 12
Stealth - Level 18
Swim - Level 5

Greater Toy Golem Skills
Adorable - Level 47
Bodyguard - Level 9
Gift of Sapience - Level NA
Golem Body - Level 34
Innocent Embrace - Level 17
Magic Resistance -Level 17

Cave Bear Skills
Animalistic Interface - NA
Claw Swipes - 58
Darkspawn - NA
Forage - 13
Growl - 2
Hibernate - 37
Scents and Sensibility - 23
Stubborn - 10
Toughness - 25

Ruler Skills
Appoint Official - Level NA
Emboldening Speech - Level 20
Identify Subject - Level 10

It's Good to be King - NA
King's Quest - Level 15
Kingsguard - Level 1
Noblesse Oblige - Level 56
Organize Minions - Level NA
Proclaim Treaty - Level NA
Royal Audience - Level 22
Simple Decree - Level 15
Swear Fealty - Level NA

Tailor Skills
Adjust Outfit - Level 5
Clean and Press - Level 20
Recycle Cloth - Level 2
Tailoring - Level 54(69)

Model Skills
Adjust Weight - Level 14
Call Outfit - Level 6
Dietary Restriction - Level 55 (+110 to all pools)
Fascination - Level 9
Flex - Level 22
Makeup - Level 12
Self-Esteem - Level 22
Sexy Pose - Level 2
Strong Pose - Level 17
Work it Baby - Level 55 (+55% to raw item bonuses)

Necromancer Skills
Assess Corpse - Level 12
Command the Dead - Level 28
Deathsight - Level 9
Drain Life - Level 8
Invite Undead - Level 12
Mana Focus - Level NA (+11% to sanity)
Skeletons - Level 19
Soulstone - Level 45
Speak With Dead - Level 24
Zombies - Level 3

Duelist Skills
Challenge - Level 12

Dazzling Entrance - Level 17
Disarm - Level 2
Fancy Flourish - Level 13 (20)
Guard Stance - Level 22
Parry - Level 27
Riposte - Level 1
Swashbuckler's Spirit - NA (+20 to cool)
Swinger - Level 2
Weapon Specialist - Level 50 (Brawling +25)

Animator Skills
Animus - Level 41
Animus Blade - Level 15
Animus Shield - Level 4
Arm Creation - Level 7
Command Animus - Level 23
Creator's Guardians - Level 70
Deanimate - Level 1
Distant Animus - Level 1
Dollseye - Level 18
Eye for Detail - Level 20
Magic Mouth - Level 18
Mend - Level 68

Enchanter Skills
Appraise - Level 30
Boost+5 - Level 25
Boost +10 - Level 5
Disenchant - Level 24
Elemental Protection - Level 18
Glowgleam - Level 26
Harden - Level 36
Soften - Level 31
Spellstore I - Level 40
Spellstore V - Level 18
Spellstore X - Level 8
Wards - Level 3

Golemist Skills
Armor Golem - Level 2
Bone Golem - Level 1
Call Golem - Level 4

Clay Golem - Level 3
Command Golem - Level 24
Flesh Golem - Level 1
Golem Animus - Level 66
Golem Guardians - NA
Greater Golem Upgrade - Level 2
Invite Golem - Level 12
Mend Golem - Level 66
Program Golem - Level 43
Toy Golem - Level 83
Wood Golem - Level 19

Smith Skills
Adjust Arms and Armor - Level 20
Refine Ore - Level 15
Smelt Down - Level 7
Smithing - Level 52

Sculptor Skills
Detect Clay - Level 8
Mend Ceramic - Level 6
Refine Clay - Level 18
Sculpting - Level 61

Shaman Skills
Beastly Skill Borrow - Level 1
Call Vines - Level 1
Dreamquest - Level 25
Fated Preserver - Level NA
Poison Resistance - Level 1
Secret Herbs and Spices - Level 5
Slow Regeneration - Level 3
Speak with Nature - Level 16

Equipment
Journeyman Tailor's Apron of fire resistance (+6 Armor, +10 Tailoring, Resist Fire 9)(+3 Armor, +5 Tailoring, +5 Resist Fire from WIB)
Okay Quality Bling
Ringtail Master's Coat of fire resistance (+5 CHA, +5 LUCK, +5 Armor, +5 Fate, +10 Resist Fire 10)(+2 CHA, LUCK, Armor, Fate, +5 Resist Fire from WIB)

Rippen Tear Cloak (+10 to brawling, +5 Armor)(+5 Brawling, +2 Armor from WIB)

Rod of Baronly Might (+5 CHA, +5 WIS, +10 Cool)(+2 CHA, WIS, +5 Cool from WIB)

Sneakypants (+5 Camouflage)(+2 Camouflage from WIB)

Yellow Belt of Bravado (+5 AGL, +5 DEX, +5 to the Fancy Flourish skill)(+2 AGL, DEX, Fancy Flourish from WIB)

Toy Top Hat (CHA +10)(+5 CHA from WIB)

Golden Laurels (Enables the REST skill, usable every two hours.)

Inventory
A Folded-steel Dagger (Dagger Level 10)
Tailor's Tools
4 vials of Green Reagent.
1 Vial of Blue Reagent
A pouch of assorted crystals, rank 1-4.
Minorphone (Enhances voice and social skills focused through it twice per day)

Quests

Unlocked Jobs

Air Elementalist, Berserker, Cleric, Cook, Cultist, Grifter, **Spirit Medium,** Tamer, Wizard.

APPENDIX I: THREADBARE'S JOBS AND SKILLS

CAVE BEAR

Cave Bears are large beasts, tough and strong and stubborn. They eat pretty much anything organic and spend most of their lives underground, emerging to forage as needed. Bears gain experience by eating bear-associated foods, roaming their territory, and defeating foes with their natural weapons.

GREATER TOY GOLEM

Toy golems are the protectors of children everywhere! And also good, reasonably cheap guardians for any fledgling golemist. They aren't the toughest of golems, but they possess a few costly powers good for helping their charges survive. Like all golems, they're sturdy, resistant to magic, and immune to a lot of things that would kill living beings. Greater golems possess sapience, and attribute ranks that lesser golems simply do not have. They can even learn jobs! Limited in that aspect only by the intelligence of their crafter, greater golems have theoretically astronomical potential. Greater Toy Golems gain experience by doing adorable things, surviving conflict by toughing it out, and defeating foes using their natural weapons.

ANIMATOR

Animators give life to inanimate objects, awakening them to serve and defend the animator. Animators gain experience by casting animator spells and defeating foes with their animi.

DUELIST

Duelists fight with their chosen weapon and swashbuckle around, using mobility and attitude to win their fights. Duelists gain experience through fighting with their specialized weapon, defeating foes with panache and style, and doing risky, flashy things in dangerous situations. Note: Specialized weapons can be changed. Practice hard, your specialized weapon will shift to your highest weapon skill.

ENCHANTER

Enchanters are one of the oddest adventuring professions. They do most of their work beforehand, and use their items to devastating effect. Enchanters gain experience by creating magical items, casting enchanter spells, and using their created items to defeat foes.

GOLEMIST

Congratulations! Through blending Animator and Enchanter, you are now a golemist! Golemists craft unique magical constructs, and use them to fight their battles. Golemists gain experience by casting golemist spells, creating golems, and using their golems to defeat their foes.

MODEL

Models improve their bodies and attitudes, displaying their glory for all to see and controlling how others look upon them. Models gain experience by using model skills, successfully controlling first impressions, and defeating their foes through social maneuvering.

NECROMANCER

Necromancers raise the dead to do their bidding, and can negotiate with powerful spirits and undead entities. Necromancers gain experience by interacting positively with the dead, casting necromancer spells, and using the undead to defeat their foes.

RULER

Rulers entice people to work for them, and organize them through decrees and rewards to do their bidding. Rulers gain experience by having their subjects do their bidding, organizing others to a common goal, and looking out for the interests of those in their charge.

SCOUT

Scouts roam the wilderness, spying upon foes and using stealth and survival to accomplish their goals. Remember, be prepared! Scouts gain experience by using scout skills, exploring new wilderness areas, and remaining undetected by foes.

SHAMAN

Shamans are wise in the ways of nature, dealing with plants, beasts, and natural forces for their own benefit and the benefit of their communities. Shamans have a wide grab bag of versatile tools, and are at home dealing with most problems that can arise in the wilderness. Shamans gain experience by living in accordance with nature, dealing with beasts, plants, and natural events, and helping their chosen tribe.

SMITH
Smiths work with metal, crafting objects with the help of a forge, anvil, and hammer.

TAILOR
Tailors work with cloth and occasionally other flexible materials, crafting objects with the help of scissors, needle, and thread.

GREATER TOY GOLEM SKILLS

ADORABLE
Level 1, Cost N/A, Duration: Passive Constant
Adorable has a chance of activating when you do something cute in front of an audience, or onlookers blame you for something that isn't your fault. It improves the attitude of anyone who fails to resist your charms.

BODYGUARD
Level: 10, Cost: 25 Sta Duration: 1 minute per toy golem level
Name a target party member when activating this skill. For the duration, you have a chance of intercepting each attack aimed at them, so long as you remain within two yards of them. Multiple attackers or overwhelming amounts of strikes may reduce the effectiveness of this defence.

GIFT OF SAPIENCE
Level 1, Cost N/A, Duration: Passive Constant
Congratulations, you now have all the attributes and can think and learn. Good luck with that. You also have 0/8 adventuring job slots open, and 2/4 crafting job slots.

GOLEM BODY
Level 1, Cost N/A, Duration: Passive Constant
Your body has no organs, and is made from inorganic or once-organic material infused with a magical force. By being exposed to effects that would kill or cripple living beings and surviving them, this skill will level up. As it levels up, you will gain immunity and resistance to a wider range of lethal effects.

INNOCENT EMBRACE
Level 5, Cost: Sanity equal to half the amount healed, Duration: Instant
Heals an embraced target 10 X the level of this skill. Will affect on other golems, is standard healing otherwise. Currently activated through Animalistic Interface, and will affect any legal target embraced. Does not affect uninjured targets.

MAGIC RESISTANCE
Level 1, Cost: N/A, Duration: Passive Constant
Has a chance of negating any non-beneficial magic cast upon you. The chance of success is dependant upon the spellcaster's level.

CAVE BEAR SKILLS

ANIMALISTIC INTERFACE
Level 1, Cost N/A, Duration: Passive Constant
Allows the beast to use their racial skills without requiring vocalization. All skills that are not constant passives may be turned on and off as the situation and instinct require.

CLAW SWIPES
Level 1, Cost 5 Sta, Duration: 5 attacks
Enhances the damage caused by your hands and feet, and adds the sharp quality for the next five strikes. Currently activated through Animalistic Interface, and will activate whenever you brawl with intent to injure.

DARKSPAWN
Level: 10, Cost: N/A Duration: Passive Constant
You gain a bonus to all attributes equal to twice your Cave Bear level while in darkness, and can see normally in darkness. Sufficient light will disrupt this effect, and the bonus does not increase the maximum size of the associated pools.

FORAGE
Level 1, Cost 10 Sta, Duration: 10 minutes
Greatly enhances your perception for the purposes of finding food, water, or other natural resources in the wilderness. At higher levels, may be used to locate specific naturally occurring resources. Currently activated through Animalistic Interface, will activate whenever you hunt for natural resources.

GROWL
Level 5, Cost 10 Mox, Duration: Instant
Growl at a target to damage their sanity.

HIBERNATE
Level 5, Cost N/A, Duration: 1-3 months
Go into a torpid sleep. Requires a cool, dark place and you cannot be affected by the Starving condition. Restores all pools to full, as per a normal rest.

SCENTS AND SENSIBILITY
Level 1, Cost 5 San, Duration: 5 minutes
Activates heightened smell, greatly increasing perception for that sense and allowing you to catalog and remember specific odors. Currently activated through Animalistic Interface, and will activate whenever you encounter an interesting scent.

STUBBORN
Level 5, Cost N/A, Duration: Passive Constant
Increases your resistance to sanity damaging effects.

TOUGHNESS
Level 1, Cost N/A, Duration: Passive Constant
Has a chance of increasing whenever you take serious damage. Raises your maximum HP by two whenever it increases.

SCULPTOR SKILLS

DETECT CLAY
Level 1, Cost 5 For, Duration: Instant
Directs you to the nearest sources of clay, pigment, and other substances useful for sculpting

MEND CERAMIC
Level 10, Cost 20 For, Duration: Instant
Mends a damaged pottery item, repairing it a small amount.

REFINE CLAY
Level 5, Cost 10 Sta, Duration: Instant
Separates any usable pottery crafting materials out of whatever material it's mixed with.

SMITH SKILLS

ADJUST ARMS AND ARMOR
Level 5, Cost 10 Sta, Duration: instant
Resizes any armor or weapons to fit the chosen wearer or wielder, and also allows minor alterations.

REFINE ORE
Level 1, Cost 10 Sta, Duration: Instant
Separates any usable crafting materials in a container or dirt, ore, or stone into neat piles of material.

SMELT DOWN
Level 10, Cost 25 Sta, Duration: 30+ Seconds
Breaks a metal item down into ingots of metal, and separates out any gems or other materials into a small heap nearby.

SMITHING
Level 1, Cost NA, Duration: 30+ seconds
Crafts the desired metal or mixed-metal-and-forgeable item desired, requiring different materials for each project and the presence of appropriate tools. Has a chance of failure.

TAILOR SKILLS

ADJUST OUTFIT
Level 5, Cost 20 Sta, Duration: Instant
Resizes any cloth outfit to fit the chosen wearer, and also allows minor alterations.

CLEAN AND PRESS
Level 1, Cost 10 Sta, Duration: Instant
Instantly cleans the selected item, and removes any wrinkles, stains,

or other blemishes. Only works on items that are primarily textiles.

RECYCLE CLOTH
Level 10, Cost 25 Sta, Duration: 30+ Seconds
Breaks a cloth item down into bolts and patches, and separates out any leather or other materials into a small heap nearby.

TAILORING
Level 1, Cost NA, Duration: 30+ seconds
Crafts the desired cloth or mixed-textile-and-sewable-materials item desired, requiring different materials for each project and the presence of appropriate tools. Has a chance of failure.

ANIMATOR SKILLS

ANIMUS
Level 1, Cost 10+ San, Duration: 10 min/level
Turns an object into an animi, capable of movement, combat, and simple tasks as ordered by its creator. Must be in its creator's party to do anything beyond defend itself. The greater the size and mass of the object, the more it costs to animate, and the more hit points, strength, and constitution it begins with. The type of material also factors in, and determines the starting armor rating of the animi.

ANIMUS BLADE
Level: 5, Cost: 15+ Sanity Duration: 10 minutes per animator level
Animates a slashing weapon and grants it minor flight, causing it to move and attack on its own. It cannot venture more than a small distance from you, and will orbit you without taking action unless invited into your party. Its weapon skill is dependent upon your weapon skill, and its equivalent strength is dependent upon your will.

ANIMUS SHIELD
Level: 10, Cost: 20+ San Duration: 10 minutes per level
Animates a shield, that moves as if wielded by an invisible warrior. Must be in a creator's party to do anything beyond defend itself.

ARM CREATION
Level: 5, Cost: 10 San Duration: N/A
Teaches an animi a weapon skill that you know, allowing it to wield and use weapons that are manageable given its size and manipulative appendages. Lasts until the animi deanimates.

COMMAND ANIMUS
Level 1, Cost 5 San, Duration: Instant
Allows the caster to issue one command to an animi that isn't currently in its creator's party. If successfully cast, the animi will follow the command to the best of its ability until it is impossible to do so.

CREATOR'S GUARDIANS
Level 1, Cost N/A, Duration: Passive Constant
Enhances animi in the creator's party, boosting all attributes. The amount buffed is influenced by the animator's will and this skill's level. Has a chance of increasing every time a new animi first joins the animator's party.

DEANIMATE
Level 15, Cost 50 San, Duration: Instant
A ray that inflicts moderate damage upon a nearby animus, construct, golem, or other animated object, and has no effect on other creatures. This damage cannot be prevented by armor, or resisted by the Resist Magic skill.

DISTANT ANIMUS
Level 15, Cost 50 San, Duration: Instant
Animates an object at range, no touch required. The animation cost must be paid on top of the distant animus cost. The range is short, equivalent to one foot per animator level.

DOLLSEYE
Level: 5, Cost: 5 San Duration: 10 minutes per animator level
Allows the animator to see through one of their animi. Lasts until the animi deactivates, or can be shut off at will. Occupies the sight capabilities of one of the Animator's eyes, so perception penalties and confusion may occur if both eyes are open at once. You cannot have more than one dollseye effect active for each functional eye your body possesses.

EYE FOR DETAIL
Level 1, Cost 5 San, Duration: 1 minute
Allows the animator to examine the status of any animi, golem, or other construct he looks upon. Also analyzes any object for animation potential and sanity cost. Can be resisted.

MAGIC MOUTH
Level: 10, Cost: 20 San Duration: 10 minutes per level
Allow the animator to speak through one of the animi currently in their party, regardless of distance. If the animi does not have a mouth, the voice issues forth from the closest approximate place a mouth would be on a living being of similar structure.

MEND
Level 1, Cost 5 San, Duration: Instant
Instantly repairs the target construct or object, restoring a small amount of HP, influenced by the level of this skill and the animator's will.

DUELIST SKILLS

CHALLENGE
Level 1, Cost 5 Mox, Duration: Instant
Calls out a target to fight you. They suffer combat penalties based on your charisma unless they are actively trying to attack you. Resistible, because some foes are just too cool for you.

DAZZLING ENTRANCE
Level 1, Cost 10 Mox, Duration: Instant
Used before revealing yourself to foes, the more dramatic your appearance the better. Boosts your charisma and cool for a short time.

DISARM
Level 10 Cost: 20 Sta Duration: Instant
Has a chance of disarming a foe's wielded item. The foe must be in melee range.

FANCY FLOURISH
Level 1, Cost 5 Sta, Duration: Instant
Unleash a fancy set of moves that won't hurt your foe but look really cool. Attacks their Moxie.

GUARD STANCE
Level 1, Cost 10 Sta, Duration: Until dropped, or the end of the fight
Assume a guard stance, and gain a bonus to your dodge skill and armor, at the cost of lowering your strength and dexterity.

PARRY

Level: 5, Cost: N/A Duration: Passive Constant
While you have your specialized weapon drawn, you have a chance of parrying any melee attack you are aware of.

RIPOSTE
Level 10 Cost: NA Duration: Passive Constant
Whenever you successfully parry an attack, you have a chance at riposting, triggering a free attack with whatever weapon you are currently wielding.

SWASHBUCKLER'S SPIRIT
Level: 5, Cost: N/A Duration: Passive Constant
Your Charisma buffs your Cool.

SWINGER
Level: 5, Cost: N/A Duration: One minute per skill level
Activate this skill to buff your agility and climb skill while swinging from ropes, chains, chandeliers, etc...

WEAPON SPECIALIST
Level 1, Cost N/A, Duration: Passive Constant
Enhances your weapon skill. Automatically assigned to your highest weapon skill. If you have two or more equal highest weapon skills, you may freely choose which to specialize in at any time.

ENCHANTER SKILLS

APPRAISE
Level 1, Cost 5 San, Duration: 5 minutes
Allows you to see all relevant information about a mundane or magical item.

BOOST +5
Level 5, Cost 25 San, Duration: Permanent
Enchants a magic item to boost an attribute or defense or magical effect by +5. Not cumulative. Consumes three doses of RED Reagents and a level 1 crystal.

BOOST +10
Level 10, Cost 50 San, Duration: Permanent
Enchants a magic item to boost an attribute or defense or magical effect by +10. Not cumulative. Consumes three doses of YELLOW

Reagents and a level 2 crystal.

DISENCHANT
Level 10, Cost 30 San, Duration: Instant
Attempts to disenchant a nearby magical item that you have created or that you control or own. Breaks it down into reagents and crystals. Chance of failure based on skill and the complexity of the item, mitigated by intelligence.

ELEMENTAL PROTECTION
Level 5, Cost 50 San, Duration: Permanent
Combine with a dedicated boost to imbue a wielded or worn item with a field that disperses or absorbs elemental energy of the chosen type, sparing you some harm. Consumes one dose of ORANGE Reagents.

GLOWGLEAM
Level 1, Cost 5 San, Duration: 1 hour per level
Infuses any object with a simple light spell. The luminescence is based upon the caster's intelligence.

HARDEN
Level 1, Cost 10 San, Duration: 10 minutes
Increases the toughness of any object or construct temporarily, adding to its armor and/or damage potential.

SOFTEN
Level 1, Cost 10 San, Duration: 10 minutes
Decreases the toughness of any object or construct temporarily, reducing its armor and/or damage potential.

SPELLSTORE I
Level 1, Cost 10 San, Duration: Permanent
Prepares an object that stores a level 1 spell or skill inside of it. Anyone can then read, break, drink, or otherwise use the object in an appropriate manner to activate the spell. Requires and consumes one dose of RED Reagents. The enchanter does not have to be the person storing the spell inside the Spellstore.

SPELLSTORE V
Level 5, Cost 20 San, Duration: Permanent
Prepares an object that stores a level 5 spell or skill inside of it.

Anyone can then read, break, drink, or otherwise use the object in an appropriate manner to activate the spell. Requires and consumes one dose of ORANGE Reagents. The enchanter does not have to be the person storing the spell inside the Spellstore.

SPELLSTORE X
Level 10, Cost 40 San, Duration: Permanent
Prepares an object that stores a level 10 spell or skill inside of it. Anyone can then read, break, drink, or otherwise use the object in an appropriate manner to activate the spell. Requires and consumes one dose of YELLOW Reagents. The enchanter does not have to be the person storing the spell inside the Spellstore.

WARDS
Level 5, Cost 50 San, Duration: Permanent until damaged or dispelled
Creates wards within an area against a particular creature type. Creatures of that type within the area are debuffed and affected with a damage-over-time effect based on the skill level. Magical effects created that are tied to that creature type may be suppressed or countered while within the area. Requires and consumes one dose of GREEN Reagents.

GOLEMIST SKILLS

ARMOR GOLEM
Level 20 Cost: 350 San Duration: Permanent
Creates an armor golem shell out of metal. Requires metal, 3 BLUE reagents and a level 4 crystal.

BONE GOLEM
Level 15, Cost 250 San, Duration: Permanent
Allows the golemist to construct a bone golem shell. Requires bones, 3 doses of GREEN reagents, and a level 3 crystal.

CALL GOLEM
Level 15, Cost 75 San, Duration: Instant
Teleports one of your golems to your side. The golem must either be in your party or within 500 feet per rank in this skill at the time of casting.

CLAY GOLEM
Level 10, Cost 200 San, Duration: Permanent
Allows the golemist to construct a clay golem shell, which may then

be baked or left unfired, as desired. Requires clay, 1 dose of GREEN reagents, and a level 2 Crystal.

COMMAND GOLEM
Level 1, Cost 20 San, Duration: 1 minute per level
Allows the caster to issue one command to a golem that isn't currently in a party. If unresisted, the golem will follow the command to the best of its ability until it is impossible to do so, or until the command wears off.

FLESH GOLEM
Level 20 Cost: 300 San Duration: Permanent
Creates a flesh golem shell out of a corpse, or corpses sewn together. The less damage there is to the corpse (or corpses), the more it will mimic life. Requires corpse(s), 1 BLUE reagent, and a level 3 crystal.

GOLEM ANIMUS
Level 1, Cost 50 San, Duration: Permanent
Turns a prepared golem shell into a functional lesser golem that will obey its creator's commands to the best of its ability.

GOLEM GUARDIANS
Level 10, Cost NA, Duration: Passive Constant
Enhances golems in the creator's party, boosting all attributes. The amount buffed is influenced by the Golemist's will.

GREATER GOLEM UPGRADE
Level 25, Cost 250 San, Duration: Permanent
Changes a lesser golem into a sapient greater golem version of itself.

INVITE GOLEM
Level 1, Cost 10 San, Duration: Instant
Used to invite golems into your party. Automatically affects golems created by the golemist, can be resisted by other golems. Will not affect golems in their creator's party.

MEND GOLEM
Level 5, Cost: 20 San Duration: Instant
Heals a golem for a moderate amount, dependent upon your intelligence and skill level.

PROGRAM GOLEM

Level 5, Cost: 50 San Duration: Permanent until changed

Allows the golemist to give conditional instructions to golems under his control. The golems will follow these instructions until it becomes impossible to do so. The higher the skill, the more instructions can be given, and the more complex they can become. Some experimentation is necessary for best results.

TOY GOLEM

Level 1, Cost 100 San, Duration: Permanent

Allows the golemist to construct a toy golem shell. Requires a toy, one dose of YELLOW reagents, and a level 1 Crystal.

WOOD GOLEM

Level 5, Cost: 150 San Duration: Permanent

Allows the golemist to construct a wood golem shell. Requires wood, three doses of YELLOW reagents, and a level 2 Crystal.

MODEL SKILLS

ADJUST WEIGHT

Level 10 Cost: 20 Sta Duration: 1 minute per skill level.

You may adjust your weight upward or downward, increasing or decreasing it by a percentage based upon your model level, or any point in between. Your body will get thinner or fatter as you do so. Getting too heavy will debuff your agility. Getting too light will debuff your strength.

CALL OUTFIT

Level: 5, Cost: 20 Mox Duration: Instant

Instantly summons one of your regular equipment sets from wherever it may be. The set must be kept together, and cannot include material heavier than leather.

DIETARY RESTRICTIONS

Level 1, Cost N/A, Duration: Until broken

So long as you have spent the last week without eating anything with the UNHEALTHY identifier you gain a small buff to all pools. This bonus is cumulative, up to twice your rank of this skill. Eating UNHEALTHY designated food immediately removes all versions of the buff.

FASCINATION

Level 1, Cost N/A, Duration: Dependant upon skill

Heal, aid, or otherwise be nice to an enemy in combat. If unresisted by mental fortitude, the foe will become temporarily fascinated with you, for a duration proportionate to this skill's level.

FLEX
Level 1, Cost 10 Sta, Duration: 1 minute per level

Buff your endurance and armor by the level of this skill.

MAKEUP
Level: 5, Cost: 10 Mox Duration: Until smeared or removed

Allows you to apply makeup that buffs any one of your skills. Form follows function, so the makeup must be appropriate to the job that contains the skill being buffed.

SELF-ESTEEM
Level 1, Cost 10 Mox, Duration: 1 minute per level

Buff your mental fortitude and cool by the level of this skill.

SEXY POSE
Level 10 Cost: 20 Sta Duration: 1 minute per model level.

Buffs your charisma, but only applies when dealing with people who are capable of being sexually attracted to you. Only one pose may be active at a time.

STRONG POSE
Level: 5, Cost: 10 Sta Duration: 1 minute per model level

Buffs your strength. Only one pose may be active at a time.

WORK IT BABY
Level 1, Cost NA, Duration: Passive Constant

Whenever one of your worn or wielded items creates a favorable impression in at least one onlooker, then this skill has a chance of increasing. All worn and wielded items that confer bonuses have their bonuses increased by a small percentage for each level of this skill. Note that the difference is harder to see with lower level gear and lower levels of the skill.

NECROMANCER SKILLS

ASSESS CORPSE
Level 1, Cost 5 San, Duration: 1 minute

Allows the animator to examine the status of any undead creature he looks upon. Also analyzes any corpse for animation potential and sanity cost. Can be resisted.

COMMAND THE DEAD
Level 1, Cost 5 San, Duration: 1 minute per level
Allows the caster to issue a command to a single undead creature. If unresisted, the creature most follow its orders to the best of its ability. Can also be used to invite unintelligent undead into a party, at which point they can be verbally commanded indefinitely by the caster.

DEATHSIGHT
Level: 5, Cost: 10 San Duration: 5 minutes per necromancer level
Automatically tells you the number of hit points any creature you can see has left. May not work on level ???? creatures.

DRAIN LIFE
Level 10, Cost: 20 San Duration: Instant
Drains a small amount of life from a nearby foe and adds it to your hit points. Will heal regardless of physical form. Does not affect certain monster types.

INVITE UNDEAD
Level: 5 Cost: 10 San Duration: 1 Hour per necromancer level
Invites the targeted undead to your party. Non-sapient undead who are not already in a party will automatically join if this spell is not resisted. Intelligent undead always have the option of refusal.

MANA FOCUS
Level 10 Cost: N/A Duration: Passive Constant
Buffs your sanity pool by a percentage equal to your necromancer level.

SKELETONS
Level: 5 Cost: 15 San Duration: Permanent
Animates one skeleton or skeletal fragment into a skeleton. Requires a spirit.

SOULSTONE
Level 1, Cost: 20 San, Duration: Permanent
Creates a soulstone crystal, which can house a newly-deceased spirit or an existing incorporeal undead. A spirit in a soulstone may be

conversed with, used to create a new undead, or simply unleashed upon the world at a time of the caster's choosing.

SPEAK WITH DEAD
Level 1, Cost: 5 San, Duration: 1 minute per level
Allows the necromancer to converse with corpses, spirits, or normally incoherent undead. In places with particularly strong spirits, the caster may be notified of the presence of conversable spirits.

ZOMBIES
Level 1, Cost: 10 San, Duration: Permanent
Turns a corpse into a zombie. Requires a spirit present in the area.

RULER SKILLS

APPOINT OFFICIAL
Level: 5, Cost: 25 Mox Duration: Permanent until changed
You may appoint one official per ruler level. This official, who must be one of your subjects, may accept oaths of fealty, and add them to your subject pool.

EMBOLDENING SPEECH
Level 1, Cost: 10 Mox, Duration: Instant
Buffs all allies Moxie and sanity by an amount related to the ruler's charisma. Only affects allies within earshot.

IDENTIFY SUBJECT
Level 1, Cost: 5 Mox, Duration: 5 minutes
Allows the ruler to examine a sworn subject's status screen. May also be used on people within your party, giving more information than the party status screen.

IT'S GOOD TO BE KING
Level: 10, Cost: N/A Duration: Passive Constant
You gain a tiny fraction of experience whenever one of your subjects does. Experience gained from higher level individuals goes directly to leveling your ruler class. Experience gained from lower level individuals may only be utilized for King's Quest rewards.

KINGSGUARD
Level 15, Cost: 50 For Duration: Until you rest
Promote one or more of your party members to Kingsguard. They

gain a buff to their weapon skills and pools affected by your charisma and ruler level.

KING'S QUEST
Level: 10, Cost: 20 Mox Duration: Permanent until changed
Decree a public quest. All your subjects within earshot may accept. Any who fulfill the quest reap the benefits of the quest immediately.

NOBLESSE OBLIGE
Level 1, Cost: N/A, Duration: Passive Constant
Buffs all sworn subjects and party members a small amount. The stat buffed is dependent upon your highest attribute.

ORGANIZE MINIONS
Level: 5, Cost: 15 Mox Duration: Permanent until changed
You may choose one quest shared among your party members or subjects. While on that quest and working toward that goal, they gain a bonus to all attributes equivalent to your ruler level.

PROCLAIM TREATY
Level 15, Cost: 200 Mox Duration: Permanent until dismissed
Choose a nation or organization. All subjects are notified of your new treaty with this group, and suffer a debuff when attacking members of this group. They also gain a charisma and perception bonus affected by your ruler level when dealing with members of this group.

ROYAL AUDIENCE
Level 1, Cost 10 Mox, Duration: 1 Minute per level
Buffs your charisma, but only when dealing with sworn subjects

SIMPLE DECREE
Level 1, Cost 10 Mox, Duration: Permanent until changed
Declare a simple command in twelve words or less. All sworn subjects are notified of the decree. Any who do not comply with this decree take Moxie damage influenced by your charisma and wisdom, resisted by cool. Only one simple decree may be in place at a time. Simple commands may not be used to inflict suicidal or self-harmful activities.

SWEAR FEALTY
Level: 5 Cost: Special Duration: Permanent until changed

Any individual may swear fealty to you, spending five Moxie while in your presence or the presence of any of your appointed officials. They become one of your subjects and are subject to many of your other ruler skills and effects.

SCOUT SKILLS

ALERTNESS
Level 5 Cost: N/A Duration: Passive Constant
Alertness has a chance to auto-activate all your sensory-enhancing skills for free in the event that you are ambushed or about to encounter unseen danger.

BEST ROUTE
Level 5 Cost: 15 San Duration: One hour per scout level
Activate while examining a visible terrain feature. Examines the best route from your current location to your destination, and marks it visibly. Everyone in your party can see the best route trail. The higher the skill, the better the route found. At high levels it will detect and detour around dangerous monsters and towards treasure and resources.

CAMOUFLAGE
Level 1, Cost 5 San/Min, Duration: Until dismissed or exhausted
Blends the Scout in with his surroundings, buffing their stealth skill. More effective in the wilderness, scales according to skill level.

FIRESTARTER
Level 1, Cost 5 San, Duration: Instant
Creates a fire, burning any flammable material it's used upon. Intensity of the starting flames depends on the skill level.

KEEN EYE
Level 1, Cost 5 Sta, Duration: A minute per scout level
Buffs a scout's perception, effects dependent upon skill level

SCOUTER
Level 10, Cost 20 San, Duration: 10 seconds per scout level
Allows the scout to view part or all of a visible target's status screen.

STURDY BACK
Level 1, Cost NA, Duration: Passive Constant
Lightens the burdens of any heavy load carried, making items literally

weigh less. Does not apply to weapons and armor equipped. Higher skill level means more weight reduction.

WAKEFUL WANDERING
Level 10, Cost 20 San, Duration: Maximum of 4 hours per Scout level

Allows the scout to ignore the need for sleep and fatigue penalties. At the end of the duration, or whenever the scout deactivates the skill, the scout is in a coma for an equal duration spent under the influence of Wakeful Wandering.

WIND'S WHISPER
Level 1, Cost 5 San, Duration: 1 message

May be activated silently. Sends a message on the wind to any named target within range. Range and amount of words speakable per message increase with skill level.

SHAMAN SKILLS

BEASTLY SKILL BORROW
Level 5, Cost 10 San, Duration: 1 minute per shaman level

Name a beast when casting this spell. You gain access to all the skills that a beast of that type would have at level one. Every skill has a rating equivalent to half your Beastly Skill Borrow level.

CALL VINES
Level 5, Cost 10 San, Duration: 1 minute per shaman level

Causes magical, mobile vines to spring out from any plant, tree, or nearby vegetation. The stronger the shaman, the stronger the vines.

DREAMQUEST
Level 5, Cost 20 San, Duration: 3-5 hours

Sends the (willing) recipient into a deep slumber for a few hours, during which time they contact the deeper forces of nature in the area and get a glimpse of the past, present, future, or all of the above. At the same time. Skilled shamans or those in the right place might be able to discern some information from a dream quest.

FATED PRESERVER
Level 1, Cost N/A, Duration: Passive Constant

Shamans are guardians of nature, and have a little more significance in the grand scheme of things. Their Fate is buffed by a number equivalent to their Shaman level.

POISON RESISTANCE
Level 1, Cost NA, Duration: Passive Constant
Reduces the damage and negative effects of poisons and the poisoned condition.

SECRET HERBS AND SPICES
Level 1, Cost 10 San, Duration: 1 minute per shaman level
Helps the shaman find herbs and natural components, and identifies unknown plants and their uses. Also counts as the Herbalism skill, when harvesting plant-based resources.

SLOW REGENERATION
Level 1, Cost 10 San, Duration: a number of minutes equal to the shaman's level
Heals the target an amount of hit points equal to the skill over the course of a minute. May be cast on uninjured targets. As usual, healing past the target's maximum hp is ignored.

SPEAK WITH NATURE
Level 1, Cost 5 San, Duration: One conversation
Allows the shaman to talk with beasts, plants, and other creatures and entities close to nature.

NOTE: General skills are self-explanatory, and do not have activation costs or require explanation.

Made in the USA
Columbia, SC
29 November 2022

72322972R00200